Like SWEET POTATO Pie

Jennifer Rogers Spinola

BARBOUR
PUBLISHING

© 2012 by Jennifer Rogers Spinola

ISBN 978-1-61626-365-2

Scripture taken from the HOLY BIBLE, NEW INTERNATIONAL VERSION®. NIV®. Copyright © 1973, 1978, 1984, 2011 by Biblica, Inc.™ Used by permission. All rights reserved worldwide.

All scripture quotations are taken from the King James Version of the Bible.

This book is a work of fiction. Names, characters, places, and incidents are either products of the author's imagination or used fictitiously. Any similarity to actual people, organizations, and/or events is purely coincidental.

For more information about Jennifer Rogers Spinola, please access the author's website at the following Internet address: www.jenniferrogersspinola.com

Cover design: Faceout Studio, www.faceoutstudio.com

Published by Barbour Publishing, Inc., P.O. Box 719, Uhrichsville, OH 44683, www.barbourbooks.com

Our mission is to publish and distribute inspirational products offering exceptional value and biblical encouragement to the masses.

ecpa Member of the
Evangelical Christian
Publishers Association

Printed in the United States of America.

Dedication

To my husband, Athos, who's sprinkled a lot of sugar and spice on this wrinkled old American sweet potato. Thanks for seven unforgettable years.

Acknowledgments

Writing a book is a bit like a recipe—a lot editing and plot twisting, a splash of re-writing, a sprinkle of wild ideas, a good dose of craziness, and a pinch of pure miracle. Whip everything together with a deadline in mind, and *voila*! Dessert's on the table. I just have to uncover my eyes before I reach in to taste the first bite.

And when it comes to baking books, nobody does a better job than Roger Bruner and his wife, Kathleen, who've coached me every step of the way, reading and rereading my rough manuscripts until their eyes burn. Roger, your own books, the fiction-writing craft books you've given me, and your urging to join ACFW has made such a difference!

Cindy Lowry, thanks for all the invaluable IRS/back tax info and for answering my questions so patiently. I'm in your debt!

Lessa Goens, one-in-a-million cousin, cop, and soulmate (how often does a girl get one of those?!)—you're the best! I'll never understand how you pull ideas out of thin air or text me back within minutes with the perfect plot fix-it I'd never considered.

Jenn Fromke, Christy Truitt, Shelly Dippel, Karen Schravemade—YOU ARE AMAZING! How on earth I'm allowed to be in the same crit group with such talented women is a pure mystery. Somebody must've been asleep the day I joined.

Since this book is as much about love as it is writing, a big thank you to Kathy Cooksey and Cherilyn Amborski, who've been my prayer/relationship/child-raising partners for years now, always putting up with my grumbling and questions and pointing me toward the Savior. I've learned so much from you! Thank you also to my sweet Aunt Lois Lambert, who—even without a husband or child—has taught me so much about love, life, and relationships. I can't ever thank you enough for your help and advice all these years. You are an inspiration!

To my editor, Rebecca Germany, plus April, Laura, Linda, and Jessie at Barbour Books, thank you for your unending patience with a newbie.

To Athos and Ethan, I love you more than I can say!

To my Lord and Savior Jesus Christ, thank you for your amazing love. I will never be the same.

Chapter 1

Saturday afternoon, and I could hardly wait to hang up my stained apron and flee Barnes & Noble. The long day of shelving books and pinch-hitting in the Starbucks café with two baristas out sick left my feet screaming for mercy. I liked drinking coffee, not steaming it. Ugh. Even my hair smelled like espresso.

But there was no time to complain about my aching back or the foaming milk roaring in my ears. I needed to get to my friend Becky—and fast. She was part of my plot. My lips twisted into a smug little smile.

I pulled up to her cozy brick house and honked the horn, hanging my head out the window. "Hurry up! We can't be late!"

"Hold yer horses, Shiloh P. Jacobs! I done got ev'rything!" Becky ran out hauling two heavy plastic bags and a cardboard mason jar box.

I lowered my sunglasses—pricey Dolce & Gabbanas, from the days when I actually had money—and gave her an exaggerated wink. "Just put the goods in the trunk."

Becky looked great. Ever since arriving in this little Virginia town from my reporter's post in Tokyo, I'd vigorously attacked her wardrobe. "The Fashion Nazi," she called me.

Still, Becky had thrown away a lot of her bulky plaid stuff and the oversize black clothes that tended to wash her out. Ditto with sloppy NASCAR and Future Farmers of America sweatshirts and the like. I'd convinced her to make charcoal gray and brown her new black and to add in softer tones like aqua and lemon yellow that made her blond hair shine.

"Fashion Nazi" is a bit over the top. I'm just a New York Yankee who knows that nobody looks good in a faded 1990s Ricky Rudd T-shirt that could fit Uncle Cletus.

Today Becky impressed even me—a frilly, sea-green eyelet top with cap sleeves that matched her eyes, plus a pair of crisp white capris. New sandals from Payless. Artsy emerald-green earrings I'd convinced her to buy at JCPenney's.

Wait a second. I squinted and leaned in closer. Did I see *nail polish?* On Becky Donaldson?

Jennifer Rogers Spinola

"Becky?" I blinked. "Who are you? Where's Becky?"

She stared at me like I'd burst into flames then put her hands on her hips. "You started this whole shindig, Miss Fashion Plate, so don't gimme no lip!"

I feigned confusion. "Aren't you always calling me Miss Independent? Which is it?"

"Yer gonna be Miss Flattened if ya don't open up yer trunk this minute!"

She grinned, and I noticed the happy color in her cheeks. I nodded in satisfaction. Becky's heart was healing.

She'd suffered through a few tough weeks after her surprise pregnancy and subsequent miscarriage, which followed four painful years of infertility. But nothing kept Becky Donaldson down for long.

"What's in the box?" I glanced over at the giant cardboard square that she cradled like eggs.

"Stuff," she sniffed, slamming the car door shut and buckling up. "You'll see soon enough."

I raised my eyebrows.

"G'won!" She pushed my head forward. "Get out that lead foot a yers or we'll be late!"

The afternoon dazzled, sun shining on the last of the season's bright yellow goldenrod blooming along the end of Becky's driveway. During my few months in Virginia, I'd learned a few things. After goldenrod comes that crisp, smoke-scented air, like a ripe apple, that warns of fall. The deep blue early October sky. Frost on the grass.

And goldenrod never lies. Splashes of pumpkin orange and dusky yellow had already rippled through the woods, whispering of chilly mornings and scattering leaves. Summer had gone without a word, leaving me only a few wild-flung days of surprising warmth.

Like today. I peeled off my jacket and tossed it in the seat, backing out of the driveway.

"That thing ya hung on yer rearview mirror's gone," said Becky abruptly, flipping down the visor to check her. . .

Lipstick? Becky considered ChapStick high-maintenance stuff. Aliens had abducted Becky. Or maybe she'd actually started listening to me.

"What'd ya do with it?" She flipped the visor shut.

"The *omamori?*"

"Yeah. That red dangly thing that said who-knows-what in Jap'nese."

"Right. A charm. You know, for good luck. I. . .well. . .decided I don't need it anymore." I smirked. "Unless you're driving, and then I need all the good luck I can get."

"Har-har," Becky snarked. "I ken drive! Jest put me on Daytona Speedway an' watch me go!"

"Exactly."

She grinned. "Well, good fer you. Good luck ain't worth a hoot anyway."

I kept my eyes on the road, trying to think of some way to break the news to Becky. She had to know. But I couldn't blast her to kingdom come either.

I flexed my fingers on the steering wheel. "I've been thinking, Becky." I kept my tone conversational, turning down a winding country road. "I really like root beer now. I don't know if I've ever told you that."

"Root beer? Naw, don't reckon so. The first time, ya told me it tasted like cheap NyQuil." She glared at me.

I flinched. Back then, yeah, I probably did say something like that. "Sorry. People change though. I really like it now."

"Well good! Yer finally startin' to get some sense in that globe-trottin' head a yers. Livin' in Japan all them years an' eatin'. . .?"

"I love sushi. Don't you dare." I waved a finger at her.

I couldn't find sushi in Staunton. Not even a measly little piece of salmon. Know what futility feels like? Try hunting for pickled ginger slices in a grocery store stocked with lard and cornmeal.

"Raw fish? Shucks, Shah-loh," she said, drawling out my name in her own distinctive Becky style. "I'd take a root beer an' sweet potater pie over some piece a raw, dead fish any day!"

"Jesus ate fish," I sniffed.

"Yeah, and He cooked it, too! That oughtta tell ya somethin'!"

Actually, He did.

She had that eyebrow up. Fixed an odd expression on me.

"What?" I glanced over.

"How'd ya know Jesus ate fish?" Becky's eyes narrowed. "You ain't set foot in a church since they started buildin' Talladega."

"Talla-what?"

"The racetrack."

I ignored her, but color flared in my cheeks. "Anyway, sushi's paradise." We came around a bend where cows lolled on green fields, oblivious to the fate of summer. "Gourmet paradise. Don't knock it 'til you've tried it."

"Over my dead redneck body." Becky'd spent all her twenty-five years living in rural Staunton, and it had morphed into her veins.

"Even deep-fried? What about all the fried dill pickles and MoonPies in the South?" I was teasing. Now. A few months ago. . . well, let's just say things were different. *And so was I.*

"You smack a piece a deep-fried sushi on my plate and see what happens!"

I choked back a laugh, remembering how I'd arrived in the summer, arrogant and judgmental and so full of hurt I fairly spewed. I probably said a lot of things to hurt Becky. And Adam. And. . .well, other people, too. I just thanked heaven they were pretty good forgivers.

"I reckon ya changed a lotta things, Shah-loh. It's the good ol' Virginia air workin' wonders on yer taste buds. Next you'll start tearin' open bags a pork rinds and goin' hog wild!"

I laughed at her unintended pun. "Over my dead Yankee body."

But I didn't want to talk about death. Not anymore. Mom's untimely passing had given me my fill of funeral flowers, cemetery visits, and regrets. And living in her house, even painted and spruced up, still took some getting used to. I hadn't been close to Mom for years—if I ever had—but it shook me nonetheless.

You're stalling. Just tell her, Shiloh P. Jacobs!

I took a deep breath and tried awkwardly to segue. "There's something else that's changed in my life besides root beer."

"Ya got another job?"

I winced. As if getting fired from the Associated Press's coveted Tokyo bureau for plagiarism at age twenty-four didn't stink sufficiently, now I worked two low-totem-pole jobs to pay off my bills. Debts. Loans. For eternity or until I sold Mom's house. Whichever came first.

"No. Better."

"Better 'n that?"

"Lots better." I tried to keep my cheeks from smiling so much, but today I couldn't manage a poker face.

Becky stared at me with that narrow-eyed look again, and her mouth slowly wobbled. "Shah-loh," she whispered. "Don't tell me ya believe in Jesus!"

I swerved.

Becky screamed. I jerked the car back into my lane, jaw dropping in surprise. "How did you. . .?"

But Becky hadn't heard me. She straightened the box on her lap and glanced inside then closed her eyes in relief. The contents remained in one piece. Or however many pieces they were supposed to.

"Well, yer gonna meet Him real soon if ya don't watch where yer goin'!"

"Sorry. You just. . .surprised me. How did you know?" My decision had been private. Personal, real, and life changing, but private. I hadn't spilled the news to a soul.

Becky's lip quivered, the radiant color in her face turning to blotches. "I don't know. There's somethin' different about ya today, like ya won the lotto or somethin'. You're sorta shinin' from the inside! Ya got stars in yer eyes! You're. . .well, you jest look beautiful. More beautiful than I've ever seen ya." She mopped her face with her hand.

"Wow," I said, tearing up myself. "It's really that obvious?"

"All over yer face," Becky sobbed.

"I just realized I needed Jesus to pay for my sins." I kept my eyes on the curvy country road, hardly believing my own words. "I saw the change in Mom's life, and then I met you and our friends, and God kept showing me something was missing. That I couldn't forgive until God forgave me. And that Jesus gave His life for me. I started reading First John like Adam said, and—"

"Adam?" Becky grinned. "I shoulda known!"

"Wipe that smirk off your face!" I ordered, trying to laugh and cry and drive at the same time. Everyone knew Adam Carter, landscaper, had a good heart—although a bit of a stuffy, straitlaced one, too. I'd written him off as a religious nut for a while.

But that's not why I said yes to God.

"I couldn't get out of my mind what I read—'The blood of Jesus his Son purifies us from all sin.' It's what Mom discovered before she died, and it changed her whole life."

I trembled, remembering the force of my decision, the strength and joy and forgiveness rushing in, breaking up the hardened anger that had closed up my heart for years.

"I found Mom's journals, how she wrote about Jesus changing her life after getting tangled in all those cults for years. And then I met Adam's brother, who's got an amazing story of forgiveness, and. . ." I glanced over in annoyance. "Are you listening?"

"Shiloh Pearl Jacobs!" Becky sat up straight, coming back to her

9

senses. "Pull over right this minute!"

"Why? What's wrong?"

"Jest do it! Now!"

"Where? Here?" I gestured to a long, dusty, gravel driveway and swerved into it. As soon as I shifted into PARK, Becky attacked me with a hug. She laughed and shouted, "Praise the Lord!"—then stuck her head out the window and whooped and hollered and waved her arms.

"Shah-loh's a Christian!" she yelled, cupping her hands around her mouth. "I been prayin' fer her a long time!"

A shiny green Chevy pickup zoomed by and honked in reply. I put my arm out the window and waved and honked back. Not that long ago I would've slumped down in the seat and tried to disappear, but not now. I felt like I did at the top of Mount Fuji: light-headed, sun dazzling my eyes, and lungs bursting with joy.

"So how's bein' a Christian?" Becky stuck her head back in the window.

"New. Different. Amazing." My hands trembled as I reached to punch on the hazard lights and pull back into the road. "And also a little scary."

"Scary? How come?"

"A lot of reasons." I pulled off my sunglasses to wipe my eyes. "I've. . .well, changed, Becky. I don't know who I am anymore, or how I'm supposed to act, or—"

"Act? Act like a woman who loves Jesus, Shah-loh! Ain't nothin' to it!"

"Sure, but it's all strange to me. I'm totally ignorant about the Bible except what I've read on my own and heard on some of Mom's old sermon CDs. I've never gone to church."

"Never?" Becky blinked.

"Nope." I played with a strand of brown hair that hung down from my ponytail, sticky with something—milk? Caramel syrup? "I don't know how I'm supposed to tell people either. I promise you, not everybody's going to be as happy about this as you are."

"Ya reckon?"

"Are you kidding? My family will just think I'm weirder than ever. . . . Not that we really act anything like family. Dad and I don't speak, you know, and my older sister just calls when she wants something." I looked out over the rolling green hillsides, rippling wheat-colored grasses lining the pasture fence. "Half sister. We're only related by Dad."

I checked the clock and pushed on the gas. "And then there's my good friend Kyoko back in Japan, who ranks Christianity up there with suicide cults. If she finds out, she'll think I'm loony. She'll. . .well, I don't know what she'll do. You get it?"

"Ya ain't told her?"

"Not exactly." I played with Mom's Virginia School for the Deaf and Blind keychain, a remnant from her life as a special-education teacher. "She knows something's up, but not the whole story."

"I reckon you'll jest have ta show her. An' ev'rybody else." Becky adjusted one of the box flaps.

I sighed. "And love, Becky? I mean, your squeaky-clean kind of God-love? I don't know anything about that."

"What's there ta know? Ya jest let Him change ya, day by day."

"Right." I turned the steering wheel slightly over a gentle rise. "But it's more complicated than that. If I'm going to marry a Christian person, well, I've got a lot to learn. I don't want to fight like Mom and Dad and end up with divorce and mental breakdowns, or hop from relationship to relationship like my old Cornell friends. I want something different. Something lasting. Something. . . What?"

Becky had teared up again.

"God's gonna teach ya all ya need to know, my friend!" She slung an arm around my shoulders. "He'll give ya the strength to tell yer friends the truth. Ain't He done showed ya ev'rything else, right on schedule? Ya won't know it all right off, but shucks—none a us do! He's a good Daddy, Shah-loh. He won't let ya down."

I wiped my eyes, still somewhat surprised at the sensation of tears. I hadn't cried in years. Literally. Almost twenty—ever since my dad walked away one winter night. Only here in this peaceful Virginia valley, with God's love pushing and prodding my shut-up heart into the sunlight, had I learned to feel again.

"I have another confession to make," I whispered. "My middle name's not Pearl."

"But ya said. . ."

"I lied. I'm sorry." I let out my breath. "But I'm not going to lie anymore. I promise, Becky. We're talking about a new Shiloh now."

"I believe ya." Her eyes were rimmed with red.

"Just don't ask me my middle name. Please. I hate it."

"I don't care if yer middle name's Possum!" Becky shouted. "Ya

11

love Jesus, an' that's all that matters!" She reached over and honked my horn, shouting out in wild excitement. I joined in, looking more like a redneck gone mad than the refined New York–Tokyo transplant I claimed to be.

Becky suddenly grabbed the box. "Uh-oh," she said, shushing me. "What? What's uh-oh? And what's in that box?"

She tried to wrestle it away from me, but I grabbed one of the cardboard flaps and jerked it back. I let out a gasp.

"It's a serprise!" Becky cried, grabbing the box back. "Yer not s'posed to see it yet!"

"Becky Donaldson!" I shrieked. "What have you done?"

★ ★ ★

It took me the entire drive home, out of Staunton (pronounced STAN-ton, not STAWN-ton, for my fellow Yankees) and into the rural outskirts of tiny Churchville to come to grips with Becky's gift. Which now yapped and whined inside the box. A cute little German shepherd puppy, all smoky black and brindle. Enormous liquid black eyes and pricked ears. Staring at me.

She yipped and whined, poking tiny paws over the rim of the box.

"Becky! We've got Faye coming over in twenty minutes, not knowing a thing, and what am I going to do with a dog?" I cried, grabbing my head in both hands.

"Hiya, cutie! Ain't ya gonna sleep some more?" Becky ignored me, massaging the puppy's velvety fur behind the ears.

"A dog?" I repeated stupidly. "You got me a dog? I'm leaving this town, Becky, as soon as I can find somebody to buy my house!" I waved my arms in the air. "I'm not a small-town girl! All I want to do is go back to Japan, and what am I going to do with a dog? I wouldn't stay in Staunton forever if somebody paid me!"

I shook my head and turned into Crawford Manor, Mom's little redneck subdivision. Passing a horse and a double-wide trailer on one side and a house with six hounds on the other.

"No offense, Becky. I love you and Tim and everybody, but I'm not settling down here. I've already stayed way longer than I planned."

"What, a couple a months?" Becky tried to cover a laugh but didn't do a very good job.

"June. July. I don't know. Whenever I came." I gestured with my free arm. "For. . .the funeral."

"Shucks. I jest thought ya might be lonely livin' by yerself, Shah-loh."

"Lonely? Give it to Faye! After all, she's the one we're trying to. . ." I clicked on my turn signal, forcing my eyes away from the box. Because if I peeked, I'd be a sucker. Hooked. Quivery wimp that I was deep down. "Besides, what if Earl doesn't like dogs? And then if he and Faye. . ."

Becky glanced up at me. "Huh? Yer blabberin', Shah-loh. An' anyway, it ain't a good idea for you to live out there all by yerself, ya know."

"My real-estate agent said I can't have any pets. They leave hair and stuff that turns off potential buyers."

"Well, Lowell Schmole ain't here, is he? He gonna tell ya what ta eat fer breakfast, too?"

"I wouldn't put it past him."

I drove down the country road lined with starter homes just like mine, with cute mailboxes and front porches decorated with American flags, dry summer geraniums, and butter-yellow football mums. I crunched across gravel and parked in front of a wooden deck flanked by fading rose bushes. Then I reluctantly pulled down the cardboard flap on the box.

"Here." Becky shoved the whole box into my hands. "Ya don't hafta keep her, but think about it, okay? I just happened ta see her at the SPCA, sorta. . .by accident. . .and couldn't pass her up."

"What were you doing at the SPCA?" I cried.

"Lookin' fer a dog fer you." Good old honest Becky. She got out and shut the door, leaving me there with the box.

Two glistening velvet-black eyes peeked up at me, framed by little fawn-colored spots like puffy eyebrows. Tiny trembling whiskers.

Something melted inside. Like sweet brown *tonkatsu* sauce poured over Japanese fried pork.

"I can't keep her, Becky! She'll pee on my carpets!" I got out, trying not to jostle the puppy or drop the box. "She'll ruin everything for Faye, after we got all this nice food ready, and. . ." I tried not to look inside the box again but couldn't help myself.

"Aw, quit whinin', woman! Faye'll love her! An' hey, maybe it'll give her some conversation with Earl, right?" Becky winked. "She don't know he's comin' yet, does she?"

"She'd better not! That's the whole point!"

Jennifer Rogers Spinola

Becky grinned as the puppy licked her chin, whining. Tail batting the sides of the box. "They said this'n's pretty close ta housebroken. Probably had a family before. An' German shepherds learn real quick!"

"She'll chew furniture! She'll cry all night!"

A quivery black nose appeared over the side of the box, followed by a curious ear.

"She'll be jest fine."

"It's a she?"

"Yep. You'll thank me later." Becky reached in to scratch her ears. "I got ya some toys jest in case."

"In case what?"

"You decide to keep her."

I stared down into the box, not liking that tonkatsu-sauce feeling. Oozing out all over and turning my will of iron into mush. "Becky, I'm not even home during the day! You know that. I work all the time."

"You're home more'n the SPCA volunteers." Her voice held a sorrowful tone. "I'm shore she'd be grateful for any attention ya gave her. An'. . .well, ya know when they cain't find homes for 'em, they. . ."

I shoved the box back at Becky then stomped out to the mailbox, trying not to think of the colorful adjectives Lowell would use when he saw that puppy. And then I spotted the fat envelope with my name in harsh block letters.

I pulled it out of the mailbox, reading and rereading the return address with a sinking lurch.

And I doubled over as if punched in the stomach.

Chapter 2

I blinked and jerked the envelope closer, turning it over in my hand to check the authenticity as my pulse pounded in my ears.

Yep. The real thing all right. A coolish breeze blew my hair and snapped the flags on nearby houses while I slowly tore the envelope open, praying silently for the whole thing to be a mistake. A dream. Anything but this.

As I pulled open the folded letter, printed and stamped on stark white paper, I felt my knees buckle.

I grabbed the metal mailbox for support, trying to make the two houses across the lawn merge into one.

Oh, God, no. . .please, no! Not now! Not when I'm trying so hard to sell the house and get out of here! I pressed a shaky hand to my forehead, mind whirling through a dozen crazy options of desperation. None of which solved my predicament in the least.

A rusty Mustang reverberated down the street in my direction, and before anyone could poke a head out the window and gape at me, still standing there with the envelope in my quivering hand, I slammed the mailbox lid shut. I trudged back to my small, rectangular country house where Becky waited with boxes, bags, and a squirming brown thing, which had begun to yap and whine.

"You okay?" She peered at me as I fumbled for my keys. "Yer white as a sheet!"

"Sure." I tried to smile and shoved the envelope in my cute Kate Spade purse a little too forcefully—a purse which probably cost more than Mom's whole house. Back, yeah, when I had money. Ironic that it was now slung over a shoulder stained with soda and red-pepper soup.

"Don't gimme that, woman! Ya done fessed up about Jesus. Might as well fess up 'bout this, too."

I unlocked the door of Mom's creamy-tan house and slipped off my shoes, Japan-style. Stepped into a pair of striped house slippers. Offered a pair to Becky, who by now knew the routine. At least it kept my floors clean now that I was trying to sell the house.

"So ya ain't gonna tell, huh? Well, no matter. Anyhow, yer gonna love havin' a dog around here fer protection! 'Specially with that murder out this way. Ya hear about it on the news? They think the guy killed her by—"

"Cut it out!" I pushed my running shoes back by the door with the tip of my slipper.

"Tim's daddy said it ain't good fer a single gal to live alone, 'specially out in the sticks."

"What? Churchville isn't the sticks." I flung my hand toward the front window, where three people across the street stood in a clump, heads together. Probably discussing in great detail the contents of my envelope, and maybe even what I ate for lunch. "I've got gobs of neighbors with prying eyes galore!"

For me, a city chick who'd never seen a live sheep until a few months ago, my new neighborhood put me in the furthest reaches of anything I could possibly imagine for myself. Crawford Manor harbored rednecks, boasted one resident in a purple house and another with truck parts adorning the front lawn, and reeked of country music. But. . .so far I wouldn't call it the projects either. Not. . .exactly.

Besides playing Hank Williams Jr. too loudly and riding their lawn mowers up and down the street, my neighbors didn't bother me. Most of the time. When they weren't squealing their jacked-up truck tires or getting into fistfights.

I pushed the button on the answering machine, which blinked an angry red *six*. "I'm fine, Becky. And I didn't say I'd keep her."

"Oh, ya will."

"What makes you so sure?"

Becky rolled her eyes.

"Oh no. They did not." I glared at the answering machine as message after message spilled out, all from Shifflet Septic Services. "I've told them to take my number off their list—how many times? Ten?" I fumed, punching buttons through the messages, all of which came courtesy of you-know-who.

Becky snickered, and I whirled on her. "You think it's funny? They've come here twice to install stuff I never asked for, and every day I get at least three or four messages. I hear their silly jingle in my sleep!"

I slapped the answering machine off, knocking my purse on the floor and scattering the hateful envelope. Becky, stifling a laugh with difficulty, glanced up at me as I tossed it on the table.

"That from them, too?"

"No." I turned away. "It's a bill, okay?"

"A bill? Fer what? I thought yer big spendin' days were over."

As much as I loved Becky Donaldson, I couldn't get the words *IRS* or *back taxes* out of my mouth. They stuck there like peanut butter, immobile.

"They *are* over. No more credit cards like I used to rack up back in Japan. And I quit my online master's, too, for a while. But. . .well, this one caught up with me," I managed, hanging up my jacket. The envelope winked at me from the table, a sliver of spiteful white. "It's from my Japan days—and before that, even when I studied at Cornell. It's bad, Becky."

"How bad?"

I swallowed hard, breath still shallow. "Mom's house just has to sell. It has to." I stared out the window at green leaves, tinged with dying gold. "If it doesn't sell in a couple of months, then. . ."

The words *lose the house* stuck in my throat like a chunk of sticky rice.

"It'll sell. We're prayin', Shah-loh. Hang in there." Becky shoved the box at me. "Here. Play mama a bit. It'll he'p ya."

Against my better judgment, I lifted out the little puppy and plopped her on the living-room floor. Legs still clumsy. Nose quivering. She wagged a stumpy tail and tottered across the carpet. Barked brightly. Sat and pricked her ears.

Smiled at me. I could swear she did.

"Oh my goodness, Becky," I groaned, feeling like a traitor. To my bills. To Lowell. "She's adorable!"

"I know." Becky squatted with her hand on her knee, looking like she might take her back if I hesitated even a second. "Don't she make ya just wanna squeeze her? She's had all her shots, too, an' ev'rything. German shepherds make the best guard dogs and pets. Bunch a people told me so."

I cradled the puppy's little warm body against my chest and felt her heart beat fast and quivery against mine. She squirmed and licked my cheek. *Checkmate.*

"Well, she's got to have a name," I said reluctantly.

"Told ya." Becky smirked. "What kind a name ya want?"

I hated to bring up the subject of names so soon after Becky miscarried her baby. I remembered her in the Barnes & Noble, baby-name book in hand. She loved names. But she put her chin up and didn't cry.

"Hmm." I thought awhile, dragging a string across the carpet and watching the puppy pounce. "I suppose I ought to keep the current trend, don't you think? NASCAR drivers. You and Adam both have dogs named after them."

"Yer funny, Shah-loh. She's a girl!"

"Who said women can't drive for NASCAR?"

She considered this. "Well, there's been a couple. Sara Christian in 1949 bein' the first."

"Appropriate name, then, don't you think?"

Becky's head came up, and she went all blotchy again. "Ya can call her Christie," she offered, sniffling.

I picked up the wiggly little body, snatching her claws and teeth away from my tennis-shoe lace. "Christie it is. And thank you, Becky. I'll just find some way to hide her from Lowell."

"Well, while yer dreamin' up hidin' places, we gotta get this place all ready fer the big event! Pronto!"

Christie toddled around the newly painted and decorated kitchen while we threw on a lace tablecloth and lit two tall candles, all courtesy of Becky and Co. Set out gleaming china plates and crystal serving dishes, along with the makings of a fabulous meal. Roast chicken and green beans. Rosemary potatoes. We nuked everything in the microwave until it steamed.

And just as I started to call Trinity, my coworker, I saw her orange Volkswagen pull into my next-door-neighbor's driveway as planned, disappearing behind Stella's big school bus.

"Here you go!" Trinity called through the screen door, coffee-brown skin gleaming in the porch light. "Delivery!"

I put the gorgeous dessert tray from The Green Tree restaurant, my other part-time wage-payer, in the refrigerator. Poured Green Tree signature roasted red-pepper soup, still piping hot, into two crystal bowls. Filled the table with yellow marigolds and the season's last roses from Mom's flower bed, and scattered petals on the lace tablecloth.

Becky and Trinity rushed around putting down silverware, unrolling cloth napkins, and pouring a cream garnish and little sprigs of fresh rosemary on the soup. We turned on some classical violin music and drizzled sparkling apple juice in glasses over ice.

And then, just to make good to my word, I got out pliers and loosened the bathroom shower faucet so it dripped. "Told Earl it was leaking again," I confessed. "Oops."

Then I shooed them out of the house and over to Stella's yard, where they crouched in the bushes, waiting for Faye Clatterbaugh's blue Escort to crunch up the driveway.

★　　★　　★

First things first. No way I'd meet Faye in cheap black pants and coffee-spattered polo shirt, my normally straight brown hair sticking out of its elastic like splayed sticks in a Japanese fan.

While Christie tugged on my house slipper with her teeth, I shook out my hair and ran a brush through it then smoothed my sideswept bangs. Stuck in a pretty clip. I untangled Christie from my feet and then the edge of the bedspread, dumped my soiled Barnes & Noble clothes in the washer, and pulled on dark blue jeans—the typical Tokyo preppy girl color. And a soft green sweater that matched the green flecks in my hazel eyes. I threw an ivory crocheted shawl around my shoulders just as headlights flickered on the curtains.

"Hi, Faye! Come on in!" I pushed open the screen door—which practically all Southern houses came with, as if issued by Mason and Dixon themselves—and heard what sounded like twenty dogs barking over on Wayburn Street. *Great. Now I've added another one. Why doesn't Becky just park a trailer in my backyard, too?*

"Where'd ya get that adorable little thing?" cried Faye, reaching out. Christie stuck out a happy pink tongue and licked Faye's chin, making us both laugh.

I didn't subject Faye to my Japanese house-slipper obsession. Just shut the door and watched her croon and scratch Christie's ears.

Faye's gently lined face reflected peace and the calm quiet of her heart. She'd collected Mom's things after her death and then practically taken me in after my life fell apart.

Faye was probably born sweet as molasses. I'd spent my twenty-four years more like a sour grapefruit, although God was heaping a little sugar on top now, thank you very much.

She sniffed. "What's that delicious smell? Did ya make dinner already?"

"Well, sort of. I know we planned to cook together, but tonight's different."

Faye single-handedly saved me from a diet of instant ramen noodles and corn flakes. Plus she helped me identify weird stuff in the grocery store like collard greens, grits, and buttermilk and turn them into something somewhat edible.

"What's tonight, sugar?" She peeked into the kitchen then did a double take. "Flowers? Fine china? What's all this about?"

My cell phone jangled abruptly. Or Adam's, rather, until I could afford to buy one. I pressed it to my ear, whacking the little dangly peach-thing out of my way. *That* was mine: the trendy Japanese *keitai* (cell phone) strap. Everybody had them in Japan. Only I lived in Churchville, Virginia, so it looked like I randomly attached fruit to my electronics.

"Sorry, Faye. Just a second." I turned back to the phone. "Becky? What's going on?" I raised my voice for Faye's benefit.

"You gotta come git me!" Becky hollered. Then she whispered to Trinity, "Quit! Yer makin' me laugh!" and some scuffling.

"Why? What's wrong?" Faye stopped petting Christie and looked up. "Oh no. You're stuck without a car. I see." It took all my concentration to keep a straight face. "No, don't worry. Just wait right there."

"Go ahead." Faye shooed me with her hand. "I'll watch yer little angel here for ya."

"Would you?" I shot her a grateful look. "I'm coming, Becky! Just hang on!"

Wow. The dog actually came in handy. I snapped the cell phone shut and ran for my purse. "Just one thing. Would you let Earl in to fix my shower in about twenty minutes? You know how Lowell carries on about having everything in the house perfect."

"Earl?" Faye gave me a strange look. "Yer shower's leakin' again?"

"Yep, sure is. You wouldn't mind, would you? I'd hate to call Earl and reschedule this late." I patted Christie's head. "You'll just have to let the puppy out a lot. I can't have my carpet reeking and turning yellow, or my Realtor will dump me."

"No, Shiloh, don't worry. I'll take care a everything."

A twinge of guilt stuck me at Faye's kindness. But not for long.

"Really? That would help so much. I mean, Earl's more than a neighbor. He's a good friend." I waggled my eyebrows at her. "Remember him? He's a deacon down at that little church just around the corner. Did you know that?"

I'd gotten that bit from my next-door neighbor Stella Farmer, who I counted on for the good stuff. Stella knew everything about everybody. I found her all-inclusive knowledge useful at times, but creepy, too.

Faye blinked. "No, I didn't. What's his name again?"

"Earl Sprouse."

"Don't ring a bell. I don't know many folks out here in Churchville."

"Well, he's the best. He loves that radio program with all the organ music. . . . What's it called? *Bible Today?*"

"That's a good one. I listen to it, too."

"Yeah, I know." I casually patted Christie. "Lowell would sell Earl's house and garden in a second if he ever put it up for sale. The way he keeps everything so nice and neat. You remember that time we took a lemon pound cake over because he—"

"I remember him, Shiloh."

I shut my mouth, afraid—with good reason—that I was chattering too much.

"Don't you worry. Earl and I have met before, an'. . ." Faye's voice trailed off. And rubbed her hands together—if I'd noticed correctly—just a tad nervously. "We'll handle things jest fine. You jest go on 'n' get poor Becky."

Poor Becky, all right. Faye would have our heads if she could see Becky falling over herself with laughter on top of Stella's petunias.

"It might take awhile, so go ahead and eat, will you, Faye? And give Earl my plate. It won't be any good by the time I get back. That's an order." I stuck my head back in the door. "Dessert's in the fridge."

She started to protest, but I waved my arms. "That soup's got a cream base! It won't reheat well. Please! Do it for me!"

I pushed through the screen door before Faye could say another word. Jumped into my—formerly Mom's—white Honda and backed down the gravel driveway into the narrow street, lined with blocky houses just like mine. All trimmed with shrubs and wooden shutters, gleaming under protective, pale streetlights. I left Mom's bright windows behind and then circled back, headlight-less. Past the house with the pink flamingos (plural). Past the creaky street sign. And into Stella's butterfly-bush-laden driveway with the parked yellow school bus.

I eased the car door closed and ran across the chilly grass to meet my co-conspirators.

★   ★   ★

Stella huddled on the porch in her trademark flowered housedress, cigarette in hand, giggling and whispering with Becky and Trinity.

I remembered the first time I met her, when she ambled past her satellite dish that loomed—and I'm not making this up—big enough to see on Google Earth.

Still, Stella had a heart of gold, and I owed her big-time for helping me land my job at The Green Tree restaurant. Owned by her brother Jerry.

"Faye fell for it!" I fingered the fringes on my shawl in the cool dusk. "I think. At least she's staying."

"Did she suspect anything?" Becky tugged on my arm. "Ya didn't overdo it, did ya? Shore took ya long enough!"

Me and my big mouth. "Um. . .I hope not. Have you seen Earl yet?" I peeked around the corner of Stella's white siding.

"Look!" Stella clapped her hand over her mouth and shushed us, even snuffing out her Marlboro. "Here he comes! Oh will ya look at that!"

We hid ourselves in the shadows as Earl Sprouse crossed the yard, toolbox in hand. He'd put on a nice dress shirt, obviously ironed, and we even caught a whiff of cologne on the crisp breeze.

He lived in the house right behind Stella and me, just a stone's throw away. All the better for our prying eyes.

"My word," breathed Stella, shuffling her hefty weight and trying not to creak the porch swing. She lowered her big hair out of sight. "I ain't seen him cleaned up like that since I don't know when. How old's he now? Fi'ty-five? Oh what I wouldn't give ta see that nice man in love again with somebody special! He's spent a lotta lonely years since he lost his wife, God bless her."

Trinity, fellow waitress and resident romantic at The Green Tree restaurant, crouched in front of me, her fragrant black curls still holding faint whiffs of fry oil. "Look at him! He's adorable!"

"This was your idea!" I poked her.

"Ow." She looked grumpy, rubbing her arm under her jacket.

"What? Did you hurt yourself?"

"I'm fine. Forget it." She sounded crabby. "Anyway, I just came up with the dinner part. The rest was yours."

I stopped gawking through the bushes and turned to her. "Hey, you okay?" I hugged a knee, noticing for the first time the dark circles under her eyes.

"Me?" Trinity jumped, the cheerful, sarcastic mask I knew so well slipping back into place. "I'm fine, Shiloh! I had to stay an hour after my shift while Jerry fixed that stupid sanitizer hose that keeps breaking, and now I'm sitting in the bushes in a redneck subdivision, shivering my tail off. Why wouldn't I be fine?"

"Good point."

"Hush, y'all!" hissed Becky, dragging Trinity to a better viewing spot behind Stella's browning hydrangea shrubs, careful not to crackle the twigs. "Jest watch!"

We stuck our heads through the leaves as Earl paused, noticing Faye's little Escort. Then he straightened his shirt, smoothed his hair, and rang the doorbell.

A yellow light cut blue evening, and Faye's silhouette appeared, classy and cool. I saw the outline of her long skirt and flats, her stylishly cut blouse and bracelet. She'd just had her hair done, looking more soft sandy-brown and less gray, and she looked great.

"What's he doing? What's he doing?" Stella whispered, heaving her way around Trinity's curly head. "I can't see!"

"He's pettin' the dog!" Becky informed her with a NASCAR-like play-by-play. "They're laughin'. There he goes! He's goin' in!"

We slipped over to my yard, creeping along the ground, and took up positions behind my bushes and the shrubby things Adam had planted behind the marigolds. Stella peeked in through the living-room sheers, crouching in her housedress and flip-flops.

"Don't know what that was all about," came Earl's voice through the screen door. "Weren't a thing wrong with the faucet. Just the washer come loose."

"Really? That's weird. Maybe it just don't tighten very well," offered Faye diplomatically. "I had a faucet like that once. Always dripped."

"Is that right." Earl scratched his head again after an awkward silence, the other hand still clutching his toolbox. "Well, if ya need any plumbin', jest. . .uh. . .lemme know."

Speak, Faye! Speak! Say something! My knees dug into the cold Virginia soil, and a prickly pyracantha shrub poked me in the thigh.

Earl just stood there, jingling the keys in his pocket. "What's all that fancy dinner about?"

We strained to watch as Earl turned to Faye, fiddling with the handle on the toolbox while she explained. They gestured back and forth, scratching their heads, checking watches, and pointing to the plates. Then finally shrugged. And sat down at the smooth wooden table, faces down-turned in the golden glow of the kitchen light and flickering candles.

Faye twirled an earring, avoiding his eyes as she reached for the serving spoon.

"Five bucks says it won't work," said Stella, fidgeting with the lighter in her pocket. "She ain't interested."

"Five bucks say it will," Trinity whispered back fiercely. "Look at her! Her hand just shook on her water glass. Did you see it?"

"Nope. She's too refined for him." Stella gestured for us to lean closer. "Word on the street's that Dreama Simmons is after Earl somethin' awful," she whispered. "Ya know, that woman who lives over on Dry Branch Road?"

Dreama who? I crossed my arms stubbornly. "No way. Faye's just shy. Haven't you read *Pride and Prejudice?*"

"What's that, a cookbook? I make a mean butterscotch puddin', y'all. Why, jest last week—"

"Forget it," Trinity groaned. "You're wrong, Stella. They're perfect for each other."

Becky peered through the curtains. "The jury's still out on this'n, Shah-loh. They're jest makin' small talk. I don't know if no romance is happenin' or they're jest eatin' some really good dinner." She rubbed her belly. "An' all that food's makin' me hungry!"

Stella looked sober for a second, face half-lit by the inside glow. "Ain't gonna work. I'm tellin' ya. Earl ain't never gonna move," she said bluntly, putting her hand in her pocket. "An' Faye don't wanna remarry. She tole me so once."

The breath caught in my throat. "She didn't."

"Shore did. Sat right here on yer porch an' said so."

I peeked through the window as they cut their chicken and almond-flecked green beans, looking for all the world like a young couple on a first date. Faye laughed easily, and Earl took off his watch and dropped it carelessly on the rose-petal-covered tablecloth.

"Don't listen to Stella." Trinity put her arm around me. "They just need an uninterrupted evening to work the magic."

"Hold on, hold on!" whispered Becky so loud we all shushed her. "She jest said somethin' about Mack! Ain't that her ol' husband who passed away?"

"She did not." Stella froze, dropping her lighter. Luckily it hit the grass instead of clattering on the porch. "She never talks about him."

"Told you." I stuck out my tongue.

I let out my breath. Finally something that didn't end in disaster in Staunton, Virginia. Before this I'd already been mugged and kicked in the side, raced friends to the hospital, and played emergency stand-in nurse.

But today? I sighed and leaned blissfully against the porch column. Sheer perfection.

Now I just had to ring the doorbell, swing open the screen door to make my entrance, and. . .

"Shiloh!" Trinity grabbed my arm with cold fingers. "Don't look now, but I think I just saw a cop car."

"A what?"

Like a bad dream unfolding, a squad car with lights flashing did indeed hover at the end of my driveway. And turn in.

Chapter 3

Becky blanched, mouth hanging open. "What on earth did ya do this time, Shah-loh?"

"I didn't do anything! Honest!" I whispered back, heart hammering.

I had no next of kin here to worry about. . . . No parking tickets . . . . My overdue bills? No. Don't be ridiculous. They'd send another collection agent, not a police officer.

Wouldn't they?

Red and blue pulsed across the yard, illuminating the front of Mom's house in eerie light as the car crept closer. Harsh CB radio messages squawked loud enough for people over in Waynesboro to hear.

Stella and Trinity fled. Becky grabbed my arm, and we ran headlong toward the car, heads down and out of the range of Faye and Earl's vision. We arrived, panting, just as the trooper stepped out and slammed the car door, hand on his gun and looking surly.

Wait a minute. Didn't this big guy with the buzz cut come into The Green Tree restaurant all the time to drink coffee and flirt with the waitresses?

"Excuse me. Who's the resident a this house?" he barked.

"I am," I whispered meekly, and he shined his light on me to check for weapons. I put my hands up. "If you're coming to talk about my dumb bills, I'm already—"

"Name, please?"

"Shiloh Jacobs. I'm the daughter of Ellen Jacobs, who used to live here."

"I just got a call about some people lurkin' around in the bushes." He shined his light on the shrubs around the house. "I'm sorry, but ya need to come with me. All of ya."

"Here's my driver's license! Read the address for yourself!" I dug in my purse and slapped it in his hand. "Just don't let the people inside know!"

He scowled and shined his light on my license then at me. Raised a curious eyebrow.

"Officer, please. Yer gonna ruin everything! It's a serprise for the people inside, and. . ." Becky squinted. "Shane? Shane Pendergrass?"

He turned his light on her in astonishment. "Becky Donaldson? That you? What on God's green earth. . .?" He put the light down and hugged her. The grizzly had dropped from his voice. "I ain't seen you in years! Since what, junior high?"

"Junior high? That was high school!" She punched his arm. "I was datin' Tim then, ya goon! An' when did you become a cop?"

Shane squared his shoulders proudly. No, boastfully. "Awhile back. Lotta work cut out for me with folks like these around." He nudged me. "So yer in on this shindig, Beckers?"

"Shore I am, an' don't call me that! Now put that light out and get outta here before you ruin the whole thing!" she ordered indignantly. "I'm serious! They probably done saw us."

Shane hastily turned off the flashing squad-car light, but two silhouettes appeared in the screen door.

"Sorry!" Shane called out, shoving me behind him. Becky ducked behind the squad car. "Wrong house, ma'am. Sorry to bother ya! Everything's fine." I hunkered down in Shane's shadow, bemoaning my bad luck.

"Sorry, ma'am!" Shane reached in the squad car and cut the headlights, too, pushing me back with his free arm. "You can go on back inside. I'm leavin'."

Around the corner of Shane's hefty back I saw one of the silhouettes disappear. Then the other. The screen door squeaked shut. I sank weakly against the cool side of the car, breath gone out of me.

"Close call." Shane helped me up. "So yer the resident." He shined his light on my driver's license again then squinted at me. "Hey, I remember you! You work at Jer's restaurant!"

"I've seen you there." I crossed my arms stiffly, remembering his suggestive comments when I refilled his glass.

He gave me the once-over, leaning against his car. Took a toothpick out of his pocket and chewed on it, studying me. "And I've definitely seen *you*. What's yer name again?" He glanced at my driver's license.

"Quit that!" snapped Becky, snatching his light. "Ya almost ruined ev'rything!"

"You," said Shane, giving Becky a steely-eyed wink. "I oughtta lock you up. You've got some explaining to do, and ya better make it good."

He gave me a too-friendly glance. "Although maybe I'll let you off for good behavior if you give me the lowdown on yer friend here."

27

Trinity slipped cautiously toward us, shiny flats barely crunching on the gravel driveway, and Shane looked up. "Friends," he amended. "Plural."

He grinned at Trinity. "You work at The Green Tree, too, don't ya?"

"And you're our best tipper." Shane shook her hand a little too long, but Trinity laughed when she pulled it away.

"Mercy, I shore stopped at the right house tonight," Shane muttered under his breath, glancing from Trinity to me. He leaned on the hood of his car, poking that toothpick in his teeth. "So, Beck, ya gonna give me the scoop on 'em or what?"

"As soon as you get outta Shah-loh's driveway I'll think about it," bossed Becky with a toss of her head. "How about we go next door with them fool lights out, real quiet-like, and I'll fill ya in?"

★　★　★

Staunton. Exhausted. Me. I couldn't reach any other conclusion as I plodded back over to Stella's yard. Shane was one of Tim's high school classmates—apparently one of the better-looking ones, which I found hard to believe—and did nothing more than halfheartedly relay my name and address back to headquarters.

"What'd ya say about bills, Shiloh?" He leaned in a little too close, profile glowing in the streetlight. Eyelashes blinking against the dark night sky.

"Me? Bills? I just thought. . . Forget it."

"Why, ya need money?" He inclined one elbow on the tree I was leaning against, invading my space like Tim's weirdo cousin Randy. "How about a night out on the town? I can hook ya up."

I shoved myself off the tree trunk and stared at him.

Shane laughed and slapped his knee at my annoyance. "Well, here's my number if you change your mind." He shoved a scrap of paper with his phone number into my startled fingers, and I took it distastefully, as if he'd slapped me with a speeding ticket.

"Ya oughtta take pride in livin' in a safe place like this, ma'am." Shane drew himself up tall and gazed longer than necessary, a whiff of his too-strong cologne wafting through the cool evening chill. "Although it's always better to have a man around." He winked at Trinity then turned back to me and crossed his beefy arms.

"I'm safe!" I snapped. "I've got a German shepherd, thank you very much."

"It's eight weeks old," Becky giggled, and I tried to kick her. So much for all her "guard dog" talk. "By the way, can ya get some info on Shah-loh for me? She never tells nobody her middle name. Cain't ya run it through again?"

After Shane got out his flashlight and checked out my driver's license for the third time, carrying on about the green and gold in my eyes—as if he hadn't ever seen hazel eyes before—I snatched my license back and told him I was going home.

Shane winked and backed his squad car out of the driveway stealthily, lights off, and gave me a slow wave out the window before cruising on back to his rounds.

Hmph. Good riddance. I turned my back on him.

"Sheewweeee!" Stella fanned herself. "That's one fine-lookin' man! Even if I am old enough ta be his mama!"

"You're not related, are you?" I scowled, feeling cranky. You could never tell with family trees in the South.

"Well. . .third cousin or somethin'. In-law, I think. Ain't sure."

Trinity covered my coughing fit at Stella's familial announcement with a laugh. "All the waitresses love it when he comes in."

"All but one." I dropped his phone number in Stella's ashtray.

"Consider yourself lucky, Shiloh. He gives good tips." Trinity pushed my shoulder. "I'm taken though. You?"

"I don't need Shane's money."

"Wale, ya shore need somebody's!" Becky teased, grabbing my arm. "Now git back over there an' see how Romeo an' Juliet are doin'!"

"Wait a second." Trinity leaned over suddenly as if sick, staring at her watch. "Is this right? Is it almost eight?"

"I think so. Why?" I glanced up at her. "I thought you didn't work at Cracker Barrel tonight."

"I don't, but. . .oh boy. I've gotta go. Sorry." She breathed frantically, shallow and fast, digging frantically for her purse and keys on Stella's porch with her hand on her forehead. She practically fell in her haste to scramble down the walkway then threw herself into her car. Her hands shook so much she dropped her purse on the gravel, fumbling with it before slamming the door.

"Trinity?" I knocked on her window, hands circling my eyes as I tried to see inside. "What's going on?"

I saw her hesitate then lower the window with an expression of unmistakable fear wide in her eyes. "Everything's fine, Shiloh. I've just gotta be back before. . . It'll be fine." Her lips quivered. "I'll see you."

She gunned the engine, backing into the street and screeching toward the highway in one fluid motion.

"What'n the world's that all about?" Becky put her hands on her hips.

"I have no idea." I stood there watching the street. "But she's acting differently lately. Sadder. Something. . . I don't know. She says everything's fine."

"Lands! She's always smilin' when we come to The Green Tree."

"Of course she is. Happy servers are one of Jerry's rules."

"Well, ya can't solve all the world's problems, my friend," said Becky, pushing me toward my yard. "Gotta take 'em one at a time! Startin' with the folks in your daggum kitchen, if they're still there!"

★ ★ ★

I plopped down at the empty kitchen table with a cup of hot green tea, replaying the way Earl had handed Faye a business card and how she'd received it graciously like a bouquet of flowers. How he'd lingered, tongue-tied, by the screen door and finally waved good-bye, nearly missing the porch step and falling into the grass.

And all Faye had said, turning to me in the doorway with Christie in her arms, was this: "So, you gonna keep this little girl, Shiloh?"

I didn't know what to make of it. Not yet. But my heart inflated with hope. I nuzzled Christie to my chin and felt her heartbeat. She closed her eyelids, yawned, and her little warm paws sagged against me.

Since I had no family except Dad and Ashley, both as distant as the moon (both geographically and emotionally), I'd gotten used to empty apartments and empty houses. But this? I scratched Christie's silky neck as she groaned and stretched. I might get used to fuzzy companionship if I wasn't careful.

The kitchen phone trilled, and I scooted back my chair and answered, cupping Christie gently in the crook of my elbow.

"Where've you been, Shiloh? I've tried to call you like six times."

I didn't recognize the voice at first. "Ashley?"

"That's me."

I sat back down and nestled Christie on my lap, my initial surprise beginning to fade into tense worry. When Ashley called, she usually had an ulterior motive. No, not usually. Always. I just had to uncover it.

An awkward silence hung between us, and I cleared my throat, fishing for conversation. "I've left messages at your house for months, Ashley. I never got any reply, so I assumed you're. . .busy?" I rested my head in one hand, scratching Christie's ears with the other.

"Sorry. Wade must've taken those. I never got them."

"Really! Then how did you get my number?"

For some reason the question seemed to catch Ashley off guard, and she stammered. "Oh, I've. . .you know. I've always had it. I used to call here all the time to talk to Mom."

I closed my eyes at the sliver of unexpected pain. I hadn't spoken to Mom in years. When she died, I didn't even know what state she lived in.

Wait. Ashley'd called her. . . "You mean *my* mom, right? Mom wasn't your. . . Never mind." I decided to shut up and sip my tea. "So when's the baby due?"

"In December. And he has a name, Shiloh. It's Carson Clay."

"Sorry. You never told me."

"It'll be expensive—all the hospital bills and baby stuff. It'll take months to pay off our credit-card bill. Maybe even years. Do you have any idea how much a sonogram costs? The insurance company says. . ."

This is going to take awhile. My empty stomach complained, and I pictured the Japanese dried fish in my cabinet, silver and crunchy.

Yep. I know. Dried fish. Japan has a way of warping people for life. You go in standing up and come out all twisted like a bonsai tree. Bowing and avoiding eye contact and giggling at things typical Americans don't find funny. Covering your mouth when you eat or laugh. Craving weird sea creatures and saying, "Excuse me, I'm sorry," ad infinitum. I once caught myself apologizing to a houseplant.

"Yes, babies are *expensive,*" Ashley repeated as I munched my fish, their hard silver sides tinkling against Adam's borrowed mug. Yet another thing of his marooned at my house for months.

"What are you crunching?"

"Dried fish." Like I said, warped for life.

"Ugh. Disgusting. Don't Japanese people eat monkey brains and rats?"

"Of course not! Gross!"

"Whatever. Your munching is annoying."

31

Oh brother. Here we go. I rolled my eyes and reached into the bag.

Come to think of it, fish showed up an awful lot in the Bible, as I was learning. Fish completed the little boy's lunch that Jesus multiplied to feed thousands and became Jesus' first meal after His resurrection. Fish, in fact, had eluded Jesus' disciples all night long when Jesus called out to them, "Throw your net on the right side!" And the net nearly broke from the heavy catch.

Maybe sushi really is divine.

"Are you listening to me?" Ashley snapped. "I just said how lucky you are to have all your house bills paid. We've got all these expensive repairs. . .and you have how many bedrooms? Two? Three?" She sighed dramatically. "Ours is so small. Just a teeny, tiny little place for three people."

I played with the phone cord, a bad feeling settling in the pit of my stomach. Ashley wanted *something*. Three times she'd used the word *expenses* or *expensive*. But if she wanted money, she was definitely barking up the wrong tree.

"Look, I have plenty of expenses," I said, trying to keep my voice calm. After all, I'd become a Christian, and Christians are supposed to be. . .uh. . .nicer or something. Right? "I work all the time at. . .well, I work."

I couldn't bear to let Ashley know that her once-headed-for-stardom half sister, who'd won awards and a promotion to the politics beat at the Associated Press, got herself fired for plagiarism—and now shelved books and took dinner orders.

Ashley's breath caught slightly. "Wait—did you say you're working there?"

"Well, how else do you expect me to pay the bills?"

I froze, realizing what I'd just blurted. Nobody in my family knew I'd burned my bridges with the Associated Press. My dad, off in Mexico City with his über-young, belly-dancing wife, couldn't care less anyway.

"You live in Japan! Why would you be working stateside?"

"Well, for a while I am." I swallowed my tea nervously, not liking this conversation.

"For how long? Aren't you selling the house?"

I set my teacup down, its little blue painted brush strokes glinting a warning like Shane's police lights. "It's on the market."

"How long will it take to sell?"

"How am I supposed to know? And what's with all the questions?"

"Me? Oh, I'm just curious, as always, about my wild, wandering sister!" She laughed, sounding too exuberant.

Sister? Has Ashley ever, in her entire life, called me sister? Something niggled in my brain, and a wave of uneasiness quivered inside. I'd felt this way when Tokyo earthquakes hit, floor shifting under my feet.

"What is it you want, Ashley?" I put my dried fish down, suddenly not hungry. "Just tell me."

"Me? Nothing," she said, her laugh chilling me. "Nothing at all."

Chapter 4

"Listen," I said, dragging my fingers through my scraggly bangs. "Let's talk another time. It's late."

"So how much do you think the house is worth?" Ashley steamrolled right over me. "I mean, just out of curiosity?"

That came out of nowhere. And now with that pristine IRS envelope glaring at me, I might never know. I'd simply find myself and my belongings stuffed in Mom's Honda.

If I got to keep the car.

"Worth? It's a prefab! A kitschy country starter home surrounded by satellite dishes and pink flamingos. Don't get your hopes up." I chuckled.

"My hopes?"

"I'm joking. I meant, if you guys visit, it won't be the Hilton. I can barely fit in the bathroom myself, and I'm just one person."

Ashley didn't laugh. An icy silence fell over the line, so I politely tried to fill it. "It's not a bad place though, for the short time I'm planning to stay. A lot of families nearby. Good yard. All the other houses are—"

"Well, it should net at least a hundred grand, right? The other prices in the area seem relatively. . ." Ashley seemed to realize she'd blundered. "I mean, I guess so, knowing Mom." She laughed nervously.

I twisted the cord around my hand, earthquake tremor increasing. "Ellen," I corrected. "She's not your mom!"

"Of course she is! You and I both cared for her dearly, despite her difficult but. . .uh. . .charming personality. She certainly doted over Carson."

Ashley made no sense. I'd lived with Mom for years after Ashley left with Dad. I, not Ashley, put up with Mom's psychological problems, depression, cults, and occasional beatings. She'd left me alone with drunk neighbors whose creepy boyfriends hit on me, and I slept at the homeless shelter after Mom got evicted. I wouldn't call any of it "charming."

Ashley Jacobs (now Sweetwater, although I found little sweet about her) sprang from one of Dad's "wild oats" before he married

34

Mom. After Dad left, I got Mom's coldwater flat, while Ashley spent her childhood skipping across Dad's marble floors.

Ashley's voice slipped into a condescending tone. "Shiloh, you two didn't really have a close relationship, right? To be quite honest, I see us—you, me, and Carson—as equals in our relationship with her."

"Ashley, Carson isn't even born yet."

She gasped, tone sharp and accusing. "Like his due date makes any difference! At least we stood by her, unlike you!"

"Now wait a minute!" I smacked my teacup down, shaking Ashley's ludicrous postulations out of my head like cold seawater. "Don't you start on my relationship with my mom! You know nothing about it, and frankly, it's none of your business!"

"Who took care of her while you ran off to Japan and did who-knows-what at Cornell?"

"Did 'who-knows-what'? Dad paid for your tuition, but I earned my academic scholarship fair and square. I worked to pay my own bills!" The blood rushed angrily to my face. "You? Taking care of Mom? You didn't even invite her to your wedding!"

"Well. . .well. . .sure I did! She came for the ceremony and then. . . uh. . .left right after. That's why she's not in any pictures."

What a big, fat lie! An *amateur* lie! Dad himself told me Ashley had banned Mom.

"Where did she live?"

"What?"

"At the time of the wedding. You did mail her an invitation, right?"

"I have no idea, Shiloh! We got married years ago."

"Five. Just name the state."

Silence. "Texas."

"Wrong, Ashley! Try Staunton, Virginia! She lived here for the past *six* years."

"No she didn't!" Ashley gasped, spluttering again. "She just. . . lived there part of the time. You know. Like migrant workers."

I choked. Fish particles spewed everywhere.

"Forget where she lived, okay? Maybe you just went off and left her, Shiloh, but we didn't!"

"Oh, right! Chicago is just down the street from Texas!"

Our voices rose and met like two angry *sumo* wrestlers.

"Don't pretend you thought so differently, Ashley! You didn't want to live near her any more than I did, and it was her fault."

An odd stillness fell over the kitchen, and the night breeze ruffled a corner of Mom's frilly, country-style curtains. Blue-and-white-checked gingham with tiebacks. I walked over and shut the window tight. Locked it, hand lingering on the sill.

"Although, toward the end Mom did change." My words fell out unintentionally, like a shrimp from an overstuffed sushi plate. As I recalled letters and packages she'd sent me after she "got Jesus." The offers to visit. My throat swelled, wishing I'd answered. Cared. But no.

I sat back down and squeezed the phone cord until my knuckles showed. "What do you want, Ashley?"

Expensive. Expenses. Her words rolled in my head.

She can't possibly think Mom's house. . .no. Not even Ashley would stoop that low.

"Want? It's not about me, but what Mom had in mind for Carson. Too bad she didn't have time to write it in her will."

"Carson. In Mom's will."

"That's right. My son. Her grandson. If you need any proof of her affection or intentions, I've got it in black and white. A letter."

"Mom writes in blue ink." My hands trembled on a silver fish.

"Okay, then blue."

"I don't believe you! Mom never planned to put Carson in her will."

"Oh no? Let me make it plain for you, Shiloh. Half of a hundred thousand, if that's what her little matchbox is worth, still makes fifty grand. Which belongs to Carson and me. After all, she was my mother, too."

The cup wavered and tipped, scattering fish all over the linoleum. I slid to the floor.

"*Stepmother!*"

"*Mother!*"

"Dad did DNA tests to see which secretary told the truth before marrying your mom," I hissed. "Before he divorced her and married *mine*. You're Susan's daughter! Not a cell in your body belongs to Ellen Amelia Jacobs."

My sumo wrestler grunted, nearly shoving Ashley out of the ring. But she roared and righted herself, slapping her thighs.

"No more playing nice!" Ashley screamed. "I gave you a chance to fix things yourself, but since you're such a selfish monster, I've hired a lawyer!"

Ashley's shrill words hit me like a redneck frying pan slathered in bacon grease.

"You. . .what?" I wobbled, plopping back down on the floor. Breath gone out.

"I've got a lawyer, and I'm contesting the will. Since you're obviously not going to do the right thing and share with family." She sniffed in triumph. "It's your fault. You're forcing me to do things the hard way."

I couldn't speak. Just opened and closed my mouth, feeling all sense bleed out of my head.

"You're the one who probably drove her to death anyway, Shiloh, with all your fighting. You know she never had high blood pressure until you two started going at it." Ashley's voice pierced into my stunned ear. "Well maybe it's time you face the truth and stop ham-fisting all her assets to yourself. Since you're the one who least deserves them."

Ashley had to be kidding. I laughed, but she didn't laugh back.

"You have no grounds to contest the will!" I finally spat, finding my voice. "Mom named me the only beneficiary."

She raised beefy sumo arms, grimacing. "Think what you want, but Mom had a different opinion—especially about Carson. Her letter proves it."

"What letter? And what does Carson have to do with anything?"

"Mom claimed Carson as her grandson. In the letter."

My sumo wrestler stumbled. Crashed. Rolled out of the ring and into the exploding stands. I sprawled on the kitchen floor, cord bonging over my head. "She didn't! You're lying!"

"Oh no. I'm not. My lawyer will be happy to provide you with a copy." Ashley's sumo wrestler raised her fists, turning in brilliant flashbulbs. "Do what Mom truly wanted. Fifty-fifty. Or I'll go for the whole thing. And I'm sure it's worth more than a hundred thousand. Quite sure."

★　★　★

No sooner had I slammed the screen door behind me than my cell phone vibrated in my pocket.

"Look, Ashley, don't call me here again—ever!" I shouted, voice echoing off Mom's siding. And started to shut it, when the name FAYE

CLATTERBAUGH glowed on the screen.

"Shiloh, darlin', what's goin' on? Everything all right?"

"Faye?" I blubbered, pulling my shawl tighter in the chill. "No, everything's wrong. Ashley called here, and. . ." I let my words die. Cold wind rustled my hair in brown chunks, and I buried my nose in Christie's soft, warm-scented fur. She licked my cheek, and I hugged her. Becky won, doggone it. No way on earth I'd part with Christie now.

"Oh, sugar. I'm so sorry. Ashley called last night and asked for your phone number. I had no idea ya didn't want me to give it."

My head jerked up. "What? Ashley called you?"

"She said she missed ya and worried about ya 'cause ya hadn't called. . . ."

"She said that?" I sputtered. A bat swooped lightning fast, dark against the sky full of stars. "Then Ashley's lying. She didn't call here all the time to talk to Mom."

"Well," said Faye, attempting diplomacy, "maybe she lost the number?"

"Maybe she's a liar! And she's got her snake eyes on my inheritance." My voice caught. "She has a lawyer."

Faye gasped. "No. Ya can't mean. . .I mean, Ellen's house ain't worth. . .forgive me, Shiloh! But ya musta misunderstood her!"

A puff of wind rattled the dry rose canes, and I hugged my knees. "Don't I wish. But I think I understood her perfectly."

I started to mumble a lame good-bye then paused. "Faye?"

"Yes, sugar?"

"Why did you call me?"

"Oh, that." She laughed, sounding nervous. Or maybe embarrassed. "Oh, doll, how can I say this?"

Great. Just what I need. More bad news. "Say what?" A sinking sensation swirled in my chest.

"Shiloh, I dunno, but it seemed kinda like maybe we'd been—"

"Who's 'we'?"

"Me an' that Earl fella. I kinda wondered if ya'd. . .ya know. Set us up or somethin'. Am I readin' things right?"

I flopped my head in my hands in surrender. Or humiliation. Whichever. All that beautiful dinner for nothing.

"Oh, honey. I'm sorry. I didn't mean to mess things up for ya. Ya worked so hard, and you're precious. Ya know that?" Faye's voice came softly as my tears dripped on the knees of my jeans. "Shiloh, sugar, I love

Like Sweet Potato Pie

ya ta pieces. Don't get me wrong. But that Earl fella? He's nice, but. . ."

"But what?" I tried to sniffle without Faye hearing me.

"It ain't gonna work, Shiloh. I'm sorry. He. . .well, I don't wanna get married again."

"It's okay, Faye. You don't have to. I just wanted to try." I scuffed my shoe on the step. *Just one more thing in my rotten life that doesn't work.*

Phones made me sick. Everything bad happened over the phone: News of Mom's death. Shouts from Dave Driscoll telling me not to come back to Tokyo. Ashley. Hang-ups. Even collection agents.

I said good-bye to Faye and huddled there under the stars, cold gusts crackling tree branches overhead, rustling mournful leaves. The wind stung, but not as much as my heart.

A chilly moon rose over looming black mountains, a far cry from hard concrete angles and millions of city lights dazzling in my beloved Tokyo. Horns and headlights crammed on the gleaming expressway, flowing all night long. The lighted subway whirring by, blowing my hair on its way to popular electronics district Akihabara, which came to life after dark like a glowing vampire.

Instead I found myself marooned in Redneckville, trying desperately to sell Mom's house. Facing what I'd lost. Reordering my messed-up life.

And stumbling straight into the arms of Jesus, who caught me by astonishing surprise.

Uh. . .yeah. That.

I scrunched my eyes closed, remembering the hardwood bedroom floor under my knees as I prayed to give my heart to God. The surge of tears after years of pent-up pain. The love which flowed, like a song I vaguely recalled, from the pages of Mom's journal and marked-up, underlined Bible.

I knew changing loyalties to Jesus didn't miraculously make everything right with the world. Becky'd told me so. And Faye. And Adam. And half the Bible, for crying out loud. Mom followed Jesus, too, toward the end of her life—and instead of pie-in-the-sky, she got a brain aneurysm.

No, Mom got better than pie. She got heaven.

But Ashley's blackmail threat, on top of my quivering Mount Fuji of other problems, seemed like a low blow, even for God.

Shouldn't He. . . I don't know. Start me off easy?

Jennifer Rogers Spinola

I stuffed my free hand in my pocket, shivering in the wind.

What options did I have anyway? I could give up on God. Turn my back on this Jesus who made the blind see and the dead raise to life. Believe what Becky called "Happy Meal" theology, which meant tossing the toy back in the box if I got one I didn't like.

Or I could take a risk and throw in my lot with Jesus. Cast my net on the other side of the boat, against all logic and say, *"I believe anyway."*

Even if it hurts.

Because it does.

I gently smoothed Christie's silky head, tears leaking out as I recalled the beautiful feel of Japanese words in my mouth. Chopsticks balanced in my fingers, slender and nimble.

And most of all, my black-and-white byline under a news story: *Shiloh P. Jacobs.* Deadlines. Dictionaries. My head bent over a laptop, Japanese documents and books sprawled on my desk in piles. *Kanji* character stickers and Japanese verb forms jotted on Post-it notes. Journalistic ethics books for my master's. My hands flitting across the keyboard as I created and polished and double-checked blocks of text, dancing with words and metaphors.

The angry countenance of my editor, Dave Driscoll, and the slight jut of his chin as he nodded gruffly. "Good story," he told me only twice.

Once when I plagiarized. The other when I rose to my feet amid applause, wending my way to the front of the auditorium to receive a coveted journalism award.

I pressed wet eyes closed, feeling the emptiness of my hands. Hands that now counted out change. Stacked dirty plates. Stickered books. Wrote checks to collection agencies. And now had to fight off my sneaky half sister, who wanted to scrape the little I had left from between my fingers.

"Blessed is anyone," Jesus said when his beloved cousin John waited on the verge of death, *"who does not stumble on account of me."*

John still lost his head. Becky still lost her baby. And I just lost the one remaining family member I thought I still had.

Can I still believe? And not fall away like a lifeless leaf, hanging by a tendril from Stella's silver maple?

I ran my palm over the rough, wooden deck where Mom had watched the sun rise so many times. *Come on, house! Just sell!* And then I'd count out the dollar bills that solved all my problems. Pay off my taxes. Even pay off Ashley, for goodness' sake, some small sum so she'd leave me alone.

Is that too much to ask, God? Just take me back to Japan! And I'll never come here again.

Christie sighed in contentment and tumbled over in my arms, pressing her fuzzy dog snout to the warmth of my neck. And I leaned into her, listening to her little heart beat strong and warm, cradled in my arms.

Trusting.

Resting.

Sound asleep, like Jesus in the storm-tossed boat when His disciples panicked, afraid they'd sink and drown.

"You of little faith," He said, *"why are you so afraid?"*

And He stilled the storm and waves with a single word.

"That's me, Jesus," I whispered, stroking Christie's tiny ears, flopped warm over my arm. "The littlest faith in the world. But if You want me, I'm still Yours."

I put my cell phone away and headed back into the house. Lowered Christie, limp with sleep, into her dog bed and started putting away the dishes Faye'd washed, cup handles out like my real-estate agent instructed.

Ashley had already left five messages, blinking red.

"Don't think you can weasel out of this, Shiloh! I told Dad about it already, and he thinks. . ." Beep.

"I don't speak to Dad!" I retorted out loud, slapping a plate in the cabinet.

"Hi, Shiloh? I'm warning you! If you want to play dirty, I'll go for everything. Even the car. Even the measly little. . ." Beep.

I turned off the answering machine and unplugged the phone. Even messages from Shifflet Septic Services were better than this. I threw the dish towel on the counter and slumped at the kitchen table, head in my hands.

And jumped as the doorbell buzzed.

At this hour? I scowled at the door.

Faye. It must be Faye. So mother-like! Or maybe she wants to tell me she's in love with Earl. I scooted off the chair and reached to unlock the door then pulled back a curtain first.

Huh? I froze, leaning closer.

Um. . .no. Not Faye. I didn't recognize the car in the driveway at all. A deep apple-red Mitsubishi, new.

I tried not to think about the murder Becky mentioned, palms suddenly sweaty. I pressed my cheek to the glass, twisting to see better.

A shadowy figure loomed at my front door, partially illuminated by the porch light.

Chapter 5

I must be dreaming. No way under the sun she'd be standing here on my front porch in a black-burgundy Bauhaus punk-rock T-shirt. Shiny tan jacket. Impatiently checking the address on a piece of paper.

I swung open the door and stared, uncomprehending, into the black-lined eyes of Kyoko Morikoshi.

"Kyoko?" I gasped, fumbling with the screen-door latch. No more words came. I just held the door half open, memories swirling like moths against the glow of the porch light: the acrid whiff of Kyoko's cigarette smoke swirling up into the Tokyo sky, late nights at the Associated Press office, and our trips to record shops (Kyoko) and Beard Papa's cream puffs (me), scarves nestling our necks. The roil of crowds at the crosswalk. Ticket booths and red Japanese maples. *Onigiri* rice triangles stuffed with shrimp and mayo. White-gloved bus drivers. Chopsticks. Skyscrapers.

Kyoko's shoulders relaxed, and she stuffed the paper in her pocket. Beep-beeped the car lock. "Well, are you going to let me in, or do I need to spend the night on the porch?"

I forced my mouth to move. "You're—you're here!"

"And bearing gifts," she announced in her coastal California accent, holding out a bag with a box inside. A skull ring twinkled from her finger next to indigo-painted nails. She looked nothing like the Japanese-American Associated Press reporter and legal expert she was supposed to be.

"It's not another puppy, is it?" My hands shook, giddy, as she stepped through the doorway. "I got one of those in a box today, too."

"If it is, you'd better call the Japanese Bureau of Health and the ATA." Kyoko slipped off black boots and stepped into proffered striped house slippers then plopped the box in my hands.

I slipped off the bag and found, to my disbelief, BEARD PAPA'S splashed across the glossy side of the box. Inside nestled six glorious cream puffs, all hugged in white tissue paper.

"Kyoko!" I screamed. "How did you do it? You know those are my favorite!"

"Dry ice." She shook off her huge, ugly purse—with green

monsters in an '80s Atari-game design—and stretched. "That's how they package them for long deliveries. And believe me, this one took long enough."

My eyes ping-ponged from the box to Kyoko.

"I did get sidetracked in Richmond awhile, too. Great music stores. Check it out—a rare Ramones LP!" She held it up, then seeing nothing registered, shook her head in pity. "Why aren't you living in Richmond, at least, instead of Pork Rind Central? I could barely find Staunton on a map!"

"Technically I live in Churchville. It's even smaller than Staunton." I poked a cream puff with my finger, mouth watering.

"Churchville. Ironic, huh? Since you're so spiritual and all lately." She smirked, shrugging off her jacket.

Kyoko didn't know the half of it. But I barely heard her. Mouth gaping at the cream puffs, the box, and Kyoko. Right there in my living room. I threw my arms around her.

Anti-affectionate Kyoko grumpily tried to disengage my hug. "What's that?" She scowled at Christie, who batted her tail.

"A dog."

"Hmmph."

Jet lag chased away sleep, so we sat on the living room floor and shared—or rather, she declined, and I ate—my box of cream puffs. Light and fluffy, dry, with a thick, silky-smooth custard filling. Exactly as I remembered them. Flavored with vanilla and dusted with powdered sugar.

"You really bought these at Beard Papa's?" I turned the box around, mouth full. Still not quite believing the vision before me.

"Well, they're not from KFC."

"I know. It's not Christmas."

Good thing Tim and Becky weren't there, or I'd have to explain how millions of Japanese preordered fast-food fried chicken for Christmas, and during the last two weeks of December, you couldn't even get a sandwich at KFC for all the backed-up Christmas orders.

I bit into another cream puff, tasting Tokyo days. Saw myself standing in line at Beard Papa's in jacket and knee boots, crisp and prim, cute expensive purse over my shoulder. Bowing politely as a uniform-clad girl with shaggy mahogany hair handed me my change in *yen*.

The scent of powdered sugar crumbling, for one moment, the

unscalable wall between yesterday and today.

I wondered if ancient Mrs. Inoue at the little neighborhood store still remembered me—if she gave ginger candy to anyone else—and whose shoes now slept in my apartment *genkan* (entranceway). Who sat in my desk at the Associated Press office? Who practiced English with the receptionist in the shiny gold apartment lobby of Carlos Torres Castro, my Argentinean ex-fiancé? (The one who unceremoniously dumped me for an Australian, mind you, after I arrived in Virginia for Mom's funeral.)

"You okay?" Kyoko turned her head sideways, narrowing black eyes at me. "Don't worry. I've got loads of Japanese stuff for you in the car."

"Never been better." I smiled, quickly sponging my face with my palm. That wasn't exactly true. But for the tiniest sliver of a moment, with sweet, familiar custard melting on my tongue, I felt like it. "Kyoko, what are you doing here?"

Christie padded into my lap, and Kyoko recoiled. Animals made her nervous, as if they'd start spewing venom and diseases just by visual contact. She picked a single dog hair off her leg and scooted farther away.

"I should ask you the same thing," she said with a suspicious arch of her sparsely plucked eyebrow, new piercing twinkling. "I thought you'd have sold this place and escaped Virginia by now."

Kyoko looked exactly the same, albeit a pound or two lighter, which I chalked up to the absence of my constant temptations with food. The fashionably purple-red sheen had brightened in her mushroom-shaped hair, more maroon than black. I'd missed her terribly.

"I'm working on it. Did you see the For Sale sign out front?"

"Yep. Do you hand out lifeboats, too? Better count 'em first."

Titanic Farm and Real Estate. I know, I know. If they didn't sell so many houses, I'd dump them for another realty company that actually paid marketing professionals.

"I especially liked the 'Farm' part." She grinned and poked me with her slippered foot. "So does this place qualify as farm or real estate? I'm thinking both. After all, I could certainly smell cows on the way down here, and those curtains look like gingham to me."

I threw a couch pillow at Kyoko. "It's not *that* bad, is it? Or maybe I'm just being assimilated."

"Let's hope not." She dusted the pillow off and stuck it under her head, lying back on the cream living room carpet. "So how many offers have you had?"

"No offers. Two visits this month. I'll be glad when it's over and I can get back to Japan. Start my master's again." I snuggled sleeping Christie against my cheek. "But I need house money to do that."

"I'm sure your place'll sell fast. To somebody with cowboy boots," Kyoko snarked then stopped in midchortle. "No offense. I know your mom lived here, and. . ."

"None taken. Want to see it?"

She groaned and covered a loud yawn with her palms. Reluctantly sat up. "Okay. Fast. But then gravity's taking over."

I walked her through the house with Christie in my arms. Memories poured back, momentarily making me forget my ache for Japan: The bedroom floors that Tim and Adam polished after taking up the carpet. The kitchen full of autumn blooms where Becky taught me to make sweet tea. The living room where we spent the last moments of her unborn baby's life, laughing, and the front porch where I'd sat with Adam in the twilight.

"What do you think?" I ran my hand across the smooth, cream kitchen walls. Adam and Tim had stripped Mom's hideous brown '70s wallpaper, and the paint still smelled new.

"Where's your stash of oversized belt buckles and cowboy hats?"

"My what?"

"Hold on." Kyoko moved things around on the counter. "There must be a spit cup here somewhere."

I rolled my eyes and sat down at the table, which was still scattered with lace and marigold petals. "So why didn't you call me? I could've met you at the airport!"

"Yeah, sorry. I know it's rude to show up out of the blue, but I had a few days off, plus two Japanese holidays. . .so I just bought a ticket and came."

She gazed around the dining room, apparently trying to reconcile herself with the fact that she'd indeed entered the South. "I can always camp out at Best Western if you need some space. I'll ask for that room you had overlooking the train tracks." She rubbed sleepy eyes, smudging her dark makeup. "Or I can stay at the Stonewall Jackson Hotel."

"Stonewall Jackson? You're making it up!"

"Wanna bet?" Kyoko slapped a printout in my hand. "Hey, you're the one who lives here. Not me."

I jerked the paper closer. "It looks nice!"

"It actually does." She bent her head to see. "I can ask for the Dixie Suite. They serve grits and pigs' feet in the morning, and a free ticket to the Civil War reenactments—complete with mugging."

I instinctively circled my side with my hand where the skinhead had kicked me with his boot, requiring lots of ice and pain medication. Then Kyoko's words registered, and I smacked her with the paper. "Don't be ridiculous! You're staying here."

"You sure? Because I don't want to intrude. Seems like you're pretty busy here, cow tipping and whatnot."

I ignored her. "I've missed you." I hugged her again, and she glowered. Got up and played with my refrigerator magnets.

I forgot—Japan and the American South had two very different rules of physical contact. Southerners hugged. Whacked. Tackled. Gave noogies. A lot. And Japanese. . .well, bowed, standing a foot apart and trying desperately to avoid eye contact.

Kyoko sat back down and gave me an awkward pat on the head, messing up my hair. "Yeah, I've missed you, too, Ro," she said with as warm a smile as she could muster.

Ro. No one else in the world used that nickname for me, made up of the last syllable of my name butchered in Japanese. Even the Japanese honorific, *-chan*, she sometimes tacked on the end reminded me of achingly beautiful Tokyo days.

"How long can you stay?"

"Can you put up with me for seven days? I know, I know. I'll smoke outside. Dog and allergies and house on the market."

"A week? That's it?" My smile collapsed. I don't know what I'd hoped for, but seven measly days? I wanted to soak up Japan from Kyoko, crab that she was, like osmosis: The office jokes. The subway. The sparkling city lights. I wanted to pretend I'd never gotten fired for plagiarism and board the plane bound for Tokyo by her side, never to return.

"Well, a week's all I've got, bucko." Kyoko yawned, stretching. "Take it or leave it. And if you leave it, give me my cream puffs back."

"I guess my choices are limited."

"Smart woman."

"Coffee? Tea?"

"Tea'd be great."

"Hot or cold?"

"Please don't tell me you've got that sweet iced-tea stuff in your fridge."

"Nope." *Because Tim and Becky drank it all when they came over to watch NASCAR.*

Kyoko relaxed. "Hot then. Maybe it'll help me sleep."

And so we sat over steaming teacups, catching up on the news. Or trying to. I couldn't describe Becky and Tim or Faye without sounding ridiculous. My prayer either. . .or Mom's journals and the decision I made that would change me forever.

Oh boy. Those would take another hour. Maybe another day. When we were both awake and Kyoko's shouts didn't wake the neighbors.

But I listened, cradling the teacup Japanese-style: one hand on the base and the other on the rim. Covering my teeth chastely with my hand when I smiled or laughed. I still did that out of habit. And bobbed my head in thanks and bowed to store clerks, too, but not quite as much anymore.

At least I'd stopped trying to pay for things with my cell phone or drive on the left.

I played with a stray rose petal while Kyoko blabbed about her new stories, how our nemesis Nora Choi blundered an article, calling the prime minister's wife "First Lady," and the fashion crimes of Yoshie-san, the office helper.

"What else?" I begged. "Tell me more! Tell me everything!"

"The same." Kyoko shrugged. "Not much changes."

"What can you possibly mean?" I set my teacup down hard enough to wake Christie. "Every single day something changes in Japan! The maple leaves turn red. They write new advertising jingles or create another TV drama. A new coffee flavor at Starbucks or a sandwich at McDonald's—like the Bacon Lettuce Burger." I swallowed hard. "And I'm missing it!"

"They don't have the Bacon Lettuce Burger here?"

I gasped. "Of course not! It's a Japan original! Like the breakfast hot dog. I loved those."

Kyoko grimaced. "You're the only one I know who's ordered the breakfast hot dog."

"Yoshie-san did. I saw him eating two of them one morning."

"Oh, and he makes it all right? I've seen that guy buy live beetles from a vending machine. He said they were pets for his son, but I think otherwise."

"Does Dave miss me?" I asked after a long pause. After bawling—and cursing—me out in my hotel room once he discovered I'd copied, Dave hadn't spoken another word to me. Most of us AP employees crept around the office in fear even though duly employed, so imagine *fired!* By Dave! I shuddered.

"Dave wouldn't miss his own mother. But in his own strange way, yes, I think he does."

"Really?"

"Well, he blew his stack at first. Everybody stayed out of his way while he stomped around on the warpath, but he eventually got over it." Kyoko leaned forward and softened her voice, fingering her skull ring. "But you know what, Ro? He never gave Nora politics. He put her on the military beat and divided politics between Kaine and me. He knows she's not cut out for it like you were. Well, are. Still."

"Thanks," I said softly, not quite believing Kyoko just complimented me. Kyoko rarely handed out praise; I hoarded it like the last drop of soy sauce in a care package.

"So, what did you do with your dumb rock?" she asked abruptly, apparently realizing she bordered on affection. She nodded curtly in the direction of my left hand.

"Oh, that." I twisted my fingers over the empty space on my ring finger. "I sent it back to Carlos by mail. In a padded envelope. With the price on the outside and no insurance."

Kyoko blanched. "You did *what?*"

"Can you believe he actually got it? He had to pay one hefty tax though. I can't imagine." I smiled in spite of myself. I probably should have retaliated. . .uh. . .behaved with more dignity, but what's done is done.

"Girl." Kyoko stared at me. "And I thought rearranging his Azuki page to make him a Brazil fanatic was clever."

Everybody in Tokyo ditched Facebook in favor of Azuki, its Japanese twin.

I managed a grin. "I wish I could've seen his face. Nationalistic Argentinean snob."

"Tell me about it." Kyoko laughed into her tea. "Carlos is one lame-o if I've ever seen one. Sorry, Ro, but it's true. You deserve better than him."

She switched topics with lightning speed. Her specialty. "So what's your middle name? You promised to tell me."

"I never promised that!"

"Peabody?"

"Keep trying. And guess female names."

"Hey, you never know."

I stared down at the yellow-green liquid in my teacup, reflecting the glass light fixture overhead. Carlos's name still stung a little. "Have you. . .seen him since then?"

"Who, Peabody?"

"Carlos."

She glared into her teacup and then at me. "I was afraid you'd ask."

"Well, have you?" The question leaped into my throat, and I trembled, looking away. Carlos had done me wrong and not thought twice, but the thought of his cologne made my pulse speed up a notch. His gorgeous face and dark eyes. Sharp Italian suits.

Beyond his good looks, I'd. . .well, loved him. Or thought I did. I turned my teacup around on the dish, trying to blot out the bitter ache that rose with his memory.

She snorted. "In person, no. Thankfully. But apparently he's modeling shirts or something now."

"What?" I jerked my head up.

"I know. I was taking the subway to Nakameguro when, *bam!* There's Carlos's ugly mug right over the subway door. Sheesh." She rolled her eyes. "Japanese companies'll slap just about any foreigner on ads these days."

"Yeah." I tried to chuckle as if it didn't bother me. "Is he still with. . .Mia?"

Kyoko gave an exasperated sigh. "As if I would know! Honestly, you're better off without him. Let him go!" She gave me a fierce look over her teacup. "Little liar! I wish he'd go model subway tracks for a while."

She sipped in angry silence. Either he still loved Mia and Kyoko refused to tell me, or she really didn't know. I decided to drop it.

"I have let him go, Kyoko. It's over. It's just hard to put the past to rest sometimes."

"Well, do it! Find a farmer or something." She jabbed at her teacup with a spoon. "Carlos didn't love you, Ro. I don't know how else to put it, but there it is."

"I know." I avoided her eyes.

"You do? I thought you bought all his drivel about. . . Never mind." Kyoko waved it away. "Well, at least you've come to your senses."

"I'm not sure I even know what love is, Kyoko." I poured some more tea from my black Japanese teapot. "I'm confused."

"Well, earth to Ro. It wasn't Carlos." Her voice softened just a touch, probably to keep me from bursting into tears again. Kyoko eschewed tears as ardently as affection.

"Yeah." My tea shimmered, wisps of steam floating heavenward. "It'll take me some time to figure out what love really is, you know? I'm thinking differently these days."

"Here we go. Your new Bible-thumping spirituality." She stared at the ceiling. "You gonna give me a gospel tract now?"

I tried to laugh like she did, pretending to go along with the joke. Then quickly picked up my teacup and turned Kyoko's own split-second subject change on her. "So what's the techie scene in Akiba? Anything interesting?"

I knew it would occupy her mind. And it did. For the next hour and a half.

I couldn't sleep with the long day clogging my head. Shane, Ashley, Kyoko, Carlos. All roiling in my exhausted brain like a Japanese typhoon.

I tossed on the pillow, eyes staring up at the shadowy wallpaper. Christie curled up next to me in a warm, fuzzy ball against the blankets. I know, I know. Dog hair. Pets. Real-estate rules. Blah, blah, blah. *I put newspapers down, okay?*

But I needed her to stop crying that pitiful little whine from her box as much as I needed her warmth. Her quivering back pressed tightly against the crook of my elbow. Her quiet, steady breath to fill the tremors of worry in my stomach.

I had a feeling. A little, nagging, uneasy feeling about why Kyoko had come without warning. Right after I got kicked by a skinhead and told her I'd started reading the Bible and the Harlem Globetrotters came to The Green Tree. Which they did. But Kyoko didn't believe a word of it.

She thinks I'm losing it, and she came to see if her assumptions from a few weeks ago are true. Maybe to get me help.

I blinked up into the dark ceiling, feeling torn in two directions.

Jennifer Rogers Spinola

As much as I regretted it, my life no longer converged with Kyoko's in Japan's cherry-blossom splendor, wending our way through subway crowds to the shiny granite steps of the AP office building. Up, up, and up to awards and glory and tomorrows.

In Staunton, Virginia, I found no glory. Just hard, painful starting over. In small-town, rural nowhere—the last place on earth I'd expect. Just like Adam's amputee brother Rick, a war hero, grunting against agony to learn to walk again.

And then there was Adam. Who, yes, drove a pickup. And hauled mulch and pruned shrubs to help care for Rick. Giving up the life he wanted for something better.

And somehow greater.

My eyes flickered to Mom's journal and Bible on a side table, their gentle lines comforting even in the dark.

Some things, I guessed, went beyond explaining. Kyoko would have to see for herself.

And when she finally figured things out, back in her cushy office chair in Tokyo, I wouldn't be around to hear her bawl me out.

Kyoko's snores wheezed from Mom's bedroom—a guest room now, while I claimed Mom's extra bedroom as mine. I eased slippered feet into the kitchen, the sky shining a dull cloudy gray through the curtains. A chill sank through the house; cold rain had spattered during my early morning run through Crawford Manor's empty neighborhood streets.

Christie stretched, toddling across the shiny floor like a ball of smoke.

I glanced nervously at Kyoko's closed bedroom door then scribbled a note. An addendum to my detailed instructions to take Christie out two hundred times an hour, don't let her eat the kitchen chairs, and so forth. I tucked it on the counter so she could find it after she'd had some tea—to minimize the impact and improve her mood first.

She's going to hate you, Shiloh!

Or maybe jet lag will take over, and she'll never figure it out.

I hesitated then kissed Christie good-bye and left her in the laundry room with her rubber chew toy. Floor well-papered with newspapers, and everything bite-able out of reach.

While Christie whined at the laundry-room door, I grabbed my purse and sunglasses. Slipped on bone-colored Jimmy Choo heels at the door, another beautiful remnant of the life I no longer had.

And backed out of the driveway, Bible on the passenger's seat.

Chapter 6

The church rose over the hills like a glimpse of sun, exactly as MapQuest predicted. I pulled into an empty parking space and turned off the car. Just sat there, wondering if I'd lost my marbles—like Kyoko already thought—by coming here. Mom had probably parked this same car, in this same parking space, and only a few irretrievable months separated us.

The sun hid again, and bitter wind tossed scarlet and brown leaves across the rain-wet parking lot. I shut the door and pulled my delicate sweater tighter around my soft ivory dress, the wispy bow trailing from my waist. Never in a million years did I guess, when I bought this combo at a trendy boutique in Shinjuku, that I'd wear it to a *church*.

I accepted a bulletin at the door, the whiff of pungent coffee spreading warmth throughout an otherwise chilly foyer lined with photo-scattered bulletin boards. A man's voice slipped through the sanctuary door—along with pale light from the stained-glass cross, dappling the carpet and wooden pew backs. Spilling nearly to my feet.

I slipped into the sanctuary with a faint squeak of the door, streaking those expensive heels with luminous color as the sun dazzled for a moment in the round glass. There, in the very back: a space on the blue-cushioned pew between a blond couple with a toddler gobbling fistfuls of Cheerios and an older African-American woman in yellow, all with plenty of room between us.

I wonder where Mom sat. I wonder what she wore. My heart pounded as I sat down, dropping my purse and Bible and glancing around the large, airy sanctuary. Globe-shaped lights suspended from a vaulted wooden ceiling, its shiny beams a homey, comforting golden brown.

The sanctuary retained a crisp coolness, despite the warm lights and rows of people, but I unwound my scarf and placed it in a soft pile over my purse. I wrinkled my nose, smelling new carpet and a hint of flowers from the altar. Chrysanthemums. Golden orange and sweetly pungent. I knew their smell.

I dropped my head, fingering a ring and trying not to think about the yellow spider chrysanthemums that covered Mom's casket, tendrils quivering in the summer breeze.

Jennifer Rogers Spinola

The man in front—who wore khakis and an open-collared shirt, not the full suit I expected to see at a pulpit—stepped down. Piano and violin music streamed, and I groped for Mom's Bible, turning my head from side to side to catch someone's movements.

No, I need a hymnal, not a Bible to sing, right? But I saw none, except a blue book tucked in a pocket of the pew in front of me. Nope. Another Bible.

People stood, and I followed them. *Should I try to find a hymnal? Should I sing? What should I do?* My clenched fingers, white on the bulletin, relaxed as the yellow-clad woman pointed to the overhead screen, on which song lyrics suddenly appeared. Oh. Easy. Okay. More modern than I'd expected.

As the music swelled, I forgot my nerves. Simply listened. And, for the first time in my life, hesitantly opened my mouth and sang with the others. About Jesus. How He died for our sins, and He is everything we need.

Strange words, but enchanting—calling my name in the same beautiful tone as Mom's journal. Wrapping around my heart like warm arms, filling the empty spaces.

All of a sudden, I needed Faye, my second mom. Needed Becky and Tim. I should have told them to expect me. Should have. . . I don't know. Done more than throw on a dress.

"Excuse me," I whispered to the woman in yellow. "You don't happen to know Tim and Becky Donaldson, do you?"

Without missing a beat, she put her arm around me and pointed.

"Thank you," I whispered back, returning her hug and gathering my purse. And I fled headlong to the space.

When I slid in beside them, Tim nearly bowled over a pewmate with his double take. He slapped me with a high five and hugged me, rattling my teeth.

"Well, I'll be!" Tim hooted. He forgot about the music, grinning so much his cheeks nearly split. Scooted his Bible and stuff to hastily make a space. "Welcome to our church, Shah-loh, and to the people a God!"

People turned and stared, chuckled at Tim, and I ducked my head. Becky just sniffled and smiled and tried to sing then dug in her purse for some tissues. I looped my arm around her shoulders, and hers around mine, and lost myself in the glorious music that had somehow become my very own song.

"I know somebody who's gonna be real excited," Becky whispered, beaming through her tears.

"Huh?" I bent closer.

And then a few rows up on the opposite side, I saw a head turn. Tall and sandy blond, dressed in a crisp blue dress shirt and tie. Arm on the shoulder of a kid who looked like Todd Carter—the little guy who stole my heart when I doled out medications for Rick while Adam rushed their dad to the emergency room with a broken arm.

Yep. That's my life. One ridiculous crisis after another.

Blue eyes swept across the congregation in midsong and then did a double take when they met mine. Adam faltered and dropped his arm. He turned partially then whispered something to Todd, who grinned and waved.

I wish I could have preserved what I saw in that shock of blue— the thousand emotions, the curiosity, and then a surprising warmth.

I waved back to Todd then glanced away. Pretending not to notice Adam's hands clench slightly against the pew back then brush nervously through his hair.

"I don't know what you're talking about," I whispered to Becky.

"Huh?" She put a hand on her hip. Mocking me.

Adam had turned back to the screen, but in the next second I saw another flash of blue. Asking.

I nodded. And a slight flush rose in his face before the smile covered it.

I could hardly look at Adam after the service. My head floated, full of the sermon, in which Jesus called Himself the Bread of Life. How He offered His broken body on our behalf. How Adam and Eve sinned by taking the first bite, but we could partake of Christ and never go hungry again.

Hunger I knew. I'd never forget digging under lockers in the elementary school hallway, starving and hoping for enough change to buy a candy bar. Mom out with her cults again, forgetting to pack me a lunch or leave food in the apartment. I'd learned to make do with powdered Jell-O packets and canned corn, and sometimes filed through the soup kitchen line at St. John's homeless shelter.

But a different hunger gnawed in me these past years: anxiety, hurt, anger. Wondering if my drive and accomplishments could fill me, could make me forget my past and give me the love I'd always wanted.

Bread of Life! Rockets fired off in my head.

"So yer gonna do that beginner's Sunday school class with Pastor Davis?" Becky stood next to me, pink leather Bible in one hand. And a camouflage-patterned cloth Bible cover snapped over it.

"His first name's not Jefferson, is it?"

"Jefferson Davis?" Becky laughed and slapped the pew. "Like the president a the Confederacy? Shucks, that's a good'n, Shah-loh! The pastor's name's Matt. Real nice guy. Former army chaplain an' pro ball player, an' his wife. . ."

But I didn't feel like meeting anybody. I needed to think. To drive. To be alone with my thoughts and sort through the surfacing questions, like shredded blossoms bobbing in a Japanese pool after the rain.

And to think of how to break the news to Kyoko, who would chalk one more tick onto her lunatic collection. "A religious nut job," she'd call me. "So you're gonna marry a truck driver and start pumping out bucktoothed kids?"

Kyoko didn't scare me.

But Kyoko being right *did*.

While Becky yakked with somebody, laughing and tugging on Tim's arm, I glanced down at my sleek Jimmy Choos and designer dress. A Versace bracelet sparkling on my wrist.

I felt like a fake, a fraud. I didn't belong here, with Tim's striped Western-style dress shirt and polished cowboy boots. Southern accents and hand slaps twanging over the pews like Confederate bullets.

I'm a Yankee snob, for crying out loud! Not a redneck denizen of the Bible Belt!

Then I noticed my nails. Clipped short and hastily slapped with cheap pinky-beige CVS nail polish, already chipping around the edges from hot dishwater and too many hand washings.

My longer-than-usual strand of brown hair curling down over my shoulder, coarse from cheap drugstore hair products and not enough time and money for expensive cuts. My old socialite friends would frown and cluck their arrogant tongues.

Fine. Let them. I didn't want to be them anyway.

Not now. Not after Jesus.

But as I stood and awkwardly shook hands with somebody, not

hearing my own words, I realized one thing: I didn't know who I was anymore.

Where do I fit, God? Who am I supposed to be?

The last time Kyoko saw me, my face kept a stone-like mask over Mom's death; I neither cried nor prayed. I knew no more about Jesus than biophysics, and I didn't care to. I could build my own kingdom, thank you very much.

The kind of kingdom Adam's brother Rick called *dust*. Because when I scooped it up, it crumbled and sifted through my fingers like cool Virginia soil.

Dust. Ashes. Death. I felt light-headed, like when I first heard about Mom's brain aneurysm back in Japan. I shouldn't have brought up death.

The scent of Mom's Avon perfume in its yellow globe mixed with funeral lilies and chrysanthemums crowded in my head as I glanced around at the sanctuary where she once sat. Once laughed, once flipped through these same Bible pages, finger on the black-and-red lines.

Before I knew her.

And now I never would.

My stomach suddenly roiled. Becky reached out to introduce me to someone, but instead I bolted for the door.

★　★　★

The main aisle out of the sanctuary crawled with strangers—albeit noisy, happy, laughing strangers—but I didn't feel like seeing anyone. I opened another door and pushed deeper into the heart of the church, finding myself in a gigantic gym, people milling around and voices echoing loudly over the high, white ceiling, which crisscrossed with bars and echoing voices. A couple with too many kids blocked the door to the parking lot.

I panicked. Veered out of the gym and into a long wing of empty rooms—probably for the nursery or Sunday school. There *must* be an exit somewhere! If not, the fire marshal would hear from me.

I'd just ducked around the corner, feeling tingly in my head and hands, when someone grabbed my sleeve.

"Where are you going?" Adam's eyebrows flicked upward. He hadn't let go of my sleeve. "And. . .Shiloh? What are you doing here?"

I caught my breath and looked up into those blue eyes I'd seen during the service, only this time I couldn't read their expression.

I clutched my Bible and purse, sweater dripping over my arm. Looked around desperately for an exit. "Um. . .which question should I answer first?"

His gaze softened. "What are you doing here?"

"Here? In the hallway?"

"No, at church."

I'd never seen Adam in a tie. Normally he displayed six feet of dust-covered dirt and mulch stains from hauling bags of gravel. I discreetly forced my eyes elsewhere.

"I thought you. . . Hey, what happened to your arm?"

"My what?" I dropped my gaze to follow his. Down to a reddish splotch on my forearm. I snatched my sleeve back and covered it.

"That wasn't one of your questions." I shifted my stuff to my other arm. "It's a burn. From The Green Tree. A hot pan or something."

Adam didn't say anything, but his eyes flashed down to a bandage on my finger, courtesy of a box of plastic wrap's razor edge. Wrapping salads.

I hid my palm under Mom's Bible, scowling. As much as I liked Adam Carter, he annoyed me sometimes. We'd even shared words once over his odd ways, right there on my front porch. "I thought you asked why I came to church."

Adam seemed to have trouble remembering his train of thought. "You rushed off without speaking to anyone."

"I know. I just feel. . ." I fumbled with my purse strap, not sure how to answer. So I didn't.

"You all right?"

"Yeah. But I need some time with my thoughts."

A man in a suit hurried past, and we both turned. Our conversation faltered.

"Of course," said Adam lightly, taking a slight step back. "I'm just . . .surprised."

"Why? Because I'm at church?"

My voice came out harsher than I meant. I tried to unstiffen my arms and breathe slowly.

Adam didn't dazzle with stunning good looks like Carlos. He struck me as sort of plain actually. On the scrawny-ish side, and kind of big ears. But Adam Carter was the sort of person who'd bring a can of gas to a perfect stranger in the middle of nowhere. Which is how I'd met him.

"I mean, Shiloh, I thought you made it clear you. . ."

"I know. That I didn't need God. Or church. Or. . .anything." I fingered Mom's Virginia School for the Deaf and Blind keychain. "Well, I was wrong. I do. More than I realized."

My voice snagged in my throat, suddenly emotional. Adam reached out and took Mom's Bible and my sweater, and I let him.

"You said yes." His voice dropped, husky.

"Like you told me to in Winchester." I turned away, irritated at my tears. *Say yes,* he'd whispered. *To God.*

"I asked Jesus to change my life." I crossed my arms and kept my chin up. "But not because of you. I mean, not entirely. I had a lot of reasons."

Adam didn't speak; he just stared at me stupidly. Tried to say something and swallowed instead. Scratched his hair and let his hand rest on the top of his head.

I shouldered my purse. "So is there an exit, or do I have to call the fire marshal?"

"Shiloh, wait." He put his hand lightly on my shoulder. "Wow. That's. . .wow. I'm so glad to hear it!"

"I know." I pawed the carpet with my shoe, afraid my throat would close again. "It's a little strange though, you know? Everything's turned on its head. Everything's. . .different. New. I'm not sure how I feel yet."

"Of course. *You're* different. You're new." He looked at me then at the floor. "I hoped. . .I mean, we all hoped you'd see how much God loves you."

"Yeah." A smile broke through, and I raised my eyes to him again. I felt self-conscious, standing there with tears piling up and my hands twisting the purse strap.

"Look, the bathrooms are down there," said Adam abruptly, pointing. "I'll wait for you."

"Thanks." I released my breath. "And then can you please get me out of here?" I rattled a nearby doorknob just in case the glow under it led outside, but it opened to an empty Sunday school room, quiet with carpet.

"Sure, but can't you at least talk to Faye before you leave? I know she'll be excited to see you. And Todd's looking for you. He's got a whole folder full of drawings for you at home. Army tanks and stuff. Some of them are really pretty good."

Todd. The kid could charm the tattoos off a *yakuza* (Japanese mafia) gangster. And then, of course, I adored Faye. My hard stance melted slightly.

"Okay, but I'm warning you. I'm not ready to see Mom's friends and talk about her. For people to cry and hug me and say how they've missed her or how they're glad I've 'come to Christ' and all that." I shook my finger. "I'm one inch away from bawling somebody out."

Or just plain bawling. Which was probably more likely.

If Adam guessed, he kept quiet. *Smart man.* "I'll get you out fast." He put his hands up. "Scout's honor."

I rolled my eyes and plunged through the bathroom door. *Adam, a Boy Scout? That explains a lot.*

But when I passed the bathroom mirror, my face gleamed as startling pink as cherry blossoms glowing in the sun. And my fingers trembled against my burning cheeks in a vain attempt to cool them.

★   ★   ★

The sanctuary had stilled. Almost empty, save a few people mingling in the corners. Light filtered in from stained-glass windows, shining red and blue on the pews. The enormous cross made me lift my eyes up, up, up—over my roiling heart to the one thing that really mattered.

"Where'd ya go?" Becky demanded, grabbing my arm and tucking it through hers so I couldn't get away. "I've been lookin' for ya! An' Todd here, too!"

"Bathroom." I gestured awkwardly as Adam whispered something in Becky's ear.

"Hey, Shiloh!" Todd grinned, mirroring Adam's blue eyes. "I didn't know you were comin' today! I'd a brought my tank drawings for you! Remember the ones I told you I'd make? The World War II versions? Rick says that first one I did used a Stromberg carburetor, so. . ."

Todd bounced against the back of a pew in excitement as he rattled on, his words carrying a thicker Southern drone than Adam's. Same sandy-blond hair as Adam though, but without the firm slant of jaw that. . .

I straightened up abruptly, smoothing my skirt. "I've got to get home. Sorry, guys. Todd." I patted his back. "But bring your drawings next week."

"Aw, don't go yet, Shah-loh! We'll go easy on ya." Becky put a protective arm around me and winked at Adam. "But say hi to yer second mama first!"

"Faye? She's here?"

"She was he'pin' in the nursery. I got her for ya!" And Becky dragged her over.

Faye grabbed me in a hug and kissed my cheek. "Becky told me about yer announcement, ya goose!" she laughed, crying at the same time. "Why didn't ya tell me last night? Is that why you had all the flowers'n such?"

No! To make you fall in love with Earl!

"Ya mean it for real?" Faye pulled me back at arm's length, blue eyes sparkling with tears behind her glasses. "Ya done asked Jesus inta yer heart?"

"I did. I mean it." I swallowed hard. "And I'm not changing my mind."

"This calls for a celebration!" Tim squished me in a happy side hug. Becky squashed on the other side, and Todd threw himself on us, laughing. It felt like a dog pile. A wonderful dog pile I never wanted to end.

"How 'bout some grub?" asked Tim, a redneck poster child with his mustache and mullet. "It's about time to eat, ain't it? That is, if ol' First Methodist ain't let out already. They's always beatin' us to the good rest'rants so all we got left is the Wal-Mart food court. I better call my cousin at First an' see if they's still goin'."

"Skatetown's got hot dogs!" Becky winked. "So does Raceway!"

"Sorry, guys. Kyoko's at home."

"Yer friend from Japan?" Becky arched an eyebrow. "She speak English?"

"She's American! We worked together back at AP." I thought hard, trying to describe Kyoko. Her dark apartment full of skull-and-crossbones, Japanese pop purses, and punk-rock stuff. Her shelves of *anime* comics.

"Well, she eats, don't she? Go'n git her! A friend a yours is a friend a ours!"

"I doubt she'll like. . .uh. . .Southern food much. Just to warn you." *And she won't be too keen on meeting a bunch of my redneck friends either!* "How about Chili's?"

"Whatever. So long's they got somethin' fried." Tim snickered, and I couldn't tell if he was joking or not.

I dialed home, and the phone rang about thirty times before Kyoko picked up.

"Sorry! Did I wake you?"

"Oh no. I'm chatting with my friend Theo on Skype. Works for a publishing company. Remember him?"

"No, but—"

"Says he wants samples of your book and wonders what's the big holdup."

"Book?"

"You know. The one that pokes 'em in the eye. *Southern Speak.* Remember? How you wrote about cowboy boots and guys with mullets who. . ."

I pressed the phone closer to my ear and hurried a few steps away.

"Oh yeah." I'd almost forgotten about the reporter's notebook I'd filled, in my early days in Virginia, with notes about belt buckles and NASCAR and processed food.

I switched subjects. "How's Christie?"

"The dog? She's all right. I took her out a bunch of times. Keeps chewing on that rubber thing."

My heart failed. "What rubber thing?"

"I dunno. It's shaped like a hamburger." I heard something muffled. "Here, you old hound. Take it and get out of here!"

I tipped my head. "Wait, you mean she's in the same room with you?"

"What was that silly note about, anyway, Ro?" Kyoko barked, not answering my question. "Where in the world are you?"

I froze. "I'm. . .uh. . .just thinking about lunch. How about it? With some friends of mine?"

"Grits and collard greens?"

"Chili's."

"Chili's? Really? Great! I can meet you downtown. I mean, Staunton doesn't really have a downtown, but. . ."

"I get it, I get it." I rolled my eyes. "You don't want me to come get you?"

"Nah. GPS, babe. You know you can change the voices? Mine has an Argentinean accent. It's the only one that gets all the roads wrong."

"Not funny! Just for that, we're going to Bubba's Diner."

"I take it back!" Kyoko shrieked. "Anything! Please! No pork rinds or grits!"

"Hmmph. I make no promises." I put my hand to my forehead.

"Wait a second, Kyoko. I've got a dog."

"No. You've got a puppy." More muffled movements. "Hey! Cut that out! Not on the carpet! Oh no. . .not the sofa. . .look at all that stuffing!"

"The sofa?" I gasped, backing into a pew. "Christie tore up the sofa?"

"Nah." Kyoko snickered. "I'm just teasing. She's fine. Just don't ask me to touch her though. I don't do dogs. Or possums. Or whatever you've got crawling around here in Virginia."

I rubbed my back where it'd hit the pew, my racing pulse calming to normal. "Well, I can't leave her alone yet, can I? She's still pretty little." I checked my watch. "I've got to work after this, and if you don't go straight home then. . ."

"You're the one who wanted a dog, Ro. Think of something."

"No, Becky wanted me to have a dog." I narrowed my eyes at Becky, and she stuck her tongue out at me. "What am I supposed to do now? Leave her with Stella?"

All that cigarette smoke? No way.

Becky's gaze suddenly lit on Faye. "I know who you can call," she said.

Faye looked up innocently from her conversation with Adam, and I tried to catch Becky's eye. Making big Xs with my hands and shaking my head furiously.

"Oh, nothin'," said Becky sweetly, shoving me toward the hallway door. "Jest tryin' ta think a who might be able ta keep Shiloh's li'l puppy a few hours. Too bad ain't none a us nearby."

Faye thought. "Well, don't Earl live out that way?"

"Why, thanks, Faye! He shore does, come to think of it. Ya got his number? I shore don't. An' Shah-loh. . .well, she's tied up right now." She gave me an extra push and shut the door in my face for good measure.

Then Faye's muffled voice. "I reckon I've got his business card here somewhere."

"Atta girl," said Becky. And I could hear her grin through the door.

"Chili's it is." I pushed open the sanctuary door. "Kyoko'll meet us there, dog-free."

"'Thanks ta Earl." Becky winked.

"Not so fast." Adam clicked off his cell phone. "Chili's says there's an hour and a half wait."

"What?" we all yelped.

"Doggone Methodists!" Tim joked, pretending to stomp.

"Try Cracker Barrel or Mrs. Rowe's," suggested Becky. "I'm starvin'!"

I shook my head. "No Southern food. Kyoko's a little particular."

"Well." Becky raised an eyebrow. "There's the Mill Street Grill, which I ain't payin' half our salary for, or fast food."

"Or The Green Tree." Adam looked at me pointedly.

I put my hands up. "Oh, no! Don't even think about it! I vote for Burger King."

They outvoted me. I sulked all the way to the car, not noticing the yellow-clad woman I'd sat next to at the beginning of the service until I saw her reflection in my car window.

"Excuse me," she said politely as I spun around. "I didn't mean to startle ya."

"Of course not." I pulled off my sunglasses. "Thanks for helping me find Tim and Becky. Me being a stranger and all."

"You're no stranger." The breeze lightly ruffled her black hair. "I knew ya'd be here today."

I gazed back at her neatly styled hairdo and sparkly flower earrings, brown hands tucked into her long winter coat. But I didn't recognize her.

"Were you. . .waiting for me?" I asked hesitantly, glancing around. Most of the crowds had dispersed already.

"Absolutely. I didn't want to intrude but wondered if I could talk to ya a minute."

"Uh. . .sure." I moved uncomfortably to check my watch.

"I'm Beulah Jackson. I knew your mother. She accepted Jesus in my livin' room."

Chapter 7

I wavered, barely feeling the cold wind ruffle my hair. "My mom?"

"Ellen Jacobs." Beulah's dark eyes echoed back tenderness. "I used to work as a temp at the Virginia School for the Deaf and Blind where she taught, and I invited her to our church one Sunday 'cause she seemed kinda lonely. I didn't think she'd wanna come back, and she didn't think so either, but she took to Faye like butter on grits. Faye's one sweet woman, ain't she?"

I nodded, my thinly veiled emotion rising so quickly I had to choke it back.

"Faye and I invited her back again, and she came. Askin' all kinds a questions. Talkin' about her hurt and anger. We met with the pastor's wife an' read the Bible and prayed together. Then I invited her to a Bible study at my house, and the small group put her at ease."

The wind blew again, and I tightened my jaw against tears, imagining Mom sitting on Beulah's sofa, Bible open in her lap. The same leather cover I now clenched in nervous fingers.

"And mostly, Shiloh, we just prayed for her. Lord knows she'd been jest about broke in half. Done lost ev'rything important to her and gave all her money away to them cults."

"Raelians. One-Spirit Life Forces. Communes. Hindu stuff. I know." Tears stung my eyes at the memories of Mom strung out on psychedelic tea, eyes unseeing. Her shaking hands reaching for a mantra to read until she fell asleep on the sofa, limp arm dangling on the cold, blistered linoleum.

Mom's story, for the first time, sounded just a little bit like mine.

No, I hadn't chased aliens or gurus, but I'd handed over my earnings to a different cult—one that promised happiness and success if I climbed corporate ladders and bought and charged. Wasting years and dollars trying to be someone that, all of a sudden, I didn't even know.

Beulah reached out, unafraid, and took my hand firmly between hers.

"But Jesus changed your mama's life inside an' out, and she became a new creation. Everything broken He made whole! Everything that caused her downfall became her strength!

"I want ya to know Ellen Jacobs lived and died a courageous woman of God, and I ain't ever seen a woman who lost so much be so filled by God's grace. She became a prayin', singin', believin', rejoicin' woman of victory through Jesus Christ, and Shiloh Papillon Jacobs, so can you!"

Beulah's forceful words startled me so much I didn't realize for a few seconds that she'd used my middle name. A gust of wind sent a rush of golden leaves across us, like my flood of emotions. Tumbling and scuttling over themselves, brittle thin.

"I believe in Jesus," I said, shivering despite my sweater. "I asked Him into my heart not long ago."

"I know ya did." Beulah didn't flinch. "The Lord revealed it to me while I prayed for ya. And I'm here to tell ya He's gonna do great things through ya! There ain't a thing in your life He can't make new. He says, 'Behold, I make all things new!' And that includes you."

She put a hand on my cheek. "Ya may be broken in spirit now, but Jesus will fill ya. 'Here I am! I stand at the door and knock,' He says. 'If anyone hears my voice and opens the door, I will come in and eat with that person, and they with me.' "

"The Bread of Life," I whispered, mind spinning back to the sermon.

"Exactly! It's no accident God brought ya here. He has plans for ya, honey! Here! Now! I don't know what ya left behind, but it's Egypt! The land of slavery. Leave Egypt behind ya! The Lord Jesus is your Promised Land now."

I didn't understand all her words, but my posture must have melted. Beulah gathered me into her arms and pressed my cheek against hers.

"I've been prayin' for ya every single day," she whispered into my ear. "Ever since I started with your mom. An' we're gonna start on the rest a your family, one at a time. Ya hear me? You're gonna see God do great things."

I drew in a ragged breath, feeling tears leak out. "How did you know my middle name?"

"Ellen told me. Said she chose it durin' one a them artsy phases and ya always hated it."

I nodded, half laughing and half crying.

"But I said, 'Doesn't *papillon* mean "butterfly" in French?' I told her God don't make mistakes, and her little girl will be transformed as much as one a them ugly caterpillars into the most beautiful butterfly she's ever seen. And I'm here talkin' to ya today to prove it."

A footstep on concrete filtered over from the distant front steps, and I looked up to see Adam and Todd politely turned away, hands on the metal railing. Tim's white pickup paused, engine running, near a clump of shrubs.

"I thought they'd all left already!" I turned slightly, shielding my moist eyes.

Oh, right. Something about getting me out of church without a bunch of crying and hugging. So much for Scout's honor!

Adam glanced back at Beulah and me, raising his palms in a questioning gesture. I shot him a thumbs-up, trying to smile.

But as I shivered in the chilly sun, which peeked briefly from behind a puff of low-flying cloud, I was glad I'd come to church—even if Kyoko complained. Glad I'd met Beulah. Glad, even, for the damp spots on my cheeks as I dug through my purse for a tissue.

Beulah glanced over to the front steps. And as she opened her mouth, I knew what she'd say. "There's a good man, Shiloh Jacobs."

"Who, Tim? Yeah, he's kind of redneck, but I like him." I played dumb.

I didn't think Beulah could roll her eyes, but she did. "I wasn't talkin' about Tim."

"Why, did God give you a revelation on Adam, too?" I asked a little tartly, pulling a tissue out of the small plastic packet. A leftover from Japan, where they passed them out on the street for advertising. The kanji characters on this particular packet proclaimed, in a riot of pink, special discounts for "bridal shaving." *What, like for Godzilla?* I dabbed at my mascara.

"You think Adam and I are supposed to be together or something?" I wiped my nose in irritation, eyes landing on the absurd cartoon drawing of a smiley bride and groom on the tissue packet. I shoved it back into my purse and zipped it forcefully.

Beulah chuckled. "I never said that! And if He did give me a revelation on it, which He *didn't*, I shore wouldn't tell ya! He don't need me to get people together. Although if He's lookin' for helpers, 'Lord, thy servant heareth!' " She spread her hands and looked toward heaven with merry dark eyes.

I couldn't help but laugh. "It's just that some people seem to think Adam and I. . . I don't know." I shrugged and dropped my gaze, fiddling with my purse strap. The way I had in the hallway with Adam, fingers trembling slightly. "He's nice and all, but. . ."

A vision of Carlos's brilliant, beautiful face flitted through me with almost palpable pain.

"Adam's not my type at all." I shook my head for emphasis. "In any possible way. And not only that, I'm just passing through town, not staying."

I fumbled with my wrinkled tissue and dropped it. Reached to pick it up off the asphalt and dropped it again then splattered my keys when I grabbed for the tissue.

"They're. . .uh. . . waiting for me." I gestured toward the steps, embarrassed. Sniffling the last of my tears.

"If ya didn't have plans, I'd invite ya home for lunch. My Frank's at home, not feelin' so well today, but we'd pull ya up another chair and feed ya 'til ya pop."

"Thanks." My eyes raised in a smile. I felt foolish suddenly, running away from Beulah, who glowed raw love and faith like a sunrise over the sloping curves of the Blue Ridge Mountains, drowning everything in gold. "We're going to The Green Tree, but maybe next time we—"

"Did you say The Green Tree?"

"Sure. That quasi-vegetarian place."

"Do you know a Trinity who works there?"

"Trinity?" My eyebrows shot up. "Trinity Jackson? Of course I do! We wait tables together! Why, just last night she came to my house to spy on—" I caught myself in case Faye could hear me, wherever she was.

"Trinity's my granddaughter!" Beulah cried out, gripping my arm. "Ya work with my son's girl! The one I've been praying about for twenty-six years now! For her to love the Lord Jesus, and you're. . . you're. . ." She broke off, tears swelling in her eyes. "Well, Shiloh, do you believe me now that God don't make mistakes? He's put you right there according to His blessed plan!"

"Huh? You mean, like on purpose?" If God's so-called "blessed plan" for me included hauling dirty plates to foul-mouthed dishwashers who hollered about NASCAR over the hiss of the steam sanitizer, He and I needed to have a chat. Pronto. "Why would He do a thing like that?"

"To bring the goodness of the Lord to Trinity, girl!" She shook my arm. "Don't ya get it? You're an answer to my prayers!"

"You mean God cares where I. . .work?" I wrinkled my nose. The thought struck me as kind of absurd. I mean, I knew it from the Bible, what few portions I'd read, but. . .The Green Tree? "I'm just trying to make money. And Jerry hired me."

I pictured the Japanese visitors in the Buddhist temples, writing their prayers on rows of wooden plaques, hoping to catch divine attention. Clapping their hands and tossing coins. Prayer ribbons flickering in the wind like lost kites.

While Beulah Jackson stood in front of me in her long gray coat and told me God planned the exact place—exact time in history, even—I'd work? And with whom?

"Does God care where ya work? Baby, He's planned every detail in your life to bring Him honor and grow ya strong and firm in Him!"

I scuffed my expensive heel in the asphalt, playing with my sunglasses. "You mean that?"

"With all my heart, sugar! He's got every hair on your head numbered."

"Well, tell Him to add a few more," I said, trying to cover the lump that suddenly swelled in my throat by picking some strands off my sweater.

Beulah winked at me. "Tell Him yourself, girl! He's waitin' on ya!"

★　★　★

My hands were still shaking when I pulled out of the church parking lot, breathing in the now-familiar scent of Mom's car interior. The berry scent of her air freshener that lingered, like her memory, suddenly sweet.

I flashed my lights as our pickup-truck-and-car parade passed a gas station. I turned in, the others honking as they headed to The Green Tree.

But instead of pulling up to the pump, I drove around behind the lot, shaded by overgrown vines and lilac shrubs. A shock of standing trees dripped green leaves mottled with cherry red across scarred concrete.

I parked, peeled off my sunglasses, and sobbed into my hands.

It took me all the way to The Green Tree to collect myself. Beulah's words. The Bible open in my lap as Pastor Davis urged us to call out to Jesus. Adam's hand on my shoulder as we stood in the hallway, purse strap twisting in my hands.

I wedged my Honda between two badly parked cars and let the engine die. Sat there in the silence, golden leaves fluttering down onto my windshield like feathers. I let my head sink down to the steering wheel. I needed quiet. Needed rest. Needed. . .

"Aw no, Kyoko! Not there!" I rolled down my window and gestured. Honked my horn. But she didn't hear. Didn't look up.

So much for quiet. I sighed and grabbed my purse, praying for God to calm my fraying nerves as I slammed the car door behind me.

Kyoko had parked her red Mitsubishi in front of a fire hydrant on the wrong side of a historic one-way street. She leaned lazily against it, tapping on her cell phone. Chunky black boots and black pants. Blue-and-black punk-rock T-shirt depicting Van Gogh's *The Scream*.

"Kyoko!" I broke into a trot. "You can't park there!"

"Huh?" She looked up, sleek hair pulled back in a twist, maroon-stained points poking up wildly. "Oh hi, Ro! Hold on. I'm trying to find that cop's number."

"Why? What cop?"

"What's his name? Shawn? Shack?"

"Shane?"

"Yeah, Shane. That's it." She tapped some more. "Think he'll come out here and try to ticket me? I wanna see if he's as good-looking as Stella says."

Of all the. . .! I halted, purse sliding off my shoulder. "When did you talk to Stella?"

"This morning. While you disappeared on your mysterious excursion." Kyoko waved her hand. "But don't worry. I'm not horning in on Shane. It's for you."

I sputtered, speechless.

She raised an eyebrow. "And don't you look all frilly today! Where've you been, Ro-chan, all dressed up? A baby shower or something?" She appraised my heels and lacy sweater with a slight nod. "Well, that cop's eyes'll bug right out of his head, anyway. So how do you spell his last name?"

Before I could even come up with a snotty retort, cowboy boots clicked on the distant sidewalk. Coming toward us. Echoing against the faded brickwork of bygone buildings, which stretched their ancient arms into a moody sky.

"That must be your posse." Kyoko attempted, somewhat, to wipe the smirk off her face. "Do they do Civil War reenactments here? That guy'd fit right in as one of the Rebs if you put a uniform on him." She smacked her forehead. "Oh, wait! Tim does that, doesn't he? In . . .where again? Winchester? Where viewers occasionally get mugged, and-or—"

"Cut it out!" I rolled my eyes and grabbed her arm as she chuckled at her own joke. "Come meet them. And be nice!"

Becky waved wildly, and Kyoko gave a lazy wave in reply, leaving her car guarding the fire hydrant.

"Well, well! Ya come all the way from Japan?" Tim grabbed Kyoko's hand and pumped it hard.

"Presumably." Kyoko squeamishly withdrew her glittery lime-green nails (repainted, apparently, from last night's deep-blue shade) and shouldered her purse. "And you must be Tim? I've. . .um. . .heard about you."

Her oh-so-innocent grin unsettled me, as did the sly way in which she said it.

"Tim Donaldson." He grinned, hugging Becky. "And this here's my cute li'l Becky. Ain't she a peach?"

"Well, she's certainly rather fruitlike. Yes." Kyoko tried to shake Becky's hand, but Becky threw her arms around Kyoko.

"Welcome to Staunton, Kyoko!" Becky bubbled, beaming. "Faye can't stay but she's comin' by to say hi, an' Adam and Todd's waitin' on us, and everybody's so pleased ta meet ya! Yer gonna jest love it here!"

"I bet I will." Kyoko showed her teeth.

<hr>

When we arrived at The Green Tree, Adam politely shook hands with Kyoko and held the door for us as we filed inside, Dawn seating us near the window. Before I could change the subject to something— anything—not involving (1) deer hunting (2) the Civil War, or (3) weapons, Todd whipped out a shockingly detailed drawing of an army tank and plopped it in front of Kyoko.

"I drew this on the way over here," he said, bending across the table and pointing. "Didn't know ya was comin' or I'd'a brought my colored pencils, but I don't have none in the truck. Sorry. Hope ya still like it."

"You did this?" Kyoko's eyebrow ring jerked upward. "What. . .

um. . .exactly is it?"

"It's a World War II tank. An M3 Lee. You know, like General Lee from the Confederacy. It's kinda shaky though, 'cause Adam's truck needs better shocks."

Kyoko choked back a laugh. "So it's for me?"

"Yeah. There's your name on the wheel well. See? I don't know your last name, so I just made one up. Hope Suzuki's okay. It's Japanese, right?"

I coughed on my ice water, but Todd didn't hear. "Anyway, I figured ya come a long way an' might be tired, so I'll show ya my other drawings some other time. Miss Shiloh's seen 'em. I got some new ones for her, too."

"Miss Shiloh?" I saw Kyoko's eyebrow flick with mirth. At least I hoped it was mirth. Kyoko's wide arsenal of dark emotions never failed to intimidate.

"Yeah. Since she's an adult and all. But you don't have to call me Mr. Todd. You can just call me Todd." He shrugged. "Unless you wanna say Mr., 'cause I don't mind."

Kyoko stared down at the drawing and then at Adam, who put his palms up and shrugged. Then at me. And shut her mouth abruptly.

Oh boy. Kyoko didn't care for kids much, or long lungfuls of chatter about army tanks. Especially coming from superpacifist Japan.

"Thirsty?" I interrupted, waving for Blake as he came by with the water pitcher. Half wishing Tim and Becky would use sign language or something so their Southern drawls didn't prickle Kyoko's sophisti-cated ears.

"So, whatcha gonna order?" Tim plopped a menu in front of Kyoko before I could intervene. "It's on the house, a course. Adam's house." Tim snickered and high-fived Becky. "Jest kiddin', y'all. After Adam gets that fancy subdivision, though, then I reckon I won't be jokin'."

"What subdivision?" I looked up from my menu. In fact, why was I reading the menu anyway? I knew everything on there by heart.

"It's not a big deal." Adam shrugged. "I probably won't get it. I put in a bid, but those jobs usually go to the big companies."

"Not a big deal?" Tim swung around in his chair to face Adam. "Every house on that lot's worth half a million bucks, Carter! And whoever does their cotton-pickin' shrubs is gonna be swimmin' in it." He pointed. "If ya get that deal, yer takin' us all out for somethin' fancier than The Green Tree. Got it?"

"Sushi?" Adam rested the side of his head on his hand and hid a smile, flipping a menu page.

"Naw. Somethin' I can eat." Tim grinned and turned to Kyoko. "As for this place, well, they don't got no grits or nothin'. Kinda weird fancy stuff, I reckon, but I find somethin' ev'ry now an' then that don't crawl off my plate!"

He leaned closer to Kyoko and dropped his voice as if revealing a secret. "Speakin' a weird stuff, you really eat raw fish like Shah-loh here? I snagged a catfish the other day, but if ya saw the inside a that'n, ya'd never eat raw fish again. I guarantee it." He whipped out his cell phone. "Hold on. I got some pitchers in here somewhere! You ever eat spaghetti? It's kinda like that, but—"

"So, Todd," Kyoko interrupted loudly. "Do you draw anything else? I mean, anything that's not catfish?" She sent a look in Tim's direction.

"Why, ya don't like 'em?" asked Todd in surprise. "They're real good eatin'. But then again, they are bottom dwellers. So go figure."

I saw Adam's face redden with laughter behind his menu, shoulders shaking. Todd calmly produced a piece of paper from his sketch pad on the seat. "I dunno. I can draw a deer real good, an' lots a other tanks. An' Dale Earnhardt's race car from NASCAR. My dog's named after him, but he died. I mean, Dale died. Not my dog. Wanna see?"

Part of the reason lunch went so smoothly is because Kyoko fell asleep halfway through it, right after Faye stopped by to say hi—slumping against the back of the booth, eyes sagging closed. I didn't blame her. A twenty-four-hour flight and half the night spent yakking would turn anybody to toast.

In fact, given my overloaded morning and wrinkled tissues post-Beulah, I could use a nap myself. But duty called. I glanced at my watch and waved for the check, grateful Kyoko couldn't hear Becky's whispers about her eyebrow ring or Tim's, "What's that psycho-lookin' thing on her shirt?"

"She's got jet lag," I explained, glancing down at Kyoko before digging out my wallet to pay. Adam ignored me, taking both Kyoko's and my check. "And knowing Kyoko, she probably hasn't slept in days anyway. She doesn't know the meaning of bedtime before three a.m."

"Poor thing." Becky shook her head, swallowing the last of her ice water and reaching over to pat Kyoko's lifeless head. "She's real sweet. Kinda funny, but I like her."

Kyoko stirred long enough to blearily watch Blake take our empty plates, walk to her car, and then fall asleep right there, seat belt halfway in its clip. Head nodding forward into the steering wheel.

"That's it." I took the keys from her. "I'm driving you home before I head back to work. Get out."

To my surprise, Kyoko obeyed, barely opening her eyes. She stretched out in my passenger's seat and yawned then dozed again as I moved her car and parallel parked in a legal spot. Then I took the long way home, meandering through the country.

We drove through tiny Churchville, with its quaint fire station and jacked-up trucks, sans stoplight, and Kyoko's eyes finally blinked open. She yawned and rubbed her face, slapping her cheeks.

"What happened, Ro? Did you guys drug my salad or something?" She scrubbed a hand across her black eyeliner.

"Jet lag." I turned my head. "You okay?"

"Yeah. I'm waking up." She grimaced at a wide horse pasture with a dumpy-looking donkey swishing its tail, gnawing on the dilapidated fence. A bumper-less car parked haphazardly in front with duct tape on the door handle. "Where in the. . . Are we in Staunton, Ro? GPS didn't bring me this way."

"Churchville. Mom's house is near here. They have a carnival in that field in the summer." I pointed as the pasture morphed into a tangle of seedy-looking shops. "With a Ferris wheel and games and stuff. Stella sat up in the dunking booth one year and yelled insults at people."

Kyoko gaped out the window and then back at me. "For heaven's sake! You're in the Twilight Zone! What are you doing here?"

"Paying off my bills," I replied meekly. "Selling Mom's house as soon as I can."

"Ro." She turned to face me, face sobering. "You really aren't planning to. . .like. . .live here, are you? I mean—"

"Never." I stopped at the intersection.

"As in, never-never? Or—"

"Never." I raised my voice. "Got it?"

"Just checking." Kyoko grinned. "It's my job, you know."

I made a face and smiled back, turning into the grocery store/gas station parking lot with the ancient Tastee Freez, conveniently located right next to the county landfill. "Want a sundae?"

"Ice cream?" She perked up. "Actually, yeah. Maybe it'll help me wake up. I'll get some tea or something, too."

"You? Iced tea?"

"No, green. What, are you nuts?" Kyoko groaned and smacked her forehead. "I'm outta luck in these parts, huh? How about Red Bull?"

"Nope. Coffee?"

She fiddled with her piercing. "I guess," she grumbled. "The sundaes don't have corn or something on them, do they?"

"No. That's Brazil."

"Corn? In ice cream?"

"Yep. Pretty good, too."

She narrowed her eyes at me. "Just how long did you stay in Rio anyway? I thought that little vacation trip of yours last year lasted just a few days." She gave a wry look. "Back when you had money to burn. Or credit cards, rather. Associated Press doesn't pay *that* much."

I winced, backing into a parking spot and turning off the ignition. "Three days."

"And you tried corn ice cream?"

"And guava and passion fruit. I loved *açai*." I shrugged. "Brazilians eat a lot of ice cream."

"Last time I checked you're not Brazilian," snapped Kyoko, glaring. "You still running every day?"

Kyoko, who could gain weight just by looking at a dish of rice, sometimes hated me.

"Pretty much. I see so many cows I've started giving them names."

"Hmmph. Well, you'd better keep it up, or you'll look like that double-wide we passed back there."

I took my keys out of the ignition and leaned back in my seat, trying to gather my courage to explain about church.

"You know, Kyoko," I began, banging Mom's keychain against my knee. "I wanted to tell you where I went this morning. I know it might sound weird, but. . ."

Her cell phone buzzed in her purse, and my words faltered. Kyoko waved it away. "Go on. Were you saying something?" She swallowed a yawn, eyes watery.

"Yeah." My gaze flickered out to the battered-looking parking lot. "About this morning. No, about more than this morning. About me and my life."

I tightened my fingers on the steering wheel. "You'll probably think it's weird, but. . ."

Her cell phone buzzed again. Loudly. I waited politely with my chin in my hand while Kyoko dug it out of her purse, her stoic expression turning angry as she tapped through lines of an incoming text message.

"Not again!" She groaned, mashing her cell phone closed. "Doggone it, Nora! Don't you know I'm in the US? Incommunicado! Go away! Do your own work!" She rolled her head in frustration against the seat back. "How on earth did she get hired at a place like AP?"

All my planned speech fizzled.

"So what was that about corn ice cream?" Kyoko turned glazed eyes to me and tried to smile. Jet lag again. I felt sorry for her.

"They sell chicken-wing ice cream in Nagoya. Tokyo's close enough. You could get some."

"Tell me you're kidding."

"And eel, too."

Kyoko rubbed her face in her hands. "Maybe a sundae isn't such a good idea."

"Trust me. You'll like this." I opened the car door before she could change her mind. "And you'll miss the opportunity to make fun of me when I move away."

"Oh no I won't. You always give me an opportunity for that no matter where you live. I just won't have such good props." She nodded to a discarded Skoal snuff can littering the asphalt.

Kyoko reluctantly got out of the car, giving the dumpy fast-food joint and "Riverside Grocery" the once-over. Then glowered at a guy with a shaggy mullet who parked his battered Ford pickup next to us, blasting country music. Confederate flag covering his rear window and two rifles in the gun rack.

"You're sure about this." She didn't move.

"Positive."

"In there."

"Yep."

I dragged Kyoko away from the Ford before she said anything rude.

"So what kind of ice cream sundaes does Tastee Freez have?" Kyoko snapped on her sunglasses in irritation as we stepped up to the door.

Country music twanged from inside, and through the glass windows a hanging ad with a cowboy hat twirled from the ceiling.

"My favorite's black raspberry."

Kyoko suddenly paused to shield her eyes, hand on the glass door. So fast I banged into her. "Wait a minute, Ro. I can't be seeing this! Tell me I'm still asleep!"

"What?" I put my hands on my hips. "Hurry up!"

"Is that the town dump?"

I pushed her inside before she could ask any more questions.

Chapter 8

Finally a quiet moment. I wiped my hands on the green Starbucks apron and brushed my sweaty hair back into its clip with sticky fingers, grateful the line of customers had disappeared. Outside glowed a gorgeous fall afternoon, all gold and brilliant blue, while my friend/workmate Jamie Rivera and I were stuck inside Barnes & Noble making espresso with Chloe and High-School Travis.

I worked with two Travises, since in the South one in approximately every five men is named Travis; the others usually falling under the category of "two-syllable-short-form-of-William-shouted-from-a-truck-window": Billy, Willy, or Bubba.

High-School Travis was personable, if not a little goofy, although our conversations mainly consisted of (1) him trying to indoctrinate me with Garth Brooks, and (2) me pretending to heave into a trash can. But dyed-black-haired Chloe scowled and kept her iPod buds in her ears against regulation when Boss Travis (the late thirty-ish one who wore ugly polyester pants and flirted with customers) left for a smoke.

At least working at Starbucks in the fall offered one benefit: Pumpkin Spice Lattes. I made them by the dozen and now knew the secret balance of milk to espresso and how many pumps of spicy syrup for the perfect cup. I could make them at home without having to wear this silly apron.

"So where's Kyoko today?" asked Jamie, stacking teacups and lids and pushing another strand of dark hair behind her ear. "I was surprised to see her at The Green Tree Sunday when I went in to get my check."

"I was even more surprised she behaved herself."

Jamie waited tables at The Green Tree, too, and she could thank me—or hate me—for the job.

She looked up with a smile, her skin the color of the fragrant latte I just made. "Kyoko came all the way from Japan just for you, Shiloh. That's pretty cool. I have relatives back in Puerto Rico I haven't seen since I was five."

"She's great." I sponged the counter halfheartedly with a wet rag, rubbing at a sticky spot. My last few days with Kyoko had spun by in such a blur. "She brought me gobs of stuff from Japan—cream puffs, dried squid, ceramic dolls. I don't know how she got it all through customs." My throat tightened. "Now she's packing up to leave."

"Already? When?"

"Tomorrow."

"Wow. Time sure flies, huh?"

"Tell me about it." I sighed. "But Kyoko has a real job to get back to."

"I know what you mean." Jamie rolled her eyes.

Making coffee for middle schoolers had to be one of the most humbling jobs ever. Too-shiny preteens with giggly laughs—who complained in shrill, annoying voices about wanting more whipped cream or insisting "something's wrong with my coffee"—all while yakking on their pink cell phones. I wanted to dump the cup right over their prissy, highlighted heads.

Beulah said God had plans for me here in Staunton, but I was fairly certain they didn't include making espresso for the rest of my life. Or carrying plates at The Green Tree.

"So did you get to do everything you wanted to with Kyoko?"

"Sort of. Some museums, Luray Caverns. But I think she really liked filming Stella throwing horseshoes at pegs in the ground. Did you know people really do that?" I guffawed.

"My relatives do sometimes."

I covered my mouth. "Oops. Sorry." Then wrinkled my brow. "Wait, *your* family? You're Puerto Rican!"

"Sure. But my dad was born here. We've been in the South for years. Too many years." We laughed together. "My uncle also spits into a cup, but I thought I'd spare you the indignity."

I shook my head, imagining the fusion foods that must show up on the Rivera dinner table: Deer fritters instead of fish? *Sopón de pollo con* hominy?

The front door glistened open in late afternoon sun rays, and a teenager wandered through, laughing into her cell phone. She hesitated at the smell of pumpkin spice and, to my relief, turned toward a magazine rack and began browsing.

"Is Trinity okay?" Jamie asked abruptly, picking up a stray plastic lid and plopping it back on the pile. "I mean, she just seems. . ."

"I know. Did she snap at you this week, too?"

Jennifer Rogers Spinola

"Sort of, but it's more. . . I don't know."

"Her eyes."

"Yeah." Jamie met my gaze. "Like something's really bothering her. I tried to talk to her, and she seemed like she might, but. . ."

I shrugged. "I can't figure her out, Jamie. She used to be pretty open about her life, but lately anytime I delve into personal territory she zips her lips. Where's the bright and spunky Trinity we know?"

"Good question. She didn't even try to insult Blake like she usually does." Jamie shook her head. "Poor kid. What is he now, nineteen?"

"I think so. He's been mooning over her for months. Maybe years." I picked at my nail polish, which definitely needed a touch-up. "Kyoko thinks Trinity's hiding something. She said her body language shows signs of 'repressed anxiety' and went on for ten minutes about the way Trinity shredded a straw paper." I rolled my eyes. "Of course Kyoko's come up with some pretty. . .um. . .colorful theories about what she's supposedly hiding. Involving illicit spy organizations or insider stock trading."

"Isn't Carlos a stockbroker?"

"Bingo! You've figured out the missing link!" I laughed, glad for once that Carlos's name didn't hurt quite so badly. "But you know something about Kyoko? She had a good time this week, but that's not why she came."

"Why, she wants to take you back to Japan?" Jamie looked up, her brown eyes reflecting that same gentle understanding that had taken me by surprise when I first started at Barnes & Noble, which seemed a century ago with all the twists and turns in my crazy life.

"No. To make sure I'm not off my rocker or something." I shook the rag into the trash.

Jamie started to laugh then apparently thought better of it. "Seriously?"

"Think about it. In the space of a few months I've lost my mom, lost my job, lost my fiancé, and on top of that, she knows I considered becoming. . .you know. A Christian." I swallowed, the last word sticking in my throat like a dry crumb of rice cracker. It still felt new to me and strange to hold it in reverence instead of making a joke or brushing it off with the rest of the world's nutsos.

"Have you told her?"

"Not exactly. We're talking about Kyoko here, Jamie! Case in point: Remember when the Harlem Globetrotters showed up at The Green Tree?"

80

"Are you kidding? How could I forget a five-hundred dollar tip?"

"Well, Kyoko refused to believe my story until Jerry showed her the autographed photos last Sunday at the restaurant. Becky still thinks the photos are staged."

"Becky? That's funny." Jamie giggled, throwing away a handful of used register receipts. "That's the first night you called me to help out at The Green Tree. No way I could forget that." Her voice softened. "I'm still amazed you thought to call me. We hadn't even known each other that long, but I really needed that job."

"And we needed you at The Green Tree." I poked her playfully. "Jerry was pulling his hair out." I chuckled. "And I'm equally amazed you came. And stayed. Now there are two of us Bible thumpers under Jerry's nose."

I shot her a smile, proud of Jamie's stalwart convictions and fearless faith. She practically sparkled. God had used Jamie to give me a push—no, more like a flying kick—in His direction.

"Well, I wouldn't peg you for a loony." Jamie shrugged, mirth tugging at the corners of her mouth. "Unless. . . Has Kyoko read about Western State?"

"The old 'lunatic asylum,' as they used to call it?" I giggled. "Right here in Staunton? Well, that certainly didn't help my case any."

Jamie laughed back, squatting under the counter for more foam coffee cups and straws. When she stood, though, arms full of stuff, her smile had faded. "Kyoko knows you better than that, doesn't she?"

"You'd think so." I moistened the rag and ran it over the now-smooth counter. "But to her, my life is so ludicrous she can't believe it's reality." My mouth straightened into a line. "Fitting, huh?"

Jamie leaned against the counter and turned to face me. "Even if she did think that, she still came. She cares about you."

"Really?" I ran my hand through my hair, confused.

"Of course. I don't know anyone who would fly across continents just to see if I was okay."

I started sweeping up crumbs from the bake case, wishing those espresso brownies and lemon bars didn't look so good. Lunch had vanished ages ago.

"She's special, Jamie. Even though she doesn't believe anything I do and probably never will. But I feel torn in half. Just like this cinnamon bun. Part of me there. Part of me here. I don't know who I am anymore."

Jennifer Rogers Spinola

I removed the bun chunks with metal tongs and cut it in little pieces for people to taste test. Unfortunately for me, eating broken goodies was against regulation. Otherwise there'd probably be a lot more severed cinnamon buns.

Jamie set a little dish of toothpicks on the counter for people to eat the cinnamon bun remains. "Well, this is probably the time you start to find out who you are, Shiloh."

I glanced back at Chloe, who dawdled in the kitchen, taking her time getting something out of the cabinet. Banging her head to whatever emo tune played on her iPod. Right or wrong, Chloe struck me as a wannabe. A rude, annoying wannabe. But Kyoko was real. Enigmatic. Deep. Unique. The woman who wrote about gruesome homicides without batting an eyelash got emotional over silly '80s romantic movies. Who rejected Carlos immediately based on his heart, not his looks—unlike dozens of women.

I puffed out my chest proudly as I thought of her, wearing her scary black garb all over Tokyo, no matter what people thought.

"But the one thing that separates us now is our beliefs. And I feel that gap growing every single day."

Jamie looked up at me, biting the edge of her lip.

"What?" I crossed my arms.

She shrugged, avoiding my gaze as she put the tongs away. "I hope this isn't out of place, Shiloh, but do you think your mom might have felt the same way about you?"

I sucked in my breath. "Mom?"

"That she loved and admired you, but you didn't see eye-to-eye about faith?"

It was far more complicated than that, but Jamie did have a point. I turned my back and straightened a plate in the bake case. "Maybe," I muttered.

"Well, did she ever do anything to reach out to you anyway? To show you she cared despite your differences?"

I felt myself bristle, the way I always did when anyone talked about Mom and our past. Mom hadn't exactly gone out of her way to make herself friendly to me until the last two years, but by then it was too late for me. Her efforts failed anyway. Still, I closed my eyes and saw the shrink-wrapped mini pecan pie she'd sent, dangling there in my bedroom—where I'd skewered it to my corkboard with a thumb tack. The one effort on her part that eventually made me cry for the first time in years.

I swallowed hard, hoping the customers milling around wouldn't order. But they did, getting a cold drink from the glass case and an espresso brownie. Jamie rang them up, head bobbing with laughter of some polite shared joke, while I heated their brownie slightly in the microwave. Stuck a plastic fork on the side of the plate.

"Mom was. . .Mom," I said, when the couple sat at a table out of earshot. "We never had many good times together. But in her last two years, she tried to show me how she'd changed without interfering. She sent me packages, like little pieces of her life to enjoy if I wanted them. And if I didn't, at least she'd tried." I picked at a chip in the counter. "At least that's what I got from her letters. The ones I. . .uh . . .actually read."

Jamie didn't say a word. Just stood there, leaning against the counter with a triumphant look in her eyes.

"What?" I glanced up.

"You just said it."

"Said what? About sending me packages and trying to——" I broke off, realizing what I'd just blurted. "Okay. I get it, Jamie."

"Do the same for Kyoko. Don't intrude or require her to believe the way you do. Just show her that you value her and be yourself. Yourself with Jesus." She poked me with a straw. "There's a big difference. She'll notice it."

"Do you think that'll be enough?"

"How could it not be?" Jamie's dark eyes met mine. "God will give you opportunities to say something more if the time is right. He'll let you know. But most of the time, you just show His love. And knowing Kyoko, she'll accept whatever you can give."

"I hope so. It'd be a lonely life without her."

"Just like your mom must have thought," whispered Jamie, patting my shoulder. "But now she'll always have you. For eternity."

I lifted my gaze to Jamie, hardly daring to believe her words were truth. "I want that. With Kyoko, too, and it seems so impossible."

"Then tell God that. That's what praying's all about. It isn't about having the right words or formulating something beautiful or convincing. It's about meeting Him exactly where you are, doubts and all. Wants and all. Sins and all. And remembering that it's His job to do the impossible."

"He already has." I stared out the glass doors, remembering the first time I'd breezed through them—so outwardly confident and yet so broken inside. Me with my top-of-the-line Japanese cell phone that wouldn't even work in Virginia.

"That's His miracle. He transforms all of us into something beautiful if we let Him."

At the word *transform,* I immediately thought of Beulah's butterfly comment. But try as I might, I couldn't imagine Kyoko as a butterfly. She was too dark and cranky. Maybe a bat instead.

"Okay, Jamie," I said as two middle schoolers giggled up to the counter. "I'll try. I'll talk to God about Kyoko, and I'm asking you to join me."

"My pleasure," she replied with a smile.

★   ★   ★

The sky turned icy blue and then violet, and I actually turned on the heat during the long drive home from Barnes & Noble in the snappy, starry night. Cool had shifted, for good, to breath-snatching cold. Time to exchange my preppy Japanese summer uniform of crisp skirt and button-up shirt for the fall/winter version: patterned tights, wool skirt, and sweater. And of course, like millions of Japanese girls, I lived in knee-high boots.

I hugged myself in the brisk chill and ran inside, breath misting, looking up at the clear moon over a black-purple landscape: the lone bright globe over darkened fields and houses.

"*Tadaima!*" I announced happily, unzipping my boots and stepping into soft slippers. "I'm home!"

"*Okairi!*" came Kyoko's voice from Mom's bedroom, returning the greeting. "Welcome home!"

I found her bent over stacks of stuff, trying to fit it all into her suitcase. There in the suitcase lid lay Christie, curled in a fuzzy ball.

"Kyoko! You let Christie within sneezing distance!" I scooped up Christie. "Aren't you afraid of vermin? Disease? Whooping cough?"

"Dogs don't get whooping cough. And I didn't say she could go there. She just did."

Still, Kyoko hadn't moved her. I smiled to myself and kissed Christie's head, sitting down on the bed among Kyoko's piles. "So you're really leaving?"

"Unless you want another waitress at The Green Tree. And believe me, I wouldn't be as nice as you guys are to some of those weirdos who come in there. Rednecks give me the creeps!" She shivered. "And those whiny, bratty preteens? Give me a break!"

She'd be fired on her first day of Starbucks duty at Barnes & Noble. Maybe even arrested.

Kyoko's return ticket lay on top of her socks. *Narita Airport,* it read, making my throat swell. "Be happy you're going back, Kyoko. I'd give just about anything to go with you."

She didn't say anything. Just folded a pair of dark jeans and stuffed it in a corner of the suitcase, picking a stray dog hair off the suitcase lid and dropping it in the trash with disdain.

"Shrimp burgers, green tea, Shibuya. . .they're all yours." I buried my face in Christie's fur and tried to blot out the rising pain that filled my chest. "They'd be mine, too, if I hadn't made such a stupid mistake. Enjoy them, Kyoko. For me."

Kyoko picked at a tiny blob of lint on a sweater, a strange look spreading across her face. Finally she cleared her throat. "I've been meaning to talk to you about that, Ro," she said, not looking up.

"About what? Japan?"

"Um. . .yes. Actually."

"What about it?"

"I'm. . .well. . . Ro-chan, I'm not going back to Japan."

I stared at her as if she'd announced her engagement to Shane the cop. "Excuse me?"

"I'm not going back to Japan." Kyoko finally looked up at me with moody black eyes.

"What are you talking about?" I snatched up her return ticket. "Of course you are!"

She grabbed it back and scowled. "Yes, brainiac! I have to go back *now!* But I've asked Dave for a transfer. I'm ready to move on."

"Move on? From Japan?" For the life of me I couldn't comprehend what she'd just said. "Why, did you get fired?"

"No, nutcase! That would be you!" She smacked me on the head with her ticket. "I'm in fine shape with Dave. But I'm just ready to leave Japan. I'd like to go home to California and then move on to somewhere new. Maybe Europe."

Kyoko's words made no sense, like her diatribes about obscure '80s bands and how nobody today knew anything about music. "What are you saying, Kyoko?"

"I've had the Japan experience. And I'm over it."

I swallowed a couple of times, trying to find words. "How," I finally choked out, "can you want to leave Japan? How?"

She stared at me with what appeared to be real concern. "Stop looking like you're going to cry, Ro-chan! Really! It's just a job! A country! I know you loved it there, but I have to break it to you that not everyone feels the way you do about Japan. For some people it. . . well, it's not home. It's not the best fit."

She put a hand gingerly on my arm, a move totally against her personal creed of affection-equals-death. "You really are crying! For Pete's sake, Ro! It's me who's leaving, not you!"

"You can't leave Japan!" I sniffled while Kyoko hastily hunted for her Tokyo-street-side-ad tissues. Most of hers, of course, read *Kinoko Records*. She patted (read, "pounded") me awkwardly on the back.

"Don't you know I'm going back? As soon as I can find a job and get a different visa, and. . ." I sniffled.

"Ro." She said my nickname almost in a whisper, and I turned. "Do you have a job yet?"

"No, but I'm working on it. I'm applying for some openings."

"Well, I don't want to hurt your feelings, but finding the right job takes time. I know you want to go back and things to be the same. But they're not. Life goes on."

Her words cut, and I flinched. "But Japan is where we. . ."

"Where we what? Worked our tails off and ate disgusting sea creatures and crammed ourselves into dainty Japanese clothes that wouldn't fit a rag doll?"

"We met there. Granted, I hadn't really known you for that long, but it matters."

"So what? It's not like I'm going to disappear and not speak to you anymore. I just won't be falling on the floor screaming about the stupid Japanese trash system. Do you know how many times I've put the burnables in the nonburnables bag and the glass out on the can day and. . ." She flopped back down on the bed. "No more! From now on I'm building a bonfire right in front of the apartment and throwing everything in it!"

"I won my awards in Japan," I went on, barely hearing her. "I sort of. . .found myself." I sniffled, twisting a corner of the tissue packet.

"No, you found Carlos." Kyoko stuck out a corner of her lip in a contemptuous expression. "Who encouraged you in your shop-'til-you-drop mania. He was so full of himself, Ro! Both of you all dolled up and stiff like robots." Her eyes lit up. "Hey, have I told you that Japan's inventing these microscopic robots that can actually go into people's veins, and then. . ."

I stared at her, tears still streaked on my cheeks, and Kyoko threw up her hands. "Okay, okay! Forget it."

"Did you think I was full of myself, too?" I eventually managed, afraid of her response. "Or just Carlos? Tell me the truth."

"A little." She attempted a smile. "But. . . I don't know. Not really. You just seemed like that Trinity woman, trying to hide something. I just couldn't ever figure out what it was."

She turned her head sideways and peered at me. "Funny thing is, you don't seem like that anymore."

How ironic that Kyoko should say that, sitting right here on my mom's empty bed. All the remnants of Mom's life, from her bedroom mirror to her carved wooden trunk, shouting back "Change! Redemption! Freedom!" I reached, hands shaking, for another tissue.

"I shouldn't have told you," Kyoko muttered, stiffly hugging her knees. Obviously not used to my new demonstrations of emotion. "I just thought you'd want to know. So you wouldn't be totally shocked and commit *hara-kiri* or something equally stupid."

Japanese ritual suicide? I choked back a laugh. "I'm just starting my life again, Kyoko. How could I do a thing like that?"

"Starting your life again?" Kyoko's eyes jerked up.

"What I mean is that. . .well, I've. . ."

"You've what? Bought a pig farm? Or wait, don't they do turkeys and stuff here in the Valley? Spill it."

I wiped my eyes and balled up the tissues then picked up one of Kyoko's black-and-silver spiked belts. Which, now that I looked at it, never should have passed airline security.

"And don't you start shredding straws like Trinity." She shook a finger at me. "You can't hide from me, Ro."

"Fine." My voice came out quivery but strong. "Since you told me the truth, I'm telling you, too. I'm a Christian, Kyoko. You can say what you want, but I'm not backing down."

Chapter 9

No one spoke. The clock ticked on the bedside table, and Christie stretched and groaned softly in her sleep.

Kyoko let go of her knees and folded her Van Gogh's *The Scream* shirt with exaggerated slowness, not meeting my eyes. I imagined her mirroring its famous image, hands on gaping cheeks. Instead her voice sounded dead. Cold. "You're serious."

"Yes."

"A Bible thumper."

"Yes." I leaned forward for emphasis, bracing myself for the big brawl that would certainly erupt any minute. The tirades on imperialism and organized religion and who-knows-what. Knowing Kyoko, she'd bring the '80s and punk rock into it somehow, too.

Kyoko tossed the shirt into the suitcase and turned to face me. "I know."

My hard stance faltered. "What? You know?"

"Yeah." She brushed back shiny red-purple-black hair that had fallen into her face. "And I know you went to church on Sunday, too."

"I did." I crossed my arms to hide my trembling. "I'm in love with Jesus, Kyoko. You can say I'm crazy. Say whatever."

Kyoko gave a derisive snort and looked away.

"What? You're not going to yell at me to come back to planet Earth and get a life?"

"Would it make any difference?"

"No." I jutted my chin out. "But at least I'd know how you feel because I don't want to. . ." I shrugged, trying not to come off too harshly. "To hurt you."

"Hurt me?"

"By changing my life. Being different from what I used to be." I picked at the belt again. "I care about you, Kyoko. A lot."

"Well." She grabbed another shirt with red Rolling Stones lips and tongue protruding. "You certainly are different these days."

"I know. Crazy, right?" My eyes filled with unexpected tears, and I reached for a pair of dark, silvery jeans and helped her fold. "Surrounded by rednecks and wackos. 'Getting religion.' Scrubbing gunk off restaurant tables."

Kyoko didn't speak for a few minutes then abruptly hurled the shirt down, half folded.

"You know what I think, Ro?" she said in a bold voice, strong enough to wake Christie. "I think you're all right."

I dropped the jeans. Right there in a pile.

"What did you just say?" I felt the room spin, dizzy-like, and slid my leg over the edge of the bed to keep from sliding off.

Kyoko sighed hard, eyeing me. Fiddling with her eyebrow piercing. "Believe me, I have no idea how it could happen in a place like *this*." She made a face. "But you've changed, Ro. It's like you're more. . .*you*. I don't know how else to explain it."

"But that's just it! I don't know who I am anymore!" I flung my arms up.

"Sure you do. You just need some more time to adjust to this new . . .uh. . .life. Post-Japan, I mean." She blew out her breath in a moody sigh.

"But I'm different."

"Yeah. Kinda."

I settled back onto the bed and picked at my nails. "Different how?"

"Well, the crying stuff is. . .well, weird, to say the least. You never did that before. But the rest of it is like you've grown up. I can't figure out how else to describe it."

"What?" My voice squeaked as I jumped from images of my crisp suit jacket back in Japan to my green Barnes & Noble apron. "You can't mean that. I'm stuck in a ten-year time warp! Half my coworkers are still in high school!"

"So? At least here you're not trying to impress anybody with your high-dollar scarves or dating some nincompoop like Carlos. Or maxing out credit cards trying to be somebody you're not."

"That's for sure. I don't have any credit cards left to max out."

Kyoko shook her head. "I still don't know how you got a Daimaru department-store card back in Tokyo. That's just not fair. Foreigners *never* get those."

"If they spend enough they do."

"Figures," Kyoko muttered under her breath. "But to tell you the truth, Ro, I think you're. . ." She paused and pulled her feet up again, stirring a striped green-and-yellow wristband with her finger. "You're

Jennifer Rogers Spinola

doing okay. More than okay. Maybe even better than in Japan. Not job-wise, of course, but. . .here." She pointed awkwardly to her heart.

I was too startled even to speak. Just swallowed. Stared. And then looked down at my crossed legs in their black patterned tights, trying to take it in.

"It makes no logical sense, Ro, with you in the Pit of Pig's Feet, but somehow you're getting something here that you needed. Something that you never found anywhere else, even Japan." She shrugged and rolled her eyes. "Go figure."

"What do you think I've found?" I stopped picking my nails. "Collard greens?"

"Ugh. Spare me." She glared at me for a long time, brooding. "I have no idea. But at the risk of sounding all icky-spiritual, it seems like you're. . .well, at peace."

"With my half sister trying to steal my house?"

"Yes."

"With collection agents breathing down my neck and a trial coming up in February? The one where I have to testify against the rednecks and skinhead who jumped me at that Civil War battle reenactment?"

"Yes. And I'll pretend I didn't hear that part about you going to a reenactment voluntarily."

"It wasn't exactly voluntary." I waved my arms. "Anyway. As I was saying. You think I'm at peace with coworkers who dip snuff and—"

"Don't push it!" Kyoko glowered. "Just take it and thank me."

"I thought you hated being thanked!"

She flicked the wristband at me.

I folded her Rolling Stones shirt back up and placed it in the suitcase, sad to see Kyoko's things packed for a flight that would take her away from me.

"Would you kill me, Kyoko, if I suggested that my peace maybe . . .comes from. . .God? From the God I've come to love?" My face burned with something akin to humiliation, but I didn't take it back.

"God?" Kyoko glared. "Don't be ridiculous."

"I'm not! I'm serious."

"Well, I just don't believe in Him the way you do, Ro-chan. And you never know. This whole thing may wear off for you, and I don't want you to be devastated when you come down off this weird high." She eyed me warily. "Just be careful. No snake handling. No mass Kool-Aid binges."

90

"Why not?" I pretended not to get it. "I love Kool-Aid."

"Because, Ro, don't you watch the news? Mass suicide? Hello?" She broke off at the smirk on my face then tried to push me off the bed. I retaliated by plopping Christie right on Kyoko's lap.

That worked. Kyoko hollered and shoved Christie off her lap into a neat little pile on the bedspread, scrubbing her palms against her jeans.

"Oh my goodness, Kyoko! You're getting sick! I can see it!" I gasped. "Canine flu!"

Christie looked up, bewildered, and toddled back onto Kyoko's lap. She curled up happily and tucked head into tail. *Yes! Chalk up one for Shiloh.*

"Aw, Ro, you know I don't like animals," Kyoko moaned, trying unsuccessfully to pull one leg away. "What am I supposed to do now?" She shuddered and gingerly patted Christie's back for a fraction of a second. Just long enough for Christie to pull out a fuzzy tail and wag it.

"What's with the tail thing?" Kyoko demanded, jerking her hands up. "Is she going to poop on me or something?"

"No! It's a sign of affection. Just pet her. You can sterilize your hands afterward, or your pants or whatever else she touched."

"Okay, but if you tell anybody I petted a dog, I'll. . ." She'd taken too long already. I grabbed her hand and patted it on Christie's furry back, at which point Christie rolled over and offered her silky snout and neck. One sleepy paw dangled over Kyoko's leg.

"Doggone it," Kyoko snarled. "She's not supposed to be like this! She's supposed to foam at the mouth or something!"

"Oh please," I groaned, flopping down on the bed. "Before you know it, you'll be sneaking one of these into your apartment in Tokyo. Or in. . .wherever you decide." The last words came out mournful.

Kyoko hesitantly stroked Christie's ears. "Sorry, Ro. I'm just not into Japan like you. I *hate* the earthquakes."

That's right. A pretty big tremor hit a few months ago. Kyoko said it broke an office clock.

"But lots of places have earthquakes!"

"It's more than that. I need a place that's less restricting, without so many rules and layers of exasperating politeness. No stroke order, remember? Writing the kanji characters any way you want, forgetting all the up-to-down, right-to-left nonsense."

Jennifer Rogers Spinola

"It's not nonsense!" I tried to protest, but Kyoko steamrollered right over me.

"A place where I can buy clothes without having to look in the 'jumbo' section, or where I don't have to go through so much rigamarole and memorized phrases just to eat *mochi* rice balls in someone's house, covering my teeth and complimenting the pattern on the teacup. Sheesh! That drives me nuts! And all the honorifics and polite language!" She covered her eyes and shook her head.

"But that's what makes Japan special!"

"That's what makes Japan tiring!"

I recoiled as if she'd punched me in the stomach.

Japan had been my refuge. My passion. I'd excelled at drawing multipronged kanji characters from the first day of Japanese language class at Cornell—so much so that my professor booted me straight to the second level in two weeks. I adored the harsh Asian study structure of copying characters again and again until each stroke gleamed. The nights of flipping through thousands of kanji flash cards, each slight variation and nuance throwing another mystery at me that somehow I excelled at solving.

Japan's almost sadistic drive for perfection suited me like my own skin: *Try harder. Achieve. Succeed.* There, for the first time, I forgot the ache of my past.

Or thought I had.

"Sorry, Ro." Kyoko looked up with a gleam of sympathy in her dark eyes, and I tried to focus on now. On her maroon-tinged hair shining in the yellowish overhead light. On Mom's flowered comforter, scrunched beneath Kyoko's suitcases. "I brought you a ton of Japanese stuff so you could remember the good times."

So that explained the boatload of presents—and even the hand-carried cream puffs from Beard Papa's.

Kyoko had brought a good-bye gift. From Japan to me.

My home phone rang, and I reluctantly turned toward the sound.

"Hey, you got a couple of calls from some septic company," said Kyoko as I climbed off the bed. "I thought they took your number off their list."

I kicked the bedpost.

Which was, of course, a really bad idea. I howled and jumped around, holding my foot.

The ringing finally stopped, and I sank down on the bed just in time to hear my cell phone vibrate against the nightstand.

I snatched it up, scowling. "What?"

"Shiloh? You. . .uh. . .all right?" came Adam's familiar voice. "I just called the house phone but nobody answered."

"Oh, hi." I sank back against the headboard. "Sorry. I thought you were somebody else."

"Who, the IRS?"

I jerked my head back so hard it cracked against the walnut headboard, and even Kyoko gasped.

"Ow." I massaged my head, mad at myself. My foot still smarted. "Why do you say that?"

He paused. "I was joking, Shiloh. Really. You sure you're okay?"

"I'm fine." I fumbled to adjust my cell phone and accidentally knocked the tissue box on the floor. "Sorry. Kyoko and I are here talking."

Kyoko raised an eyebrow as I stretched over the side of the bed to retrieve the tissue box, grunting.

"Don't worry. I won't keep you. I wanted to let you know your headlight's out. My dad passed you this morning in town and saw it."

"Really?" I rubbed my head some more. "My front one or my back one?"

Adam didn't speak for a second. "Huh? You mean the. . ."

"Sorry. The right or the front?" I waved my hand in irritation, knocking the tissue box off again. "The right or the left?"

"The left one. He said. . ." I heard speaking, and Adam broke off abruptly. "Sorry, Shiloh. Gotta go. One of my guys just cut his thumb."

When I pressed the phone off, Kyoko had leaned back on an elbow, studying me with a sly smile.

"What?" I knocked the tissue box off a third time as I reached to set my phone on the nightstand and finally just left it there. "Why are you looking at me like that?"

"Like what?" Kyoko grinned. "No reason. Who called just now?"

"Oh." I shrugged, catching a black sweater in midslide over the edge of the bed. "A friend. Not the septic service."

She waggled her eyebrows. "Who?"

"Just. . .Adam. You met him." I shook out the sweater and then sniffed it. "This smells like incense, Kyoko. What do you do, burn it in your bedroom?"

Kyoko laced her fingers together, nodding with a smirky wide-eyed look that reminded me of a deranged psychologist. "Adam. Really. How interesting."

"Cut it out, Kyoko." I grimaced and waved her away. "We're just friends. Forget it."

"It's just that you're suddenly so. . .pink."

"Pink?" I hollered, dropping the sweater. "I am not! For your information, I—"

"Did you see the way he held the door for you, Ro? Even for me?"

"Well, of course! That's only because he—"

"He paid our bill. And he made sure to leave a good tip for the waiter, even though I can tell he doesn't have much money. Am I right?" She raised an eyebrow. "Ro? What are you doing?"

I realized I was twisting a ring on my finger and jerked my hands down. "Nothing. And to answer your question, no. Adam doesn't have much money. He gave up a college scholarship to help take care of his brother Rick, who lost a leg and a foot in Afghanistan. A double amputee."

"Ouch."

"So now Adam runs a landscaping business. Planting stuff, building decks."

She looked up suddenly, giving me a sneaky Cheshire-cat grin. "So now I see why your house is so well landscaped! All the shrubs trimmed and everything."

"Please. He does that for everybody." I crossed my arms uncomfortably. "Besides, he's way younger than I am. I told you that already."

"Oh, a year and a half." Kyoko rolled her eyes. "Heaven forbid."

"Still."

"What on earth does that have to do with anything?" Kyoko waved her arms as if to jog some sense into me. "Join the twenty-first century, will ya? He's no baby. At least he's legal, Ro. I once dated a guy who was. . ." She bit her lip. "Never mind."

My jaw wobbled.

Kyoko ignored me. "So when's he coming over? I'll make myself scarce."

I pressed my hands to my cheeks, trying to stop the heat from flooding. "Stop it, Kyoko! He's not coming over. And I don't have feelings for Adam like that. He's a friend! He's not even cute at all, and. . ." I waved my arms. "I have no idea why he unnerves me. It's probably because he's so weird and stuffy all the time, asking goofy questions, and he makes me nervous. But at least we're not arguing like we used to, right?"

Kyoko the legal reporter missed nothing. She squinted at me, twisting her head. "That's an awful lot of vociferation, don't you think?"

"Well, it's true." I crossed my arms grumpily. "He just. . . I don't know. Forget about him."

"Guys don't hold the door for me, especially in Japan. But he did. And. . . I appreciated it."

"You what?"

"It was nice." She coolly picked at some chipped nail polish.

"I didn't think you cared about that stuff!"

"Sometimes. I might be fat and scary, but I'm still a girl."

"You're not fat!" I smacked her leg so hard she yelped, waking Christie. "Scary, yes. But fat, no. Don't ever say that again!"

"Ow!" She glared and rubbed her leg. "Glad you agree I'm scary. I try."

"I know. You do a good job."

Kyoko stayed quiet awhile, bending a ticket stub into a rounded arch. "I have to tell you something, Ro."

"It better not be about Adam." I bristled. "Or I'll—"

"Huh? No. Not this time." She grinned. "But coming to see you is what reminded me how ready I am to go home."

"Coming here? Why?"

A funny look passed across Kyoko's face. "Let me back up. I don't know exactly how to say this, but I came thinking maybe you needed help. That you're maybe. . .overstressed or something."

"I know."

"You do?"

"Yeah. You sort of hinted at it over the phone. I'm not a dummy, Kyoko."

She looked away. "Oh. Well. Sorry, but I was worried about you. All you've been through could wear anybody down. But I have to tell you that your life isn't quite like I expected."

"What do you mean?"

"They love you, Ro," she said bluntly, looking up at me. Her piercing glinted in the overhead light. "I don't know where you met that bunch of friends, and they're weird all right—especially that Tim guy. But he's really nice. Becky, too."

"What did you say?" I did a double take. "You *liked* them?" Kyoko the stoic hadn't uttered one word after our Sunday lunch at The Green Tree. "But I thought. . ."

"I never said I *liked* them. Let's not get carried away." She coolly stuck her ticket in a leather travel wallet-thing, hiding a smile. "But. . . They're okay, I guess. If you must associate with people from Staunton."

"You gave them those looks! And when Tim said that about catfish, you. . ." I crossed my arms stiffly. "I don't believe you. You're just making fun of me."

"I'm not!" Kyoko shoved my shoulder. "Don't make me say this twice because I swear when I get back to Tokyo I'll go back to giving you grief. Hear me?" She shook a stray sock at me for emphasis. "I liked them, okay? I admit it. And I don't like people very often. You should know that by now."

"You can say that again."

"Yeah, well, I had a million reasons not to. But when I saw how they treated you. The way they. . ." She threw the sock in the suitcase, and for a split second her eyes looked watery.

"Are you crying?" I recoiled in surprise.

"No! My contact's bugging me." Kyoko rubbed her eye harshly, smearing her glittery green eyeliner. "Anyway, those friends of yours talk to you like you really *matter*. They hear you. They protect you, in a weird way. Even your redneck boss man, hovering around our table and making sure we got the best service and bragging about what a good job you do."

I smiled faintly. "Jerry does that to everybody."

"And that Todd kid? What a cutie."

Kyoko Morikoshi calling someone a cutie? Impossible. "I can't believe this! I thought Todd got on your last nerve."

"What? No way!" Kyoko ran a hand over his army-tank drawing. "He's gonna be an artist. Did you see the detail on that fender? Man! I'm going to show this to my friend Makoto who draws anime comics. It'll blow his ponytail off!"

My friends had outdone me. Just like Jamie said, they showed her our life to enjoy if she wanted to. Rolled out their red carpet, tattered as it might be. And striped with stars and bars.

I heard the tick of the clock on Mom's bedside table and wished I could somehow stop time. That Kyoko could stay forever, and at the same time she'd change her mind and forget Europe. Tell Dave she made a mistake. That she'd misjudged Japan the way she'd misjudged

Virginia—and wanted to give it another try.

"I've missed this, Ro. I miss having friends who care for me. Japanese people can be wonderfully polite, but a foreigner is almost always outside looking in. And I'm ready to be on the inside again."

"You're always on the inside here." I wanted to say more, but my lip quivered, and I felt my throat choke up.

"Ah." She patted my shoulder, smooshing my hair. "You're all right, Ro. I'm glad I came. After all, who else can I pick on back at the office? They're all a bunch of dorks."

I reached up and squeezed her hand as she pulled it away. "Thanks."

"For what? You're a dork, too. But with a more intimate knowledge of fried chicken and biscuits."

"I meant thank you for coming here and caring," I said, ignoring her attempt at humor/affection. "I mean it."

She yawned, leaning back on her elbows in an *I-don't-care* position. "Yeah. Well. I do what I can. Just try not to get attacked at any more battlefields because I can't exactly send you ninja throwing stars through the mail. Well, actually I *can*, but I'd have to. . .never mind. I'd better just do it because then you can claim you didn't know if you get caught."

Kyoko's skills, legal and otherwise, never failed to impress.

"Just one thing."

I looked up. "What?"

"That Stella woman is one weirdo with a capital *w*."

My blood ran cold. I hadn't seen Stella in a few days. "Why? You didn't say anything rude to her, did you?"

"No. But I sure made up some good stories about your neighbors." She snickered. "I bet she's off investigating them now."

"Kyoko! You didn't!" My eyes popped out.

"Kept her busy, didn't it?"

"That's evil!"

"I know." She beamed. "You should hear the stuff I said about you!"

The following morning frost painted the grass velvet-white. Kyoko took the remaining vestiges of summer with her, leaving me standing on the front porch in a cold, dazzly, hazy-breathed dawn. I'd hoped to drive her to Richmond, but she refused on the spot. Probably the emotion thing.

"I'll do anything for you, Ro," she said in an uncharacteristic spout of tenderness, patting my head with more force than necessary. "Just let me know."

It stung. I rubbed the spot and fixed my hair. "Want to buy a house in western Virginia?"

"Ha! Don't kid yourself. I'd go insane." She flicked my shoulder. "Like you."

I hugged her as long as she'd let me (about one-and-a-half seconds), and then she jumped in the car and left. Honked at the end of the driveway and pulled away.

I thought I saw her wipe her face with her free hand. And then never look back.

Leaving me with a mouthful of unsaid good-byes.

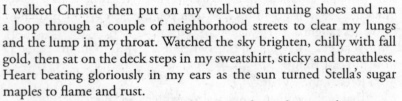

I walked Christie then put on my well-used running shoes and ran a loop through a couple of neighborhood streets to clear my lungs and the lump in my throat. Watched the sky brighten, chilly with fall gold, then sat on the deck steps in my sweatshirt, sticky and breathless. Heart beating gloriously in my ears as the sun turned Stella's sugar maples to flame and rust.

And when I stood to open the screen door, they caught my eye: Mom's last white Kobe roses of the season frozen in a shock of fine, diamond-like frost, as if sprayed with glitter starch. Breathtakingly beautiful for their last moment.

Just like Mom. Taken in an unexpected instant, the bloom still in their cheeks. Fearless. Bold. Standing strong in the face of death.

"Come, fall! Come, winter!" Mom had written in her journal. "*I am not afraid! I will keep on singing until my last petal falls.*"

My breath misted as I touched the papery petals, frozen in time. Their last bloom before winter. I knelt on the cold mulch, sun sparkling on the tiny ice crystals that formed on each delicate white petal like shards of spun glass.

I raced inside and grabbed my camera.

Squatting next to her roses, I snap-snapped away, trying to keep my cloudy breath out of the frame.

I could still see Mom's words, written in her distinctive loopy script, so different from the angry words I remembered from my childhood:

> *Even though the canes are bare, life stirs beneath the surface. How do I know? Because that's what faith is. Belief in an unseen God. Belief in grace and second chances even when all else shouts otherwise. Belief that one day the evil will fall away, and what we see now will be transformed. Renewed. Made perfect.*
>
> *Belief that somewhere, under this cold, earthly flesh, is a heart made to sing His glory—now and for eternity!*

My camera groaned, sluggish with cold, and my fingers turned red. I rubbed them together and took a few more shots. Then I gently touched one of the chilly canes, which had burst forth in glorious bloom in the late summer sun.

"I'll miss you," I whispered, thinking of Mom's smiles from her photos. Of Japan, slipping steadily from my grasp. Of Kyoko's retreating car, when I'd finally lost it from view behind a neighbor's white siding.

Good-byes were becoming part of me. A little ache just below the surface, always holding back a tear.

But spring would come.

I believed it now.

"I'll see you when winter's over," I said, touching a cold leaf in the morning glow. "I can't wait to be together again. To say hello instead of good-bye."

To you, roses. And to you, Mom.

I can't wait for our reunion.

Chapter 10

Somebody should have warned me about fall in Virginia.

Whole mountainsides roared with red and orange flame. Gypsy Hill Park turned to gold, leaves sifting down to brilliant carpets where I used to see grass. The air crackled, crisp as the endless apples people gave away in bulging bags to ease the weight on their groaning trees. Our clear blue mountain ridges turned a distinctive smoky purple. My marigolds glowed.

Even the sun shone differently—muted apricot, a little bit sad and a little bit joyful, slanting across railroad tracks and evergreens with cool blue shadows.

Another color sprouted across the hillsides: blaze orange. Tim informed me "huntin' season" was about to open and it was almost "deer time." His gun rack bloomed with actual rifles, while he dressed in an odd combination of neon and camouflage. Eye-smarting, synthetic orange popped up everywhere—on caps, on vests, and gleaming from endless trucks and cars that winked in the receding fall sun.

While the local guys huddled at the gun range in plaid-wearing clumps to sight in their rifles, Wal-Mart set out a huge hunting display—complete with taxidermied deer and mannequins clad in shaggy, leaf-covered coats. Rows of camouflage caps, hand warmers, bows and arrows, rifle scopes, and shotgun shells stacked all the way to the counter, which bristled with rifles. They issued hunting licenses for the opening of deer season by the hundred—first for bows, then for muzzleloaders, and in November, the long-awaited rifle season. The waiting line snaked around the corner and into the photo area. I listened to them chat about "twelve pointers" and "three-fi'ty-sevens" and "black powder" as they inched forward in their blaze orange and camo, cleaning their nails with pocket knives or fingering boxes of shiny gold ammo cartridges.

The most astonishing fact of all: Becky told me that local schools gave excused absences for hunting!

Tim mysteriously disappeared three different weekends, and Adam and Todd, one. Staunton's general male population shrank. Everybody—including the membership of my "new believers" Sunday school class—jawed about buckshot and synthetic pheromones, and my Sunday school teacher even drew deer-stand diagrams on the white board.

And then I started seeing dead deer strapped to tops of cars and in beds of trucks.

It horrified me to stomp on my brakes at a red light and find myself staring into the cold eyes of a buck just a few feet ahead. And I told Tim so the night they invited me over for rice and venison.

"It's barbaric! How can you kill a deer? They don't even have any natural defenses!"

He looked up from packing another Ziploc full of red stuff, fresh from his meat grinder. "Well cows don't neither, and ya eat them up mighty quick."

"Well, that's different. They're raised for food."

"Ain't no differ'nt. Fact is, deer got the better end of the stick. They live their lives free an' wild, an' then I take 'em out before they know what hit 'em. One clean shot. Ya ever been in a slaughterhouse?"

I hadn't. And I didn't like the way this conversation was going. "Maybe I should become a vegetarian."

"Try it." Becky slid a plate of tender venison and gravy in front of me as Tim slammed the freezer door shut. I tried not to notice the scarlet-stained rinse water as he washed his hands in the sink. Gordon, the hound, obviously undisturbed by such moral dilemmas, whapped his tail and stared at me in expectation of a handout.

"Fact is, if we don't keep the doggone deer population down, they'd overrun the place," said Tim, pulling out his chair. "Few years back they was beggin' us to bag as many as we could 'cause they was destroyin' farmers' crops and gettin' hit by cars. I take out a few of 'em nice and quick, and we eat the proceeds. Sounds like a fair deal to me."

As liberally as people gave away apples and zucchini (which I still couldn't figure out why God created), they also gave away deer. Faye's freezer bulged. Even Earl presented me with a couple of Ziplocs—the traditional redneck packaging—of frozen red stuff. They'd probably remain under my TV dinners until the next Ice Age.

"So, you gonna sit there all day, Yankee, or you gonna try it?" Tim slung an arm over his chair.

I stared down into my plate of venison, slivers of onion peeking out from the creamy gravy, and felt like a traitor to Bambi. Worst of all, it smelled delicious.

"Don't they have diseases and things?" I sounded like Kyoko. "I mean, just running around outside with. . .you know. . .ticks and worms and. . .?"

"You tell me"—Tim took a bite and shook his spoon at me—"which one breeds more diseases—a cattle pen packed full a hundred head a cattle gettin' fed artificial soy feed and hormones, all squished together in the mud, or a bunch a deer runnin' free an' wild in God's green woods?"

The little cubes of brown venison sounded more appetizing all the time. I took a bite and swallowed. Gordon bayed and wagged his tail.

"All right," I said grumpily. "I tasted it. Happy now?"

I ate two more platefuls.

"Now ya gotta try squirrel since ya et that up so fast!"

I dropped my spoon and gawked from Tim to Becky, and she finally burst into laughter. "Now, Tee-um, take it easy! She done ate yer deer. Let's take things slow-like. Right, Shah-loh?"

"You eat squirrel?" My hand still hung open from the falling spoon. "I mean, like the squirrels that run around in my yard?"

"Have some more venison," said Becky, ladling some more onto my plate. So tasty, all covered in that nice, peppery gravy, that I forgot what we were talking about.

★　★　★

Lowell's news about my house, though, shocked me more than dead deer. Even after days of Tim's venison stew, chili, jerky, and steaks, I couldn't get his words out of my head.

"You won't believe what Lowell said about my house. Ever. In a million years."

I stabbed another sweet potato as Tim's NASCAR clock made a zooming sound to mark the hour and jerked my head up to see the time. Fumbled with my knife. Swallowing my nerves at the thought of tonight's ridiculous agenda. And why should I be nervous? I'd already decided not to go. Probably.

"Is that clock right?" I tried to sound casual.

"Shore it's right. We got plenty a time. Why?"

Tim chewed, looking at me for a response. "Why? Ya got somethin' after the big shindig?"

"Shah-loh?" Becky waved her hand in front of my face. "You breathin'?"

"What?" I jerked straight and turned away from the clock, remembering to inhale. And putting tonight out of my mind. "Sorry. I'm just. . ." I took a bite of sweet potato, not sure how to frame my hesitation.

"So what did Lowell say?"

"Empty." I wiped my mouth with a napkin and forced myself to focus on now, on one problem at a time. "Lowell said the last two people who looked at my house said it was empty!"

I smacked my palm on the red-and-white checked tablecloth for emphasis. "Two separate couples! Can you believe it?"

"Empty?" Becky peeled the foil off a baked sweet potato and sliced it open. Steam rushed up in curls from its tender flesh, the color of Tim's bright orange hunting cap. "What, like ya don't got nothin' in it? What'd ya do, give away all yer furniture?"

"No. They said it 'felt' "—I curled my fingers in exaggerated quotation marks—"empty."

"Well, that's plumb ridiculous. Ain't a house fer sale s'pposed ta be empty? Kinda?"

"That's what I thought." I held up the packet of Lowell's "house staging" mumbo jumbo. "Anyway, he said the walls had to be painted off-white. All the personal photos and decorations taken down and something generic put up instead. I did that! How on earth could people call it 'empty'? 'Soulless'? That's what somebody else said."

Christie was shredding a newspaper in gray shards across the brown-and-white linoleum floor, which reminded me vaguely of Mom's ugly '70s wallpaper. Before Tim and Adam replaced it with sleek, cream-colored paint.

"Please. It's a house, for crying out loud! How can it have a soul anyway? It's a blank canvas, according to Lowell. And that's what I've made it." I fished out a piece of venison for Gordon, who'd slung himself across my high-heeled boot in anticipation.

Tim shook his head at me in pity. "Bunch a Yankee weirdos with too much money, I reckon."

Um. . .Connecticut and Maine, respectively. Not that I'd tell Tim that.

"Like them. . .whadda they call 'em. . .pet whisperers?" His shoulders shuddered. "People plunk down a hundred bucks ta hear about their hound's problem with his grandma! That's what happens when people got too much money an' not enough ta do." He tittered. "I'm thinkin' a gettin' me a license fer pet psychology. Whaddaya think?"

My fist tightened on the fork, and my laughter wrenched suddenly toward tears. "You don't understand. I need this house to sell. Badly."

"It's gonna." Becky touched my arm.

"Yeah. I keep telling myself that." I wiped my eyes. "My horrible half sister wants a copy of Mom's will and said if she doesn't receive it by the end of the month she'll turn the case over to her lawyer."

Becky looked up in horror. "Ya ain't gonna send it, are ya?"

"Not until I get a court order."

Ugh. Court. With a bunch of rednecks and a skinhead. Why on earth did I have to bring that up? I stabbed at my sweet potato, mentally counting off the months until February. Like a condemned man savoring his last moments.

And what did I get for my last meal? Deer.

"Everything's against me! Why is it so hard to sell this place and move on?" I smeared butter on my sweet potato and sprinkled it with cinnamon.

"Maybe God wants ya here." Tim grinned at me.

"In Staunton?" I glared then silenced the wrath that threatened to spill. After all, they *were* feeding me. "I'm made for big cities, Tim. For major newspapers. For. . .well, different things than Staunton can offer. You know that. So does God." I forced a smile that I hoped didn't look too farcical. "But thanks. . .uh. . .anyway."

Gordon nudged my foot under the table, and I slipped him another morsel.

"It's funny, though, Shah-loh, them sayin' about yer house bein' empty," said Becky, shaking the ice cubes in her glass. "Fact is, a house is s'pposed ta have soul! Life! To hold in the mem'ries. The way that Lowell fella says it, it sounds almost like a skeleton."

"He'd better not find any skeletons at my house, or I'm moving in here!"

I meant it as a joke, but Tim got this funny, faraway look in his eyes that usually preceded one of his more serious statements. "Ever'body's got a few skeletons hangin' around in their closet, don't ya reckon? Goodness knows we ain't born holy."

"Who, you and Becky?" I teased.

"The people a God." Tim shook his spoon at me, dripping gravy. "No matter how saved we look, we all got stuff we'd prefer ta fergit. Ev'ry last one of us. But ya know somethin'? Jesus comes ta kick all them skeletons outta the closet one by one! Just face 'em! A couple a old bones ain't nothin' to be scared of. B'sides, ain't He the one who made the dead rise and walk again?"

Tim looked almost tearful then he reached out with rare emotion and clasped Becky's hand. "We're the most blessed folks on earth, ain't we, Shah-loh Jacobs?"

It struck me that Tim was calling himself blessed—*blessed!*—just months after Becky lost her miracle baby.

"I guess so." I smiled back at them both in admiration, Gordon nosing my ankle for more handouts. "You guys deserve all the blessings in the world."

"Deserve?" Becky nearly dropped her fork. "Shucks, Shah-loh! Ain't none a us deserve nothin'! 'Cept Tim, who, when he ain't preachin', deserves a kick in the pants from time to time."

I choked on my tea as they smooched over the napkin basket. Then I turned away, affecting great interest in a Remington rifle cartridge wall calendar, complete with a wild turkey gobbling on the November page.

"Hurry up, y'all!" Becky finally said, scooting her chair back. "We gotta hit the road! It's gonna start at what, around six?"

"Maybe you guys can go without me. I'll stay here and shop eBay for tapestries and lamps and stuff. Since my real-estate agent is so set on me spending more money." I rolled my eyes and scraped the last of my rice with my fork.

"Well, if it's fancy decorations he wants, I got ya some NASCAR posters and ol' pitchers a Jeff Gordon!" Gordon howled at his name, tail thumping and tags jingling. Becky poked my arm on the way to the sink with plate in hand, grinning. "That'll give yer house some soul! Prob'ly got a ol' set a deer antlers 'round here somewhere, too."

My eyes popped. "I know! That stuffed groundhog Tim shot when he was. . .how old again? Seven?"

"Twelve." Becky rolled her eyes.

Tim scowled at me over his rice. "Uh-uh, Shah-loh Jacobs! Don't you be gettin' no notions about my Brownie! He's mine fair and square."

"Please!" begged Becky. "Let 'er have it!"

"It ain't a 'it.' It's a he, if ya don't mind. An' Brownie ain't goin' nowhere." He leaned down the hallway and hollered. "Hear that, Brownie? Don't ya worry! I ain't gonna give you away!" He shook his head. "Ya made the poor thing cry."

I stared at him, leaning my head on my hand in disbelief.

"Tim's awful attached to that rodent," Becky whispered. "Sleeps with it sometimes when I'm outta town."

"*Shh!* Don't you say that in front a comp'ny, woman! She'll think I'm weird!"

"Well, she done figgered that out by now." Becky carried her plate to the sink. "Goodness only knows! Don't even git me started on the Cheez Whiz an' badger episode!"

"The what episode?" She was joking. She had to be.

"Woman? Shush!" Tim glanced over at me, choking back laughter. "Did you say somethin', Shah-loh? Thought I heard some high-pitched noises, but it didn't make no sense ta me."

"I got pitchers!" Becky called on her way down the hall. "So don't sass me, boy!"

He pretended to pound the table in frustration.

Becky was still yelling. "Y'all better hurry up if we're gonna make it over ta Adam's before dark! I don't know 'bout you, but I ain't missin' that pie an' bonfire fer his birthday!"

"Oh yeah." Tim shoveled his rice and gravy into his mouth and swigged the last of his sweet tea, which Southerners drank no matter how cold it got outside. "Honey? Did we get him a present?"

"I'm wrappin' it right now!"

"What is it?"

"Oh, just that ol'. . .what'd ya call it? Brownie?"

His eyes bugged out. "Now hold on just a cotton-pickin' minute!" And he pushed his chair back and dashed down the hall.

I twirled my empty fork on my plate, envying the warmth that welled up between Tim and Becky. I missed being known by someone—and still loved.

Loved, like Tim said, no matter what kind of skeletons hung in my closet. "*A relationship,*" Adam had called life with God last summer, as he and Becky and Tim sat over take-out pizza in my living room.

"*A romance,*" amended Tim.

I glanced out the frilly tan curtains at a poplar branch, which shook lemon-yellow leaves in the late afternoon sunlight. Remembering—for some odd, inexplicable reason—the long, pale scar that stretched across Adam's knuckles on his left hand. I'd seen it before but never asked what happened.

A bike accident? Chopping firewood? Or did he fall off the roof like his dad a few months ago, necessitating (1) a rush to the emergency room and (2) the laughable "help" of one clueless waitress—*moi*—at The Green Tree to administer Rick's medications?

I'm just glad I didn't overdose the poor guy; Rick was certainly one of my favorite people, next to Todd, of course, and Adam, and. . .

Why am I thinking about Adam anyway? I scooted my chair back abruptly and took my plate to the sink. Stepping over Christie, who had fallen asleep on a heap of torn newspaper bits. One shred hung in the fuzzy fur of her right ear.

"Shah-loh? Yer goin', too, right?" Becky poked her head around the corner, mouth foamy with toothpaste.

"Going where?" I ran some water over the sponge.

"Aw, quit that!" She smacked the sponge out of my hand. "I don't bring ya over here ta clean my house! That's what husbands'r for."

She grinned and scrubbed her teeth some more, hand on her hip. "Whaddaya mean, 'where'? Didn't Adam invite ya? He said he did!"

"He sort of mentioned it on Sunday." I put both hands on a kitchen chair back, balancing it back and forth. Yep. Uneven flooring. Lowell said that took money off property value.

"Ya got him a present! What's the matter with you?"

I shrugged, pushing the chair back into place and running my hands through my hair. "Nothing's wrong, Becky. I just. . .maybe I shouldn't. I don't know." My laughter sounded nervous, and I tried to relax, sitting down at the table and straightening napkins in the basket. "Maybe I'll stay here and watch the dogs. Gordon ate a lot of deer meat, and that can't be good for his digestive system."

"What on earth?" Becky stared, toothpaste dripping.

"Okay. Gordon'll be fine. But I've got Christie. Todd wanted me to bring her, and I think it's a bad idea."

"Why? She's an angel!"

"Right. Because she's asleep now."

Becky marched over and put her hand on my forehead. "Lands, Shah-loh, yer fingers are tremblin'! You comin' down with somethin'? Ya ain't got a fever, but ya look all funny all of a sudden."

"I'm not trembling!" I thrust the napkin basket away. "And I'm not sick either. But about tonight? I mean, it's going to be Adam's family mostly, and I'm not family. I haven't even known him that long. Isn't a family birthday party kind of. . .private?"

Becky didn't even listen to the rest of my little speech. I caught a glimpse of her as she headed down the hall, toothbrush in hand— shaking her head and rolling her eyes.

Chapter 11

"Trinity's what?" I pressed my other ear closed, trying to hear Jerry on my cell phone over the loud breathing of two dogs, the squeak of Tim's shocks, his rumbly engine, and Hank Williams on the tape player up front. Yes, Tim's truck still had a tape player. "She hasn't shown up to work yet?"

"Nope. You seen her?"

"What do you mean she's not there? Trinity's never late. She helped train me, for crying out loud." I shoved another rifle in a cloth case over to the side as Tim turned a corner, piling dogs and crossbows and an army-green camping chair against my legs.

"Well, she's an hour late, an' nobody's seen her." Jerry sighed, and I heard the clatter of dishes in the background. Flash's muffled voice calling an order to José, the newest short-order cook.

"I'm kinda worried about her, Shiloh. She ain't all there these days. I don't wanna let her go, but. . ."

"I'm worried about her, too, Jerry. I'll call her. Thanks for letting me know."

I told Jerry good-bye and dialed Trinity, my forehead tight with worry. Nothing. I dialed again, hanging on to the back of the seat with one hand while Gordon drooled wet patches across my nice jeans. Christie put both front paws on the window and whined.

"Get off, hound," I whispered, trying to gently push Gordon away and then finally elbowing him off my legs. Groaning at the endless ring of Trinity's phone that abruptly shifted into voice mail.

"What's goin' on back there?" Becky called back, scrunching her head around to see me as she disentangled Christie from the gearshift. "You seem awful stressed fer somebody who's got the night off!"

"I'm not stressed. I'm. . ." A black metal crossbow slid sideways, skewering me in the ribs, followed by a rain of musty-smelling camouflage hunting coats. "Smashed." I unclipped my seat belt and turned sideways in the seat, shoving stuff on the floor.

"Well, I'm real pleased ya decided to come." Becky raised an eyebrow. "Ya had me worried there fer a minute."

I dialed Trinity a fifth time and left a message then reluctantly

Jennifer Rogers Spinola

closed my phone and stuffed it into my purse. "Yeah, well, I can't stay long. I'm busy. I've got tons of stuff to do to fix up the house, and then I've still got to iron my clothes for work tomorrow."

I felt bad for complaining. It was nice of Adam to invite me, especially when I knew he didn't have much time off. Fall kept him busy with more than hunting: pruning, winterizing lawns, hauling leaves, putting in walkways and walls, and planting bulbs. So much so that he didn't even have time for a real party—just a couple of pies before a long night of balancing ledgers and updating flyers.

Two of his employees hadn't shown up for work, so Adam spent the previous week scrambling to hire new guys and smoothing over problems at one construction site. He told me at church he'd pulled three all-nighters, finishing up blueprints for a new project in record time and dozing in his car as he waited for the copy shop to open.

I knew how he felt. Last Friday I nodded off at The Green Tree, rolling silverware. Face-planted right on the table. Jerry sent me home early and gave me the following night off.

"How does he find time to sleep?" I asked as we jolted along then realized I'd spoken out loud. "I didn't mean that. I just wondered. . ."

"Who, Brownie?" asked Tim. "With me. Oops. Did I say that? I meant on the shelf!"

Becky smacked him. At least she'd put on her nice jeans and a fuzzy gray sweater, topped by a fitted jacket, so she smacked with style.

"I was asking about Adam." I rolled down the window a crack to rid my nose of doggy smell, pulling Christie back on my lap. "How does he sleep with all the stuff he has to do?"

"He don't get much, I reckon. Landscapin' is like that. Ya work yer tail off all spring an' summer long an' into the fall, and then durin' the winter ya get yer breaks."

"Well, what does he do in the winter? He can't hibernate."

"He works on new plans an' blueprints and orders new supplies. Sometimes he takes a class, like that one he did last year to learn how ta put in stone walls and ponds an' stuff like that. Buildin' decks. An' then there's snow. Lots a shovelin', but there's money there."

"Shoveling snow?" I wrinkled my nose. "Doesn't sound like great work, huh?"

"Neither does waitin' tables, but it pays the bills." Tim grinned at me in the rearview mirror.

"Touché."

110

"I think he's wantin' to start takin' college classes," interjected Becky. "He didn't say nothin', but I keep seein' him look at college stuff. Wouldn't be su'prised if he starts his course again now that Rick's doin' a little better. Maybe rent a place of his own."

"Rent a place? Why?"

"Well, he's twenty-three."

"And that means something? Kyoko dated a forty-one-year-old who still lived with his mom."

"Ha!" Tim shook his head. "'Round these parts a man like that's called a freeloader. An' Adam ain't one, last I checked."

"Wait," I said, stopping in midpat on Christie's head. "Is Adam thinking of moving? Or only moving to a new place?"

My question came out a little too quickly. "I'm just curious," I added, in case they got any wild ideas. "I mean, I'm planning to leave town as soon as I can sell Mom's house. So." I shrugged.

Tim finally turned down the tape player. "Well, I don't reckon he's thinkin' a movin' away until Rick's in a little better shape. Wouldn't ya say, honey bun?" He turned to Becky, tapping out the rhythm to the music on his worn steering wheel. "'Course with his business and all, it's gonna be awful hard fer him ta ever move."

"Right." I leaned against the seat back and shifted my legs around Gordon. "I sort of figured that."

We turned into the narrow gravel driveway and parked in front of the two-story Carter house, its wood-and-brick exterior gleaming in the last rays of evening. The first time I'd come in such a rush to help Rick that I barely noticed a thing. Now the gardens Adam had skillfully designed glowed, jewel-like, in the pale blue evening: stone walkways, small burgundy-tinged dogwood and dark spruce trees, and flower beds bursting with cheery marigolds and thick, broccoli-shaped clumps of rust-red sedum, all interlaced with leafy coleus exploding in chartreuse and pinky-red tones. Ice-blue asters poking up petaled heads among yellow-faced pansies. Even in the ruins of summer, Adam's garden lived—breathed—sang—a kaleidoscope of last hopes before the snow.

A dying sun spilled over the mountains, twinkling through the tree limbs that sifted quivering leaves onto a golden carpet.

"They're here! They're here!" Todd shouted, throwing open the front door. Two chocolate labs bounded down the front walk—named, if I remembered Todd's explanation correctly, after NASCAR drivers

Jennifer Rogers Spinola

Dennis Hamlin and Dale Earnhardt. "And you brought Christie! Thank you, Miss Shiloh! Thank you!"

I doubt your family will be thanking me in five minutes, after she's chewed on the kitchen table and torn holes in the sofa, I thought, warily holding her out for Todd.

We met in a happy mass on the sidewalk. Todd grabbed Becky and me by the hands and dragged us into the bright yellow foyer, Christie squirming under one arm. We shook hands with Adam's dad, Cliff, a high school math teacher, minus the arm cast I remembered from his summer accident. His mom Vanna giving hugs with her cute pink-cheeked smile. An elderly couple who I guessed must be Adam's grandparents.

And then Christie wiggled loose, dropping to the carpet. Nails skidding on the shiny floor. She darted through the arched doorway and into the living room.

"Christie!" I hollered, panting, running after her for the fourth time, as Todd grabbed her from gnawing an armchair. Denny and Dale in curious pursuit, noses quivering. "Todd, you've got to hold her tight. Like this." I stuffed her in the crook of my elbow.

"I'll hold her! I promise!" He reached out, eyes pleading.

I shook my head, wishing I'd never brought her. Or better, agreed to Becky's silly dog idea. "If she pees on the rug, your parents will kill me."

"Oh, she won't. I'll—"

Christie, sensing a challenge, stuck her nose under my elbow and somehow managed to slip through both my grasp and Todd's. Careened toward the hallway. I ran to grab her, practically bowling over Adam's older brother, Rick—maneuvering his wheelchair through the bedroom doorway with obvious effort.

Droopy pants hung over the empty places where his leg and left foot should be, but his shoulders showed new strength. The weight benches and physical therapy gave him a good workout.

I stopped short as Todd snatched up Christie, laughing, and bounded outside with her under his arm.

"Hiya, Shiloh. Brought me a dog, eh?" Rick laughed, watching them go.

"Don't I wish."

Rick's grown-out brown military cut fell over his forehead like Adam's. He'd made such an impact on my decision to trust God that I wished I could say it, put it into words. Instead I remembered myself and dug in my purse. Then dropped a little shopping bag in his lap.

"What's this?" Rick asked, rolling his wheelchair to a better-lit corner. "It's Adam's birthday, not mine."

I bent awkwardly to hug him. "Open it!"

He dug in the bag and pulled out a CD of the Psalms. Just reading and some background music. Thanks to my employee discount at Barnes & Noble.

"Guns N' Roses?" Rick turned the CD cover over. "Uh. . .thanks. I'll have to grow my hair out now."

"What?" I snatched the CD back and realized he was teasing me again.

"Really, Shiloh," he said, dark eyes meeting mine. "I appreciate it. That's really nice." His voice had lost its characteristic wry laugh.

I shrugged. "I just thought you might like to have it, especially when you're not feeling so great. Adam said you've been training a lot to walk, and. . ."

My voice trailed off, remembering his face pale with agony. The pills I'd handed him in shaking fingers.

"Read to me how we are made," Rick had begged as pain swept over him. *"How we are fearfully and wonderfully made."* And never before had the scriptures entered my heart so deeply, so personally.

"The Psalms are my favorite."

"I know. You're going to make it, Rick. You're going to do far better things than you imagine."

"We both are. Hang in there, Shiloh. Things'll get better for you, too."

Outside I heard Todd shouting Christie's name, and I laughed and shook my head. "Don't be so sure."

★　★　★

We stood under a sunset-painted sky, warming ourselves by the crackling flames, when I heard the familiar rumble in the distance. The sound of a truck door slamming. And my heart made a funny little miss-beat.

How ridiculous. I turned my back and tossed another stick in the fire. *It's just Adam—and he's not my type at all!*

Ever since I learned that men lost their senses over soft hair and sugar-sweet smiles, I'd always dated "high" on the food chain: rich, good-looking guys with hearts of ice. A pro basketball player. An Issey Miyake model. Stockbrokers like my black-eyed heartbreaker Carlos. It formed a society ladder—work your way up to the top and never look back.

I'd definitely never wasted a second glance on somebody who drove a pickup truck and hauled gravel.

But when Adam came into the backyard in work boots and a thick jacket, carrying heavy gloves and a pair of pruning shears, that little miss-beat tickled again. He strode so confidently—a man who worked with his hands and knew what he wanted out of life.

"Hey everybody!" He waved as Todd raced toward him in the sweet, leaf-scented twilight, laced with fragrant smoke, and caught him in a hug. Christie racing after him with a stick in her mouth. "I'll just change and be right down."

He headed inside, and I saw a light come on in his bedroom behind the curtains then blink off, and then Denny and Dale bounded down the back steps ahead of Adam in a chocolate-brown escort. He cradled Christie, who nestled down against his jacket like she belonged there. Warm against the crisp November breeze, fur blowing.

"Well, look who's here!" crowed Becky, high-fiving Adam. "The birthday boy himself!"

"Birthday?" asked Tim, looking lost. "You gotta be kiddin'! I'm here fer pie!"

Cliff pushed Rick's wheelchair across the leaves, squeaking and crunching, and we all merged in front of the fire, amber light flickering on our faces. Faye came across the yard like a shadow, rosy from cold, and we pulled her over into the cozy circle as sparks danced and showered in the air. Smoke blew in a shift of wind and Todd fled, choking.

The happy conversation and spilled laughter warmed me as much as the flames, offering a glimpse of what it must feel like to have family. A simple family, yes, but a happy one. Cliff wrapped his arm around Adam's shoulders, the way they must have talked for years.

Adam said something in reply, making them both chuckle. I saw Adam shift Christie in his arms as he scratched her velvety ears, and then I turned to watch Rick and his mischievous smile, teasing Todd about something. Their heads bent together, laughing, and all of us somehow caught up in it all.

I couldn't remember ever feeling this way about family—not even for a moment.

Losing Mom packed a hard punch, but I'd never really known her. Ashley's dagger wound, on the other hand, still stung. And try as I might, I still struggled to forgive my dad for leaving Mom.

For leaving me.

Just about everyone I'd ever known, including my fiancé, had walked out of my life and never looked back.

I closed my eyes and tried to press all of *now* into my memory: the lighthearted voices, the crackle and roar of flames, the snap of twigs and puffs of smoke. A sapphire sky crisscrossed with dark holly branches, and the last gasp of greenish turquoise on the western horizon. Christie gnawing Adam's jacket button. That sweet fall chill wafting up from carpets of fallen leaves, so sharp and cold it hurt my nose.

After a song and a prayer, Becky and Faye went in to help Vanna. I followed awkwardly, not sure of my role at the Carter house.

We carried pies down to a table, already laid out with paper plates and cutlery. And a big crock of hot, spicy apple cider. A smaller one of coffee.

I weighed down the napkins and plates with decorative gourds to keep the cold wind from grabbing them and made a space for the famous tub of Cool Whip. If there's one topping Southerners can't live without, it's Cool Whip. Processed and full of chemicals, yes, but I caught myself licking the plastic lid before tossing it in the trash.

Vanna turned on an outdoor light, and then everyone attacked the table. Reaching for plastic forks. The glint of carving knives. Pouring steaming cider into paper cups. Tim stealing the cup out of Adam's hand. Faye cutting slices of cinnamon-scented pie, bright orange like fall leaves. Pumpkin, perhaps?

I was still hugging my jacket in the cold and remembering my years without family when someone thrust a plate into my hands. "Looks like you got a second chance."

"Sorry?" I accepted the plate and looked up at Adam in surprise.

"It's pecan." His eyes were luminous. "The kind your mom sent you back in Japan."

I remembered it there in its plastic wrapping, symbolizing everything ridiculous I thought Mom's life—and our relationship—represented.

And I was wrong.

Jennifer Rogers Spinola

I gazed at the dark triangle on my plate in surprise then back at Adam.

"Thanks." I dropped my eyes and fumbled with a napkin, remembering how rude I'd been to him, too, during my first days in Staunton. How infuriated he made me, along with everyone else, and the way he dug napkins out of a paper bag to stanch my tears. Instead of hating me, Adam took me fishing.

Gave me a second chance to start over. To discover the Mom I never knew and the pieces of her life I'd missed.

"What's the other one?" I pointed to his orange slice, picking up my plastic utensils with clumsy fingers.

"This? Sweet potato."

"Sweet potato pie?" I nudged it with my fork. "You're serious?"

"Sure. We always make it this time of year. Try it." He held his plate closer. I hovered my fork, remembering purple-skinned *satsuma imo* sweet potatoes back in Japan, roasted and passed piping hot from the vendor's truck as he sang his wares in an eerie, lilting voice.

I shaved off a little piece and tasted cinnamon. Cloves. Something thick and intensely creamy. "I'm surprised." I took another bite. "Not bad."

"Want to trade?"

"How about we share?"

"Even better." He tugged a plastic knife down the middle of both slices, and I plopped a wobbly half on his plate.

Then he touched his plastic fork to mine in a kind of "cheers," and we both dug into our pie. Crunchy with pecans, just as I'd remembered. A perfect salty crust. That ying-yang mix of crunchy and gooey. Mom would have loved it.

I wondered, briefly, what she would have thought of me standing here under the deep blue Virginia sky, eating pie with a teacher's son.

"How's your burn?"

"My what?" My mouth bulged with pie. And Cool Whip, which someone had applied liberally on top.

"The burn on your arm."

At church. Our conversation in the hallway. I pulled my sweater sleeve down across my wrist. "It's fine. It's not a big deal."

Adam took another bite before speaking. "Do you get them a lot?"

"What, burns?" I shrugged. "I don't know. Sometimes. The milk steamers get really hot."

116

I saw him glance down at my finger with the bandage, but the curve of the plate covered it.

"You're one to talk." I nodded at the deep scar across his left hand. "I'm surprised your fingers are still attached. Stitches?"

"That? Yeah. A bad machete swing. But. . ." He scratched his hand through his hair.

"But what?" I prompted, feeling my old irritation crop up. It was always like this with Adam—me prodding it out of him and, usually, getting ticked off at what he said.

"I don't know. It's just different."

"What's different?"

Adam shuffled against the wooden railing. "I just hate to see you covered in bandages. You're not a man, Shiloh."

"And?" My words came out testy. I'd spent nearly twenty-five years living by myself, and no guy was going to tell me I couldn't do my job. I even knew how to tie a tie, thank you very much! For my superstarched Green Tree uniform. "It's okay for you to hack yourself with machetes, but I can't break plates and burn myself with hot appliances?"

Adam soberly sized me up. "Yes."

And nothing else. We ate in silence, and I forced myself to choke back the angry speech that rose—with frightening swiftness—to the tip of my tongue. *Things are just different here, that's all. Where the Civil War still lives and chauvinistic guys blast deer and possums with their stupid twelve gauges!*

"Do you like coffee or cider?"

"This is your birthday." I started for the table, but Adam's hand on my elbow stopped me. He had two plastic cups there, one of each, resting on a railing.

"Coffee. Thanks." I smiled in spite of myself.

Stubborn Adam. If I married somebody from the South, I'd better get used to weird male machismo. And probably deer heads mounted on my wall.

"It was nice of him to hold the door for me," Kyoko had said. *"I might be fat and scary, but I'm still a girl."*

My cup shook just a little, and I wiped coffee off my chin.

Adam winked at me, something I'd never seen him do. "Come on over with the others." He gestured with his head toward the warm circle around the fire. "Don't stand over here all by yourself. You're not alone anymore."

★　★　★

For the rest of the night his words played in my head—as we threw away the plates and carried empty dishes back inside, and as Adam sat on a log near the fire and opened presents: a new sweater from Becky, some business books from Tim, and my meager contribution—a (discount) book on garden design from Barnes & Noble.

Christie frolicked with the wrapping paper, leaving shreds all over the leaves, finally falling asleep in a heap on Todd's dirty jeans. The chill increased to a sharp cold, and most of the crowd headed for the warm, yellow interior.

But several of us lingered, warming our hands by the fire and slowly feeding it logs. Every now and then Tim or Adam would go off into the dark trees with a knife and come back with fresh branches, sending sparks soaring.

"You're not alone anymore."

What did he mean by that? That this band of friends had become my family? Or that he. . .? I scuffed my shoe in the leaves, darting cautious glances at his worn brown leather work coat and then back to the fire, trying to figure him out.

Tim was competing with Todd to see who'd eaten the most pie when Becky suddenly smacked me. "Doggone it, Shah-loh, you didn't give him yer present!"

"Yes I did! The book. Remember?"

"That ain't yer present! At least that ain't what's in the back a the truck."

I turned scarlet-oak red. "It's not a present. I mean, not exactly. I just thought he might want it, but it's not all that."

Becky lifted her chin and harrumphed at me. "I think ya oughtta let him decide that, don't you?"

Adam looked up from the dry pine branch he was snapping against his knee. "What's in the truck?"

"Now don't you go braggin' about yer doggone eight-pointer again, Yankee!" Tim complained. "That's all I heard all day!"

Adam's eyes bugged. "You shot a deer?" He laughed in disbelief, hands frozen on the branch as his head swiveled from me to Tim.

I scowled. "Don't be silly! Tim's lucky I'm even eating the stuff."

"Eatin' it? You scarf it up like there ain't no t'morrow. Tell the truth, woman, er you ain't gettin' no more a my rice an' gravy!" He shook his finger at me. "Say, 'I like it!' "

"All right! All right!" I put my hands up. "You win. I like it."

"A lot!" ordered Tim.

"A lot."

"Enough ta wash my truck every weekend an' clean my rifles."

"Enough to. . ." I looked around for something to throw.

"What's in the truck?" asked Todd, cheeks red from cold.

"It's. . ." I shoved my hands into my pockets, wishing Becky hadn't brought this up. I'd nearly decided not to give it to him after all, especially after his "you're not a man" comments. Hmmph. "Well, you just have to see, I guess. But I don't think you'll want it."

We put out the fire and crunched through pungently sweet fallen leaves to Tim's truck, and there it sat in the truck bed—a curious bulky thing covered with a tarp and tied down with rope. I felt foolish. It had seemed like a good idea at the time, but now I regretted it.

"What is it?" Adam peered in.

Tim jumped up into the bed of the truck and squatted down, picking up the bundle without unwrapping it. He handed it down to Adam, who dropped the heavy thing onto the ground with a thud.

Todd tried to peek under the blanket. "Is it a toilet, Shiloh? Did you give him a toilet?" He laughed. "That'd be a weird birthday present. Then again, the one upstairs don't work so well, so maybe it's a good idea."

Adam looked up at me, and I shrugged. "Go ahead."

He let the rope fall and then peeled off a layer of tarp. Unwrapped the old blanket taped around it. And when the light shone on it, I was afraid to open my eyes.

Chapter 12

It was a birdbath. An old ceramic birdbath I'd found in Mom's storage building and intended to throw away, before Earl convinced me to keep it. He told me it had a nice, wide basin and could be used again, especially if I painted over the ugly stained gray. Which gave me an idea.

I'd seen some beautiful garden art in the books at Barnes & Noble, and Earl helped me paint the whole birdbath a rich cobalt blue. Then we added some antique gold paint and partially sanded it off, gilding the corners and leaving the blue to shine through. Lacquering it to leave a shiny gloss.

A few swipes of the brush in gold paint along the bottom in Japanese-style fish shapes, and voilà. Unique and striking—or so I imagined at the time—and I thought it might look nice filled with water in one of Adam's garden displays. But now I could hardly look at Adam. He built decks, not birdbaths.

"Shiloh?" Adam looked up in astonishment. "You painted this?"

I gave a nervous laugh and shoved my hands into my pockets. "You can tell, right?"

He turned it around in the dim glow of the porch light, running his hands along the base and the bowl.

"Look, you don't have to keep it. It was Mom's, and Earl and I just gave it a new paint job. I know right where I can put it if you don't have room."

"Who's Earl?" He abruptly glanced up.

"My neighbor. The one we tried to set up with Faye."

"Oh. Him." He ran his hand along the gilded lip of the basin. "You painted this?" he asked again, scratching his head in disbelief. "For me?"

"I mean. . .sort of. Yes. It's garden art, or something like that. And you're a landscaper. I guess the birds will like it."

"Shiloh, it's. . ." He squatted there a few minutes and ran his hand over his jaw, eyeing the blue birdbath. Then without warning grabbed my hand, pulling me along toward the house. "Come with me!"

I had no idea what his reaction meant, but I figured it must be. . . uh. . .good.

It took my stunned brain a moment to realize he was *holding my hand*—warm, strong fingers laced between mine—and to catch the rising breath that fluttered in my throat. Adam's hands were hardworking hands. Hands that hauled boulders and heavy bags of gravel and soil. Dug postholes and planted trees. Hoisted heavy posts into the ground and nailed trellises. I felt lightheaded.

"Where are we going?" My breath puffed out in a little cloud as we came around a bright corner of porch light and dim fire glow to the wooden back deck. He pulled me up the steps, and I shivered as he dug around in the shadows by the pine tables.

"Hold this." Adam plopped a chilly pot of scarlet chrysanthemums into my hands, and the heat dissipated from my fingers immediately.

He picked up another matching pot and headed back to the truck, Becky staring after us with a sneaky, open-mouthed smile.

"I've got an idea!" He beamed his flashlight on the birdbath. "Can you help me bring it over here, Tim?"

And they hauled it over to a shadowy spot on the other side of the house, all landscaped with flat stone walkways and juniper shrubs. Faint light from the lanterns in the front cast a pale yellow glow.

"Here." Adam gestured with his work boot. "Right next to this patch of Irish moss." And they dumped it upright in a swirl of white gravel, tamping it down around the base.

"Todd, can you fill one of those buckets out back with water?"

Todd sprinted off. Adam clicked open a pocketknife and sliced off some deep red chrysanthemum blooms right under the flower head, making a pile on the gravel. Todd returned with the bucket, grunting and sloshing, and Adam helped him pour the water into the birdbath. It glinted there like black satin ribbons shot through with gold from the flashlight beam.

"What are you going to do?" I asked, shivering. Pulling my jacket collar as tight as it would go and wishing I'd brought my scarf.

"Watch." Adam set a concrete brick in the very center and set the pot of whole flowers on top, making it appear to float on the water. Then he sprinkled the cut blooms right-side up in the water like little crimson suns. They drifted there lazily, bobbing around the rim in a gorgeous contrast of deep red and blue. Almost Asian, like colors on a bright lacquer vase.

"Wow," said Tim, scratching his head. "I reckon that looks perty nice if I do say so myself. Ya done good, Yankee!"

Adam crossed his arms with satisfaction. "It looks fantastic! I can use it as one of my trademark gardening displays for my website. Or even better—my flyers! Come take a look."

We tramped inside, cheeks and hands red from cold, to Adam's cramped bedroom upstairs, which groaned with stacks of files earmarked with yellow stickers. Bags of advertising flyers and posters. A tiny desk crowded with Bible, pencils, and markers, and rolls and rolls of blueprints in various states of unroll and completeness. Paper sketches taped up all over the walls.

The rest comprised an odd array of gardening tools, bags of gravel samples, color swatches, and leather work gloves.

I felt sorry for him. He barely had room to pull out the desk chair and offer it to me then unfold a chair for Becky. Who promptly scooted it over to Adam's ancient desktop computer and checked her e-mail.

"Hey, check yers real quick," she giggled, pulling me around to the screen. "I jest sent ya something."

"Now?"

"Yeah. It's real funny."

While Adam dug in the closet for his buried flyers, I tapped in my password and dragged the mouse down my inbox list. Clicked on Becky's message, which blared red flashing hearts. Something about love advice and Adam's name. . .? I gasped and clicked out of it, hissing something at Becky under my breath.

She doubled over with laughter. "Read it!" she whispered.

"Read it yourself!" I started to close my inbox in a huff and then froze right next to the name in bold black and white: *Ashley Sweetwater*. I clicked on it.

And then the room seemed to still. I leaned back in my chair with a gasp, knocking a book off the shelf.

"What's a matter?" Becky crowded around. "What, yer half sister send ya somethin'?"

"Well, I'll be. She wasn't kiddin'." Tim stroked his chin, poking his head around Adam's.

"Nope. It's a real law firm." I clicked through the website again and shook my head. "They're legit."

"I can't believe it, Shah-loh! She ain't really gonna. . ." Becky's voice trailed off. "Why, I thought she was jest full a talk!"

"Maybe she is, but if she's really hired somebody from this firm, then I'm in big trouble." I scanned through her brief e-mail, which told me to expect a letter from J. Prufrock.

"That guy from the T. S. Eliot poem? No way. She made this up!" I laughed out loud, scrolling through the list of attorneys on the site.

"Who?" Becky peered up at me. "Don't he drive fer Shell?"

There it stood, in block letters: JAMES REUBEN PRUFROCK III, ATTORNEY AT LAW. I skimmed his bio then rested my forehead on my hand. Closed my eyes and mentally pounded the keyboard. "What am I supposed to do now? Hire somebody, too? You know I can't afford a lawyer."

Shoot, I couldn't afford the frozen chicken on sale at Wal-Mart last week. I bought eggs instead and ate them scrambled over rice.

"Shucks, Shah-loh, yer always in trouble," Tim teased, noogie-ing my hair and trying to make me smile. "Ain't nothin' new."

"Don't do anything." Adam reached over me and clicked through the site. "Wait until they contact you. You're not obligated to do anything at this point. If you do, it'll just make a bigger mess."

I made a face at Tim, trying vainly to smooth my hair. "A bigger mess hardly sounds possible."

"You shore she ain't pullin' yer leg?" Tim ran his hand through his brown mullet as I clicked out of the site and closed my e-mail.

"No, but how can I be sure? I can't trust Ashley for two seconds." I played listlessly with the mouse, remembering Adam's "you're not alone anymore" speech. I sure felt like it sometimes. Especially now, when the last person in my family had deserted me. "Mom's house isn't worth much, but she's right. Fifty thousand is still a sizeable chunk. Which is why I need it to sell."

Because the IRS is going to carve a huge chunk out of my front porch if I don't.

I turned my chair away from the computer. "So where are your flyers, Adam? Let me look at something positive for a change."

"Ha. Then you don't want to see these. They're pretty bad." He dug a pile out of a box and plopped it in my lap. "See what you think."

CARTER LANDSCAPING, they read in a basic (ugly) font. Cheap-quality paper. A faded ink foldout part with information about the kinds of landscaping and light construction jobs Adam did. But I had to squint to make out the dark, fuzzy pictures, several sizes too small. The whole thing needed a dose of good old Virginia fall color.

"I think I'll go back to that lawyer site," I teased.

"I know." He rubbed his forehead. "Not that great, huh?"

"How old are they?"

"Old enough. I'd like to update them this year, but I don't have much experience with all that."

"That birdbath thing'd make a nice pitcher," said Tim, picking his teeth with a toothpick he found somewhere. "All them colors. Whadja think, honey bun?"

"Real nice," said Becky. "With them red flowers. Looks kinda Asian."

Before I could comment, Adam stuck a business card in my hand. ADAM J. CARTER, LANDSCAPER.

I turned the flyer over again. "What's your budget for these?"

"Dirt cheap," he said with a wry smile.

"Can you be more specific?"

He pointed to some numbers in a ledger. "Basically paper and printing. I do all the layout on my computer."

"I could help you with design if you want," I said hesitantly. "I did take some photography and design classes in college. Just about every reporter does. I mean, I'm not great, but. . ."

"You could do that?" Adam took a step back, blinking in surprise. "You're serious?"

"Me? Sure." I leaned forward. "I mean, you wouldn't mind if I tried? I can't guarantee anything, but I've got some ideas." My heart pounded suddenly, thinking of something—anything—I could do that wouldn't fall flat on its face here in Staunton, Virginia.

Adam leaned against the bookshelf, eyes bright with excitement. "I'd pay you, of course."

"Fine. And I'll pay you for painting my kitchen."

He smiled briefly and arranged some papers on the desk. "Well, if you designed these for me, I could print out some new ones to include my new services. And take them to some new businesses that will probably need work soon."

I looked around his room at the hanging plans and rolls of blueprints. The Bible half covered by receipts and colored pencils. I tapped a pen thoughtfully to my chin.

"You need a new name," I blurted. "Something catchy."

"What do you have in mind?" Adam scratched his head, one wary eyebrow raised.

"Eden. Eden Landscaping."

Tim nodded, and Becky hugged herself in excitement. "That's

perfect, Adam! The Bah-ble an' the garden an' all that! An' you bein' named Adam. Ain't that funny?"

Adam reddened. "Yeah. I get that from time to time. Not exactly my idea of funny."

"But that's just it!" I looked up from the flyers. "That's your tagline. People will remember you. It's corny, but it sticks." I grabbed a pencil and doodled on some scrap paper hanging off his desk. "Look. If you made a logo like this, like the tree in the garden"—I drew some roots sticking out—"or a leaf, or—"

"A fig leaf," snickered Tim, and we all roared. Even Adam.

"A normal leaf," I retorted. "Whatever. Make that your logo, maybe add in your initials like this and put it on everything you print, and people will start to remember you."

"Look at Miss Artiste!" Becky cooed, leaning over my shoulder.

"Really? You think so?" I felt shy suddenly, nearly losing my courage. But this might help Adam, so I kept sketching an *A*. "I minored in art, but I don't think I'm that great. What's your middle name, Adam?"

Adam pretended not to hear. I slowly lowered my pencil. "You do have a middle name, right?"

"It starts with *J*."

We all exchanged glances, and Becky shook her head. "Good luck gettin' it outta him," she grinned. "Y'all and yer weird middle names! Mine's Louise if anybody's askin'!"

"You're really not going to tell?" Adam with a goofy middle name. It struck me as funny, the way he came off as so sober and proper about everything.

"If you tell yours first."

"Forget it." I sketched in a *C*. "You'll just be middle nameless then."

"Boy, do I wish," Adam muttered under his breath, stacking up some boxes to make more room for Tim.

"Mercy, Shah-loh! I didn't know ya could draw like that! Yer real good!" Becky crowed. "I can't hardly do a stick man; although once I drew a donkey fer a Christmas program at church. Folks thought it was a cotton-pickin' monkey!" Her eyes lit suddenly. "Hey, you could put a verse on yer stuff, Adam!"

"I actually had one here. Look." He turned over the flyer. "In small print down at the bottom."

"I see it. But it's not connected to anything," I said. "If you choose a nature verse—like one from the Psalms—then it would all fit together."

Adam's gaze pierced mine with that excited glow I saw from time to time. " 'The earth is the Lord's,' " he quoted. " 'And everything in it.' "

"That's it! You need a catchy theme to stick in people's minds, with lots of colors and pictures. Ad stickers on your truck. Go on the radio. Do some free work for publicity." I turned his card over. "And you should call yourself a 'landscape designer.' It sounds more professional."

"Sheewwweeee!" said Becky, standing up and slapping me with a high five. "I think our little Shah-loh done hit another home run!"

And the way she said it, looking from me to Adam with that sneaky grin, I didn't think she meant just the flyers.

"Then your business will have soul," I said, ignoring Becky as color crept up my cheeks. "Unlike my house."

"Your house?" Adam looked confused.

"Lowell told her it's too empty," said Becky. "That it don't got no soul an' that's why folks ain't buyin' it. I offered her nice posters 'n' artwork, but I doubt she'll take me up on my offer." She snickered.

"And she ain't takin' Brownie!" glared Tim. "We done been through that a'ready. So don't even ask!"

Adam lifted an eyebrow. "Is Brownie that. . .you know, that. . .?"

"Yessir! An' he ain't goin' nowhere."

"Well." Adam put his hands on his hips. "That does present a problem."

His large, rough knuckles were close enough for me to touch, and I forced my eyes elsewhere. Mentally screamed at myself to *stop looking at Adam* and get my mind where it belonged—on staging Mom's house and leaving Staunton.

"But they're wrong, Shiloh," said Adam, voice piercing my thoughts—which, at the moment, included throttling Becky for her sneaky grins. "Your house isn't empty. It's full of you. Your new life. Your mom's life."

"But I'm not supposed to show me. It's supposed to be a blank slate. A canvas. A skeleton."

"Impossible." Adam crossed his arms. "A house reflects the heart. That's what it's made to do—to shelter and protect." He gazed down at me in a way that made my pulse beat faster, despite my best intentions.

"Just let your house reflect your new heart. It's. . .well, beautiful."

Oh boy. I shaded my tree some more, hands shaking so that I had to erase one edge.

A little spark leaped up into my mind, glowing, just like the golden spots of color that had danced over the fire. Only this one didn't fizzle. It burned like an ember under my thoughts all the rest of the evening until Adam walked us out to Tim's truck to say good-bye.

Overhead the moon had risen, sharp and cold, over the smoky black land as Tim and Becky slapped hands one last time with Todd on the other side of the truck. Christie, blessedly, hung limp with sleep in Becky's arms, while Gordon panted and made sticky swirls on the truck window with his wet nose.

Adam opened the truck door and pushed back the front seat for me then offered me his hand to jump into the back.

I stood there looking at his hand in the moonlight then slowly grasped it. Squeezed in behind the seat and tucked in my knees, breath curling softly in the chilly air.

Adam hadn't let go of my hand.

Then instead of releasing me as I expected, he pulled me toward him ever so slightly. "Shiloh," he said in a strange, tender tone of voice that I'd never heard before. I loved the way he said my name—rolling it over his tongue like a song. "Thank you. For everything."

His face came so close to mine that it startled me, and a tremor quivered through my stomach. I felt the heat in my cheeks as I stammered to say something—anything—that wouldn't sound stupid.

But I didn't need to. Without another word Adam kissed me lightly on the forehead. He released my hand and stepped back to adjust the seat. Then he stood off to the side with his hands in his pockets, jacket collar up against the wind.

"Shah-loh?" Becky hollered, striding around the darkened yard, swiveling her head. "Where'd ya go?"

"I'm here!" I leaned over Tim's hunting stuff and banged on the window, cheeks flaming.

Tim threw his hands up in the air in mock exasperation and waved good-bye to Adam then let in a frigid blast of air as he threw open the truck door.

Tim and Becky laughed as we pulled away, bantering back and forth and playing with sleepy Christie, and I joined in. But I don't remember a word of what we said. I sat in the darkness, face hot in the cold cab. Touched the tips of my fingers to my forehead. *Adam just kissed me.*

Sure, he could have kissed a sister that way, or his mom—but it was still a kiss. A sign of affection and even—dare I say it?—possession.

I wondered there in the darkness, with Tim's gun rack behind me and headlights dazzling my eyes, how it would feel to be known as Adam's. To have his strength and protection all around me like the sturdy walls of a house, sheltering me against the cold and loneliness of life. To spend my days in peace, knowing that I was no longer alone.

Just as he'd said before drawing me into the warmth and glow of the party.

The spark that had twinkled in my mind suddenly blazed up, bright and burning. *Light. Laughter. Life.* Just like Adam's fall-blooming garden, spilling out color no matter how short the days.

I stared out at the darkened fields, telephone poles flashing by as my thoughts gathered momentum. Counted off things on my fingers. Then reached out and whapped the back of Becky's seat so abruptly that she yelped.

"What in the name a Pete?" she exclaimed, lurching around to scowl at me.

"That's it!" I cried. "Adam figured it out! I know what I'm going to do with Mom's house!"

Chapter 13

Cold wind whipped my hair as I carried the giant photo prints out to the car, looking them over in the bright parking lot. I wished the November sun would warm the chilly asphalt and even chillier car, but no such luck.

My roses in the flower bed had long since faded, withered like the brown and yellow leaves that still clung to barren trees, but I had preserved vivid fall. Here. On glossy printouts of Kodak paper with matching black frames: Mom's spiraled Kobe blooms all rimmed with ice. A lone tree on a hillside. Leaves beaded with raindrops, all in bright colors that popped against the white matting.

All these photos would form a gallery on the cream-colored kitchen and living-room walls. My house fairly sang with simple touches here and there: a bouquet of dry hydrangea blooms, their once-blue petals turned to paper-thin sepia. Bare forsythia branches in a vase. Bible verses. The Bible open to 1 John. Fragrant walnuts in a bowl. Golden pumpkins. Fall leaves.

Everything fresh and joyful, just like my new heart.

The house didn't need more expensive stuff. It needed my *soul*. It mirrored me, Shiloh P. Jacobs, the butterfly-to-be—the no longer empty, who came to life, day after day, like a green tendril waking from winter sleep.

Looking around at her new world and finding a gift here, a surprise there. A touch of God's hand in the smallest of things. Things that might otherwise be overlooked in my former rush for beauty, polish, and poise.

For the first time I didn't care a bit what Lowell thought.

My house would sell soon. I felt it.

Which meant I needed to figure out what on earth to do about Adam Carter. And soon.

"Thanks again, Pastor," I said, shaking Matt Davis's hand as I left the Sunday school room. Behind me a couple of guys still argued over whether soft point or hollow point bullets worked better for deer hunting, and a woman named Tammy wrangled over who had doughnut duty next week.

Donut duty. Another reason for my fervent interest in the class.

"No problem, Shiloh." Pastor Davis beamed, patting my elbow. "We're glad you're here."

The class had finished early, so I slipped down the hall toward the still-cold sanctuary to wait for Tim and Becky and Faye. And try as I might to deny it, a certain Virginia landscaper.

I clutched my Bible under one arm, thinking of the blue-violet asters Adam brought to The Green Tree as a centerpiece for my kitchen table. Something warm had crept into his eyes when he looked at me, and I found myself tongue-tied when we spoke, blood rushing to my face. Me, a fearless reporter who'd interviewed the Japanese prime minister without batting an eyelash.

Despite all my inner scoldings to the contrary, my hands still trembled when Adam and I bent together over his computer screen to design the layout of his flyers, our fingers barely touching on the mouse.

We walked through the cold grass and shrubs of his late-autumn gardens in early morning, the grass painted with frost and a silver, low-hanging mist sifting down through the trees. I stood next to him with unexpected closeness, squatting to take photos of his work and feeling flushed as I stood up. Stilling as he brushed a single eyelash off my cheek, his eyes just inches from mine.

We did all the work together: going over the final draft, picking up the printing with jittery hands, distributing them all over town, designing new business cards.

And wonder of wonders: it *worked*. For once I'd done something right, something that didn't fall apart into burning pieces splattered across the ground.

Adam had to hire two more employees to deal with the unexpected increase in clients, more than he'd ever had in the fall. Not to mention two orders for cobalt-blue birdbaths—complete with scarlet-red mums, just like the one in the picture.

In return for my help, Adam gave me a Greek-style fish tile in colorful mosaic, carefully chiseled out of an old garden wall he'd torn down at some sprawling estate. Baskets of wrinkly, citron-scented osage oranges and red bittersweet berries. Which now adorned my newly be-souled house.

He even went so far as to pick me up from The Green Tree on our way to Thanksgiving dinner. A big, noisy family shindig at Becky's parents' house over in Stuarts Draft—out in the farthest reaches of the county—and I inhaled the musty smell of his truck, like mulch and burlap and a whisper of cologne. We laughed together over glorious orange sweet potato casserole topped with melting marshmallows, piling our plates full of green beans, turkey with cornbread stuffing, and quivery Jell-O salad. His eyes tender as the golden yeast rolls he passed me, our fingers barely brushing on the basket.

Whoever this Adam J. Carter was, I found him invading my thoughts and carefully laid plans a little too often for my comfort. And with the worst timing possible—right as I scheduled house showings and turned mug handles in the same direction and polished a stove someone else would soon own.

How could I even consider him? Especially so soon after my debacle with Carlos?

For years I eschewed marriage, telling myself I'd never be like Mom and Dad, arguing hours into the night and slamming doors in icy good-byes. Not me. Not alive and vulnerable, afraid to weep. Even Carlos had remained more or less at a painful distance, which served me well when he cut the ropes with one swift, magnificent, coldhearted swipe.

But Adam? I laced my fingers together tightly, wondering if maybe he could be different, could be. . .

"Sugar?" Faye had stroked a strand of hair behind my ear the night before as I sat at my kitchen table, hands clumped with biscuit dough. My eyes fixed on the fish tile and its red, blue, and yellow mosaic squares. "That's real pretty. Who gave it to ya?"

"That?" My voice had come out sort of squeaky, and I tried to shrug. Plopped the blob of dough down on the flour-covered table. "Oh. Just Adam. Sort of as a thank-you for. . .um. . .work stuff."

Faye didn't reply. She just leveled her eyes at me behind her glasses and moved the biscuit pan out of the way. Handed me the rolling pin. "Adam's a real nice guy," she finally said, clearing her throat. "He's got a good heart, Shiloh. I wonder if ya. . ."

I scraped some dough off my fingers with the spoon and looked up, my pulse beating faster.

"Ya ever. . .well. . .think of him as more than jest a friend?"

"Adam?" My sticky fingers shook, and I picked up the rolling pin and gently flattened the dough. Like so many of my reservations, smooshed thin and pliable. "I don't know. I guess I thought he's. . . all right." My shoulders shrugged again, and I curved the rolling pin around a circular edge. "He's not that good-looking, Faye. I mean he's not ugly or anything, but he's not. . .you know." My face flamed. "Okay, maybe I've thought of him that way. A little. Yes."

I couldn't look at Faye. Couldn't raise my head. I just kept rhythmically rolling the dough.

Her voice came so soft I almost didn't hear: "Have ya told him?"

"What? Of course not."

"Well, maybe ya should." Faye tipped my chin up with one flour-covered finger. "Or at least let him know ya feel the same way."

"Why? I'm leaving anyway. It won't do any good."

"I think ya oughtta let him decide that." Her words hung in the air. "He's old enough to recognize love, Shiloh. And so are you. Trust God and tell him the truth."

That night I burned the biscuits. But they were the sweetest ones I'd ever eaten, crisp and brown on the bottom, drizzled with strawberry jam. I thought of the words *love* and *Adam Carter,* and a small voice inside me murmured a hesitant *yes*.

I stopped briefly by the church bathroom in the chilly Sunday school wing to fix my hair, wondering how to put into words what I needed to say to Adam. Maybe after church, as we stood outside in the bright wintry sun, the vast sapphire sky cold and magnificent. The last days of fall swirling around us like dried leaves on the wind.

Maybe I'd ask him what he meant by that kiss. Or maybe I'd just say it: "You're all wrong for me, but I like you anyway."

No. That sounded horrible. I smoothed the clip in my hair and straightened my sweater, amazed that for once words eluded me. Me, a journalist, whose life and craft wove words—and suddenly my tongue could only stammer.

But I would find those words and exchange them as a gift, like that little fish tile and pot of asters he placed so eagerly in my open hands.

I pushed open the bathroom door and stepped into the hall, checking my watch. Voices echoed against the corridor walls as classes let out, strains of music just beginning to filter over from the sanctuary.

And then I saw it—a figure that looked like Adam's as I brushed past an empty Sunday school room.

"Well, it's good to see you again, Adam," said a female voice, wafting faintly through the doorway.

A *young* female voice. I scrunched to a stop on the carpet—and put myself in reverse.

"I'm so glad." She giggled. "That's great. I've been thinking about you so much lately, and. . ."

I knew I shouldn't have peeked. I knew it. Something inside me, over the sudden pounding of my heart, shouted at me to mind my own business. To stop eavesdropping and "skedaddle," as Becky always said, as fast as I could toward the sanctuary.

But my feet didn't obey. I caught my breath, peeking around the open door at a carroty-blond woman about my height standing with startling proximity to Adam Carter, her back partially toward me. But visible enough for me to see blushed cheeks and delicate pearl earrings. Down-turned eyes as she clutched her Bible to her heart. Adam's head bent toward her.

The surprising tenderness of the sight took me aback. What on earth was Adam doing in an empty Sunday school room talking to a girl? A girl who, from all outward appearances, he knew. . .um. . . quite well?

He opened his mouth to speak, and I caught my breath and leaned forward.

"I know you and I have gone through a lot together," he said, voice low over the empty folding chairs. "And we've always known. . ."

We've always known *what?* My mouth turned to sand.

Adam shifted slightly, and I caught a glimpse of her face: not particularly pretty, especially in that ugly patterned dress framed by a horrible square pilgrim collar—but focused on Adam's gaze. I saw her reach out, as if in slow motion, to put a hand on his arm.

"We were meant to get married," Adam said in such low tones I had to scrunch myself against the wall to hear. "From the beginning. You and I."

My wool dress coat fell off my elbow and onto the floor. Right there in a pile. I jerked back and tried to breathe, unable even to swallow, as I caught snatches of their hushed voices—*"us"* and *"together"*—right there in Covenant Baptist Church's Sunday school room, in Adam's husky tenor voice with a touch of Southern drawl.

There must be some mistake. I snatched up my coat and leaned back against the wall, heart pounding. Trying to draw some other conclusion than the sinister one that formed in my brain, but coming up empty. The Bible quivered in my hands.

"I know," I heard her say back, although I didn't dare peek again. "You're one in a million, Adam. I've always thought of you that way, you know."

The floor trembled and the ground shook. I backed away, trying to regain my balance, and nearly knocked into a woman hurrying by with two kids. I managed to lurch into another corridor, barely seeing the people that jabbered and laughed, scattered in little clumps outside the rooms.

"Shiloh? How's your work going?" somebody called as I pulled on my coat and whipped my scarf violently around my neck.

I stuck my hands in my coat pockets and walked faster, dodging deacons and robed choir members and children waving crayoned pictures of Jonah in the belly of the whale. Where, as I flung myself toward the nearest door, seemed like a pretty good place to be.

I stalked out of the church and into the parking lot, stuffing my fingers into my gloves with shaking fingers. Striding faster and faster toward my car, breath coming loud and furious. I jerked open the door and threw my stuff inside then jammed my keys into the ignition and shifted into REVERSE.

"You're one in a million."

I pressed my Prada heel to the accelerator, not looking back.

Chapter 14

won't cry. I won't cry. I drove as fast as I could away from the parking lot, bursting out of town and down side streets toward. . .well, anywhere that wasn't Covenant Baptist Church. In three hours I'd clock in at The Green Stinkin' Tree, and only God knew if I could keep my composure long enough to carry a tray of steaming plates without dropping them all over someone's table.

My gloved hands clenched the steering wheel, knuckles tense and bulging, as my mind reeled over the images of Adam and Red-Blond Chick in an endless, roiling succession.

I couldn't have seen right. I couldn't have. . . . I lifted one hand and pressed it to my cheek, still stunned. Did he really say *marriage?*

A red light blinked on the dash, but I barely glanced at it. I clenched my jaw and kept driving, wondering how on earth I'd gotten myself in such a mess. Adam wasn't even my style, for crying out loud! My. . .anything! He wasn't even handsome. Not really.

And now *I* felt like the heel, not even understanding why I cared so much about somebody like Adam Carter in the first place. For crying out loud—I wasn't staying in Staunton anyway!

Stupid birdbath. I turned right at the stoplight, heart boiling, and veered down a lonely country road. A brown rump stared back at me from a slow-moving horse trailer, and I stepped on the gas and passed it. Wishing I could do the same thing with this awful portion of my life—just leave it behind in the dust.

I barreled through the next intersection, pausing at the STOP sign, and flashed past a smooth field lined with fiery red oaks, the color of my bursting pulse. Rolled hay bales scattered across the faded green like just-baked dinner rolls.

And out of nowhere, I felt the car slow. The steering wheel tighten.

What on earth? My jaw dropped, and I jerked off my sunglasses. Fumbling for the console with my free hand, running my finger over the lights and dials. *I've got plenty of gas!*

A burned smell wafted in, mingled with the sharp stench of cow, and white puffs curled from under the hood.

"No, no, no!" I moaned, banging the steering wheel. "Not the car!

Jennifer Rogers Spinola

Not now! Please, God! I haven't even fixed the headlight yet!"

I pulled over in the gravel and threw the car into PARK. Then I climbed out and squatted awkwardly by the car in my dress to pop the hood. I pulled off my gloves and jerked the hood open, and smoke poured out. Something dripped, stinking like charred rubber.

I thought of Adam in that horrible Sunday school room. Ashley. The IRS. The hefty fee I'd have to pay to have my car towed then repaired—if it could be repaired—by some quack mechanic who'd take one look at my high heels and sunglasses and charge me double.

I buried my face in my hands and bawled.

★ ★ ★

I was still sponging my face and trying to think of who to call when, over the hill on a gray ribbon of country road, I spotted a squad car.

Oh no. Please not. . .

The car slowed, and a familiar buzz cut poked out the window. Shane put up his sunglasses. "Well, well, well. If it ain't Shiloh Jacobs."

I wiped frantically at my mascara then stuffed the tissues in my purse and zipped it shut.

"What ya tryin' ta do? Send smoke signals over to Charlottesville?"

Shane pulled in behind me, and as much as I hated to admit it, I felt my shoulders sink in relief when he parked. He walked over to my car and checked the console then stuck the hood prop under the hood and leaned under to see what was dripping. Smoke billowed out.

"Looks like ya got a oil leak. Yer car's overheated."

"How much is that going to set me back?" I kept my chin high and my gaze detached. I felt awkward, though, since Shane had sent me red roses—a towering, expensive bouquet—to The Green Tree. And called me, too, after getting my phone number from his cronies at the Department of Motor Vehicles.

Shane grinned and dug a toothpick out of his pocket. He stuck it in his teeth and leaned against my car, dropping his sunglasses back down over his eyes. Presumably so he could check me out, as he did most women, without showing his pupils.

"It'll cost ya upward of a thousand bucks. Maybe two." He showed a broad smile at the look on my face. "How 'bout I take ya home? I'll have a lunch break here in a bit."

"I can't go home. I work after this." I swallowed hard, trying to keep my emotions down.

"Ain't a problem. I'll take ya there."

I glanced at my Honda and back at Shane. "No thanks. I'll just call somebody to come pick me up."

Church. I sank my head in my hand. *Everybody's at church with their cell phones off. Shoot.* And no way under the sun would I dial Adam Carter or anybody who'd ever called him "friend." I dumped my cell phone back in the seat and stuck my hands on my hips. "Fine," I sighed.

Shane seemed to enjoy my frustration more than anything. He smiled and crossed his arms, not moving from my car. "Jest one little thing."

"What?"

"Ya gotta go out with me. Jest one time."

"Forget it. I'll call a taxi."

"A taxi?" Shane guffawed. "Go ahead. It'll cost ya another thousand this far out, if ya can find one open on Sunday mornin'."

A brisk, sunny wind blew my hair, and I hugged myself, shivering. Something dripped under the hood, and my hair reeked of smoke.

"Come on. I'll take ya to lunch."

"And then the restaurant?"

"Of course. I'll even call somebody ta come get yer car." He punched some numbers on his shiny new smartphone.

I reluctantly followed him, taking my purse and Bible from the front seat. "It's not a date," I reminded him, grumbling as he held the door open for me with a too-gallant sweep of his arm.

"Oh yes it is." He winked at me.

"Whatever." I rolled my eyes and slid in.

★ ★ ★

"This is a bar," I snapped as Shane opened the door wider for the woman behind me, who sported a low-cut tank top. How in the world she could bare so much skin in the dead of November I'll never know. But Shane didn't seem to mind.

"Yep. Club 21. It's a sweet little joint." He put his hand on my back and walked me toward a table. I walked faster so he wouldn't have to touch me.

I could hardly breathe in the dark, smoky, musty interior, gleaming with neon beer advertisements. "You come here all the time?" I arched an eyebrow, raising my voice over the pulse of rock music as I scooted out my chair and reluctantly peeled off my coat and scarf. I draped them over the chair back next to me and rubbed a spot on the table disdainfully with a paper napkin.

"Yep. Every weekend. More'n that after grouse huntin'."

"What?" The bass blared, and I twisted my head to hear.

"Grouse huntin'."

"What's a grouse?"

"Huh?" We both leaned forward and knocked heads.

I rubbed mine irritably. "Never mind." *Probably some kind of rodent.*

Shane caressed my hand, which rested on the table. Then laced his fingers through mine as if he knew me a little too well. He didn't. I snatched my hand away and mentally paged through my list of phone numbers for someone who could possibly pick me up. Stella? I dug out my cell phone and dialed her, turning away from the table. Dialed again. Then a third time as Shane scooted his chair closer. Sickly sweet aftershave invading my nostrils.

"Drink, Shiloh?"

"Water," I said purposefully, glancing around at the beer bottles sprouting from nearby tables.

Oh, Lord. . .what have I done?

"So ya still gettin' them calls from the septic service?" Shane put his face close to mine with a leering grin.

"Yes. Almost every single day." I stopped short at the sight of his teeth, startlingly white in the dull overhead light. "Why, is it you?"

"Me? Naw. Ha-ha." He chuckled and pulled his chair closer. "Becky told me 'bout it. They's prob'ly jest tryin' ta hit on ya. Not that I'm s'prised, you bein' such a looker an' all. Lands, look at them eyes!"

"Looks have nothing to do with it." I untangled my hand a second time. "It's simple disrespect to a woman to keep calling when I've asked eleven times for them to remove my number from their phone list."

"Oh, I respect women." Shane grinned again. "A lot."

The waitress came, and Shane followed her with his eyes until he noticed me staring.

"So, Shiloh," said Shane, leaning closer. "What's this I hear about you an' Adam Carter?"

"Adam?" I stiffened, fingers tightening on my water glass. "Nothing whatsoever."

"Aw. Come on. I hear through the grapevine that ya'll might have a li'l somethin' goin' on. Not officially, of course, but—"

"He's a friend," I snapped, bristling. "Or he *was*. And. . ." I pulled my sweater tighter, feeling bile pour back into my stomach. "That's all you need to know."

"Some water under the bridge between you two, eh? Well, maybe it's a good thing yer not tangled up with him the way I thought 'cause I hear Eliza Harrison's back in town."

"As if I care." I took a sip of my water and stared over Shane's head at a flickering TV tuned to a NASCAR prerace interview. "Whoever she is."

"They were real close, ya know. Grew up together. She ain't real good-lookin'—kinda like him—but an all-right gal, I reckon. Seemed like they was gonna get married awhile back, an' now that she's back, I bet they're gonna—"

I pulled out my cell phone and scrolled through my numbers again in irritation, pretending not to pay attention to anything Shane said.

"Ah." Shane snickered. "I see. Well, good thing, 'cause he ain't good for ya. No sirree." He swigged his water and scooted closer. "Adam's a nice guy an' all, Shiloh. Don't get me wrong. But he's kinda stiff. If ya know what I mean."

"What?" I glanced up in irritation, remembering—with a pang— Adam standing on my front porch after nightfall and declining to come inside. The scent of dewy grass and moist earth filling my lungs.

Shane snorted. "Some weird religion a his, I reckon. His brother's all right, though, jest ain't gonna be able to do much now without his legs." He moved the toothpick to the other side of his mouth.

Something angry stirred in my chest as I listened to Shane ramble on about people I knew as if they valued no more than pocket lint.

Shane dug in his back pocket and tossed his (fat) wallet on the table. "Adam works hard, but he couldn't give ya a dime. You deserve more'n that." He dropped a heavy, cologne-laden arm over mine. "Ain't you tryin' to sell that house an' pay stuff off?"

I scooted away and pulled my arm free, metal chair legs scraping on the sticky floor. Before I could answer Shane's question, he pushed his wallet toward me with the bottom of his glass. "G'won. Open it."

"Your wallet?" I jerked my head up incredulously. "You must be joking."

"Here." Shane opened it and let the bills splay in glorious shades of green. "The mark of a real man, Shiloh. He always has enough to take care of the woman he loves. Yessirree."

I closed his wallet and shoved it back, struggling to keep my voice calm. "I'm just fine."

But instead of arguing, he dropped his head and found my gaze. "You clip coupons, Shiloh. I done saw ya in the Food Lion. An' yer scared to death a how much that car's gonna cost ya. Why don't ya just let somebody he'p ya fer a change?"

"I'm just fine, Shane!" I said louder, grabbing my purse and pushing my chair away from the table. My hands shook on the chair back. Afraid of Shane's roving eyes, but even more afraid of how my mouth went dry when I glanced at that wallet. *For shame, Shiloh!*

And yet I was hungry. Cold. Bleary-eyed from too many back-to-back shifts and skipped meals, and getting ready to head right back to work. I wanted to crumple right there under the table and wake up next century, when everything had been paid off or repossessed or whatever needed to be done.

"Aw, simmer down," said Shane, chuckling as he put his wallet away. "I'm jest kiddin'. C'mon. I'll leave ya alone. Honest Injun." He put his palms up, reminding me of Adam's ridiculous "Scout's honor" nonsense, and scooted his chair a few inches back. "Sit down. Let's have lunch."

If I wasn't so hungry, I would have walked out the door anyway, but instead I plopped back down and grabbed the menu.

Chapter 15

So you got your car back, Ro-chan?"

"Yeah. A few days ago." I tucked my old Bluetooth tighter in my ear and listened to her voice crackle over the bad international connection as I steered the car around a fence-lined bend toward home. A shower of dry burnt-orange and brown leaves rained up from the asphalt. "I'm driving it now. Thank goodness for that."

"How much did it cost?"

"Two thousand." I sighed, flicking the wipers to scoot away stray leaf bits in the darkening gray-blue glower of evening. "Plus another seventy to replace that broken headlight."

"Two thousand?" Kyoko yelped. "That's more than you make in what, six months?"

"Very funny." I reached over with one gloved hand to turn up the heat. "Although you're not that far off."

"How did you manage to pay two thousand bucks up front? Or did they let you break it up in payments?"

"Well. . .neither."

"What's that supposed to mean?"

I sighed again, hating that I had to answer. "Shane paid for it." My lips quivered in humiliation. Especially after practically EVERYBODY in the state of Virginia had gossiped about my dumb nondate with Shane.

"Who? That good-lookin' cop Stella told me about?"

Argh. *Stella!* "Yes, him." I scowled. "And he's not that good-looking."

I flexed my fingers on the steering wheel, troubled. He'd sent me roses two more times since I got my car back, calling and asking me out, and all I'd done was blow him off. Why? Why couldn't I just tell him to take his roving eyes somewhere else and leave me alone? I never had trouble saying that to guys before.

My eyes fell on a small, white rectangle that had fallen out of my purse and onto the passenger's seat: Adam's business card. The one we designed. The one with the new leaf logo, courtesy of yours truly, announcing the new Bible verse and "landscape designer" bit.

"Well, what's wrong with him, Ro? Stella said he's a decent guy."

"Who?"

"Shane! Who else?"

"Oh. Right." I jerked my eyes off the business card and back on the road then reached over and covered Adam's business card with a fold of my scarf. "Stella thinks everybody's decent. She tried to set me up with the water-meter reader, who's got a criminal record! Divorced twice and three kids, all by the age of twenty-three."

"Wow. That's impressive, actually. He certainly keeps himself busy."

"Well, I'm not going after anybody like that. Forget it. Shane just paid for my car without asking, and none of my arguing did any good. So what am I supposed to do? It's not like I have two thousand dollars in my pocket to pay him back. I told him I'd reimburse him a little each month."

I felt the car accelerate as I came down a small hill, murky lights from country houses twinkling across the cold gloom. "I'm not Esau, Kyoko. Shane doesn't tempt me."

"Wait, Esau. . . Isn't he the lead guitar player in that British band?"

"Huh? No. Esau from the Bible. I read about him in the book of Genesis." I glanced down at my gas gauge, its insolent red needle pointing to EMPTY. Did I really put in that many miles between work and home?

"So what about Esau?"

"He traded his birthright for a bowl of stew."

"That sounds like you." Kyoko snickered. "If anything would lead you into temptation, it'd be food."

"Very funny. Stella's marble cake might do the trick though. I've been trying to convince her for weeks to sell desserts to Jerry's restaurant. Have you tasted her caramel chocolate chip cookies?"

"No, but I'm sure you'll tell me about them."

"Oh, Kyoko," I sighed. "Stella's an incredible cook. If only she'd leave me alone about Shane."

I dug in my purse with my free hand to see how much money I had for gas—and counted out ten one-dollar bills. No, wait. Eleven. Somebody actually gave me a one-dollar tip tonight, the cheapskate. And after I had the kitchen make him a special vegan plate. *See what I put in your sandwich next time, buddy!*

Kyoko remained quiet, and I jiggled the Bluetooth in my ear to hear better. "Hello? You still there?"

"I'm here, Ro. Just thinking."

I felt my stomach lurch. "What?"

"See, here's the thing, Ro-chan—Shane's not asking you to marry him, you know. Why can't you just date him awhile? And take advantage of his. . .uh. . .financial procurements?"

"What?" I threw my head back. "*You* would do something like that?"

"No. But I'm not serving coffee to thirteen-year-olds either."

I know Kyoko didn't mean to hurt me, but it stung. I swallowed and clenched my jaw tighter, wanting to prove I wasn't some desperate waif.

But who was I kidding? In ten minutes I'd arrive at an empty, freezing house in rural Virginia with bad heating and half my furniture chewed up/torn/peed on by a dog that I hid from my real-estate agent. My hair still greasy from fry oil and nothing for dinner but a package of frozen corn. And, yeah, maybe some deer meat buried under there somewhere.

"I didn't mean that the way it sounded," said Kyoko, her voice gentler than before. "I'm just worried about you, Ro. I've put money in your bank account, but I can't fix your problem long-term. Maybe Shane's. . . I don't know. A temporary solution."

"Thanks again for the money, Kyoko. Really. I've already used it to pay for—"

"Quit thanking me. I did it for the tax refund. You being a charity and all," she quipped.

I made a face. "But no to Shane. He's a temporary. . .um. . . temptation. Or his money is. The Bible says we'll always have to fight against temptation from the wrong things in life."

"Temptation? C'mon, Ro-chan. You really believe that?"

"Sure I do. I live it every single day." I wiped at a spot on the windshield, wishing the defroster worked better. "Temptation to knock snooty customers through the wall. Steal somebody else's money. Which, yes, I did lots of times as a kid. And I can't even repeat what I'd like to do to Ashley." And maybe Adam, too. With his little Eliza Harrison and her pilgrim collar. Give me a break!

Ashley's newest letter sat on my kitchen table, unopened. Or indirectly from her, I suppose. The official-looking letterhead read JAMES REUBEN PRUFROCK III, ATTORNEY AT LAW. With a real Chicago address.

"Well, then, do it! Stop being so repressed."

"Right. Maybe I'll just copy a story on the prime minister's wife and send it to Dave."

Even Kyoko's words faltered.

"Nope. I'm done living my own way." I stretched my neck and back, stiff from a too-long day of carrying heavy trays and ferrying orders. "I'm trusting God, Kyoko. You'll see. He'll provide what I need without Shane's dumb money."

I tried to sound confident, but something in my voice wavered, edged with bitterness. And I left it hanging in the air, not bothering to try to convince Kyoko I meant it.

"What about that farmer?"

"Huh? Farmer?" My foot pressed the gas a little too hard, and I eased on the brake.

"I forgot what he does. Something with vegetables. Or. . .no. Plants."

"Vegetables?" I hollered, as Kyoko collapsed into laughs. But for some reason I couldn't laugh back. Couldn't even smile. Thinking of how I'd suddenly cut contact. Skipped church on Sunday. Not returned any of Adam's calls.

"Adam's a landscaper, Kyoko," I finally replied, staring out at a patch of barren trees, which still clung to a few wrinkled mahogany leaves.

"Whatever. How is he? And that kid brother of his?"

"I don't know. Fine, I guess. Don't ask me."

"What do you mean? I thought you two. . ."

"No. I told you we're just friends." My voice rose, hard and sharp. I forced myself to relax, as if it didn't bother me. And why should it? Adam was just. . .Adam.

I glanced over at Adam's business card, one little corner still visible in the shadowy darkness. "He's got a girlfriend, or whatever she is. Besides, I'm not staying in this town any longer than I have to. Adam and I. . ." I paused, feeling my pulse quicken slightly at the combination of those three words, bound together in unexpected unity. "We've both got separate lives and separate. . .callings."

"Callings. Wow. You sound so spiritual."

"Stop making fun of me, Kyoko," I said, voice flat. "I'm too tired for this."

"I actually wasn't. I just wondered if. . ." The characteristic ping-pong sound of Kyoko's Japanese doorbell chimed in the background. "Sorry, Ro. Gotta go. Pizza's here."

"At eight in the morning?" My eyes fluttered to the clock on the dash.

"Sure! Why not? Breakfast!"

"Which kind?" I asked, trying to brighten my waning spirits with memories of the Tokyo I loved. "Curry or tuna?"

"Neither. I found this cool place that sells *natto* pizza. Can you believe it?"

Fermented soybeans? On pizza? I gagged. "Do they have those long strings of slime hanging between them?"

"Like week-old dishes in my sink? Uh, yeah. Actually." I heard her speaking Japanese in the background, laughing with the pizza guy. Words I still saw in my sleep, their complicated kanji strokes like elaborate works of art, each one a perfect riddle that I somehow knew how to unravel. Now they hovered on my lips just out of reach, like a prayer I didn't have the courage to lift to heaven.

"Kyoko?" I heard her pick up the phone again. "I know you've got to go, but do you think I should maybe. . .call him?"

"Call who? Pizza delivery?"

"No. Adam." I bit my lips together. "I mean, we were friends. Good friends."

Her voice turned sober. "Do you miss him?"

"Me? No way! I just. . . I don't know. Maybe a little. He's a great guy, and we. . ." I shrugged. "I probably should call him, right? Maybe when I get home I'll try and see if he's there."

"Huh? Hold on. I didn't give the pizza guy the right change." Something jingled. "You don't have two hundred yen, do you, Ro?"

"Sorry. You should have asked me that a year ago." I made a sour face. "Bye, Kyoko."

I started to take out my Bluetooth, for once entirely glad that when I ordered pizza, it came from Virginia—not Japan. Then I heard Kyoko call my name again.

"Ro? Don't give up. You'll find him."

"Find who?"

"The right guy. And it'll just. . .fit. Hang in there."

"Sure. Maybe ten years from now. But thanks anyway."

I told her good-bye and dropped my Bluetooth on the seat. I drove silently, staring out at the darkening fields and remembering the bright photo prints on my walls. The beautiful fish tile in its lonely square. The pot of purple asters Adam had given me, wilting brown and limp around the edges. They needed water. Needed care. Needed. . .

Gas station. I jerked my car over into the gravel entrance, glad I'd caught it before it closed—which happened shockingly early out here in the country. A frosty crescent moon peeked from a brooding sky as I pulled up to the pump, and scattered stars twinkled. Reminding me of long walks down sparkling Tokyo streets, a million miles and memories away.

Instead my eyes fell across my rumpled Green Tree shirt and tie, hanging half out of my duffel bag. Dirty Mary Janes strewn across the floorboard, a smashed spaghetti noodle stuck to the bottom of one.

I grabbed my purse and scooted out, slamming the car door behind me. Just as a patron with a sleek, new Prius came around the corner of the pump and grabbed the windshield washer squeegee.

I reached for the gas cap, not realizing his speed, and whammed right into Carlos Torres Castro, Argentinean ex-fiancé and heartbreaker extraordinaire.

Chapter 16

My knees buckled. The shock of seeing Carlos was one thing—but finding him at a run-down gas station on the side of a country road outside Staunton, Virginia—was another. Context slapped me in the face.

I felt myself sinking toward gravel, my breath squeezed out, when Carlos rushed around the pump and grabbed my shoulders, clumsily hauling me to my feet.

I wobbled there stupidly, not able to form a single word, as my senses came back in a muddled rush. Then I jerked myself away from his grip.

"What on earth are you doing here, Carlos?" I hollered, hands on my hips. My lips trembled as chilly wind whipped my hair from my once-smooth ponytail.

Am I dreaming? I must be dreaming. I just hope this isn't the one where I'm being chased by a herd of black-eyed peas because that one always ends with. . .

I felt my knees sinking again and leaned against the side of my car with both hands, trying to force some sense or breath—whichever came sooner—back into my spinning head. Trying to make the two images of Carlos form into one.

"Oh, thank goodness it's you," he said breezily, leaning against the gas pump as if we'd planned this moment all along. His face achingly beautiful in the harsh shadows of the overhead fluorescent lights: proud cheekbones and strong chin, those black, almond-shaped eyes. His longish curly hair cut shorter, sleeker than I remembered it. "I'm lost. I'd just stopped to get directions."

I had to remember, for a split second, that I was supposed to despise Carlos. So handsome he was in his fitted winter coat, preppy dark knit scarf around his neck.

"What do you mean thank goodness it's me?" I spat, taking a step back. "You better not be looking for me, you. . ."

"*Amor*. I missed you. Come on." He opened his arms and had the audacity to smile. "Please. Let's talk."

"Talk?" I shouted, so loud a woman with a blond 'do the size of

Jennifer Rogers Spinola

Texas gawked out the window of her broken-down car. I forced myself to lower my voice. "Are you here to see *me?*"

"I'd hoped so. Yes." A hint of Spanish accent hung on Carlos's perfect lips.

I stared, jaw wobbling open. "Doesn't anybody from Japan bother to call me before showing up?" I shouted, forgetting my brief attempt at propriety. "You're all nuts, you know that? Haven't you ever heard of a phone?"

Carlos blinked in confusion. "Who else came from Japan, *mi amor?* I had no idea."

Bunch of stalkers. "How did you find my address?" I spoke through clenched teeth, fumbling for the gas cap. Angrily jerking the nozzle off the pump and turning my back on Carlos—in part so I wouldn't have to look at his gorgeous face. "Kyoko wouldn't give it to you, that's for sure. And I'll knock her lights out if she did."

"Mrs. Inoue at that shop you like. She said you sent it in a letter."

"You went to Mrs. Inoue's shop?" Angry color rose to my cheeks, and my eyes burned as I jammed the nozzle into the Honda. "*My* favorite shop? Where I used to buy green onions and jasmine tea?"

"Shiloh," Carlos whispered my name. In that tone of voice that used to thrill me. But I felt dead, motionless.

"I'm sorry." He reached out to take my arm, but I shook it away. "Leaving you for Mia showed my. . .well, absolute stupidity. I didn't deserve you, and I certainly don't blame you for hating me."

I whirled around, brushing my hair back again as the wind tossed it in my eyes. "Excuse me?"

"I broke up with Mia, *princesa*. And I miss you. I—I *love* you, Shiloh. I've always loved you." He pushed himself off the pump, taking a step toward me. His perfectly fitting, trendy-classy jeans and nice sneakers contrasted with the gas-splattered, pockmarked asphalt littered with cigarette butts and blackened bubble gum.

"Don't 'princesa' me!" I ordered, voice loud and tight. "Love? What are you talking about?"

"Shiloh, please. Just listen. I messed up. And I'm asking your forgiveness. You Christians know about forgiveness, right?"

"Oh, did Mrs. Inoue tell you about that, too?"

My voice came out harsh, but tears rose as Carlos's sultry accent played in my ear, reminding me of old walks through the crowds at Shibuya, arm in arm. Spiky-haired Japanese teenagers milling past us,

148

the girls giggling at Carlos and calling out "Haro!" in broken, butchered English. Cherry blossoms sprinkling pale pink all over the sidewalks.

In the middle of all this, as if seeing my ex-fiancé just a couple of miles from my house wasn't enough, Carlos's cell phone trilled in his pocket, and he pulled it out and turned away slightly, finger to his ear.

I felt dizzy again, gripping the back of my car to keep standing up straight.

"Yes," I heard him say. "That's right. Make sure you turn it in by Friday, or it'll be. . .right. Good." He lifted a finger at me, shrugging in apology. "But you have to. . .no. No. Let me explain again."

I shook my head in disbelief as he rattled on in an ugly combination of Spanish and Japanese, the latter of which wasn't Carlos's strong point. I considered grabbing the phone to correct all his mangled verbs.

Without warning, he laughed a good-bye and flipped the cell phone closed. "Sorry about that. My work. They're always bothering me, especially with this new intern. She's hopeless. She has a thing for me though, for some reason, which. . .whatever. Forget it."

I didn't reply, mind still reeling over the fact that (1) Carlos was here, and (2) he'd interrupted an apology to answer some intern back in Tokyo.

"Listen. I had to talk to you, princesa," he said, suddenly standing so close that I had to twist my neck to look up at him. A whiff of his sweet-smelling cologne slipped past my nostrils on the cold wind, over the stench of gasoline and an overfilled trash can. "I count the minutes without you. My heart is empty." He dropped his voice to a whisper. "*Te necesito.*"

The same old Carlos, golden-tongued, that whisked my heart away two years ago. I don't know if he practiced these lines in front of a mirror or something, but they worked.

I stood motionless, like one of those sparkling ice statues at the snow festival in northern Japan. People carved them with chain saws, crystalline shards flying against white drifts.

"Did you hear me, mi princesa? I love you. Will you think about us? Can we at least. . .talk? Please? Let me come home with you. I was just searching for the right road. See? It makes no sense to me. Look." He pulled a printout map from his pocket, looking so pathetically helpless with his raised palms that for a fraction of a second my heart went out to him.

A flicker of dead hope twinkled against my will.

Jennifer Rogers Spinola

"Please, amor." Carlos reached out and stroked his fingers through my hair, curling the strands behind my ear. Surveying my post-Green Tree knee boots, coat, tights, and wool winter dress with approval. "Do it for me. You look beautiful. Did I tell you that? Just look at you." He kissed his fingertips and burst them open, like a blooming flower.

I stared at him, not saying a word, and then heard a sickening *thunk*. I squeezed the gas nozzle, and it thunked again.

"Oh no. I didn't." I spun around, dripping gas, to find the tank filled to the brim. At a total of more than sixty dollars. I let out a long groan. "I just. . .hold on a minute, Carlos. I've got to. . ."

Eleven bucks. That summed up all my cash. I left him there and dug in the car for my checkbook, paging desperately through the stubs to check my balance. Exactly ninety-two dollars in my checking account. Which meant I'd have to use money from somewhere else to keep my light bill from going off this week before they drafted it out of my account, slapping me with a nasty overdraft charge. Did this gas station even accept checks? I stood on tiptoe in my boots, muttering to myself as I searched for a No Checks sign.

"You okay, princesa?" Carlos reached out and brushed my cheek. "Need something?"

"No thanks."

"Can I follow you home? Please?"

"Forget it."

I turned on my heel, halfway to the lighted gas station building, thinking of how I'd become a prude practically overnight after Adam's old "what-would-the-neighbors-think" speech.

Eliza Harrison's down-turned face popped into my mind. The fiend.

Or no. Maybe Adam was the fiend.

"You know what? Fine," I said, shoving my hands in my pockets. "Whatever. But just to talk." I glared at Carlos. "Don't get any ideas."

And I turned my back on him, pushing through the glass doors, which greeted my arrival with a tinkling bell, a rack of Slim Jim sausages, a mounted deer head, and a shelf full of NASCAR lottery tickets.

★　★　★

Shiloh P. Jacobs. What on earth are you doing?

The thought pulsed through me with almost palpable power, so

150

strong I jerked my head up from my checkbook. The pen quivered in my fingers as I signed my name with a flourish. I deserved it; I'd argued a good five minutes with the frizzy-permed woman behind the counter before I thought to mention Earl Sprouse. She granted me approval on the spot. "He fixed my toilet once in the dead a winter an' didn't charge me nothin'," she said. "We'll take yer check."

So this is how people did business in Staunton, Virginia. Or somewhere between Staunton, Churchville, and Nowhere, because a couple of rickety barns and dilapidated farmhouses served as the only sign of civilization along this desolate road. One silo sported a chunk of an old Holiday Inn hotel sign to patch a hole.

"Hey, yer that gal who went out with Shane the cop, ain't ya?"

My fingers stopped on the checkbook. "Excuse me?"

"That Pendergrass boy. I know him."

"It wasn't a date," I said through my teeth. "It was blackmail."

I slapped the cap on my pen and waited for my receipt, staring angrily over cartons of glassed-in cigarettes and—with a shock of surprise—right at the woman's faded "What Would Jesus Do?" sweatshirt.

I closed my checkbook then leaned forward to rest my elbows on the greasy counter to massage the bridge of my nose, where a headache started to pulse.

What would *Jesus do, Shiloh? What would He want* you *to do?*

I sighed and rubbed my eyes, probably smearing my mascara. The cheap stuff from Rite Aid, by the way. No more fancy cosmetics-counter Dior for me. Although to tell the truth, I really couldn't tell much difference between the two. Which said a lot about the stuff I used to plunk my money down for so quickly back in Japan.

"You okay, hon?"

"Huh?" I stopped rubbing my forehead.

"Y'all right?" She paused her gum chewing and leaned toward me, earrings jingling.

I straightened up and stuffed my pen and checkbook back in my purse. "Sure."

"Sorry. Ya jest looked a little upset."

I took my receipt. "I'll be fine. I just wish life were simpler."

"Don't we all." She patted my hand with be-ringed fingers, her short, ridged nails painted an ugly puke-rose color. "Jest lean upon the Savior, doll. He'll he'p ya make it through."

Jennifer Rogers Spinola

I grasped her hand tightly as if reaching out for hope, for one sliver of solid sanity in my frazzled brain. And felt my throat choke up as she shook it firmly in hers, patting it with her other veiny one.

The bell on the door tinkled, and I abruptly grabbed my purse and keys and marched toward the brightly lit gas pumps, pulling on my gloves as I went. A rusty Chevy truck pulled in front of Carlos's car, blasting something by the Dixie Chicks.

Pray. I need to pray. I managed to think something along the lines of, *Please, Jesus, don't let me mess up my life more than it already is,* and then took a deep breath and plunged through the double doors.

Chapter 17

The dull parking lot lights glowed down on my car in coppery ribbons as I squeezed into a parking space. Carlos switched on a turn signal behind me and eased to a stop by a potted tree.

I turned off the ignition and looked out over the shadowy parking lot in the quiet, remembering when I'd first met Adam standing over by that concrete divider, baseball cap pulled low in the summer sun. Me in my black funeral dress and Adam covered with mulch.

I hadn't known Jesus then. Hadn't known Mom, or even cared to.

Now the puffs of green on the tree Adam mulched had long since shriveled and vanished, leaving bare twigs. A few remnants of tattered leaves lingered, as if clinging to crumbly memories.

A tap on the window startled me, and I quickly fumbled with my keys and grabbed my purse.

Carlos hugged himself in the cold, raising an eyebrow in a look that—from the time I'd spent with him—meant annoyance. "What is this, princesa?" he asked, gesturing to the Best Western lobby, which glowed golden in the murky evening. "I thought. . . I mean, I thought you said you. . ."

I didn't hear the rest of what he said. "Is that a *Yomiuri Shimbun*?" I stared at the newspaper under his arm with longing, my eyes following the news columns of Japanese kanji characters. Newsprint and words and Japanese phrases that used to roll in my head like music.

"This?" He shook it. "You want it? I was going to throw it away. I can't read those kanji anyway."

"Please." I reached out greedily, and Carlos dropped it in my hands. The annoyed look increasing to a line between his brows. "Whatever. But can't we go to your place?"

"I changed my mind," I said, avoiding his eyes as I ran my gloved fingers over the thick folds of newsprint. "I think you'll be more comfortable here. They've got. . .uh. . .coffeemakers in the room, and I only have instant. And they don't have a dog."

"But I could have found this place myself." He put two hands on either side of my cheeks in what I guessed was supposed to be a tender gesture. "It's you I want to see. To talk to. I miss you."

"Then talk." I broke away from his gaze and strode toward the lobby. "And let's get you checked in while you say whatever it is you came to say."

The first person I saw when I pushed open the doors, Carlos trailing behind me in a sort of feet-dragging defiance, was none other than Shane Pendergrass. Leaning against the counter in full uniform, toothpick in his teeth, laughing and flirting with one of the front-desk clerks.

He spun around when I marched up to the counter, glancing from me to Carlos and back again. Eyebrows lifting until they almost touched his buzz cut. Even the young blond desk clerk—whose name tag read JUDY—turned to stare at me.

"Hi, Shane," I finally said, lifting a hand in a friendly wave to cut the silence. "How's it going?"

He shifted his weight and pushed himself taller, crossing his arms over his chest. "I'm good, Shiloh. You?" The corner of his mouth still turned up in a smug grin of either contempt or curiosity at my obvious discomfort, or both. "Haven't seen ya since our last date." He leaned forward, emphasizing the last word.

"Date?" Carlos and I said at the same time, spinning around.

"It wasn't a date." My face blazed. "I told you that! It was. . . You made me. . . You. . ."

Judy coughed, obviously holding back laughter, and disappeared into the back.

"What's that, Shiloh? Can't hear ya." Shane froze me with a merciless smile then looked over me at Carlos. "Hey, man, is she always like this?"

"Her? Pretty much," Carlos muttered, shaking his head.

"Well, good luck." Shane raised an eyebrow. "She's a tough one."

"Tell me about it."

My cheeks pulsed livid red, and I turned my back on Shane. "Excuse me. I'll just. . . How many nights again, Carlos?" I crossed my arms, shaking with fury.

I felt like an idiot standing there while Carlos hemmed and hawed, obviously uncomfortable. "Come on, princesa. I don't want to stay here. Let me go with you." His voice hushed, touched with that unique Spanish slur that smacked of sultry Argentina, of tangos and kisses. He pulled off his gloves and draped his arm over my shoulder. "Please." He stroked a warm hand through my hair. "It's you I came to see."

I tried to pull away, aware of whispers between Shane and Judy, and also aware that Judy's stares had shifted from me to Carlos. Who, yes, smelled heavenly, like cologne, coffee, and fresh wind. I took a step back to make sure his scent didn't cloud my faculties.

"No, Carlos. I'm sorry." I stood my ground. "You can stay here, or there's a Hampton Inn on the other side of town, and—"

"Hampton Inn's already booked fer the night," Judy interjected a little too helpfully, flushing slightly as she smoothed her curling-iron-puffed bangs. Gaze still fixed on Carlos. "Ain't nothin' at the Holiday Inn neither."

"Look. . .all right. All right." Carlos put his palms up. "One night. Okay?" He nodded at Judy. "No smoking, please. I can't stand smoke."

"You're leaving tomorrow?" I whispered, keeping my back to Shane and pulling Carlos out of Judy's nosy earshot.

"No. I. . .just want us to talk, and then we can decide where I stay. All right? It's important to me, amor." He gestured to his heart. "Just do this for me, please? It'll be like old times. You'll see."

"Do what for you?"

Judy put her hand out for Carlos's credit card, her fingers trembling slightly as she sneaked glances at him, color rising in her cheeks. Carlos sighed and fished it from his black leather wallet, his eyes piercing me with a pained, suffering gaze.

Shane's shoulders shook as he turned away with poorly concealed laughter.

As soon as Carlos accepted his key, he put his hand on my shoulder and steered me gently toward the elevator. But for once in my life, even under Carlos's spell, I didn't move.

"Let's go, *linda*. Aren't you coming?" His dark brows flicked irritation. "What's wrong? I thought. . ."

"It's late, Carlos. I've been on the clock since eight this morning. I'm tired. I need to go home." I rubbed my eyes, aware that Shane and Judy were still watching us, heads tipped toward each other at the front desk. "We can talk tomorrow."

"Amor." Carlos actually sounded angry, flinging down his arms. "I came all this way. I need to talk now."

I sighed, rolling my eyes toward the ceiling. "Fine." I crossed my arms, remembering—against my will—Adam standing there stubbornly on my front porch after nightfall, reminding me that Churchville was a small, small town. "Then we'll do it in the lobby."

"In the lobby?" Carlos's eyes flashed dark-brown fire. "Why are you going all prudish on me? This isn't the 1950s. You didn't used to be so. . .stiff." He waved his hands.

I flinched, aware that he'd slapped me with the exact same adjective Shane used to describe Adam.

"Yeah, well, things are different. I'm different. Don't you get it?" I raised my voice just a touch, irritated. "I'll wait for you over there at that table." I started to stride past him, my precious *Yomiuri Shimbun* cradled under my arm.

Carlos's lip curled in mild derision. "Amor. You are not so different as you think you are." His words came staccato and soft, piercing through every single layer of hurt, anger, and defensiveness I'd wrapped around my heart. So powerful that I paused in midstep, purse still swinging.

I turned back, one glance at his familiar face taking me back months. Years. To a time when nothing mattered except my own life, my own dreams. No need for religion or rules or clipping coupons.

"But for you, I'll do this." Carlos didn't smile. He put his hand on my shoulder and accompanied me over to the sofas gathered around a too-shiny coffee table, which the hotel staff had topped with ugly pink silk flowers and an advertisement for Doug's Cable TV and Satellite Dishes.

★　★　★

My watch showed nearly three in the morning when I finally pulled out of the Best Western parking lot, Carlos's muscular physique cutting an angular shape against the golden glow of the lobby window.

I switched between noisy music and talk-radio stations to keep myself awake then finally cut the sound altogether and drove in silence. Trying to push Carlos's tears out of my mind. His apologies. His promises to love me, if only I would let him.

And my promise to meet him again tomorrow when I got off work.

My eyes shifted over to the folded *Yomiuri Shimbun* on my

passenger's seat, its black-and-white lines barely visible in the passing streetlights. Each kanji character crying out mystery. Adventure. Life beyond deer hunting and NASCAR and processed Cheez Whiz in a spray can.

I thought of my stained Green Tree apron and felt exhaustion tugging at my already strained back.

I stopped at a red light, mind wandering to the Greek-style fish tile Adam had given me. Reminding me of multiplied miracles and a miraculous catch. Jesus' promise not to give a snake if I asked for a fish.

Could Carlos really have come all the way here just for me?

My brow wrinkled, uneasy, and I leaned the side of my head against my hand, my elbow resting on the window ledge. Recalling fragments from Sunday school and sermons: *"Do not be unequally yoked with unbelievers. . . . Trust in the Lord with all your heart, and lean not unto your own understanding. . . . Wait for the Lord, and He will deliver you. . . ."*

Wait. . .wait. . .wait. . .

I was sick of waiting.

Why in the world did Jesus make things so hard? If you read some of the gospel tracts out there, you'd think utopia dawned the moment you said yes—and everything after that swirled in butterflies and roses.

Ha! I got nettles and wasps.

The light turned green. I whispered another prayer, feeling as empty as the darkened Staunton streets around me.

Chapter 18

As it turned out, that gas station check was the last I'd write in a long, long time. When I dug in my mailbox back at home, eyes bleary from too-little sleep and mind racing into frantic dreams, there it lay: the warning letter from the IRS, giving me ten days before slapping a lien on my bank account. Since I had no stocks, no investments, and none of the thousands they wanted in back taxes.

Well, help yourselves, I thought, sucking back tears. *There might be enough in there to buy a cup of coffee.*

I thought of calling Tim the accountant and begging him for help, but he and Becky'd helped me already—both financially and with advice. I was sick of whining, sick of people's pity.

As I tossed and turned and tried unsuccessfully to sleep, I peeked out my bedroom curtains to find snow falling—an unexpected snow that surprised all the local weather commentators. Flakes sifting down over the brown and rust-colored land, gathering in hollows on tree trunks and in the curves of fallen leaves like my silent thoughts. Covering my front lawn with a thin coverlet of white, grass blades poking through.

But nothing felt calm in my heart as I prepared myself for tomorrow's talk with Carlos. I could see my car turning into the Best Western parking lot, the tall lights dimmed by flickering dots of snow shadows, and my heart stuck in my throat.

★ ★ ★

"Where have you been, amor?" Carlos demanded, standing up from the sofa, tossing the magazine back on the coffee table. "You're late. You said you'd be here at seven. I. . . . Hold on." His cell phone jingled in his pocket, and he turned his back to me, waving his arms as he spoke in Spanish. Work stuff, I figured.

I cradled my injured hand in my other gloved one, still too tender to try to stuff it even into a mitten, and eased into the sofa. Grateful to rest my tired toes, which really hurt. Especially after I dropped a heavy serving bowl on my left foot.

Carlos sat down next to me and leaned forward, laughing. Running his hands through his thick black hair as I caught snatches of words: *Beautiful. Boca Juniors. Three seconds.*

Wait a second. "Boca Juniors?" I turned to him incredulously. "Are you talking about soccer?"

Carlos glanced up then hastily ended the conversation. His smile faded as he stuck his cell phone back in his pocket. "Sorry about that. He's kind of a work buddy, and I have to. . .but that makes no difference. Where were you? I've waited all evening." His dark eyes glinted, wounded and moody.

"Emergency room," I replied in humiliation, stuffing my bandaged finger in my pocket. "Didn't you get the message?"

"No! Did you leave one?" His hand fluttered to his cell phone pocket. "I'm so sorry. I didn't see it."

"No big deal. Just three stitches." A drinking glass that cracked as I loaded it into the too-full Green Tree sink. Apparently I didn't do the whole "carry-heavy-trays-without-maiming-yourself" thing very well.

"Stitches?" He ran a hand through my hair. "You should be more careful, amor."

We sat there in strained silence until he finally caressed my arm. "You. . .okay? Are you hurt? Where did you cut yourself?"

"I'm fine. I just. . . I'm fine." I kept my arms crossed.

Carlos ran his hand through my hair. "Listen. Let's get something to eat. You look hungry."

"I'm not hungry. I just want to know why you're suddenly here. You haven't called me for months."

"I know. I'm sorry. I just thought. . . Why should we have all this distance between us? You're beautiful, Shiloh. Special. I need you."

I kept my gaze shifted away, praying for words. Something exciting but menacing tingling in my heart, like a flash of lightning over the mountains. "I don't know if I'm ready for. . .well, what we had before, Carlos."

"Ready? Why not? It's me, Shiloh. I even brought your ring back." His eyes glowed as he reached into his pants pocket. Not jeans this time, but good-quality khakis from Banana Republic that fit him flawlessly. Ironed. Nobody I knew around here wore khakis like that, even to church.

When Carlos opened his fingers, my engagement diamond glittered in his palm like ice. "I've even forgiven you for all the stupid taxes I had to pay on it. Although I really wish you hadn't put the full price on the envelope. But. . .that's all in the past now."

Carlos reached out and grasped my left hand, and before I could think what to do, slid it on my ring finger. It sparkled there in breathtaking defiance.

"Leave it on," he murmured, that lush voice of his whispering gently. "I bought it for you."

I stared at it there in the yellowish lamplight, snow falling outside the darkened window. A thousand words stuck, frozen, on my tongue.

"You're still the same inside, princesa," he whispered. "There's nothing to be afraid of. We'll pick up where we left off. I love you." His voice trailed, husky. And he leaned forward to kiss me. Not on the forehead, but on the lips.

I shook myself out of my stupor long enough to pull away, scooting abruptly across the sofa and opening a wide space between us.

"I'm not ready yet, Carlos," I said in warning tones, slipping the ring off with shaking fingers and handing it back to him. "You dumped me for some lousy housemate and haven't spoken to me for months. I don't know you anymore. What do you even want out of life?"

My heart beat out a plaintive cry as I remembered Adam asking me that same question, sitting on my deck steps in silver summery dawn. Everything that had previously mattered to me falling on its knees in the light of this strange and wonderful Jesus, whose light seared each empty corner of my heart.

Carlos stared down at the ring in his hand then finally put it back in his pocket, rubbing his forehead in irritation. "What do I want out of life? I don't know. That's kind of a heavy question for me right now." He shrugged and checked his cell phone, a gesture that annoyed me. "I think. . .happiness, right? There's nothing greater in life than to be happy. And I could be happy with you."

I could be happy with you. The words didn't bring the stunning force I expected. I could be *happy. With you.*

I remembered Kyoko's question hanging there in my Japanese cell phone in block text letters and the cursor blinking. Waiting for my response. DOES HE LOVE YOU?

I cleared my throat. "So, happiness?"

"Sure."

Adam told me he wanted to honor God. The thought sprang into my mind without any warning, and I guiltily shoved it down.

"Let me stay with you." Carlos's eyes pleaded. "Just for a week or so—how's that? And then we can talk about our future. I'll do anything. I'll clean your place. I'll fix it up. I'll have dinner waiting when you come home. Whatever you need."

I hesitated, ever so slightly, and Carlos saw it. He reached out and took my hand in his, lightly kissing my fingers. "Please, princesa."

My free hand bumped, with shocking accuracy, into a blue hardbound Gideon Bible on the end table, right next to the lamp. I ran my fingers along the pages, feeling them flutter like flakes, a soft rustle of silver.

Maybe I'm wrong about this whole Jesus thing, I thought, staring out at the snow. *Maybe my Jimmy Choos are telling the truth about who I really am.*

I pressed my palm to the Bible cover, wishing I could draw warmth from its words. This confusion of Carlos twisted around my neck like a too-tight scarf, cutting off the circulation I thought I had.

Is it so wrong, God, to want happiness? To want wholeness? Life? Purpose?

To want out of this mess of bank liens and back taxes and house seizures?

Ice beaded on the windows, diamond-like, in sparkling patches like my engagement ring. Each tiny point sharp and dazzling. Frozen like my thoughts, my breath.

A thousand glittering eyes staring into my roiling heart.

I abruptly excused myself, untangling my hand, and fled for the lobby bathroom. Closing the door behind me. Leaning, trembling, against the cool painted wood.

"Oh, Jesus," I whispered, covering my face and trying to pray. All my former confidence swept away like the sun. "Please show me the way! I am weak. I am tired. I am a lost sheep.

"Worse than that, I am Esau."

I imagined a brown helping of stew, steam curling up its bowl. And I reached for it. With my one unbandaged hand, of course.

I got out my keys and pulled on my coat, marching out to the lobby and straight to the exit. Not trusting myself to go and sit beside Carlos. "I need to think," I said, wrapping my scarf around my neck. "I'll call you tomorrow."

And I plunged out into the bitter night, leaving him standing at the glass door with stiff hands on his hips, watching me go.

★　★　★

My cold feet must have been an omen.

Stella called the next morning to announce another snowstorm and people packing the Food Lion to buy bread and milk. Misty Wilcox had her eye on Shane again, Stella informed me, and if I wanted him, I'd better move fast.

"Which one's the most urgent? Food Lion or Shane?" I stood at the window, watching the snow. Not daring to mouth a word about Carlos.

"Well, duh! Shane of course! He's a good-lookin' man, and Misty's on the prowl. I jest hope he's got enough sense ta stay away from that gal. She ain't nothin' but trouble, Shiloh. You gotta save him!"

"The only thing I'm saving is my skin from collection agencies," I replied, padding through the kitchen in my house slippers to pull out the rusty ironing board. Can of spray starch (per Jerry's picky requirements) and white-collared shirt waiting on the kitchen table. "Shane will have to fend for himself. Besides, I've got a house showing at six. I'm busy."

I was trying to scrub wrinkles out of my stubborn shirtsleeve when the phone trilled again. "Stella? I've got extra bread. How much do you need?"

"Lowell Armstrong here."

"My Realtor. Oh. Sorry. The house'll be ready by six. I promise."

"Did I hear right, Shiloh? You went out with Shane Pendergrass?"

The iron hissed as I set it upright. "Yes, Lowell. And we're getting married this afternoon," I snapped, sick of chasing down this stupid rumor. "Satisfied?"

Lowell didn't speak for a long time, and I ironed in angry silence. "Are you serious?" he finally sputtered. "What about your house? I thought. . ."

"I was kidding, Lowell." My voice stretched taut. "No. I didn't go out with Shane. I'm not interested; never will be. Okay? So I'll call you tonight after the showing. I'm kind of in a hurry here."

"Listen, Shiloh—I know we agreed on six, but the snow's supposed to get worse, and they want to come early. Can you do it? I've got a good feeling about these guys."

"Early?" My eyes flickered to the clock, which pointed to just after eight.

"Oh, just maybe. . .ten? You can do it by ten, right?"

"Ten o'clock in the morning? In this snow?" I yelped. "Are you kidding? I've got to scrape my car, dig out of here, and get ready for work, Lowell! I'll never get the house together in time!"

"I believe in you, Shiloh. This is your moment!"

Right. I slammed the iron down. *Of course you believe in me, busting my tail getting ready for work and cleaning the house while you sit behind your cushy office desk, probably with your feet up on it!*

I ran a hand through my messy hair. Snowbound outside of my own house, with just a few minutes to pick dog hairs off the furniture. "Fine. I'll go to work early. I'm on the clock for eleven thirty anyway." I mashed the wrinkled sleeve with the iron.

"Atta girl. Believe me, nobody wants your house to sell more than I do, Shiloh. Hey, and say hi to Shane for me, will you? His dad and I are buddies. Tell him to come by sometime and let me know if he still wants to sell that—"

I slammed the phone back into the receiver.

★ ★ ★

I pushed through the frosty glass doors at The Green Tree, and there sat Beulah Jackson at a side table, sipping the remnants of a cold-looking cup of coffee.

"Beulah?" I shook snow from my hair and leaned over to hug her. "What are you doing here? Trinity doesn't come in until this evening."

She patted my cheek affectionately. "Oh don't worry. I ain't here to see Trinity. I'm here to see you. And what a cute thing you are, too! Just like one of Santa's elves, all rosy and bright."

"Well, for heaven's sake, please don't say anything about Shane. I didn't go out with him. Not like he thinks I did."

"Who?" Beulah swiped snowflakes off my eyelashes and brushed my shoulders. "No, that ain't why I'm here. But take these." She held out a flowered gift bag. "I made 'em for ya. Can't vouch for how they taste."

"For me?" I peeked inside. The bag bulged with heavenly smelling chocolate chip cookies and a jar of homemade hot cocoa mix. "Beulah, you didn't have to bring me anything!"

Beulah and Stella were a dieting girl's worst nightmare. Good thing Kyoko wasn't here, or she'd bark at me to run around the block.

Beulah patted my arm. "But I wanted to. It's good to see you, Shiloh. I prayed you'd come in early today." She slid out of the booth and pulled on her gray wool winter coat. "C'mon." She held out her arm. "Take a walk with me. I've paid already."

"A walk? Now?"

"Yep. When's the last time you actually slowed down enough to enjoy somethin'?"

"You win. Let's walk."

I held the door for Beulah, and we stepped out onto the wintry sidewalk. Cars slushed through the wet streets, dotted with falling snowflakes. Snow carpeted the leaves of a potted tree, dusting its brown branches like a striped candy stick.

I stuck my hands in my pockets and inhaled deeply: the scent of snow, fresh and clean and cold.

"Snow that covers," Mom had written in her journal. *"Snow that blots out. Snow that promises shouts of victory just beneath the surface. All the roots and shoots and stirrings waiting, joyfully, to erupt at the just proper time. . . . A picture of the gospel: 'Though your sins are like scarlet, they shall be as white as snow.' "*

Beulah put her arm around me, looking up at the old brickwork and church steeples. Pearl-gray clouds scuttling overhead. "Beautiful, ain't it?"

"Yeah." My breath misted, and I thought suddenly of Adam. The way he'd looked at me standing at Tim's truck door, and the way he'd called my new heart "beautiful." His lips briefly brushing my forehead.

I twisted my bandaged finger inside my coat pocket. "Did you really come just to see me?"

"Shore did." She took my arm and walked with me, catching my eyes with her dark ones. "Lord put ya on my mind, an' I wanted ta see how ya were doin'."

"You mean like about the house?"

"No. About your heart. Your faith."

I wrapped an errant scarf end around my shoulder, not sure how to answer. "I'm trying," I replied, not meeting her gaze. "It's. . .well, it's hard sometimes, Beulah. I'm not as strong as I thought."

A gust of wind puffed my bangs back from my face, and I covered my ear with my free hand. Wind, expressive as it might be, sometimes stung.

"God ain't asked ya to be strong. He's asked us to lean on *His* strength and call on His name for help. He says no temptation is too strong to overcome."

"Well, that's just it, Beulah. I. . .just don't know what to do sometimes."

"About?"

I swallowed hard and played with the fringes on my scarf. "Stuff," I mumbled. "Men. One I used to date. Plus a lot of other. . .uh. . . problems."

She stopped there on the sidewalk, and my black Mary Janes scuffed to a halt in the thin layer of snow. "What? I haven't actually done anything yet about any of them. I'm just. . ." I shrugged. "Considering."

Beulah's eyes suddenly brimmed over, and she cupped my cold cheek in her brown hand. " 'Simon, Simon, Satan has asked to sift all of you as wheat. But I have prayed for you, Simon, that your faith may not fail.' " Her voice caught in a sob.

I couldn't move. Couldn't speak. She looked so serious it frightened me. "Who's Simon?" I managed, lips quivering with cold.

"We know him now as the Lord Jesus' disciple Peter."

Beulah's black hair, threaded with a few strands of gray, ruffled as she steadied her voice, still heavy with tears. "It ain't easy bein' a Christian, Shiloh. Jesus knew it. Even Saint Pete failed Him, which is why Jesus prayed for his faith. Because He knows how hard it is sometimes to follow. To hear His voice."

I played with a silver earring, which chilled against my skin. "I'm trying to. And you're right. It's hard."

"Nobody ever said it would be easy." Beulah took my arm again and walked by my side, wiping her face with her free glove. "But you've got God on your side, woman! Do ya trust Him?"

"I guess so."

"No, Shiloh. Do ya *trust* Him? Ya can't guess about this." She turned again to face me. "Trust and faith, in the face of all that's hopeless, is what it's all about! Either ya do or ya don't. If ya don't, then jest walk away now 'cause ya ain't never gonna make it. But I'm here to tell ya that nothin' on the face of this earth satisfies like my Lord Jesus Christ and His plans! They may be nothin' like ya had for yourself, but that don't mean a thing." She patted my arm. "You ever plant seeds, Shiloh?"

"Seeds? Like for plants?"

Plants again. And those rough hands patting soil around a tender green seedling. Why didn't Adam Carter just stay out of my head?

"The Bible talks about seeds. Says Jesus is kinda like the sower. You know—a person who plants crops. But not all the seeds grow up into healthy plants. Some grow where the soil is dry and wither before they take root. Some get choked out by thorns or fall away when the problems get too big. Only a few of 'em make it strong and tall and healthy." She poked me. "So you gotta choose, baby. Who ya gonna be?"

I pursed my lips, which burned in the icy wind. Desperately needing a new coat of lip gloss.

"I want to be the healthy plant. I love Jesus. I really do." My hands tightened in my pocket. "But. . ."

"No buts about it! He *loves* you, Shiloh Jacobs! Don't ya get that?"

"No, I don't." I didn't mean to be so blunt, but that's how I felt. "Everybody talks about love, but nobody seems to know what it means. My mom used to say she loved me when she beat me. Now Carlos says he loves me again, but he. . . I don't know. I give up."

" 'Love is patient,' " Beulah quoted, putting her hand on my shoulder. " 'Love is kind.' Read it. It's in His Word. Jesus loves ya more than ya can possibly imagine. He created ya before the foundation of the earth. Do ya know that? He's the Good Shepherd, who gave up His life for His sheep. For you. While ya still hated Him."

"Then why is life so hard? Why don't things. . .fix themselves? Go easy for a change?" I kicked a blob of snow. "Why don't the wrong guys just stay away and the right one only show up when everything's in place? With some magic fanfare to show me he's the one?"

"You're lookin' for Eden, baby! An' you ain't gonna find it here. No, until ya die you're gonna live in a war zone."

"War? For what? I've already chosen His side. What else is there to fight over?" I stuffed my hands deeper in my pockets.

"Ya think that's it? That once ya said yes and handed over your weapons all the bullets gonna stop flyin'? Lands, people in this state still fightin' over the Civil War, an' that ended more than a hundred years ago! Can ya imagine what's goin' on in the spiritual realm? How much Satan would like to see ya fall? To ruin your witness? Your life? Your faith?"

Tears reddened Beulah's eyes. "That precious faith is what my sweet Trinity needs to see. She's lost. She needs Jesus shining out of you. And nobody would love to smother your light more than the old devil, who the Bible calls a 'thief.' Says he comes to wreck your life."

I brushed some snowflakes out of my bangs and smoothed them to the side. "You really think God wants to use me, Beulah? I've lied. I've cheated. I've. . . Well, why on earth would He use me to reach Trinity? I just went to church for the first time not long ago, and I wasn't very good at it."

"Good at it? Like you gotta practice your pitchin' arm first?" She chuckled.

I laughed, too, but it fizzled quickly like the lacey snowflakes on my coat. "Why would Satan care about ruining my life, Beulah? I'm not important. I'm not a missionary or a preacher. Do you really think he cares about messing up my crummy situation even more?" I scuffed snow off my shoe into the curb. "I mean, isn't that what my life has always been? One mess after another?"

But Beulah leaned her face close to mine, unafraid. " 'Your enemy the devil prowls around like a roaring lion looking for someone to devour. Resist him, standing firm in the faith!' " She poked me. "That's 1 Peter 5:8 and 9. You need to put His words in your soul. Read them! Memorize them! Hold them up like a shield when Satan whispers in your ear!"

She took something out of her pocket and handed it to me. "Here."

I looked down in surprise at the little Gideon New Testament, nearly identical to the one I usually packed in my purse.

"Ya got one, don't ya?"

"Sure I do. I just. . .didn't bring it today." I wiped my nose with a tissue from my pocket.

"I know. God sorta reminded me that ya might need this one." She took my arm.

"He what?"

Beulah shrugged. "I don't know. I'm not important either. But I pray, and I listen. And I hear His voice. Ya see, ya don't have to be a missionary or a preacher to come under attack. Satan hates us because we love the Lord Jesus and can't wait to destroy our lives and faith. But don't fear—just keep your eyes on Jesus and let His powerful words take root in your soul!" She caught my eye. "Don't be fooled, child! We're *always* at war!"

I looked over at her in surprise. "Why did you come today, Beulah?

Jennifer Rogers Spinola

How did you know. . .?" I let my words trail off.

"Forget about me. I'm just the Lord's servant. And I feel that He wants me to tell ya to *wait on Him*. Wait on the Lord, Shiloh, *and He will deliver you!* I promise ya that."

My throat suddenly choked.

"Ain't one of His good promises ever failed, baby. Trust Him! He'll show ya the way. Here. Pray with me." And she took my other hand and prayed for me right there on the corner of the sidewalk while I shivered, sniffling back tears. Feet freezing in those flimsy Mary Janes.

"That young man a believer in Jesus?"

"Of course he is!" I hugged myself in the cold. "You know him from. . ." I smacked my forehead with a gloved fist. "Oh. You meant Carlos. Um. . .no. I don't think so."

"Why, who did ya think I meant?"

"Nobody. At least nobody I could be with."

"Why not, baby? There's always a way."

"Not for us. Everything's all wrong." I stuck my hands in my pockets. "And he doesn't even. . .forget it. It doesn't matter anyway."

"God can change things in a New York minute, Shiloh."

"Exactly. I wish He would and park me right in West Village with a good-paying reporting job. This isn't my kind of town, or my kind of life. Jesus should know that."

"Jesus knew ya before ya drew your first breath." Her words came out soft, like snow that barely grazed my cheek. She put her arm around me. "Well, why are ya considerin' some other fella if he ain't following the Lord?"

"Maybe he will." I looked down uneasily. "Maybe it's God's plan for me to tell him what I've found, and we'll. . . I don't know." I broke off, looking at my watch. "But I've got to clock in, Beulah."

"Okay, sugar. But that ain't exactly the way it's supposed to work. When ya look for a man, honey, he oughtta be saved and walkin' with the Lord Jesus. Not perfect, mind you. But saved."

"Does it count if he's really handsome? And rich?"

Beulah laughed and slapped my back. "You're a funny one, Shiloh Jacobs. Ya ever thought a doin' stand-up comedy?"

"It depends. Would it help pay my bills?"

Beulah harrumphed. "How many bills ya got?"

I hesitated, gazing gloomily up into gray puffs of cloud. "Never mind. I'd better stick with waiting tables."

168

Chapter 19

"No." I drew my chin up to face Carlos, crossing my arms tightly against a gust of freezing wind. "The answer's no."

He drew back, those too-thick lashes blinking in confusion. "What do you mean no, amor? To stay at your house? I thought we decided to talk about this." He put his hands on his hips, irritation flashing across his sun-browned face. The cold breeze carrying a hint of his aftershave, like stumbling upon a long-forgotten memory of our hands entwined, his breath stirring my hair against my cheek.

I quickly turned my head and purposefully inhaled the smell of icy asphalt, trying to clear my lungs. It hurt, pulsing like the still-healing gash on my finger.

"That, too. But I mean *you*. I'm sorry, but I can't be. . .well, anything with you. Ever. We're done."

Bare branches from a nearby tree scraped against the wall by the lobby as we stood outside the double doors, headlights of passing cars reflecting in glossy smears across the glass.

It had taken me awhile to decide, but somewhere over the clatter of dishes and squeak of shoes on the kitchen floor, Beulah's words and verses solidified something in my head. Something that just wouldn't budge, like the scar across Adam's knuckles even after years had passed.

Carlos opened his mouth, but no sound came out. Then he shook his head, eyes burning. "Wait a minute. Let me get this straight. *You're* breaking up with *me?*"

"Technically, no. We're not together. We were just. . .discussing. And I'm saying no." The last words stung, but I got them out. I covered my ears with my hands as the wind blew, wishing I could just as easily block out the aching fierceness of Carlos's voice.

"I come across the entire world for you, and you say no? Before I've even asked you anything?" Carlos's voice rose in a blaze of Latin temper, and I stepped back.

"What are you saying? You tried to give me my ring back. You told me. . ." I couldn't bring my cold lips to form the word *love*.

"I never said I wanted you back."

"Excuse me?" The words hit me with an unexpectedly blunt blow, and I drew in a sharp breath.

"I gave you the ring because I have a big heart. Not because I want some kind of commitment. You're—you're all wrong for me. You and your religion. I like the old Shiloh better." He turned away, facing the snow-dusted, leafless woods and long, lonely train tracks behind the hotel. "At least back then you were fun."

I flinched again, forcing my chin up. "At least back then I thought you loved me." I pressed my lips together to keep them from quivering. "I know better now."

Carlos opened his mouth to retort, but his cell phone rang inside his pocket. I watched in disbelief as he put it to his ear, gesturing me to wait by lifting a finger. "Hold on a second." His voice scratched me like a rough branch—harsh and prickly. "This is important. Just five minutes." And he rambled over somebody's stock balance in great detail, turning away from me. His breath misting up into the bitter night sky.

I stood there for a few minutes, shivering, then stalked off to my car, which glinted under the apricot-colored parking lot lights. I'd just put the keys into the ignition when I heard the low vibrating of my cell phone, indicating old messages from sometime during the day.

I took off my gloves again and pressed the button. And saw, to my surprise, Carlos's number.

"Carlos here. Listen, do you still have that newspaper I gave you? I just remembered something. Would you mind dropping it off during your break? It's important. I just need to. . .uh. . .check something."

I pressed it again, brow wrinkling. "Carlos here again. What's your work address? I'll just get the newspaper from your car myself so I don't bother you."

I flipped my phone closed and tapped it to my chin, feeling something creepy in the pit of my stomach like I did when Ashley called me. Wanting something. But what on earth could Carlos possibly want from me?

The *Yomiuri Shimbun* still lay in the passenger's seat, now stuffed under my duffel bag, Beulah's cookies, and the little Bible she'd given me. I pulled the newspaper out, inhaling the sharp, musty scent of newsprint, and opened it. Wondering why Carlos was making a fuss over a week-old Japanese newspaper that, by his own admission, he could barely read.

I held it up to the dim artificial light, curious, and then switched on the interior light for a closer look at the rows of intricate black kanji characters. Crinkling my way through the pages until a shaft of yellow landed on a square outlined in pen. Noted with little translations in the margin, in Carlos's bumpy ink handwriting: *Boston. Alexandria. Fairfax. New York. Washington, DC.* Topped with the printed words *Northeast Fashion Month* and listing some Japanese designers and locations for shows. A couple of (mostly female) names and initials penciled in by the various cities.

Including mine. With a tiny note: *Maybe too far.* I leaned closer, trying to understand. *But + g.c. = perfect.*

"Northeast Fashion Week?" I said out loud, eyes jumping from the newspaper to Carlos's distant figure, partially illuminated in the glow of the bright windows. "What's the big deal about that? And who's G. C.?"

I started to fold up the newspaper in disgust, its beautiful, kanji-lined pages retreating into an insipid black-and-white rectangle.

The dates. I halted, something ominous twisting at my stomach as a little square of paper fell out of the pages, notes and numbers scribbled in Carlos's block handwriting.

Certainly not. Not Carlos. Not. . .

All at once it hit me.

I grabbed the newspaper and reached for my purse, slamming the car door behind me as I stalked toward the hotel lobby.

Chapter 20

Northeast Fashion Week?" I said, waving the *Yomiuri Shimbun*. "Is this what you tried to hide from me?"

Carlos, who stood outside the glass door in a black leather jacket and navy-and-tan striped scarf, finally ended his conversation, phone bobbing in surprise, and faced me. "What's that supposed to mean, amor?" But something awful darted across his face a second before he smiled.

"Did you decide if I'm too far away from Fairfax or not? Because I'd hate to make you miss the big event on my account—seeing as how you're a model now and all. It's a long drive out here to rural Virginia. You must want *something*." My throat knotted, unable to swallow.

"Give me that." His smile faded like the headlights of a passing truck, taking the sudden flash of brilliance with it. He stretched his hand for the newspaper, but I tucked it under my arm, just out of reach.

"You're a stockbroker. What do you make now, six figures?"

"I don't need to tell you my business." His voice dropped to a growl.

"But that's just it. You're after something that all your money can't buy. You think I didn't figure out why you drove here to find me, apologizing and offering to make me dinner?" I poked him in the chest defiantly. "You thought you could get away with it. That I wouldn't find out."

"You're crazy! Find out what?"

I stood on tiptoe to meet his eyes, surprising even myself. "That you want to use me for a green card. By marriage. So you can go on with your next venture. Start your own clothing line or something." My words hovered there, frosty, in a breath of smoke. "But my house and my heart don't come free, Carlos. I don't take in boarders. Or freeloaders." I forced my voice to hold itself steady, although something underneath wanted to crumble. "Spare me the love speeches. You left your green card notes inside the sports pages." A sob caught in my throat.

He took a step forward, eyes snapping. A cold wind whisked

between us, and the front doors opened and closed. We moved away from the entrance as a bellman rolled a shiny gold cart through, and we faced each other in the shadows.

"Are you accusing me?" Carlos's eyes snapped, his voice raising a touch. "You're calling *me* a freeloader?"

"Did you think you could buy me off so easily by flashing a ring and spouting all this 'I love you' nonsense?"

"Is that what you think? That my words are nonsense?" He jabbed a finger at his heart, breath loud and angry. "I wanted to see you, amor. That's all that ever mattered to me."

His eyes flickered away from me when he said it.

"I don't need your help with anything." His voice rose, cold and proud.

"I'll bet."

Without warning, Carlos caught my eye and dropped his voice to ice. "You're just jealous because I'm doing something better with my life than you are, Shiloh. Look where you live—a small-town dump. Doing what? Waiting tables?" His lip curled up in a sneer, and he shook his head in disgust. "You don't even have your master's yet, do you?"

I opened my mouth in a silent cry, wrapping both arms around my middle to hold in the pain.

"You do what you want with your life." My teeth chattered as I struggled to keep tears from rising. "But I won't help you. But maybe Kristi can, in Boston, whoever she is." I flung the newspaper at him.

"Ah." Carlos threw his arms up, kicking the newspaper aside with his shoe like an old hamburger wrapper. "You're despicable, amor. To think something like that about me."

"Don't call me amor. You never loved me. Whatever you had for me, it wasn't love."

"Love." He spat out the word, gazing out over the darkened landscape. Trees, dark and spindly, spotted with snow. "What is love, Shiloh? Tell me that. I think it means something different for you than it does for me."

"Maybe so." I felt tears well up as wind stung my cheeks, and I put my hands in my pockets to keep back my emotion. "We're done, Carlos. Go. Don't try to call me. Don't. . .anything."

"You're really serious?" Carlos laughed again, a bitter laugh, but it died out. Lost in the sound of wind shivering in the dry shrubs.

Neither of us spoke.

Finally Carlos let out a long sigh, throwing his head up to the cloudy night sky. "Why, Shiloh? Why do you have to be this way? We did have something special, you know. At least back then."

I swallowed the lump in my throat with difficulty, remembering how not long ago I would have fallen into his embrace despite my misgivings, inhaling the painful sweetness of his cologne-tinged sweater: a warm scent of wool and comfort. And let his golden words fall soft in my ears, willing myself to believe them.

But this time I didn't move, arms taut like ropes pulled painfully tight.

"You're not Hachiko," I whispered.

"What?" he cried. Obviously he didn't remember the little statue of a dog in Shibuya, Tokyo, that moved me more than anything else in Japan. Every day Hachiko waited at the station for his master at the time of the evening train. Day after day, year after year. Until the day his master never came home.

And still Hachiko waited at the time of the train. For ten whole years, until they found his stiff, lifeless body on Shibuya streets.

Talk about love. Faithfulness. And I would never find it in Carlos Torres Castro, no matter how his radiant good looks cried out to me.

He sputtered in indignation. "What does an iron dog have to do with this?"

It was bronze, but I didn't correct him. "Good-bye, Carlos."

"Nobody's going to want you, Shiloh! You're washed up."

"Then I'll stay single."

"You're crazy! I've wasted too much time on you."

"Please don't call me or come here again. Ever."

I picked up the battered *Yomiuri Shimbun* from the concrete and marched toward the desolate parking lot, turning my back on an angry flurry of Spanish. I wanted to weep, but no tears came. I had cried them long ago. Strips of snow had hardened like my resolve into little crystalline patches, sparkling under the tall parking-lot lights.

I ducked my head into the wind, my eyes barely seeing the shadows and frozen, snow-scuffed cars scattered across the parking lot as I trudged between the cars.

Everything dark, everything cold, everything terrible.

And then at the last minute as I turned toward my Honda, I lunged and gasped. Barely missing the dark shadow that seemed to appear from nowhere, between an SUV and a station wagon, heading toward the hotel. Inches from me.

"Sorry! I didn't. . . Sorry!" I flung my hands up, almost dropping my purse and newspaper.

He jerked out of the way with a quick apology, which the wind snatched away, and I watched him go, sensing something uncomfortably familiar in that gait, that coat. Wishing the light would shine a little more clearly on his obscured face under its cap. His footprints left hollow marks in the blanket of snow.

I dug for my keys, heart pounding, as he paused a few feet away, turning abruptly back in my direction.

He swiveled his head between me and Carlos, who still stood at the door, laughing, blowing me a spiteful kiss.

A streak of light illuminated his arms full of newly printed flyers, sleek and colorful in a flash of overhead light. And without reading the print, I knew what those business cards tucked under the rubber band said: *Adam J. Carter, landscape designer.*

Chapter 21

Good! Now try that on." I pointed, hands on my hips. "I'm telling you, you'll like it."

Becky regarded the bag skeptically. "Well, I'll try it. But the jury's still out on this'n."

Becky Donaldson made me proud. She looked great these days, a little more polished and pulled together, and every few weeks she ditched something else: the oversized overalls, fuzzy pink ponytail holders that didn't match anything, bulky sweaters and sweatshirts that made her look lumpy.

What she didn't ditch, I hid. Simple.

"We need to make you look more girly," I'd told Becky. "You're a beautiful woman, not the Abominable Snowman!"

To her credit, she'd done the unthinkable. For the first time ever, Becky traded in her scuffed green Nikes for a pair of brown boots from Payless. NICE boots! With *heels!* And when she paired them with jeans—her new boot-cut jeans in trendy dark blue I'd practically forced her to buy—she looked fabulous.

But then my plan backfired. Becky wore them every. . .single . . .day.

"You need to wear skirts. Dresses." I'd taken her to Goodwill, Target, and T.J.Maxx, where we did most of our discount shopping. Even Wal-Mart had a few surprising grabs every now and then.

"But I don't got nothin' to wear no skirt with! An' I git too cold."

"Long boots," I suggested, pointing to mine. Knee length à la Tokyo, topped with tights and a wool skirt. "Longer than your brown ones. They're warm."

She shook her head. "It works on you, Shah-loh, but they ain't my style. I ain't all fancy like that."

So we shopped, and I mulled. And finally had a breakthrough. I convinced her to buy a couple of things and rushed her home. Winter tights were delicate—so as much as I loved Gordon, he had to go. He sat outside the bedroom door mournfully, scratching his stinky collar and baying.

"I ain't never worn a dress in the winter," grumbled Becky,

reluctantly opening the shopping bag. "It's too cold, an' doggone if I'm gonna freeze durin' church on account a some frippy li'l dress!"

"Frippy?"

"Frilly. Whatever." She held up the fabulous dress: a warm brown print that came just to her knees. Tiny pale blue flowers. Long sleeves. Brown satin ribbon around the empire waist.

"Trust me. Put these on."

"Those are tights." She glared at them and at me, like I was asking her to wear a hula skirt. "I wore 'em when I was two."

"Well, they're back in style now. Put them on."

I waited, hands on my hips, while she tore open the package and scrunched one leg in at a time. Nice, thick, ivory tights, soft and patterned. Then she pulled the tags off the dress with her teeth (even though I always scolded her to use scissors) and shoved it over her head. I tied the bow in the back and fluffed out the skirt. "There. Now the shoes."

I always snapped into "bossy" mode when shopping with Becky. If I didn't, she'd wind up in that same gargantuan Virginia Tech sweatshirt with one of Tim's plaid button-ups over the top. The most hideous combination I'd seen yet.

"It ain't so bad, I reckon." Becky raised an eyebrow as she stepped into the shoes. Brown leather Mary Janes with an extra-thick sole.

"Ain't so bad?" I muttered. "You're gorgeous! Look at you!" I pushed her over to the mirror, and she turned around, smoothing the skirt. "The Fashion Nazi strikes again."

"I reckon it's kinda nice." She gave a lopsided grin. "Tim'll like it, won't he? He always says I'm cute in a dress. I jest don't wear 'em much. But mebbe. . ."

"Told you." I pretended to blow on my nails. "What can I say?"

"But what if I get cold?"

"Beauty hurts," I said unsympathetically. "And you need to do your eyebrows again."

"Again?"

"They grow back. Numb them with ice." I surveyed her stock of wraps and sweaters, ignoring her ranting. "Now. Back to the dress. You can use one of those new cardigan sweaters we bought a couple of weeks ago. The light-blue crocheted one that ties in the front." I riffled through her closet and held it up. "See? Gorgeous. Now all you need is a good winter coat."

"I got one." She pointed to a hideous army-green thing hanging in plastic. I jerked it closer for a second look. *Camo? Please tell me I'm not seeing. . .*

"What? It's real warm."

Sheesh! Tim could use it during hunting season! I snatched my fingers away. "Like I said, now all you need is a good winter coat."

"I jest told ya—"

"Do you really want me to start? Because I'm not budging on this one."

Becky laughed and rolled her eyes. "Yer awful picky, Shah-loh, fer somebody on a budget!" She punched me. "And hey, yer carryin' a lotta cash these days. I ain't seen ya use yer checkbook or cards in ages. Ya doin' Tim's envelope method?"

I swallowed hard, not wanting to blab about my bank lien. I just cashed my checks at a gas station and lived on the cash. "Just because I'm on a budget doesn't mean I eat peanut butter crackers three meals a day," I replied, breezing over her question. "You have to look hard for deals, but they're there. Now the last one! Hurry up."

The room chilled me. I pulled my sweater tighter, sniffling and rubbing my cold hands together. For a so-called Southern state, Virginia sure laid on the snow and frigid temperatures with all the gusto of upstate New York. I wouldn't be fooled so easily next time.

"Tim's gonna keell me, buyin' all this stuff!"

"No he's not, and you know it! His jaw's going to hit the floor."

She grinned at her reflection, playing with the shawl. And then her eyes in the mirror turned to mine, and the smile faded like a slowly melting snowflake on my jacket sleeve.

"What?" I looked away.

"Yer just real sad lately, is all." Becky turned her head downward. "You and. . .ya know. Adam." She shrugged. "I don't think either one of ya's said a word ta each other durin' church lately. Sittin' as far apart as the ushers and the choir."

Church. Why did Becky have to remind me of that empty Sunday school room echoing with whispers and Eliza's hand reaching for Adam's arm?

When we met by accident at the coffee table in the church foyer, he poured his cup in silence, setting the pot barely close enough for me to reach. I turned my back, pretending not to see him. Reading the bulletin boards as I stirred my lifeless black brew.

Becky shrugged. "I know neither one of y'all wanna talk about it, but I jest hoped. . . Oh well."

I didn't reply, picking up receipts and tossing them in the trash.

"Did'ja know he got that big landscaping bid for next summer? That'll be the most money he's made in ages. Ain't it swell?"

"Adam's not really speaking to me, so what's the point?" I smushed up a shopping bag, jamming the plastic hanger inside.

Becky waited a few seconds before answering, head still bowed. "I know. He won't breathe a word about why, but lands—I shore wish I could figger things out an' patch 'em back together. Y'all seemed like a nice couple, you and Adam."

You and Adam. The juxtaposition of our names again. I threw away the bag, ignoring a slight jolt of something painful through my chest.

"But. . .yer differ'nt, too, Shah-loh. I don't wanna make ya mad or nothin', but I been noticin' it for a while. Seems like ya don't wanna to talk to him neither. Did y'all have a fight or somethin'?"

"No." I kept my lips in a straight line.

"Wale, then, what gives?" She lifted her head, and I shrugged, turning away.

"He's just not who I thought he was." I threw a handful of tags in the trash. "Please, Becky. Let's talk about something else."

I abruptly opened the door and shooed in Gordon, who practically bowled me over with his toothy smile and whapping tail, baying in relief. I gathered him up, toenails and stinky fur and all, and pressed my cheek to his floppy ears. Arms feeling inexplicably empty.

"Hey, ya old hound," said Becky, pausing in midpull of her new beige corduroy pants to kiss the top of his head. "Still recognize me? Or did my new la-tee-da fragrance throw ya off?" She sniffed her wrist and held it out to him. "It's some ol' vanilla-jasmine-somethin'-or-other the Fashion Nazi made me buy."

"Maybe you should put some on Gordon." I gagged, pulling my head away. "And you got a great deal on that perfume, so don't complain! Clinique, seventy-five percent off?"

"I reckon so." Becky grinned and reached for her sweater—a nice green-and-gray Fair Isle knit that lightly hugged, not flooded, her slender figure. "I's jest joshin' ya. I like it all right."

She poked her head through the sweater like a turtle, eyeing me. "An' don't worry, Shah-loh. God'll show ya when it's the right one."

"Right one what?"

"The right man for ya."

Goose bumps raised on my arms again, but this time with a measure of creeped-out-ness. Anytime someone talked about "the one," I worried that I'd miss it. That out of all the billions of people in the world, I'd bungle it somehow, like I'd already done with so many other things in my life—and wind up with, say, a balding meat packer from Queens.

Then again, I'd be in New York.

"I never thought in a million years I'd say this, but you sound like Kyoko." I rolled my eyes. "Telling me the right one will come by at just the right time." I patted Gordon and put him down, flicking dog hair off my skirt. "To tell the truth, I don't know if I believe there's 'the one' anymore."

"Oh, I do."

"You really think that God makes—"

"Yessiree." Becky straightened her sweater and smoothed her hair, which looked cute smoothed back with a clip on each side. All wavy and tousled in the cold. "With all my heart."

I moved closer to Becky's cranky bedroom heater, which smelled perpetually of burnt dust. And sat in front of it a minute, chin in hand, thinking. "How did you know Tim was the right guy? And don't say—"

"Ya just know." She clasped her hands under her chin and fluttered her eyelashes.

"Not funny!" I scowled.

Becky giggled and dropped the act. "'Course I'm kiddin'! I didn't just know."

"You didn't?"

"Nope."

"Then how?" I checked my watch. "And make it fast because I've got to work."

Becky thought a moment, hands on her hips. "I have no idea! Really! I didn't get into all that 'how do ya know' stuff. I had a crush on Tim fer about two years, and when he asked me out, I thought I done died 'n' gone to heaven! But ya know what? Once all the fireworks fizzled out a bit, he was jest a reg'lar, nice Christian fella."

I bit back a smile, trying to imagine "Tim" and "fireworks" together. I liked Tim, but seeing his hands stained red with deer blood would've crossed him off any list of mine.

180

"And I figgered if a nice Christian guy asks me to marry him, and I wanna get married, why not? An' bingo! There ya have it. Best decision I ever made, 'cept fer Jesus Christ." Becky giggled gleefully. "Might not be the most romantic story, but hey, that's what I got! Have ya ever seen a happier woman?"

"It *is* romantic. More than you think."

"Wale, that's just it! They's all romantic! Ev'ry bride is beautiful! People jest need to stop bein' afraid an' start livin', instead of sittin' around and waitin' for some neon sign to pop on overhead. God never gave a snake instead of a fish. We might have problems, but that's life. Who don't?"

I glanced at Becky's belly involuntarily, my smile fading. "So. . . you're okay with having problems?"

The room fell so quiet I could hear Gordon's rattly breath, turning quickly into a snore, and I prayed I hadn't overstepped my bounds.

"Oh, I'd have problems if I was single, too, or widowed, or whatever. God's ways ain't our ways, ya know. The prophet Jeremiah got thrown in a pit, an' ya know what they did to Jesus. Life ain't fair."

She reached over on her bookshelf and picked up the baby-names book she'd bought at Barnes & Noble back when she'd first bounced in with her happy news.

I froze, recalling her shining face as she flipped through the pages.

"I'm still hopin' fer the Lord to give me another miracle. And when He does, I'm gonna be ready! Look." She showed me with her finger. "There it is—the name I'm gonna give my little girl. Macy Alyssa."

"Wow. It's. . .it's beautiful. It's you. I love it."

"An' if He don't give me what I want, the way I want it, I'll still believe in Him." Her eyes suddenly filled. "Hear me?"

I tried to think of something deep to say, but instead Becky shut the book and plopped it back on her bookshelf.

"You're an amazing woman." I stroked a hand through her hair, wishing I could somehow heal her pain. "I admire you so much."

Becky leaned her head against my shoulder and wiped her eyes. "Aw, yer real sweet. But I ain't really in a cryin' mood today. I'm in a put-my-nose-in-somebody-else's-business mood. So watch out!"

"Well, there isn't anything to tell," I retorted, whacking her with my Barnes & Noble lanyard to make her smile. "And nothing else to report on the house or new jobs either, except another rejection letter."

"From them newspapers ya keep applyin' to?"

"Yep. *Washington Post* this time."

"Aw, Shah-loh! Ya wanted that'n!"

"Well. That's the way it goes." I gathered up my stuff and checked my watch. "And Ashley tried to sic Dad on me. He called my cell phone twice this week. I'm thinking of changing my number."

"Why don't ya jest talk to him a little?"

"No way."

"Not even—?"

"No."

I slid on my wool coat, a gorgeous shade of avocado that matched the golden flecks in my eyes, and buttoned it up. Belted it at the waist.

"Well, how's Shane doin'?" Becky smirked and threw away her tissue.

"Don't you start." I shook a finger at her. "I told you what happened, and it's the truth."

"I hear he was pretty tore up."

"Well, too bad. I'm done with guys like him. When I find the right one, he's going to be different. He's going to love Jesus." I raised my head, meeting her gaze. "And he's going to love *me*. I'm serious, Becky. I'm not the same girl I used to be."

"I'm real proud of ya." She beamed and patted me on the shoulder. "An' Shane's gonna be real sorry he missed out."

"Oh, I wouldn't worry about Shane. Seems like he's got his eye on somebody else at The Green Tree." I grinned and pressed an ivory knitted cap on my head.

"Who? That cute li'l Jamie?"

"No. That cute little Trinity."

"Red roses?"

"Precisely." I smiled. "Now if you'll excuse me, I have dirty tables to scrub and dishes to break."

"Fun, fun." Becky shot me a sympathetic smile. "I gotta scrub the rings outta the bathtub. Wanna trade?"

I gagged. "No thanks. Just pray for me, Becky. Pray that I can have one calm night free of problems and go home by nine and get a good night's sleep. Just once. Will you? Please?"

"Yes, ma'am!" She saluted me.

"Shiloh Phyllis Jacobs! Git in here right now!" A bespectacled Jerry waved me into his tiny office—a renovated closet, actually, ceiling and walls crisscrossed with thick pipes and gobs of Jerry's recipes and Post-it notes.

"What'd she do now?" Blake shook his head, refilling glasses from the ice pitcher.

"Oh no," I moaned, dropping my head into my gloves. "I'm not even clocked in yet, Jerry! If you're going to ream me out, can't you at least pay me for it?"

"Git on in here an' quit whinin'!" Jerry held the door for me. "Pronto! I'm in a hurry!"

I edged uneasily into his office. "And my middle name's not Phyllis."

"I don't care if it's Persimmon. Sit." Jerry pointed to a tiny folding chair jammed against the too-tight wall and pushed the door closed a crack.

"I didn't break those plates on purpose, Jerry. And those people didn't tell me they were allergic to dairy. I promise!" I stood there in my coat and hat, palms up. "Ask Jamie. She was there, too. And I had nothing to do with the samosas! You didn't even have me scheduled because—"

"For gracious' sakes! Sit!" Jerry shoved me lightly into the chair and plopped down on the other side of the desk. "Lands, you'd drive the Pope insane! Here. Read this."

I sat, warily regarding Jerry as he stuffed a card into my surprised hands.

Marble pound cake by the slice, it read, as I leaned forward to make out the curly script in Jerry's dim office light. *Caramel chocolate chip cookies.* The paper wavered, and I looked up to see Jerry's grinning mustache. "These are Stella's recipes!"

"Guess they taught ya pretty well at that fancy Cornell a yers, didn't they?"

I turned the card over. "What is this?"

"Green Tree's new dessert menu. Already sellin'." He beamed. "Stel's tickled pink! Says she always wanted to do somethin' like this, to make some extra money, and she tole me it's yer idea. Ya helped her choose the recipes and ev'rything." He leaned back in his chair and crossed his arms. "I think we're gonna work real well together, me an' Stel. She's had a rough go of it in life, ya know. And this jest made her day."

"Really?" A smile spread over my whole face, making me temporarily forget the ache in my heart. "Maybe if her baking takes off she can open a catering business—like for parties and things? She's a good cook, Jerry. I'm serious. I'll help her."

"Reckon she could." His gaze softened. "You're great with all that logo stuff. Think ya could give her some ideas?"

"Absolutely." I closed my eyes, picturing her new business cards. *Country Confections,* I'd call it.

Jerry's eyes watered as he reached to shake my hand. "Jest wanted to say thank ya. Yer gold, ya know that? An angel. Thanks for helpin' out my ol' sis."

"She's a good friend, Jerry."

"Well, we can always use more a them, can't we?" He smiled. "An' listen, since yer so good with high-falutin' international cuisine an' whatnot, yer got any ideas for the rest'rant? We need some fresh updates. Don't hafta be vegetarian, but in the ballpark."

"Sushi?"

"Don't even go there."

I raised my palms in a laugh. "Well, I had to try."

Jerry guffawed and then opened his mouth to retort then abruptly checked his watch. "Did Trinity clock in yet? She's on the schedule for half an hour ago."

"Trinity?" I felt my stomach lurch. "I—I don't know. I just got here."

"Wait just a second. I'll be right back." Jerry pushed back his chair and disappeared into the busy kitchen, hands on his hips. A muscle in his jaw clenching.

Uh-oh. I blew out a deep breath and hastily dialed Trinity, praying hard that she'd pick up. *Answer, Trinity! For goodness' sake!*

Trinity's voice mail clicked off as Jerry pushed open the door. He slumped down at his desk, eyes sorrowful. "I reckon I'm gonna hafta let her go." His Adam's apple bobbed as he swallowed. "I don't wanna do it, but she can't leave us in the lurch like this. We run a tight ship here, and. . ." He tapped a pen on the table, staring into space. "It's the third time in two weeks."

"Jerry, please don't." I put my phone away. "I don't know what's going on, but Trinity's not herself. Something's wrong."

"I know." He scratched his hand through his brown redneck bowl cut, frowning. "But I got a rest'rant to run, Shiloh. I jest don't know what to do sometimes. She seems like she wants to talk ev'ry now an' then, but. . ."

"She called me this week." I held up my cell phone. "Four times. Trinity never calls me. But every time she started to say something about what's bothering her, she broke off and hung up. I'm worried about her."

"Yeah. Me, too." Jerry just sat there with his face sadly slumped, fingers twiddling a pen. "Well, I reckon it's time for you ta clock in, ain't it?"

"Jerry." I leaned forward, mouth suddenly dry. "Let me go."

"What? Ya want me to fire you, too?" He jerked his head up.

"No. Let me go find Trinity. I think I know where she is."

"What? Now?" He threw his arms up. "You've got that big group from Mary Baldwin College s'posed ta come in tonight—an' they're yers! You scheduled 'em, an' they asked specifically for that cute li'l Shiloh Jacobs. Somethin' like thirty of 'em! You wanna give your tips to Blake?"

I hesitated, imagining those stacks of green bills tucked in Blake's apron pocket as he waved them a cheery good night. *Great. I needed that cash to pay my light bill.* I bowed my head and shot a silent prayer toward heaven.

"I'll go talk to Trinity," I said with a sigh, raising my head. "I don't have any other choice."

"Yes you do. You can work your hours and let Trinity fend for herself. She's a big girl."

"She's in trouble, Jerry." I picked up my purse. "I can sense it. And I'm going."

I slipped my jacket back on, leaving Jerry shaking his head under all those pipes.

As soon as I opened the office door, I almost ran smack into Jamie—dressed post-shift in nice jeans, a milky jade-green sweater in a gorgeous weave, and a fitted gray wool peacoat that suited her perfectly. None of which smelled like fry oil.

On the contrary. Something sunshiny and floral. I sniffed closer.

"Wow, Jamie Rivera. Did Shane ask you out, too?"

"Me? Not this week." She giggled.

185

"You mean he has before?"

"Of course. This is Shane we're talking about." She poked my shoulder. "Although he only sent me roses once, not three times. He was pretty smitten with you, I must say."

"Well. I'm sorry for that." I switched my bag to the other shoulder. "He's nice and everything, but he gives me the creeps, too."

"Tell me about it. But listen, Shiloh. I'm just waiting for you before I talk to Jerry." Jamie grinned and plopped a piece of paper in my hand.

"You want to talk to me?" I checked my watch and then turned the paper over. An address. In Ohio. I looked up at her in confusion. "This has your name on it. But you live here."

"Not anymore." Jamie took my arm and pulled me over to the side so Blake could squeeze through, carrying a huge bucket of blue-cheese salad dressing. "I'm starting college again in January and scheduled to graduate next June."

"What?" I covered my mouth. "You are? How?"

"This job," replied Jamie, wrapping her arm around me as we stood there together at the edge of the noisy kitchen, Flash alternately hollering orders to José and belting out something from Randy Travis. "My income has more than doubled since I started here—way more than I ever made at Barnes & Noble. I've saved up enough to replace the scholarship they canceled." She sniffled and fumbled with her gloves. "I just couldn't wait to tell you. To thank you."

"Thank me? For what?"

"You're the one who invited me to work here. Remember that night?"

"The Harlem Globetrotters. How could I forget?" I felt my smile grow misty, thinking of Jamie walking to the front of a crowded auditorium to receive her diploma in a roar of applause. No more community college and financial-aid meetings and taking semesters off. "And you don't need to thank me, Jamie. I always knew you'd finish well."

I traced her new address with my finger. "Can I keep this?"

"Of course. It's for you. And I'll hunt you down if you don't come for a visit."

Jamie looked up at the framed black-and-white autographed photo of all of us standing next to the Harlem Globetrotters, their huge arms draped around our shoulders like octopus tentacles. We looked like midgets. "You know something, Shiloh? Just before you called that night, I read in the Bible about the miraculous catch of fish."

"Fish?"

"You know the story, right?" Jamie blinked at me, her dark hair shining like the tears that glittered in her eyes. " 'Throw your net on the right side of the boat' and all that?"

"I know it." My throat constricted as I thought of Adam's Greek fish tile still perched on my kitchen wall, its glossy, colorful surface motionless and cold.

"Well, I'd just prayed over my finances. . .and then you called. I guess God still overflows our nets in ways we'd never expect, doesn't He?"

I stared down at my feet, wondering how to answer. "I know He does. I just haven't seen it yet. But I will."

I raised my eyes, remembering the cold sliver of moon over the Best Western parking lot as I pulled out, leaving behind Adam as well as Carlos. I'd paused at the red light to dig, through my tears, under my stuff and pull out Beulah's tiny Bible. Flipping through the pages in the red glare and following with my finger the lines she'd marked: "Love is patient, love is kind. It does not envy, it does not boast, it is not proud."

And then, there in the book of John, as if waiting to remind me—to circle my aching heart with a strong reminder, like a hug so tight it nearly squeezed my breath out: "For God so loved the world that he gave his one and only Son, that whoever believes in him shall not perish but have eternal life."

I'd bowed my head right there and wept and prayed the rest of the way home, feeling the hardness ease inside my heart. Replaced by something soft and tender.

"This is love, Shiloh," He seemed to whisper, holding out two scarred hands. *"Never forget it."*

And I reached out in my mind and took His hands, feeling as if I'd never let go.

Jamie put her arm around my shoulders, and we just stood there. Me dreading the thought of another good-bye. Another figure retreating slowly into patches of memory. "So you're leaving us?"

"I'm going in now to give Jerry my notice."

I played with the address card, feeling lonely. Picturing our green Barnes & Noble aprons covered in espresso. Her book-scanning gun.

Her heartfelt smile, urging me to love Jesus. "We'll miss you, Jamie. You. . .helped point me to God." My eyes filled.

"And now you'll be holding down the fort."

"What do you mean?"

"For Him." She pointed up. "You're the one who needs to pray for Jerry and Trinity and everybody else. To shine His light in a world that needs Him."

"Me?" I shook my head. "Jamie, I'm not like you. I'm not all bright and shiny and. . ." I swallowed hard, playing with a curl of dark hair that fell over her shoulder.

"And what?" She leveled her chin at me. "You have your own gifts. Don't be me. Be Shiloh." She winked. "On steroids."

"Ha." I tried to steady my voice. "The restaurant would explode."

"Well," she teased, putting her hands up, "you win some, you lose some."

I laughed and hugged her, and she patted the back of my head. "You can do this, Shiloh," she whispered. "God's using you. I'm so glad you came to Staunton."

"Then pray for me," I said, giving her a final hug and turning toward the door. "Because Trinity might not be so glad when I find her."

It took me longer to weave my way through the dilapidated streets than I expected, each house getting ricketier as I turned the corner. Stray dogs barked, running loose alongside my car as the woods thickened into a dark smear.

I idled my car at the entrance to the unpaved driveway, flanked by a broken mailbox and SOLD sign, and checked the address again in a pale shaft of moonlight. Then I cut the engine and got out of the car. My boots crunched softly over earth and gravel as I peeked down the driveway between the pines.

Bingo. Trinity's orange Volkswagen Beetle, hidden in the shadows.

I pursed my lips together, wondering if I actually had the courage— or stupidity, I wasn't sure which—to go after her. The wind cut like redneck pocketknives, shivering a lone wind chime in the distance, which mingled with the sound of barking dogs.

"Trinity?" I whispered into the phone as her voice mail switched on. Not answering? Fine. I switched to text. I'M STANDING OUT BY YOUR CAR. PLEASE COME TALK TO ME.

And I waited, shifting from one freezing foot to the other, until I saw my cell phone light up.

THERE'S NO WAY YOU KNOW WHERE I AM, Trinity texted. I'M NOT EVEN AT HOME.

IS THAT A DATSUN NEXT TO YOUR CAR? I texted back. I CAN'T TELL BECAUSE THE BACK BUMPER'S RUSTED OFF IN A PILE BY THE DOGHOUSE.

Wind whished through the pine trees, blowing a few bits of leftover snow as my cell phone remained silent. And then, as if rocked by surprise: GIVE ME TWO MINUTES.

I saw the porch light go off outside the double-wide trailer parked deep in the trees.

Chapter 22

"Shiloh P. Jacobs. What on earth are you doing out here?" Trinity hissed, looking so furious I started to think I'd made a mistake. "You could get us both—" She broke off and looked away, shivering in a too-big puffy coat. "Are you out of your mind?"

"I could get us both what?" I stood my ground, urging my teeth not to chatter.

"Forget it. Just get out of here. Please."

"Jerry's going to fire you, Trinity." I stuck my shivering hands inside my pockets, trying not to stare as she flinched. Her eyes filling with sudden tears.

"Fine. I knew he would eventually." Her face fell, and she brushed at her eye with a gesture of irritation.

"But he won't if you come back and tell him the truth. I'm certain of it. He's worried about you." I hunched my shoulders against the wind. "We all are. I just wish we knew how to help."

Trinity scrubbed a foot in the gravel, looking back over her shoulder at the trailer. "Aren't you on the clock at The Green Tree tonight?" she asked abruptly. She rubbed her nose, red from tears and cold.

"Yes." I held her gaze as it turned watery again. "You're important to us all, Trinity. Please talk to me. Name the place, time, anything. I'll be there."

She lifted her chin, sizing me up. "How'd you find this place? I never told you a word about it."

"No, but when you called me I heard somebody in the background playing that music on a keyboard and changing the words around."

"What music?"

"The tune from the septic-service ads. Don't you remember?" I hummed it. "And when I checked my answering machine yesterday, they'd updated the song. Get it?"

"No." She shook her head.

"Flash told me the name of the guy who does all the music and voices for local ads." *Poorly done local ads, mind you.* "Like that clothing store and mechanics shop in Churchville. Their jingles all kind of sound the same. Am I right?"

Trinity winced and turned away, crossing her arms rigidly. "Okay. You win. This is Chase's place. He's. . .yes. . . got a keyboard."

I shrugged, trying to lighten her tight gaze. "Good thing I found him. Now I can ask him to write something for Jerry. Since he's so open to my restaurant ideas these days."

"Oh no. You don't want to go in there." Trinity shook her head hastily. "Don't worry though. That ad company won't be around much longer."

A couple of dogs howled in the distance, and we both lifted our heads. Waiting for the wind to groan in the pine limbs, covering us with quiet.

"You really want to talk?" She pulled the coat tighter.

"I do."

"Waffle House, then. Two a.m." Trinity took a few steps toward the trailer. "Sit in the back."

"I'll be there."

I waited until the trailer door eased closed, and then I started my car and did a U-turn on the lonely road. Wondering, as I so often did, what on earth I'd just gotten myself into.

"So you really waited for me." Trinity pushed open the door and slid into the too-warm booth across from me, her fitted black leather coat beaded with drops. Two men looked up from their pancakes, eyes flitting to her dark lashes and long, slim jeans. Trinity coolly ignored them, obviously used to such attention.

"Of course I did." I moved my purse and took my legs off the opposite seat, sweat trickling inside my sweater. Short of disrobing completely, there wasn't much I could do for relief under Waffle House's exuberant heating system. Too bad I couldn't funnel some of it to Mom's house, where the cranky heating system left me freezing.

"I'd wait all night if I thought you'd really come." Although they'd probably scrape me off the floor, sound asleep.

Trinity flicked her light brown eyes in my direction, surprisingly soft. "Why, Shiloh? You don't even know me that well."

"So?" I shrugged. "Why not?"

Trinity didn't answer, blinking back what looked like sudden moisture in her eyes as she paged listlessly through a menu. She gave a nervous glance once or twice over her shoulder then settled back in the booth. "You hungry?"

"Are you kidding? I'm trying to decide which pancake platter to order."

"After whatever else you ate already?" She nodded to my empty plate, which previously cradled a chicken Caesar salad.

"I might order two." I fanned myself with the plastic menu page. "With eggs and bacon."

She raised an eyebrow. "You need to. My grandma's worried about you. Says you're turning into a skeleton."

"She's worried about you, too." I closed the menu.

"I know." Trinity sighed and pushed the menu away. "But not about my weight."

"Nope. You look gorgeous." I tried to flatten my frazzled hair, which didn't bend into thick spirals like Trinity's did, even in the snow-flurry-turned-weepy-rain and humid streets. "But unhappy."

"Yeah." She sighed again and waited until the waitress brought some ice water and took our orders then sipped in silence. "You going to the surprise birthday party Grandma's throwing for my grandpa?"

"Sure. She's sweet to invite me. How about you?"

"Sorry. I've got to work at Cracker Barrel tomorrow and Friday, too. And at The Green Tree, if I can talk Jerry into letting me stay on." Trinity shook her head sadly and played with her straw paper.

"Do you want to stay on?" I asked bluntly.

My question seemed to surprise her, and she flinched and dropped the straw paper. "I do." Her eyes watered. "I really do. I just don't know if I can."

"What do you mean 'if you can'?"

The waitress appeared with Trinity's coffee, and then Trinity just sat there, twisting her hands together. Her lips sealed even after the waitress left, down-turned in a frown. She twirled a fork back and forth between perfectly manicured red nails.

"Look," I said, leaning forward and softening my voice. "I'm not trying to be nosy, Trinity. You don't have to tell me anything you don't want to. I just. . .want you to be okay."

I thought she wasn't going to reply, by the way she kept twiddling the fork and not meeting my eyes, but all at once her words slipped out. "It's Chase."

"Who?" I set my water glass, which had nearly reached my lips, back on the table.

"Chase. My boyfriend." She practically whispered the words, eyes flashing up to the nearly empty tables and booths.

"That big guy who comes in to ask for you sometimes?"

"Yep. That's Chase Fletcher." She tore off the corner of a sugar packet and dumped half of it in her coffee. Stirred it with a spoon.

"The owner of the company that does music and voices for ads."

"Right."

Trinity was shivering, even under her sweater and leather coat. I picked up my expensive Japanese scarf, which lay in a shimmering pile of mother-of-pearl tones, and leaned forward to wrap it around her neck. Fluffing the ends and straightening her earrings. Trinity fingered the soft ends, nodding her thanks.

"Why, did you and Chase have a fight or something?" I settled back in the booth.

Trinity sighed, turning her water glass in the light. "Well, yeah. Kinda. See, here's the thing." She leaned closer. "He's got a temper, Shiloh. A really bad one. I mean, it's not his fault. He works hard, and his ex-girlfriend was a jerk, and—"

"Huh?" My fingers tensed on my glass, and I forced myself to react as little as possible. "What do you mean 'he's got a temper'?"

"Well, if he finds out I'm here with you, he'll hit the roof. He'll. . ." She sat back in the booth, shaking her head. "I don't know what he'll do. I told him I saw a possum after the dog food in order to meet you outside."

"What?" I yelped. "Why can't you have coffee with me? I don't even know the guy!"

"I know!" Trinity's voice clipped in irritation. "It has nothing to do with you. He's just. . .possessive. Doesn't want anybody spending time with me that's not. . .well, him. If he finds out Shane sent me roses, he'll blow his stack." She rubbed her hands together, looking away. "I gave them to my sister. Told her Grandma sent them."

"Trinity," I began, suddenly not hungry.

Her teeth chattered, and she tugged down the sleeve of her coat, the same way I did to hide my burn from Adam.

I sat up straighter. "Are you sick? It's a million degrees in here."

"I'm not sick." Her eyebrows flicked irritation. "And don't give me a speech about Chase! He loves me." She punched her ice water with her straw. "I know he loves me. He wouldn't act this way if he didn't care so much."

God, what am I supposed to do now? I'm completely the wrong person for this!

"Is that why you haven't been coming in to the restaurant?"

"Yeah. Chase says he needs me, and after he's had too much to drink, he's just unreasonable and doesn't care about the time or my commitments. I mean, he needs to drink a little, of course. He has a hard job. And now with his new plans he's. . ." She stopped, resting her forehead in her hand. "Well, he calls me all the time, Shiloh. He's always got to know where I am. He thinks I'm at home packing now."

I drank some water, trying to formulate words and not show the despair that flickered through my weary brain. I'd seen these women before. Denying reality. Making excuses. A lot like me in a nasty dating relationship I had back in my late teens. Which ended, I might add, with him getting arrested for assaulting a coworker. And I went on with my life and tried to be smarter next time.

"Why did you want to talk to me then?" I finally asked, wondering what kind of scumbag would treat Trinity like a criminal, watching and checking up on her.

"Because I'm. . .scared." She twisted a sparkly red ring, not touching her coffee. "He's pretty intense sometimes, and now he wants me to move to California with him—first thing in the morning. He's sold the trailer and everything."

"What? You? To California?" I sputtered.

"Yeah. He says he needs me, and he'll throw a fit if I say no. The last time I said no about something he. . . Well, things didn't go so well." She stirred her coffee again, finally lifting the cup to her lips. "And I love him, so I should probably go."

I shook my head in disbelief. "What about his ad business?"

"That?" She rolled her eyes. "There's really not much business there. Which is what got him into his next endeavor." She put her coffee cup down with a nervous clatter, shifting her gaze around the restaurant. "Can they hear us over there?"

"Where?" I turned around. "I don't think so."

Trinity shrugged and leaned closer, voice barely audible. "I don't know what he's into, but it's bad. Drugs and stuff. I found documents and pieces of a fake passport once, and. . .well, he got pretty upset." She pulled her arms closer to her.

The waitress came and set my plate in front of me, and I nodded in thanks. But didn't move to pick up my fork.

"Where is he now?" I asked when the waitress walked out of earshot.

"At a friend's house over in Waynesboro. He left home around one o'clock, so I slipped out to meet you. But he's got a key to my apartment. If I'm not there when he gets back by five this morning, I don't know what he'll do."

"Trinity." I pushed my plate aside and reached for her hand. "Do you want to go to California with him and be involved in all this stuff?"

"No." She sighed. "I mean, I love him, but he's wrong on this one."

"Has he ever. . .you know. Hit you? Or. . .?"

Trinity snatched her hand away, scowling. "No. Of course not! He loves me! Why would you ask a thing like that?" Her voice raised just a touch.

"Sorry." I put my hands up. "You just said he was possessive, and . . . Sorry."

She didn't speak for a while, playing with her straw. "Okay. Maybe once." She let out a shuddering breath, and I jerked my head up to see tears shimmering in her eyes. "He said it wouldn't happen again. He was drunk. Didn't know what he was doing. But then last week he. . . Okay. More than once."

My eyes flicked to her jacket. Long-sleeved sweater. She crossed her arms, fingers tracing the outline of what seemed to be a tender spot on her upper arm.

I covered my face with my hands.

Trinity fumbled with the metal dispenser for a napkin and mopped her cheek. "I'm a mess, Shiloh. I don't know what to do. I'm stuck. That's why I called you this week, but every time I tried to talk he interrupted me, hovering over the phone."

I came to my senses and fished a tissue out of my purse and handed it to her, my own fingers shaking. "Well, I'm a mess, too. I'm not sure my advice'll do you much good."

"Yeah, but you seem like you. . ." She sniffled and steadied her breath. "I don't know. You have something that I don't."

"Stitches?" I showed the scar on my finger.

See, God? I told you I'm the wrong person for this. I don't know what to say. What to tell her. I don't know anything! Love? Relationships?

Jennifer Rogers Spinola

Give me a break!

"No." Trinity rolled her eyes and laughed. "You just seem like you have a *heart*."

"What? I was born on the wrong side of the bed."

She laughed again, a tear spilling down her cheek. "That's the thing though. When I thought of who to talk to, I kept coming back to you. I have no idea why. You just seem to have this. . .I don't know . . .something, and I need help. I love Chase, and he loves me, but. . ."

"What he's doing to you isn't love, Trinity," I said soberly, raising my eyes to her. "Please understand me. Love isn't like that."

She recoiled again, tears still burning in her eyes. She sponged at them, trying not to smudge her graphite-colored eye shadow. "How do you know? You haven't even met Chase."

"I'd like to." *So I can knock him into next week!*

"Do you know what love is? Is Adam the one for you?"

"Adam?" I jumped, my gaze jolting from the glistening shadow of my glass on the table to her eyes. "Why'd you ask that?"

"I don't know. I just saw the way you guys looked at each other in the restaurant that time. With your Japanese friend." She raised a palm. "Maybe I'm wrong, but I thought you made a good match."

I blinked quickly and looked away, trying to recover. "I don't know about Adam. He's a nice guy, and at one time I thought maybe we. . . But he's with somebody else." I tried to shrug in indifference, but it came out more like a shiver. *A good match.* I pulled my coat on, hugging myself to calm my sudden jitters. "But regardless, I can't see him. . .you know, treating a woman badly."

On the contrary. Adam noticed my bandages. Lent me his cell phone. Held the door. I stuffed my scarred finger in my pocket, wishing Trinity hadn't brought him up.

"How am I supposed to know whether a guy is good or not?" she asked in a voice that almost pleaded. "How? Why is it so hard?"

I shook my head and shrugged. "It *is* hard. But you look at his life. You see how he treats other people. That's what Faye told me, anyway. If he loses his temper and mistreats other people, then he'll probably do it to you, too." I twirled my glass. "Don't look at me. I'm hardly the expert. But I know you have to go into relationships with both eyes open and let God show you his true character. Pray a lot."

Trinity thought a long while, tracing the edges of the sugar packet with slender fingers. The way I'd traced Adam's business card.

"Real love just feels different from anything I've ever known before, Trinity. I'm still learning about it."

"How?"

I sat silently a long time, trying to choose my words. Then reached out and cautiously took Trinity's hand again. She didn't pull away.

" 'Love is patient,' " I began from memory, feeling an inexplicable lump swell in my throat. " 'Love is kind. It does not envy, it does not boast, it is not proud. . .' "

★ ★ ★

So much for Becky's prayer for a night without crisis. Which ended. . . oh, around four in the morning.

I should have included the following afternoon in my prayer as well, when I drove home from Barnes & Noble, taking back roads and checking my rearview mirror over every rise, every turn. Keeping an eye out for Chase's red Blazer.

And why not? I'd absconded with his favorite punching bag. Hidden her inside Mom's cream-colored walls and blue-and-white-checked gingham curtains, begging her to talk to Jerry and call in a sick day at Cracker Barrel. Or maybe three or four of them until Chase got tired of looking for her.

What on earth have you gotten yourself into, Shiloh Jacobs? I scolded myself, slipping on a pretty gray sweater dress. Stockings. Nice, trendy Mary Janes—unlike the scuffed ones I wore to the restaurant. I pinned up my hair and grabbed my plate of cheap Rice Krispie squares, the three-ingredient budget dessert, just in time for Frank's birthday party.

"Don't you dare call Chase, Trinity." I pulled on a winter white jacket that probably wasn't warm enough and slung my purse over my shoulder, giving Christie one last scratch behind the ears. "Promise?"

"I won't. And he'll leave, Shiloh. I'm sure of it. He's got everything all lined up in California. The trailer is sold. He can't stay here very long."

"He might bash your stuff in when he finds you missing." I propped my sunglasses over my hair. "Just to warn you."

"I know." She stood at the window, avoiding my eyes. "He's done that before, too."

Jerk. I watched her there, arms folded on the sill and eyes reflecting

197

barren trees and soft sunny skies of early winter, and I felt suddenly thankful for God's new love opening up in my heart. No matter what Carlos said about my pitiful life.

"You sure you don't want to go to your grandfather's party?" I hesitated, gloves in hand.

"No. Chase might look for me at Grandma's. Or my car, anyway."

"He won't find it here." Not hidden behind Stella's bus, just like the night we spied on Faye and Earl. "As long as you—" I broke off, words sticking in my throat at Trinity's focused frown. Her eyes turned past me toward the front yard. "What?"

"I thought I saw a car."

"What? Here?"

We both jumped as someone banged at the front door. Loudly. The glass of water on the table shook, and Christie leaped from my arms, hackles raised.

Chapter 23

reat. Great. Great. I ran my hand through my bangs, trying to decide what to do. Keep quiet? Answer it? Confront him? *God, this is getting over my head! What are You doing to me?*

"Wait—that's not Chase's car." Trinity spoke in low tones, peering through the living-room curtains.

"You can't trust anybody, Trinity. Don't you get it? He'll—"

"It says U.S. Mail."

"Mail?" I jerked my head to the split in the curtains. "What?"

The door pounded again. I clenched a hand over my racing heart and shoved Trinity out of the room then moved to open the door a crack. "Can I help you?"

"Sign here." The uniformed guy shoved a clipboard at me.

"For what?"

"Registered mail. I need your signature." He held up an envelope.

I stepped through the screen door and scrawled my name with the attached pen then reached for the envelope.

And there grinned the words in crisp, no-nonsense font: James Reuben Prufrock III.

I fumed all the way through winding back roads to Beulah's, trying to avoid the main highways. I know, I know. A surprise party. I was supposed to be cheerful. But I couldn't tear my thoughts from that stupid letter by Ashley's lawyer. Lying on the passenger's seat, a malevolent block of black and white. And all the while, keeping an eye out for Chase's Blazer.

My cell phone trilled. "Trinity?" I shook off my gloves and jerked my phone up to my ear, against my own driving regulations. "What's up? You okay?"

"I'm fine. It's just. . . Christie sort of chewed on one of the couch cushions."

I drove over a bump of roadkill. "You're kidding, right?"

"No, she really did. Just the corner where you. . . Well, you can see some split threads. I can try to sew it back."

Of all the. . .! I covered the phone and groaned. "Just keep her out of the living room," I replied, trying to keep my voice steady. "Don't worry, Trinity. She does it with me, too. I have to watch her constantly. She's getting better, but. . ." I stopped at a desolate intersection, not sure whether to go right or left. I snatched up a map from the passenger's seat and turned it one way. Then the other. Turn signal blinking as I tried to find the road.

"Oh, and some guy named Carlos called."

"What?" I hollered. My foot slipped off the brake, and the car rolled a few feet.

"He just said he'd call back later."

"No!" I pounded the steering wheel. "I don't want him to call back! Ever!"

"Sorry, Shiloh. I—I didn't know."

"No, it's not your fault." I felt like blubbering again. I gave up trying to read the map and turned down the road to the right, which forked at an unmarked intersection. Right again, and the two-lane road meandered into a cow-spangled distance. "We're done. Over. Period. Why can't Carlos leave things alone?"

"I don't know if I should tell you this or not, but. . ."

"But what?" I swallowed hard and drove over a weedy hill then down into a long stretch of pasture. Not seeing any of the landmarks the map suggested.

"Right after Carlos, somebody from that septic service called, saying you'd scheduled some maintenance work."

"I did NOT! Wait 'til I get my hands on those. . . Wait a second. What is this?" I turned, cell phone to my ear, as the road narrowed down to a sparse one-lane, lined with gravel on either side. Marked with flagging tape.

The road coiled around several turns with dusty, brush-choked shoulders, and paint faded into unmarked asphalt.

"This can't be right." I slowed and tried to turn, but the overgrown woods hemmed me in. Asphalt under my tires littered with layers of rust-brown pine needles and decaying leaves.

The road bumped off pavement into dirt and then abruptly dead-ended. Right in an unfinished patch of dry, tan soil, grasses waving. Land surveyors were already checking the area for construction readiness, as evidenced by the perk holes—scattered brown mounds of fresh earth like fresh cow pies. Snow melting between them in pale patches.

"Shiloh? You still there?"

"I'm here." I let out a sigh and pulled to a stop. I checked the map again then tossed the useless thing on the seat. "You don't know where Smokewood Meade is, do you?" I peered out the window at a COMING SOON construction sign next to some roped-off areas marked with flagging tape.

"Where? I don't think so."

"Great. Then you can't tell me how to get to your grandma's place from here."

Trinity paused. "Um. . .sorry, but no. What's the nearest main road?" I checked the map, turned it right and left, and tried to find the name with my finger. None of the route numbers on the map made sense.

"I have no idea. I came from that road by the barn."

"What barn? There are tons of barns."

"The red one. The one near that church. What is it, Route 254?" I shook out the map. "No. Not that one. I don't know." I looked out the window again, phone under my chin. "How about if I call you when I get out of here and figure out where I am?"

"Sure. I'll stay by the phone."

"Thanks. And stay safe, Trinity."

"I will. Thanks for your help. Really." Her voice quivered. "I don't know what I'd do without you."

"Are you kidding? I don't even know what county I'm in."

I tried to turn my car around on the loose jumble of rocks and branches, pausing only when an out-of-state number vibrated on my cell phone. I answered, holding it under my chin as I turned the wheel sharply to the left, steering column complaining.

"Shiloh Jacobs? This is Doreen from *USA Today*. How are you?"

I jammed on the brakes. "Fine, thanks. You received my résumé?"

"We did. It looks great. You've got a lot of experience."

My heart hammered loudly in my ears. "Thank you. I'd be glad to send my portfolio, or—"

"Well, actually we're not hiring for news-desk positions right now. But we've got a receptionist job if you're interested."

Receptionist? A *receptionist* job? Answering phones while all the big-shot reporters laughed together in the lobby, lanyards over their

Jennifer Rogers Spinola

perfect trendy suits, all laden down with Starbucks cups and briefcases?

Tears burned in my eyes as I sucked back my pride, eyes landing on James Prufrock's envelope. My Green Tree to-go bag still on the floorboard. "What's the salary?"

She told me, and I slumped against the back of the seat. Barely more than I made already, but without the free rent.

"Um. . .thanks," I mumbled, trying to force a little politeness in my voice. "I'm probably not interested, but I'll let you know if I change my mind."

As soon as I pressed off the phone, I gunned the engine and abruptly hit something hard. It reverberated through the entire undercarriage, and my wheels on one side spun in the muddy, snow-slushy dirt. I shifted into REVERSE, horrified, and something—a rock, tree branch—hung against the back of my wheel, refusing to budge.

Oh. My. Goodness. I turned off the car and sat there in perfect silence, a single pine needle sifting down onto my windshield. Crows over the field flapping soundless wings as they soared off into soft blue sky, making black specks in the distance.

I thought of banging the steering wheel, but what would that do? I'd probably destroyed Mom's Honda enough.

"Great. Now I've got to call Beulah and tell her I'll be late," I muttered through my teeth, scrolling through my cell phone numbers.

Just as my cell phone vibrated again, buzzing against my hand.

"Whoever you are, go away!" I hollered, trying to keep back the tears.

I fumbled with the phone, pressing all the wrong buttons before finally hitting the right one and snapping a crabby, "What?" Then I saw—out of the corner of my eye—a familiar number on the screen. "Adam?" I shoved it to my ear in disbelief.

"Shiloh? You. . .uh. . .okay?"

It took me a minute to realize that (1) Adam Carter had called me and (2) was still waiting on the line for me to respond. The breath went out of me as I tried to gather my words.

"Me?" I swallowed, my fingers fluttering nervously on the cell phone. "Sure. I'm just fine. Thanks." I tried to sound cheery and—most importantly—indifferent.

He stayed silent awhile then cleared his throat. "Actually I was wondering if maybe we could. . .talk."

"You want to talk? To me?" I almost laughed then thought better

202

of it. "What about?"

Adam sighed. "I don't know, Shiloh. Our friendship. I just wish we could. . .settle some things."

"Okay." I responded like a robot. Afraid that if I talked too long I'd either cry or spill all my problems—neither of which sounded either wise or appealing. Especially not in front of Adam Carter.

I just sat there, drumming my fingers nervously on the steering wheel.

"You sure you're okay?"

His voice hit me with an unexpected tenderness, despite the stiff layer of formality over his words, and before I could stop myself, hot tears coursed down my cheeks. I mopped them silently, not daring to breathe.

"Shiloh?"

"I'm here. And I'm perfectly fine." I turned my head away from the phone to wipe my nose with a tissue. "Never been better."

I turned on the ignition and revved the gas, trying to move the car. Something scraped along the undercarriage with a sick grinding sound, and I threw it into PARK again, the tail end still pointing toward the road at a crazy angle. "I'm just a little stuck is all. But I'll figure something out."

"Stuck? Where are you?"

"I have no idea." I glared at the map and mopped my cheeks. I leaned closer to the window, trying to make out the words on the sign. "Smokewood Meade. I'm lost, and I think I hit something."

"Oh, I know where you are. That new construction site, right? They're going to put in a subdivision."

"You know it?" I brightened slightly. "Can you tell me how to get out of here and over to Beulah's?"

"Well, I'm actually not far away. Want me to come by there and take a look at your car?"

"Would you?" I wiped my nose. "Thanks. Not because I. . .you know. . .am a woman and can't drive or read maps. I'm just. . ." My throat choked again.

"Do you want me to come?"

"Sure. Thanks."

"I'll be there in about five minutes."

I pressed off the phone then dropped my head on the steering wheel and whispered a prayer for the mess of my life. For Ashley. For

Jennifer Rogers Spinola

Trinity. For my car even, lodged against whatever I'd run over.

"It's not like things can get any worse, God," I sniffled, reluctantly opening my door and crunching through the mucky dry grass and patches of white snow. Kneeling down among the scattered pinecones to see what I'd hit.

No good. I dug back inside the passenger's seat for my purse and tried to shine my mini flashlight under the car, but the weak battery flickered and went out, leaving me just as stumped as before.

I heard a sound. The low drone of an engine. And when I popped my head up over the hood, what should stare back at me but a bright red Blazer—standing out against the bleached landscape like a warning flare.

Chapter 24

I stood up quickly and brushed myself off, but not before Chase had screeched the Blazer to a stop behind my car and slammed the door. He strode across the frozen ground in a dark, sleek leather jacket, thick and burly, fallen limbs crunching under his heavy boots. Face creased in a dark scowl.

"Where is she?" he demanded, voice coming out like a snarl. Shoulders bulging under his jacket, hands on his hips.

"Excuse me?" There was no time to hide. I leaned against the hood of my car in a casual position, tapping out a text message. Just in case I . . .uh. . .needed to call for help. And to hide my shaking fingers. "Who are you?"

"You know who I am." He took a step closer. "Where's Trinity?"

"I've never met you before in my life." I looked up from my cell phone with a look of disdain and pushed off the hood. Moving ever so carefully as to keep the car between us.

Chase cursed and kicked my tire, and I felt its shock vibrate against my shoe.

"Hey! Stay away from my car!" I shouted, trying to make my face look stern. "What's the matter with you?"

"I know who you are!" he hollered, striding around the car like a bull, steam snorting from his fancy pierced ears. "You work at the restaurant, and you went looking for Trinity last night! Somebody in the kitchen told me."

"Somebody in the kitchen? That's your source?" I laughed in derision. "And how do you know my car anyway? What are you, some kind of a stalker?"

"Apparently even the dishwashers know your car. What does that say about you?"

Marcos. Nosy, weasly little Marcos, always blabbing about everybody's business! Wait 'til I clock in tomorrow!

"It says that they've got nothing better to do than spy on other people."

Chase circled around the hood of my car toward me, glaring ominously. "He told me you live out this way. Where's Trinity?" His voice rose. I kept walking, keeping the car between us. Although it was getting difficult with Chase's long strides. "Why would I know where Trinity is? I don't keep tabs on people's whereabouts. Especially somebody Trinity's age, who's certainly old enough to take care of herself. Now get out of here and leave me alone, or I'll call the police!"

I shouldn't have said that last part. I should have just done it.

But today wasn't my day. Chase narrowed his eyes at me and, in a lightning second, lunged around the side of the Honda and grabbed me by the arm. He tore the cell phone out of my hand and threw it across the snow then shoved me hard against the side of the car. Knocking the breath out of me. My purse and keys fell down into the grass.

"You listen here," he rasped, tattoo on his neck bulging. "You tell me where she is, or I'll. . ."

At the faint sound of an engine motor, I screamed at the top of my lungs. I punched Chase away from me, trying to squirm free from his grasp.

As Adam's truck grew closer, Chase abruptly dropped my arm and backed away, breathing hard. He crossed his arms angrily, beefy biceps bulging, then took a few steps toward his SUV.

"Whoa, whoa, whoa," shouted Adam, leaping from his truck and jerking up a metal construction stake, ripping it from a section of faded orange netting. "Who do you think you are? Shiloh, what's going on?"

"He's nuts!" I hollered back, stumbling over the grass as I dug for my cell phone. "Stay away from him!"

"Oh yeah? You think I'm nuts? I oughtta. . ." Chase kicked my car again as Adam and I circled around toward each other, Adam still brandishing the metal stake.

Before anyone could speak, another rumble came over the hill, and a cloud of dust lifted as two battered cars roared through the trees. Rolling to a stop, one on either side of Chase's Blazer, like a bad movie.

Well, well, well. My brain raced, frantic, as I backed away, completely out of plans and out of luck. *Party at Smokewood Meade. And all I have are Rice Krispie squares.*

Car doors squeaked open.

"Uh-oh," I whispered, taking a step closer to Adam as two scary-looking guys got out, one dressed in leather and the other with a bandana tied around his head. "What now?"

"Run!" Adam whispered back, pushing me across the snow-littered ground and toward the trees.

Chapter 25

Good thing I'd worn Mary Janes and not the high-heeled boots I'd originally planned for Frank's party. We tore through the underbrush at the edge of the clearing, stumbling over limbs and scattered logs as footsteps pounded and shouts raised behind us.

"What did you do?" Adam hollered, cheeks red with cold as he threw a thick fallen tree branch behind us to block our path. The construction stake still tucked under one arm.

"Why does everybody always think I did something?" I yelped, waving my arms as we came to a ditch-like gully. "And why did you call me anyway?"

"Call you?" He awkwardly grabbed my hand and helped me jump over a muddy section choked with dried limbs and withered leaves, jerking me so hard through a clump of pines that my teeth rattled. "I told you I wanted to talk. You haven't spoken to me for how long?"

"Of course I haven't. Not after you kissed me and then—" I twisted around, hearing the shouts closer, and ran harder, straining my lungs and the muscles in my calves. Good thing I ran nearly every day; my life might depend on it.

"And then what?" Adam jumped to a slightly dryer section of mud and pushed me ahead of him, through a thicket of brambly stuff that grabbed at my tights and dress. Snatching at the ends of my scarf.

I left my scarf hanging in the briars, but Adam indignantly grabbed it up and stuffed it under his coat. "Don't leave anything behind, Shiloh! They'll follow us!" He jerked my arm toward a stand of winter-gray elms, framing the bleached sky with spindly branches. "Over there! Go! Hurry!"

Twigs clawed at my face and arms as I jumped over a jumble of rough stones protruding through the tattered carpet of brown leaves and pushed through the elm limbs. Between broken strands of rusted barbed wire and rotten fence posts and a scatter of empty Guinness bottles where people with snootier tastes in beer apparently indulged after dark.

"Eliza Harrison," I gasped, scrambling over a tangle of twisted tree roots. "Need I say more?"

"What?" Adam yelped, coming to a complete halt in mid-duck under a thick tree limb. "What does she have to do with anything?"

"I saw you," I panted, pausing just long enough to turn and meet his eyes before I bent over to catch my breath, hands on my knees. "In the Sunday school room."

"What Sunday school room?" Adam shook his head in bewilderment and lowered the stake, a twirling, taupe-colored leaf landing on his head. He brushed it off in irritation, chest rising and falling as he let out his breath. "What are you talking about? Especially when—"

Someone tore through the briars behind us, and I lunged ahead, sprinting through the muddy, pine-needle-littered ground. "Especially when what?"

Adam caught up with me, pulling me faster by the elbow of my jacket as a loud *pow* rang out through the trees. "Those guys might have guns, Shiloh! This is serious!"

"Finish what you started to say," I gasped, ducking a jumble of broken limbs.

"Rumor has it you went out with Shane Pendergrass. Are you dating him?"

I ran smack into a branch, right between my eyes, and fell on my bottom. Knocking the breath out of my lungs.

"Are you kidding? Shane?" I gasped, as Adam dragged me to my feet. "I never went out with Shane!"

My tailbone smarted. I jumped over a tangle of briars and scooted up a muddy hill, stumbling twice and catching myself on my knees and elbow. Pushing free with one hand. "How dare you accuse me of something like that! My car broke down, and he picked me up. I never—" I flailed my fists through a patch of thick dried weeds. "Why on earth am I explaining this to you anyway?"

"I believe you." He skidded down the other side of the rise, swerving around a tree stump, and grabbed some branches for support. "But this is a small town, Shiloh. News travels fast."

"Don't give me that!" I hissed, shaking my finger at him. "You're one to talk, whispering in a Sunday school room with Eliza Harrison! Talking about marriage? I'm not stupid, Adam. I've learned quite a bit about the male species these days, and it's all been pretty rotten."

The land leveled, and we turned in a circle, not sure which direction to go.

"Are they gone?" I whispered as an eerie silence descended on the woods. Just faint cheeping of nuthatches and a low whistle of wind in the pines. I shivered, suddenly feeling the bitter chill. My fingers smarted, red with cold.

Something crashed in the underbrush, and we both whirled around. Just as a coat-clad figure shouted, lunging for my arm. I screamed, jerking away and sprinting through a patchy grove of trees with peeling bark. Just as a bullet whined past me, splintering some dried limbs of a white pine tree. They quivered and fell to the ground in a heap.

"Watch out!" Adam shouted. "They've split up!"

Chase dove at me from around a shadowy bend, and I managed to squeeze through a couple of tight-fitting trees and out of his grasp. Crawling on my belly under a rusty fence and into a patchy thicket that bled into a cow pasture.

I glanced over my shoulder just in time to see Adam lean into Chase with the construction stake, doubling him over, and then scoot under the fence right behind me. Shouts ringing up through the trees.

"Use your cell phone!" I hollered, wind cutting across my face in the open field and nearly sucking my words from my mouth. "Call the police!"

"It's in the truck!" Adam hollered back.

I groaned, sprinting to the edge of the cow pasture, where black-and-white Holsteins lolled in comatose bliss under the waning December sun. Adam caught up with me, breathing hard, and then abruptly jerked my arm back under a thick canopy of hemlock trees with pungent branches of tiny green needles.

"I know where we are."

"What?" I swiveled to glare at him, out of breath. "What do mean where we are? We're being chased by a couple of madmen who—"

Adam surprised me by slapping a hand over my mouth. "Can you be quiet for two seconds, Shiloh? Just wait. I know this pasture. It loops around near the truck. If we can get them to pass by us, we can double back."

"And get in your truck," I finished, pulling his hand away from my mouth with shaking fingers and lowering my voice. Still annoyed at his "be quiet for two seconds" comment. "Do you have your keys? Because I don't have mine."

Adam jingled his pocket in reply.

"But you have to be quiet. And get down." He pushed through a thick section of limbs, opening a shadowy hollow, and ducked his head, motioning with his hand. We crouched there against the tree trunk, branches around us so thick I could hardly see out.

I pulled my skirt tightly around my knees, gaping holes ripped in my once-sleek stockings. Shoes caked with mud.

"Sorry about your clothes," Adam whispered, nodding toward them as I hugged myself, shivering.

"I'm more sorry about Eliza Harrison."

Adam shook his head and let out a sigh, resting his forehead against the dirty metal stake. "You don't understand, Shiloh. I've never even dated her!"

"What?" I tried to keep my teeth from knocking together as I massaged my cold fingers. "But you said. . ."

He peeled off his coat and stuck it around my shoulders in an annoyed sort of huff, not the gentlemanly way I'd expected. Then he shushed me again with a glare, putting a finger to his lips. "Let me finish. I said something to Eliza about marriage, right? Well, our parents had this. . .I don't know. . .'thing' about us getting married. Since we were practically babies."

I bristled, reluctantly sticking my arms through his coat. Which smelled. . .like Adam. I tried to push it out of my mind.

"You *shh* this time." I smacked his shoulder, which now sported only a dark blue sweater and some kind of ugly plaid shirt underneath. "I hear somebody."

I caught my breath as one of the guys stomped past us, shaking the leaves. Adam tucked his head down, pressing my head practically into the dirt with his arm. We huddled there in breathless silence, listening to him snap a twig and kick old clumps of branches, cursing in low tones.

I squeezed my eyes closed, praying, until silence fell again. A squirrel whisked across a branch overhead, chattering, and I thought briefly of Tim's deer stew. Wonder what wild animal Becky'd tossed in the Crock-Pot for tonight?

"So go on. Tell me about Miss Harrison," I sniffed, sitting up slightly and pulling Adam's coat tight against my neck and—although I'd never admit it—basking in its delirious warmth.

"There isn't anything to tell," he whispered, brushing hemlock mulch from the side of my face. "That's how we grew up, Shiloh. Eliza

210

and I actually had nothing to do with it. Our parents thought the idea was cute." He rolled his eyes, voice barely audible over the gentle brush of wind through the leaves. "And then when she left Staunton to go to college, she eloped with this guy named Greg without so much as an e-mail to any of us."

"So she's. . .married?" I clapped a hand over my mouth.

"For nearly two years. Her mom found out by accident, and everybody was upset at her and worried about me."

"So how did you feel?" I scowled. "Heartbroken?"

Adam scowled back. "No. I just wanted her to stop feeling guilty and go on with her life. She's not right for me anyway. Just. . .not my type at all."

Yeah, and you're not mine either, buddy! I wiped at a muddy spot on my skirt.

Adam released a long breath. "And then she showed up on Sunday, and we had our little awkward talk about leaving everything in the past and being friends."

"And you let her put her hand on your arm."

"Man, Shiloh. Did you really spy on us?" he snapped, looking truly angry for the first time.

"You shouldn't have had anything to hide." I raised my eyes and chin level with his, brushing aside prickly twigs. "And I didn't mean to see you. I just. . .did."

"Well, she didn't touch me. I moved away before she did. Eliza was always a little too touchy. If you know what I mean."

"I don't." I held his hard gaze then finally let it drift. "She said you're one in a million." The words whispered off my lips before I could stop them.

Another guy tromped by in the distance, mumbling all kinds of murderous threats, and Adam waited before whispering back. "You're one to talk. I saw you and your Argentinean boyfriend at the hotel, Shiloh."

"Boyfriend?" I yelped, and Adam whirled around, glaring. Pressing a finger to his lips.

"Fiancé, then. Whatever he is. He blew you a kiss."

"He's neither." I dropped my voice to an indignant whisper. "Blew me a kiss? Please. He hates my guts. He just showed up out of the blue wanting to stay at my house and marry me for a green card. And I said no. I took him to the Best Western instead. Satisfied?" I felt like sticking my tongue out, but restrained myself.

Adam's face blanched. "You mean you—you're not. . .?"

"Seeing Carlos? No. I'm not even returning his phone calls. And we did nothing more than talk in the lobby. Go ask the front-desk clerks if you doubt my story. Judy was pretty taken with Carlos; I'm sure she'll tell you all you want to know."

My cheeks burned, and I looked away, shaking against the cold ground.

Adam's hand on my elbow startled me. "I don't doubt your story. About Shane or anybody. I just. . .didn't know."

"Well, you should have asked," I said, facing him. "You judged me."

"You should have asked me, too." He held my gaze, not flinching. Until I finally turned away, still reeling from his news about Eliza. "And no, I didn't judge you. I called you to find out the truth, which you never cared enough to do with me."

"I never said I didn't care," I whispered, digging scratchy bark bits out of my scalp.

His eyes met mine briefly then flitted away. "How was I supposed to know that?"

The shouts faded around us, and overhead I heard the low groan of the tall hemlock, bending in the winter wind. Adam inched forward on his knees and parted the thick branches then motioned for me to follow him.

"I hope you don't mind getting dirty," he whispered, lips barely moving.

"Oh, I do. I definitely do."

We crawled through the damp leaves, scattered with patches of beaded snow, and Adam paused long enough to ball up my scarf and hurl it as hard as he could. It hung there in a distant bramble patch, fluttering.

"Sorry. I had to throw them off our trail."

"I know. I'm just glad I didn't bring my silk one, or I'd make you go get it."

Adam motioned me behind him, and we crept through the underbrush and across the gully, slipping over fallen logs and piles of snow-speckled leaves until the edge of the new development land glimmered through the trees. He inched forward to make sure the field was clear then waved me forward—just as voices tangled through the trees behind us. Someone found my scarf.

"Let's go!" Adam grabbed my arm and half dragged me toward the truck at top speed. He shoved the key into the lock and boosted me up then climbed in and locked the door behind him.

Adam gunned the ignition and threw the truck into REVERSE, spinning the steering wheel and jerking us over a hard bump, just as two of the guys appeared in the clearing. A bullet zinged off the metal construction sign, and I ducked, covering my head. Adam stepped on the gas and roared out of the subdivision, raising a giant cloud of dust behind us. Barreling down the narrow dirt road and bursting through a piece of flagging tape, knocking over a cone.

"Put your seat belt on!" he yelled between gear shifts, gesturing wildly as I plastered myself to the seat, hands on the dash. "There's black ice all over this road!"

We looked horrifying. My hair hung in damp strings, studded with leaves, and my entire dress and stockings torn and muddy under Adam's too-big coat. Brown patches of what looked—and, unfortunately, smelled—like cow poo clinging to my shoes and the elbow of his coat.

I fumbled with the seat belt, clicking it in just as Adam swerved around a curve, tires screeching.

"Ouch." I massaged my head where it had banged against the glass. "Where'd you learn to drive, New York?"

"Funny." He glanced in his rearview mirror, breathing fast, then stepped on the gas.

"Are they following us?"

"Maybe. There's dust back there."

"Oh great." I groaned, flopping back against the seat and trying to catch my breath as he jammed the truck into gear and swerved down a side road scattered with distant houses and cars. We sped left and then left again, leaving the cow pastures behind in a rush of roads and stoplights.

Adam turned to me again, the sun sinking toward the mountains in a wash of red and blue. "Shiloh Jacobs,"—he shook his head, chest heaving—"you make more enemies than anyone I've ever met. Care to explain?"

Chapter 26

So you're really not dating Carlos?" Adam asked when I'd spilled everything about Trinity.

"Huh? No."

Adam didn't reply for a while, clenching his dirty hands on the steering wheel. "I guess you think I went too far the night I. . .uh. . .at my house, after you gave me. . ."

"No." My forthrightness surprised me. "Not at all."

Adam swerved. It was slight, but I felt it. Apparently he didn't expect my response at all. He raised his hand and brushed it through his hair, messing up the back, and then let it fall back to the steering wheel.

"Black ice. You have to be careful because it. . ." He looked over at me as I sat back in my seat, loosening the seat belt that suddenly felt tight. "What did you say again?"

"Is it hot in here?" I cracked the window.

"Hot?" He was still staring at me.

"Yeah. Can you turn that thing down?"

"What thing?" *Hopeless. We are hopeless.* I fumbled at the dash until Adam clicked the heat off.

"So you do feel. . .uh. . .something?" Adam's knuckles clenched on the steering wheel. "Toward. . ."

"Toward who?"

"Well, maybe. . .me?"

My hands, which suddenly started to tremble, knotted themselves together. "Maybe. A little."

Neither of us spoke for a long while, and Adam turned away, face toward the window.

"Where were you going again?"

"Beulah's house. For Frank's surprise party."

"Want me to take you there?"

I didn't answer. Just raised an eyebrow as Adam glanced at my torn stockings and leafy hair, one side of which hung in my eyes.

"I guess not, huh?"

"Um. . .no."

Adam flicked on his windshield wiper to loosen the pine needles stuck underneath. "How about some coffee then?"

"Coffee? Like a date?" I tried to keep the smile back, reaching on the floorboard to move Adam's work boots and a bag of mulch away from my dirty shoes. It sounded tacky to ask, maybe, but I was sick of guessing. If some guy wanted to go out with me, he'd better say it up front.

"Not a date. . .per se." Adam reached over with an apology and chucked the boots and stuff in the back with his free arm. "See, here's the thing: I don't date. I mean, not exactly."

"You what?" I threw my arms up. "I need an aspirin. Right now." I pressed my eyes closed and rubbed my forehead.

"What? I don't date. I'd rather get to know a woman truthfully, the way we are in real life. Almost like a courtship. Meeting her family. Seeing if we're right for. . ."

You can NOT be serious. I opened one eye in disbelief. "Right for what? Marriage?"

"Yeah." He downshifted to a lower speed. "Marriage. A life together. That's what the whole point is, right?"

I laughed, sort of, but Adam didn't. And the rest of my laugh froze there, like the frosty skin of ice on a pond as we drove past. "Um. . . okay," I heard myself say. "Sure." As politely as if he'd offered me a discount on rose fertilizer. Not sure if I was being serious or sarcastic.

"Tastee Freez okay? The one out in Churchville where those guys won't come looking for us?" He glanced down at his muddy jeans. "And where we won't get too many odd looks dressed like this?"

Right. That makes perfect sense. Get chased by lunatics and soiled by cow manure then go out in public.

"Then we can go back and get your car. If. . .if that's all right with you."

I dug a twig out of my hair. "Are you sure I'm not keeping you from something?"

"No. I'm okay. You?"

For the life of me, I couldn't believe why I'd agreed to coffee with Adam Carter after tromping through the woods at breakneck speed, risking our necks at the mercy of Creepo Chase Fletcher.

Adam's hair stuck up like a rooster's comb on one side, flattened on the other. A stray branch had sliced him across the cheek, leaving a bleeding red scratch.

215

Jennifer Rogers Spinola

"Shiloh?"

"What?"

"I asked you a question."

"Sorry. What was it again?"

I should have screamed and thrown myself out of the truck window. Instead I chitchatted about who knows what as we meandered toward Churchville until Adam backed into a parking space. Indigo nightfall sifted over the land, and headlights and streetlights flickered on.

Adam got out and slammed the door, and I wordlessly unclipped my seat belt, waiting for him to come around and help me out of the truck.

I, Shiloh P. Jacobs, just climbed out of a pickup truck in a run-down, Podunk parking lot next to a greasy fast-food place and the town dump. Reeking of dirt and cow manure, with a cash-strapped landscaper from Virginia talking about marriage. *I have definitely lost my mind.*

Outside the stars burned brighter than I'd ever seen them, pulsing silver through breaks in the heavy clouds. I walked side by side with Adam, our breath smoky, avoiding his gaze as he opened the door for me and put his gloves and keys on a little side booth.

"What can I get for you?" His voice held a funny mix of nervousness and fearlessness over the twanging country music.

"Coffee." My hands shook just a little. I stuck them in my pockets, feeling a bit overdressed in my delicate winter outfit in a place that served Big Country Combos and root beer. Or I would have, if I didn't look like I'd crawled out of a hole in the ground.

"Are you sure? Anything else?"

"No thanks. Just coffee, really hot. With cream and sugar."

I watched him go up to the counter and order, and the fifteen-ish-year-old girl who rang him up neither blushed nor fumbled like Judy had done with Carlos. Of course not. This was Adam Carter, after all. Humble and plain. So simple you almost missed him, like one of those multiple-choice answers that you can't believe they'd be dumb enough to put right there on the test.

"Here you go." Adam set my coffee down on the table complete with napkin, stirrer, and little packets of cream and sugar. He went back to the counter to get his cup and sat down across from me. Right next to his head hung an old framed photo of a long brick building, reading, BUFFALO GAP HIGH SCHOOL.

"Is that a joke?" I pointed, avoiding the stares of patrons on our dirty backs.

"The high school?"

"The name. That can't be real."

He smiled into his cup. "Do you really want me to answer that?"

I'd sort of stopped jotting down stuff like ridiculous truck names and lawn ornamentation in my *Southern Speak* journal, but this was pretty good. I considered.

"You don't put sugar in your coffee?" I dumped in my second packet.

"No. Southerners like their tea with sugar and their coffee without."

"That figures. In Japan we like our coffee with sugar and our tea without. And tea, by the way, should be green."

"Tea should be black."

I didn't flinch. "Tea should be hot."

"Tea should be cold."

"Beans should be sweet."

Adam grimaced. "Don't even. . .no. Let's not go there."

I enjoyed my victory, smirking to myself. Picturing the dark reddish-brown, sugary *azuki* bean paste stuffed in traditional little Japanese cakes. Imagine those lined up on Kroger's shelves next to the ham hocks and cornmeal.

We sat there silently until Adam awkwardly ran his hand through the chunk of sandy hair on his forehead. "Sorry if I freaked you out with the no-dating thing. I just. . .want something different for my life, Shiloh. I don't like seeing people tying themselves together as a couple right off or slinking off to dark places to make out or whatever. It's. . .I don't know. Tacky."

I choked on my coffee, grabbing frantically at the stack of napkins. Two patrons with cowboy hats, who'd already gawked at our unusual attire, turned again in our direction.

He shouldn't have mentioned kissing. Not Adam. Not with such a serious face, our tightly wound nerves, and that goofy chili ad with a grinning groundhog dangling just over his head. I burst out laughing before I could help myself.

"What? I just meant. . ." Adam reddened.

"I know. I know. It's just. . ." I turned my head to where I couldn't see the groundhog. "I didn't expect you to say that. Sorry. Go on."

"I know I'm weird, Shiloh. I don't do things conventionally sometimes."

"Yeah. The muddy sweater is a nice touch."

Adam chuckled then wiped a patch of brown stuff with his napkin. "My way isn't the only way to do things. But these are the standards I've set for myself after. . .um. . .significant failure otherwise." He sipped his coffee. "Forgive me if I come across like I know it all. I don't."

"I didn't think that." I poured in another packet of sugar and stirred it. "You're. . .well, different, to say the least."

I stirred awhile longer, trying to unjumble my words. My thoughts, even. "But it's a good different." *I think. Maybe.*

"Really?" He looked up as if relieved and reddened slightly. "Thanks."

For goodness' sake! We looked like two petrified high schoolers from that Buffalo Crack whatever. My hand wobbled, and I spilled my cream down the side of the cup. He wiped it off for me with his napkin.

If Kyoko could see me now, she'd slap me silly.

"You're. . .well, something special, Shiloh." That Southern drawl resurfaced, and I lifted my head. "I'd just like to get to know you better. And see what God has planned for your life."

I loved the way he said it, as if God had big things ready for me, just waiting to burst out. Maybe He did. I didn't know how, surrounded by dinky two-lane roads and cows, but Beulah sure believed Him. I drank my coffee and thought, playing with my stirrer.

Not dating? Not kissing? Not coming inside? What, were we supposed to sit in the parlor and crochet?

"What did you. . .um. . .have in mind?" I attempted tact.

"Well, I don't have anything planned exactly because I thought you. . .you know. Felt differently." Adam turned his cup around on the scratched table, avoiding my eyes. "But. . .um. . .talking about things, maybe with your family and friends."

"I don't have any family. And what things?"

"Yes you do have family. Faye. Beulah. People who love you." A corner of his mouth turned up wistfully. "And what to talk about? I don't know. Your dreams for your life and your future, maybe. Where you think God is leading you and what you plan to do after you sell your house."

He took a deep breath. "And that's all. I just wanted to make my. . .uh. . .intentions clear. So you don't think I'm playing games with you."

At the mention of playing games, Shane's greasy smile slid into my mind, along with his fat wallet of bills. My eyes bounced to Adam's worn coat and then back to my fingers on the coffee cup, one of which still wore a bandage.

My hopeful expression slowly faded. Like the last gasp of a country music croon on the scratchy overhead system, leaving us in a few embarrassing seconds of silence.

"But there's one thing." I leaned forward, tucking stray brown hair behind my ear. "My house. Regardless of what we think, and. . . um. . .feel. . ."

My voice faltered, and I crossed my mud-caked shoes uncomfortably. "I can't stay here in Staunton. If the house doesn't sell, I'm going to be in big trouble."

"Why?"

"Just. . .because." I sipped my coffee, too embarrassed to splatter my mess about back taxes and overdue Gucci credit cards across the greasy Tastee Freez table. "You know I've got a lot of bills and. . .and stuff. That waiting tables and putting price stickers on books won't even begin to put a dent in. And then there's Ashley." I sighed. "The house *has* to sell, and by the end of March."

"Why, because of tax time?"

I jumped so sharply coffee spilled from my cup. "No. Not exactly. It doesn't work that way. But don't you see? If I do sell, then. . .?" I shrugged and took a nervous sip of my coffee. It was back to arguing about tea again.

Adam didn't answer.

I peeked up at him sitting there in the booth, plaid shirt collar poking out from under his sweater. Rough hands holding his coffee cup. Youthful face, but mature from his years of experience. Not so long ago he'd been a virtual stranger, pouring gas in my rental-car tank while I wiped horse slobber off my hands.

"Well, I'm here to see what God has for you, and maybe it isn't Staunton." He looked up soberly. "Maybe it isn't me."

I nodded, hardly daring to breathe.

"But I'd like to find out."

"Okay." I picked up my cup.

"Really?"

"Sure."

Relief and joy spread over Adam's face. But he covered it quickly and lifted his cup to mine. I thought he was going to say, "To us," which freaked me out a little. But instead he announced, "To the starlings."

His old bird joke from the first day I met him. I laughed.

"To the starlings," I grinned, tapping my cup against his.

★　★　★

Starlight flickered over the darkened meadow when Adam eased into the Smokewood Meade development plot, Tim rumbling in behind us in his white pickup. Armed, I might add, with more than enough deer-hunting weapons of all sorts to keep us sufficiently protected.

But nothing Adam or Tim said could have prepared me for the sight of Mom's battered Honda, its sides dented in and windshield wipers and side mirrors torn off. The windshield smashed, littering the dry November grass with glistening shards.

My brand-new, just-fixed, seventy-dollar headlight bashed in.

AND MY RICE KRISPIE SQUARE PLATE EMPTY. *The nerve!*

I slid out of the truck to my knees right there in the snowy ground, unable even to cry.

Chapter 27

The Christmas season had announced its arrival in Staunton with gaudy strings of colorful blinking lights and tacky light-up reindeer. The nicer houses put up more "refined" white lights, but not the purple house down the street. Oh no. They decided to decorate with orange candles in every window, giving the whole place a creepy Halloween glow.

Trinity surprised me. Not only had she moved out of my place, but she'd left her old apartment and moved in with a cousin. The dark circles slowly disappeared from under her eyes, and although I know she still missed Chase on some level, I saw her smile again.

I stood on a stepladder at The Green Tree, helping Jerry dust the evergreen boughs and red ribbons. *Merry Christmas, Chase ol' pal!* I thought spitefully, adjusting the wreath over the door.

Jerry had given Trinity some extra shifts to keep her busy, and surprise of all surprises, handed me an envelope with nearly three hundred crisp dollar bills. Courtesy of Blake, who'd taken my Mary Baldwin College party of thirty—and graciously saved me my tip.

Which meant that, during the month of December, I got to pay my light bill and buy groceries.

As for my car, Beulah paid for my entire repair bill when she heard the news, and Tim and Becky and Adam threw in enough to get my house and car-door locks replaced, since I never found my wallet and keys.

Just my purse, lying there in the empty snow.

★ ★ ★

For Christmas I got invited to more places than I could humanly attend: Christmas Eve with Faye and her Sunday school class, a bash with Stella and Jerry, Christmas dinner with the Carters. Beulah and both generations of Donaldsons haggled with me over the remaining days.

I hauled home more gifts of homemade spice cookies and chocolate-covered pretzels than I could eat, plus new gloves and doggie toys and ice scrapers for my car. Peppermint-scented candles and creamy goat's milk soap from Cracker Barrel's gift shop. And a fat seventy-five-dollar gift card for JCPenney, which I hoarded like Scrooge himself, dreaming of soft knits and clean wool pleats. Fancy designer or not. It had been, after all, a long time since I'd plunked down money for new clothes.

We all showed up for the church's candlelight service on Christmas Eve, too, cold and happy and laughing and excited. Whispering about our Christmas plans. Until the spotlight beamed down on the baby in the manger, and I remembered why Jesus had come. How He'd shown up unceremoniously, much like I had in Virginia, and taken on flesh so He could know our pain. Our joy. Our temptations and struggles.

And not just to know them, but to heal them.

We circled the shadowy sanctuary with flickering candles in our hands: a shimmering group of faces, of uncertainties and memories, both sweet and painful, all joined in solidarity.

The ancient verses gleamed comfort into our souls: "But the angel said to them, 'Do not be afraid. I bring you good news that will cause great joy for all the people. Today in the town of David a Savior has been born to you; he is the Messiah, the Lord.' "

Becky stared into the flickering flame with eyes brimming over, remembering perhaps her empty womb but the full manger. Faye held my hand, her face lit with hope for the new year. Adam stood next to me, one hand on Rick's wheelchair and the other around Todd, eyes glinting gold.

I'd never seen anything like it. The swelling music, throbbing in my throat, as I lifted my voice for hymns. The mystery of simplicity and sacrifice, power and humility. The rustle of Bible pages, whispering, "Draw closer! Draw near on your knees! Come see the One who came in flesh. . .for you!"

For one shimmering moment I knew—without a cloud of doubt in an inky-black winter sky—who I was.

I am Shiloh P. Jacobs, redeemed of God. I will never be the same.

My hands shook as I held my candle, spilling wax teardrops down onto the paper holder.

Like Sweet Potato Pie

★ ★ ★

I could still feel the warmth of flame and candlelight in my soul when Adam led me out into his backyard after Christmas dinner, a light snow sifting down from the laden boughs like powder. It was crazy enough that I'd spent a whole day with his family, helping Vanna bake cranberry-apple pies and playing G.I. Joe action figures with Todd.

My eyes playing hide-and-seek with Adam's blue ones as we set out gold-rimmed china and unfolded red cloth napkins. Firelight glowing on the curves of his face, his sweater smelling of wood smoke and snow, and our fingers intertwined as we bowed our heads for prayer. Now I stared up at evergreen branches and bare twigs stretched across gray—a gaping, open sky, bare and exposed, in contrast to the lush, sheltering canopy of fall. My sapphire blue birdbath wore a crown of ice, fallen maple leaves enshrined as if in glass.

"Is that where you got my Christmas tree?" I asked, breath making a white puff. Adam knew I hated cut Christmas trees, chopped down in the prime of their lives, so he dug up a little pine for me, root ball and all, and potted it. In the spring I'd replant it out in my backyard—for whoever bought the house to enjoy it.

"Over that way." He pointed. Our footsteps crunched in soft snow, and my nose smarted with cold. Began to run. Not the best way to make an impression.

"*Shh*. See that?" He moved his head close to mine and pointed.

"What?"

"There. In the tree." His breath stirred the hair against my cheek, and I could smell the faint fragrance of his aftershave, masculine and woodsy like he'd been hauling in firewood. Actually he had. Maybe it wasn't aftershave.

"Um. . .where?" I gulped.

"To the right of that big turkey oak."

"Turkey what?"

Adam's shoulders jumped with poorly concealed laughter. "Just look." He turned my head with his hand and pointed. "See that red dot?"

"What is it?" I squinted.

"A cardinal."

I shielded my eyes and gazed at the shock of crimson on deep-green boughs, like an oversized holly berry. I'd seen pictures of them before, but never an actual, live cardinal.

Brooklyn claimed one kind of bird—pigeons. Flocks of them, everywhere, always underfoot. And the oversized Tokyo crows that swooped down on people with huge, outstretched wings, smart enough to break into color-coded trash? Don't even get me started.

We watched as the cardinal preened and shook his feathers then flitted off with a dusting of snow. Soundless. Like the silent world around us, as if all noise had vanished with summer. We stood apart again, a cold wind rushing between us. Adam tipped his head back and looked up.

"It's beautiful, isn't it?"

I shivered and pulled my scarf tighter. "It looks kind of sad, if you ask me. All the leaves fallen. All the empty and barren places. So much gray. I guess I'm not much of a winter person."

"Oh, I am. It's my favorite season."

"Winter? Really? I thought summer would be your favorite. It's when you get the most work."

"If you like sweating in the hot sun, it's great. Winter is the only time I really get a break." He smiled. "Not much demand for water gardens and tulips at ten below zero."

"Good point." I shoved my hands deeper into my pockets. "But I like leaves."

"So do I, but there's beauty even in the bareness of it all. See? Look at the branches."

"I know. Empty."

"Okay, yes, maybe. But look at the lines. The sharp contrast of light and dark, cutting across the sky like a knife. Their intersections and shapes. I think it's beautiful."

I watched as my breath puffed mist that dissipated into the cold branches overhead. "You sound like my mom," I said softly, remembering her words.

"Me?"

"Yeah." I shifted uncomfortably. "But I mean that in a good way."

He didn't ask, but I felt I owed him some sliver of explanation. "She changed a lot before she passed away. God did an amazing work in her heart. I think. . ." I pressed my lips together, wind stinging my face. "I think I would have loved her. Maybe I did. Maybe I do now."

If I wasn't careful, I could even say the same words about Adam.

A twinge of embarrassment crept up like a chill. *Why are we even out here anyway?* I shivered, knees knocking together.

"Come on. You're cold. Let me show you your present." He put his hand on my elbow and led the way.

"My present? I thought you gave me one." I followed him, chattering. "The basket of flower-seed packets. Right?"

Odd but nice. A gardener's gift: little dry flecks that would burst with color in the summer.

I'd sifted through them: a blue-and-white Japanese morning glory, a strange ivory flowering vine that trapped and released moths, a burgundy poppy, a sapphire-blue nasturtium, and several others. Some heirloom varieties.

And a short note about something all the seeds and I had in common.

Blue? No. The Japanese thing? No again. They all grew leaves. . .?

His riddle stumped me, but I thanked him anyway. Fortunately Vanna was ready with a pretty, and much less thought-provoking, ivory knit scarf that matched my wool dress coat, and I exchanged it for a tin of homemade chocolate chip oatmeal cookies with dried cherries.

Adam swung open the creaking door of a large, musty-smelling outbuilding, its interior dark and cave-like. It smelled of secrets, bound and stored for years upon years. I leaned forward and peeked inside, tiny snowflakes stinging my cheeks.

"A weed eater? You shouldn't have."

"Funny. Although you could use one around your shrubs." He reached in to a shadowy shelf and produced what looked like an ugly potted stick studded with some gleaming red fruits. "Merry Christmas."

Huh? I took the pot, chilly through my gloves. *Is this some kind of a joke?*

But Adam looked so excited that I studied the pot again, figuring one of us had a screw loose. Then. . .wait. . .that familiar knobby trunk, the corkscrew turns and twiggy branches.

"Is this a bonsai?" My voice raised in shock. I held the pot up to eye level and inspected it in bewilderment, brushing stray snowflakes off the winter-gray twigs.

"Yeah. Sorry it doesn't look much like one right now because it's dormant. But it'll bloom in the spring."

"A bonsai?" I repeated. "A real bonsai?"

"It's a crab-apple tree. I'm keeping it out in the toolshed to maintain a cool temperature without freezing. It should sprout buds around March or April if you bring it inside."

I looked from the pot to Adam in disbelief. "A crab apple? Those gnarly trees you see on farms? Does it have flowers?"

"Pink ones. They'll come out before the leaves if you raise the ambient temperature."

I opened my mouth and closed it, not even teasing him about his garden-ese. "I've always wanted a bonsai! And even in Tokyo, I never, ever had one. How did you know?"

"Just a guess."

I turned the pot around, heart pounding so fast I could hardly look at him. The form curved meticulously, as if it had popped off the pages of a Japanese magazine. "Did you trim it yourself?"

"Yeah, but I've only had a few months. I started it. . .well, awhile ago." In fact, Adam had only known me a few months. Still. Impressive, to say the least.

"But how? How did you learn how to do it?"

"Internet. You can learn to build a spaceship on the Internet if you want to."

I circled the little tree with my hand as if protecting it from the cold. He'd even studded the soil with moss and tiny white Japanese-style stones.

"Did you know that you could sell these and make tons of money, Adam? You're really good. And Asian stuff is all over the design magazines now."

He stuck his hands in his pockets as snow shivered off an overhead branch like fine mist. "Maybe. But that's not what I'm interested in at the moment."

"What are you interested in, then?" I fingered the cold twigs.

"Giving you something to remember Japan."

It struck me suddenly that a crab-apple bonsai was as east-south as the deep-fried sushi I'd joked about with Becky. A farm tree turned Japanese artwork. I let out a silvery breath, feeling something tender rise in my chest.

"And maybe see you smile again, the way you do when you remember your life back in Japan."

My mouth stuck shut. It was too much, all the thought Adam

had put into my little tree. The months and weeks of trimming and pruning without saying a word. The research and shaping and careful arrangement of stones.

Molding his ways to mine in the smallest of details. My heart flickered like the Christmas candle, and I wondered, ever so briefly, if I could do the same.

★　★　★

I was still thinking about my little bonsai, so bare and beautiful and full of promise, when Adam surprised me one sunny afternoon by appearing in Barnes & Noble toward the end of January while I shelved and organized books.

"Do you have a free evening this weekend, Shiloh?"

"What?" I asked, nearly dropping a heavy motorcycle encyclopedia. I stepped down off the step stool and smoothed my hair behind my ear.

"An evening to go somewhere. I've found a place I think you'll like."

"In Staunton?"

"In Charlottesville." Adam's dark khaki coat, which fit him surprisingly well compared to his bulky work stuff, nearly matched his hair.

"Where's that?"

"A city big enough to have what I wanted."

The air glinted with cool Brazilian guitar music and the scent of espresso. "Sure." I smiled, turning my eyes down in sudden self-consciousness. "Who else is going?"

"Tim and Becky, and I've asked Faye, too." Adam cocked his head. "Hey, is she seeing Earl or something?"

"Earl? No. We tried that already." I scooted some books together on the shelf. "It didn't work. Just like most other things in my life. Why do you ask?"

"Well, she said the funniest thing. She said we might think of inviting Earl, since she feels sad he has to be alone this time of year."

My heart skipped a beat. "She said that?"

"Ask her yourself." Adam shrugged. "Should I invite him?"

"Definitely." I took a book from the cart, imagining our triple date. Or since Adam was arranging it, triple nondate. Or whatever I was supposed to call it.

★　★　★

"Where are we going?" I pressed my nose to Adam's truck window like a kid, eyes searching unfamiliar six-lane roads and restaurants. Charlottesville lights and bigger-city traffic sprawling for blocks. "And where did Tim and everybody go? I thought they were following us!" I checked the rearview mirror again.

"They'll be here," said Adam, flicking on his turn signal and veering off the crowded street. "Tim had to stop for gas."

"What's this place? Aren't we going to. . .?"

My voice failed me. I broke off, staring at a building with a dark, Asian-style slanted roof. Tips turned up like bells on a jester's shoes. Low, sculpted pines. Bare Japanese maples. A Japanese-style stone lantern arching over a wooden footbridge.

"You didn't." I let out my breath.

KATO JAPANESE STEAKHOUSE read the sign.

"You did!" I grabbed Adam's arm in delight, scrambling out of the truck before he could even help me out. "It's a Japanese place!"

"Probably not the fancy stuff you're used to, but it's as close as I could find to good Japanese food." Adam slammed my truck door and leaned against it, bracing his coat against the winter cold.

"You're serious? They have sushi here?" I felt tears burning in the corners of my eyes, and not just from the harsh wind.

"I can't guarantee the quality. But they're supposed to. Yes."

"Real sushi?"

"I hope so." Adam smiled. "You hungry?"

I didn't even answer him, my mind so busy sifting through beautiful Japanese memories like handfuls of pearls: salty *miso* soup, deep-green-circled sushi rolls, pink shrimp perched on rice, cups of steaming tea. Earthy, briny, brown soy sauce and pungent ginger slices. Slender chopsticks. The things I had come to love as my own.

"You want to go back to Japan, don't you?"

"Of course. It'll always be part of me. But. . ." I stuck my hands in my pockets. "I guess I can wait to go back."

"Why?"

We stood in silence, watching the cars go by and wind rustle the fawn-colored winter grasses that grew along the edge of the parking lot. Little winter juncos pecked at something by a red Camry.

"Well, my goals are different than last year," I finally replied, playing with the ends of my scarf.

"How?"

"I don't want to live for myself anymore. I'm God's now." Beulah's verse tingled in my ears. *Behold! I make all things new!* I dropped my scarf back in place. "And at the same time I have to keep in mind that—" I broke off, looking away.

"That what?" he prodded gently.

"Well, things are probably going to change pretty drastically if Mom's house doesn't sell." I swallowed hard and glanced at the Japanese restaurant, each stone lantern and sculpted juniper tree catching in my throat.

"Right. The whole house without soul thing."

"Oh, it's got soul, all right. Lowell said the last three people loved it. Said it shined from the inside. But they didn't make good offers, so I'm still in the same place I started." I sighed, eyes smarting in the late afternoon sun. "I don't know what I'll do or where I'll go. But I'm starting to realize it probably won't be Japan."

"Are you okay with that?"

"Maybe. But I have to do. . .something. I can't keep waiting tables at The Green Tree forever. You know that." I scuffed the heel of my boot on the smooth asphalt. "How about you, Adam? What do you want to do with your life?"

Adam stuck his hands in his pockets and looked away, the slight gesture sending a whisper of something lonely through me. As if my future and his forked, irrevocably, into different horizons.

"Well, there's always my business, which keeps expanding. I need to move out and find more space for my tools and things. Hire some new people. If I could, I'd even set up an office. I can thank you for all the ringing phones and new contracts." He nudged me with his elbow.

"Nah. It's nothing. You do good work."

I meant it. From the little I'd seen of Adam actually on the job, I liked the way his hands circled the tiny trees, packing earth around their roots like a blanket. Shoveling and leveling the rocky ground. Cradling his seedlings, moving their pots into shade as the sun shifted. Matching colors and textures like my university art-minor days, filled with swatches and oil colors and paint-stained clothes.

Maybe we weren't so different after all.

Jennifer Rogers Spinola

"So you've always wanted to work with plants?"

"Not really."

"No?" I turned in surprise. "I thought you loved landscaping. You're really talented." A recollection of Adam's neatly pruned shrubs and ferns in contrasting textures flitted through my mind like one of his beautiful variegated basil leaves, striking and fragrant.

"I did people's yards and gardens in high school to earn some money, and people liked my work, so. . ." He crossed his arms over his chest. "I mean, I like being outside and working with my hands. But I didn't grow up dreaming of mulching trees at hotels, if that's what you mean."

Which is exactly what he was doing when I met him.

"But then Rick got hurt, and even though the military pays for most of his treatments, it still changed our lives a lot. Mom had to quit substitute teaching to stay home with Rick. So Dad picked up an extra job after school, but then Todd started to suffer, so I just went full-time and let Dad quit and just teach math. And that's. . .where I'm at now. Don't know when that'll change."

I leaned against the deep blue side of Adam's truck, feeling an unexpected spark of kinship. Both of us stuck in Staunton, doing what we never really wanted to do.

A sports car turned into the parking lot, and we both turned. A noisy gaggle of twenty-somethings emerged, slamming doors, and laughed their way into the restaurant, tearing our silence. The big Japanese-style wooden door fell closed behind them, and I heard the wind again. The trickle of water over the garden pond, all decorated with lanterns and shrubby trees.

"Hey, that looks like my neighbor's garden back in Tokyo." I pointed. "See those ponds and lanterns in the garden?"

We strolled through the white-stoned garden, stepping over a curved wooden bridge where sluggish water flowed through a pond stocked with gigantic spotted *koi* goldfish. I felt sorry for them, so cold and silver, huddled on the bottom, not moving. Streaks of gold and rust on their chilly scales flashing like sequins.

Fish are cold-blooded; apparently they keep right on breathing even when ice glasses the surface. I felt like that suddenly, looking up at Adam and wishing—for the first time in my life—that I could stay in Staunton a little longer. That I could stop time, hovering there in my motionless world, and come to life when everything had straightened itself out. When Adam and I could maybe, just maybe. . .

Adam was saying something about a horse.

"Sorry?" I tilted my head. "A what?"

"Equine therapy. For Rick."

"Oh, like for riding," I said slowly, showing my vast knowledge of all things equine.

"Right. Sitting around is killing him. He aches to walk again. And riding is something he can do without depending on his legs."

I studied Adam there, his reflection glassing the smooth mirror of water. Making him twice his size.

Come to think of it, anyone who'd do for Rick what Adam had done deserved to stand taller than everyone else.

"You gave up a college scholarship for Rick." It misted out before I could catch myself. Empty branches rattling as if by the force of my words. "Jerry told me."

Adam tossed a small white stone from the garden before answering. "It's not a big deal. Rick lost his legs, Shiloh. I hardly think putting off college a few years qualifies as major suffering. And he's. . .well, he's a great brother. I love him."

"I know you do. But anytime we give up something for someone else it's suffering. It's what Jesus did, in a different way. A choice of the heart," I said, looking across the garden at Adam in a sudden burst of courage. "You know something? Rick's a fighter, and so are you. I've never seen people so determined as both of you. You're. . .well, amazing."

I meant *you* as in the plural *you* to include Rick, but it just sort of came out that way. I blushed and ducked down to look at the goldfish, but not before noticing the warmth that suddenly crept into Adam's eyes as he looked at me, like seeing me for the first time. The way he'd looked at me in church, and if I pressed my memory hard enough, maybe before that.

Adam cleared his throat. "I think you're pretty amazing yourself, Shiloh," he said in a tone of voice I'd never heard him use.

"Me?" I squeaked, wishing desperately that Tim and Becky would arrive. And at the same time, over the hammering of my heart, that they wouldn't. That the low gurgle of the water and wind through the shivering shrubs would keep our silence. "I haven't ever given up anything for anybody. Not in my entire life."

Kyoko'd said that exact thing about Carlos. I nearly blurted that, too, then slapped my lips shut.

"Sure you have. For Jesus. You left the old life behind for the new," said Adam, not taking his gaze from mine. "That takes courage. You're here on your own, and it's not easy to step into something new and not look back."

"Oh, I look back," I said, taking off a glove and kneeling to stir the icy water. "All the time. But the funny thing is that old just doesn't look so tempting anymore."

"You've changed a lot." Adam's voice came out bold and direct, just like when he asked to know me better. Unafraid. "We're all proud of you. I'm proud of you." He emphasized the last sentence, just in case I thought he'd pulled a collective *we* as I had done.

Now my face burned poinsettia red. I'd never seen Adam so intense or his eyes so blue.

"Well, you're mistaken when you said I'm on my own here. Not anymore. You've all been my family," I said, finally meeting his eyes. "And I don't know what I'd do without all of you. Tim. Becky. Everybody. Thank you for being in my life." I meant it. My heart suddenly overflowed, and I closed my mouth to keep it in.

All this time I'd longed for family, and here it stood, right in front of me. "Who are my mother and my brothers?" Jesus had asked.

Adam reached out with his palm, both cold and warm, and brushed the hair back from my cheek. He looked as if he wanted to say more, but at that very moment, my cell phone vibrated in my purse.

I sighed and dug it out, the perfect moment ruined once again.

"Becky Donaldson, where in the world are you, West Virginia?" I snapped then looked up as Adam stepped off the maze of barren Japanese maples and lanterns to wave at someone in the parking lot. Tim yakking and slamming the truck door, and Faye following politely alongside Earl, hands clasped.

"Oh, sorry. Hello?" I put the phone back to my ear. *You really need to stop with your preprogrammed messages, Shiloh!*

"Shiloh Jacobs? This is Kevin Lopez from *The News Leader*."

"The Staunton newspaper?" I pressed my ear closed, trying to hear over the crackle of the bad connection and Becky laughing. Earl stomping his feet in the bitter cold.

"That's correct. I see here you. . ."

I lost him. "Hello? Mr. Lopez? I can't hear you." I stepped through the shrubs and mulch in search of a better connection. "But if it's about my mom's subscription, I canceled it. I noticed you guys made a mistake and sent the notice again."

"I'm losing you here, Shiloh. Did you say something about a subscription?"

I pressed my ear closed. "Yes. I canceled it."

"No, it's not about. . .it's. . ." The line went dead. I turned the phone over, moving to call him back and then remembering we'd stopped in Charlottesville, not Staunton. Roaming charges galore. Which I didn't want to strap Adam with, since he technically owned the phone plan.

"Shah-loh?" Becky waved at me. "We got lost! Ya comin'? Or am I gonna have to eat all the sushi without ya?"

Chapter 28

I let myself in with the key under Faye's orange clay flowerpot, its terra-cotta glow deceitfully warm in the winter chill, and checked my watch six times while I waited for her. Paged through a JCPenney catalog, chin in hand, and thought of Kato Japanese Steakhouse. The rice bowls with MADE IN CHINA etched on the bottom, and our Mexican waiter who mispronounced all the Japanese sushi names. The sushi wasn't even authentic—using cheap dyed yellow daikon radishes in place of ginger.

But it was unforgettable. Every bite a poem—of my past and present, all tangled together in one inseparable mystery.

Kyoko. I have to talk to Kyoko.

I checked my watch again then dug a glossy international phone card out of my wallet and dialed on Faye's phone.

"Moshi moshi?" Her voice distracted, soft as if not to wake the neighbors. Of course. Noon here meant after midnight in Tokyo. Not that Kyoko, of all people, cared much for something as frivolous as sleep.

"Kyoko! I got a job!" I slumped back, head resting against the fabric of Faye's blue-flowered sofa. Unexpected delirium swirling in my head. I could imagine my Barnes & Noble lanyard folded neatly in a drawer. My Starbucks apron hung on a peg. Those filthy Green Tree clothes washed. Or no—burned.

"What kind of job? Where? In New York?" Her breath caught. "Are you coming back to Japan?"

My wind sort of deflated, but I refused to let the glow dwindle like a winter sunset, low and pale over blue mountains. "It's here, Kyoko. At a local paper. But isn't that better than waiting tables?"

I scrubbed a hand through my silky bangs, still fragrant from Trixie's scissors at Crystal. "They still had my résumé from last year. And when I interviewed this morning, they practically hired me on the spot. A crime reporter, Kyoko! I'm going to do the crime map and updates and investigations. I start right away. Tuesday. Tomorrow. Jerry's going to kill me."

"Wow, you mean it?" She gasped. "With a full-time salary?"

"Benefits, too. It's not much, you know, compared to"—my face colored—"you. And what I used to have. But it'll do."

"Aw, Ro, that's fantastic! I'm so happy for you!" I heard the chair squeak as Kyoko bounced. "You didn't tell the paper you're moving when the house sells, did you?"

"Of course not. Although I've been thinking about things lately, and maybe—" I broke off, staring into the patch of sun coming through Faye's curtains as I pictured Adam's face. "It makes no sense, but I just wonder sometimes. Maybe I should stay a little longer and just. . .see how things go with him. At least until my house gets taken in March, and then I'll decide what to do." I twisted off my heels, wiggling my toes.

Kyoko apparently hadn't heard me, still hooting her congratulations. "Let's just hope they don't find out about your fiasco with AP, right?"

"The editor knows. I. . .uh. . .told him."

Dead silence. "You WHAT?"

I held the phone out, grimacing. "I figured they'd find out anyway, and I wanted to be on the level. He raked me over the coals about journalistic ethics and then thanked me for being honest."

Static popped for a second while Kyoko seemed to scramble for words. "Seriously? How. . .I mean, how on earth did that happen?"

" 'Then you will know the truth, and the truth will set you free.' "

Something fell off Kyoko's desk, and I heard rustling paper as she shoved it back on her bookshelf with a muffled bang. "What is that? What did you just say?"

"I told the truth." I shrugged. "I'm changing, Kyoko. I'm not hiding anymore."

"Please. No religious stuff, Ro," Kyoko shot back with a snort. "Just let me be happy for you." Her voice softened. "Really. You've been through a lot, and this is good news."

"Thanks." I adjusted the phone, feeling like crying and celebrating at the same time. I mean, here I sat, getting all emotional about a dinky newspaper that wrote up stories on bear hunting and livestock shows.

"What about that farmer? Does he know?"

"No, but maybe it'll show him that I'm really. . .interested. Because I think I might. . .maybe. . .I don't know. I like him a lot, Kyoko." I twisted a ring back and forth, suddenly jittery. "I didn't really before, but. . ."

"You said he's not your type at all!"

"He isn't."

I could almost see Kyoko tapping her nails, probably painted black or that moody plum she liked so much. "Just how interested are you?" Her voice suddenly turned suspicious. "Are you dating? More? What?"

"Not exactly. He. . .uh. . .doesn't date. Per se."

"He WHAT?" Kyoko blew her breath out in disgust. "You're wacko! All of you! I swear!" She muttered something about religious nut jobs.

"I don't know. It seemed a little weird at the beginning, but not so much anymore. You don't have to date to get to know someone, Kyoko. Really. You watch him live. Meet his family and friends. It might not be conventional, but it works."

"Not conventional? Ro, it's absurd!"

I rubbed my feet on the carpet. "You really think it's that strange?"

"You're all just weird down there. Must be something in the pork rinds."

"I don't eat pork rinds."

"Of course not. They're pure fat. Fried fat, if that's even possible." She sighed and shuffled some papers around, waiting so long to speak that I wondered, briefly, if she'd hung up.

"You're not rebounding, are you?" she snapped.

"I don't think I am."

"Nobody thinks they are."

"No, really! He's. . .way different than anything. . .anyone I. . . anyone."

"You can stop stammering, Juliet. I get your point. Just don't wind up in a double-wide eating MoonPies."

I grimaced. "I'll do my best. Although the image is tempting."

"At least you're not seeing Carlos. I still can't believe that little creep showed up in Staunton! If I ever see him again, I'll beat the stuffing out of his pretty Argentinean head." Kyoko let out a long string of heinous threats and then expired into a yawn. "Well. It's about that time."

"For bed? You never sleep!"

"Who said anything about sleeping? I've got a date."

"A date?" I shouted. "At this hour? What time is it there, midnight?"

"Ten after two. It's a Japanese holiday. We're going to Daikeien Game Center in Ichikawa. Ever heard of it? It's this insanely huge place with tons of arcades. Batting cages and stuff. And it costs a hundred yen to get in, Ro! A buck! Can you beat it?"

"With who? You didn't tell me!"

"Of course not! I didn't know until yesterday afternoon. And it's with *whom*. Have you forgotten your grammar there in the verb-impaired South? Tsk-tsk!"

"Tell me!"

"Tell me your middle name, and I'll spill."

"What?"

"Oh well. Time's up."

I bit my lip and considered making up another name, but I felt guilty. Lying didn't come so easily anymore. "Really? You're not going to tell me?"

I must have sounded so pitiful that Kyoko felt sorry for me. She made an annoyed groaning sound. "All right, all right. Kaine, okay?"

"Kaine? As in, AP Kaine? The guy who flirts with the Japanese secretaries and saves all the mayo packets from his nasty fast-food lunchboxes and eats them on saltines?"

Pause. "Yes, that's Kaine," she retorted a little crabbily. "Thanks for spoiling my night out on the town." She sighed. "I've stooped to dating a coworker. That's how bad my life is."

"Don't you even complain about how bad your life is! I doubt you have neighbors who set up plastic deer in their front yards to plink with .22 rifles, do you?"

"You?" Kyoko hooted. "If you ask me, it looks like your life's starting to look up a bit. Next thing you know that farmer will be out on your lawn playing Peter Gabriel. Remember that movie?"

Great. If I argued with her, we'd have a full-scale conversation about constructivism, counterculture, the '80s, and a lack of modern soul, complete with musical references, with poor Kaine standing at her door until two in the afternoon.

I chose diversion. "So you'd better go get ready, right?"

"Ready? You think I'm gonna get dolled up for somebody who eats mayo packets?" I heard her cell phone tweetle. "Hold on." Some muffled talking. "It's him, Ro. I'd better go."

"Have fun." I grinned.

"One last thing. Did you know that John Cusack, the '80s cult-classic heartthrob for more than two decades, never married? One of the greatest ironies of all time."

"Wow. Really?"

"Yep. Then again, neither did Morrissey. Go figure."

Jennifer Rogers Spinola

If I ever figured out who Kyoko was talking about half the time, I'd be a happy woman.

I hung up and listened to the silence of the room then shuffled over to Faye's computer and logged onto the Internet to disperse my good news to the world.

And as I scrolled through my in-box, the cursor hovered over a name I vaguely recognized—an old family friend. I clicked, startled at the brightly colored photos that spilled out. Baby blues and pink of cheeks and Ashley's dark wheat-colored hair falling over her exuberant dimples. Dimples that reminded me of Trinity and, with a deeper pang, of Dad.

Ashley's motherly smile took me by surprise. Proud and exhausted and tender, hands circling a pale-blue receiving blanket, minus the bulk of her pregnancy weight. Her husband, Wade, grinning that goofy smile as he tried to change diapers.

My half sister was a mom. I had a nephew. A half nephew.

She hadn't even told me he was born.

Of course not. I passed a hand along my smooth hair, tied back in its sophisticated ponytail, wondering how things got so ugly between us. Ashley certainly couldn't blame *me*. Even so, I felt a bit left out, a mere onlooker in this important event. Worse, a lurker. Just passing through their photos like any other stranger.

"Hello, doll!" said Faye brightly, making me jump as she rattled her key in the door. "Who's the darlin' baby?"

I spun around. "Faye? You're home!"

"Home and waitin' for yer news, sugar! My lands, yer in a suit! Well, don't ya look like a million bucks!" She hugged me, smelling of spicy jasmine perfume. Something flirtier than she usually wore.

"You got new glasses!" I traced the wire frame. Younger and slimmer than her other roundish ones, in a modern tone of brownish-red.

"Ya like 'em? I figgered I'd try somethin' different." She set down her grocery bags as I moved to log out and turn off the computer screen. "That little smiler somebody ya know?"

"Carson?" I reluctantly dragged the mouse down his photos. Which, I had to admit, looked pretty good. I could almost smell his sweet baby-powder scent. "He's Ashley's baby. Just a month old."

"Things with Ashley any better?" Faye rested a hand on my shoulder.

"What? How? I got a letter from her lawyer demanding copies of the will, but until Shane Pendergrass comes to haul me to jail, I'm not giving her anything. Not one measly penny."

Faye sat down next to me. "Well, of course not, sugar. You aren't obligated to do anything."

I studied her. "But you think I should."

"Not at all. But there might be other ways ya could keep the door open."

"What door?"

"Relationships, sweetheart. Keep the door open to a relationship. Maybe not now, but someday."

"With Ashley?" My mouth gaped. "Are you kidding, Faye? I don't want a relationship with her! Or Dad! Ever!" I crossed my arms.

Faye hesitated. "I know, doll, but not so long ago ya thought the same way about yer mama."

I winced and fresh anger stirred. "Mom was different. Mom changed her life and recognized her mistakes. Ashley and Dad just go on living the way they want and couldn't care less about anyone else."

"Well then, maybe ya can be the one to show 'em a different way." Faye's words came out soft, her arm around my shoulders.

"Me?" I gasped. "What do I have to do with anything?"

"The Lord loves us all, sugar. He died for us while we were still His enemies. Ya might not want a close relationship with Ashley, an' that's fine, but I wonder if ya might consider shinin' a little bit a His love through the crack in that door. So if she wants to change one day, she can."

Great. Here we go again. As if my episode with Chase wasn't enough. Now I'm supposed to be a light to Ashley, too? *Why don't You dump all the weirdos and creeps in my lap, God?*

"I can't help Ashley, Faye. I'm barely a Christian myself."

"A little bit a light on a dark night is better than none at all." She patted my hand as she moved to hang up her coat. "And I think you'll find that when the Lord's in ya, it don't matter if ya been a Christian one day or a hundred. He still works through ya. Still speaks through ya. And still uses ya to draw others to Himself."

Faye had just stepped around me when I reached up suddenly and snatched her hand back.

"What on earth?"

Her *ring* hand.

Chapter 29

Faye tried to pull away, but I was too quick for her. The smooth wedding band I remembered had vanished. Instead a small ring of silvery gold glittered in its place, antique, affixed with a sparkling lavender stone.

"What is this?" I hollered, knowing full well. But I wanted to hear her say it—hear Earl's name slip from her lips like a secret—hear Faye Clatterbaugh tell me, in her own words, that she'd found love.

Love. The sound reverberated through me like a roar of distant thunder.

"I was gonna tell ya anyway." Faye cast bright eyes downward, running her finger along the ring. "We jest. . .we. . ."

"We who?" I shouted, even though she sat right next to me on the piano bench, pretty pink sweater contrasting with the purple stone.

"Me an' Earl. I reckon we. . .well, seems like God's doin' somethin' we didn't expect."

"Well, everybody else sure did!" I felt tears brim in my eyes. Faye enfolded me, and I leaned into her shoulder, gasping back a sudden rush of emotion.

For all my ridiculous mishaps in Staunton, this *actually worked!*

"Are you all really going to. . .?"

"Get married? Yep. I reckon we're gonna."

"What? That fast?" I blotted my eyes, wondering if I'd actually encouraged Faye to take leave of her senses. "You've only known him for what, a couple of months?"

"I know, sugar, but when it's right, well, why wait?"

I couldn't argue. Just hugged her tight, mind reeling over all the implications of Faye Clatterbaugh becoming Faye Sprouse.

"You're going to be a wife again!" I blabbered, releasing her to hunt for a tissue. I shouldn't have said "again," I suppose. It sounded gauche. But Faye didn't seem to notice.

"I'm no spring chicken!" Faye chuckled, taking off her glasses to wipe her eyes. "But I shore feel like one! Like I've done lost my mind, as giddy as back in high school when I met Mack. Dear Lord! I didn't know I had any a them emotions left!"

Her teary face turned toward the photo of Mack on the end table. I wanted to snatch it away, to hide it, to bury it somewhere in an attic, but Faye's hands found it. She turned over the glass gently, stroking the frame.

Two golds touching—one around her ring finger and one curved around the photo.

"I thought you didn't want to get married again," I said hesitantly, scrubbing my face with a tissue as Faye's face darkened slightly, like a cloud passing over the sun.

"I didn't." She swallowed hard, looking down at the photo. "I loved Mack. Maybe I still do."

Neither of us spoke for a minute, and I stared down at the beige carpet.

"Ya see, Shiloh, love ain't what ya see in the books and movies. Forget all the sultry eyes and trips to Paris and women chasin' after yer gorgeous, mysterious man. That ain't real life. My Mack wasn't even real good-lookin', to tell the truth. Nobody ever hit on him or chased me around askin' if he had a brother, like they always show in romance books. But he was my love."

I looked up in surprise at her tender tone.

"Ya know somethin', honey?" Faye leaned forward, looking at me with blazing determination. "There ain't no Mr. Right," she whispered fiercely.

"What do you mean? I thought you just said that Earl. . ."

She grasped my hand and turned me toward her. "Men are *flesh*, Shiloh. They're *human*. Do ya hear me? They ain't all movie stars an' muscles an' bouquets of flowers. That's Hollywood! Young women fill their heads with this idiotic nonsense an' then run out and divorce their man 'cause he ain't what they wanted. He ain't what they read about. Thing is, they cain't never find it 'cause *it. . .don't. . .exist.*"

Faye's bird clock on the wall tweeted the bottom of the hour, but I didn't move an eyelash.

"Listen to me, sugar. If ya don't remember a thing I say, remember this: Love is what you live out every single day, good times or bad. Givin' up things for the other. Changing to accommodate somebody else. Learning to love without all the bells an' whistles. It ain't always pretty, and it definitely ain't perfect. But it's good."

She patted my hand and let it go.

"It's like. . .well. . .like sweet potato pie."

"Pie?" I choked, heart still racing from her speech.

"Sweet potatoes ain't the prettiest vegetable, Shiloh, once ya dig 'em outta the dirt. Ya ever seen one?"

"I guess so. In the grocery store."

"They're all lumpy and crooked and got knobby purple skin. Kinda ugly shape. But once ya cook 'em awhile over God's good ol' refining fire and sprinkle on some sugar and spice, a little laughter and a lotta forgiveness, a heap a mistakes, you'll make a dessert fit fer a king. Lands, one a the best things I ever put in my mouth!"

"Didn't we have that at. . .um. . .Adam's house?" I asked hesitantly, afraid to meet her eyes. "For his birthday?"

"Yep. That's the one."

I twisted my fingers together, remembering the way he'd put the plate in my hands. That scar across his knuckles.

"God's heroes are real, Shiloh," said Faye, tears welling up in her blue eyes. "They fail and make mistakes. They can't complete ya or fulfill ya 'cause only Jesus can do that. They ain't always gorgeous or even good-lookin'. But they'll hold yer hand 'til the day they die an' lay down their life for ya like the Good Shepherd Himself. Now *that* is *real.*"

I heard my cell phone vibrate in my purse. But I didn't move to pick it up. I couldn't.

They'll lay down their life.

Kyoko's voice rang in my head just like I'd heard it on the Tokyo subway: *"Carlos has never given up* anything *for you!"*

And then I felt the weight of Adam's cell phone in my pocket. The cream-colored table skirt reminding me of my newly painted kitchen. The bandage on my finger and his hand reaching out to touch it.

Faye chuckled. "Ain't much mysterious 'bout a man when ya wipe his hair an' stubble outta the bathroom sink. When ya pick up his dirty, sweaty clothes off the floor and clean his toilet. But I tell ya one thing—there ain't a love on this earth that can compare. Do ya hear me, Shiloh Jacobs?"

I moved my mouth, and my voice could only squeak out a whisper. "Tell me, Faye. Tell me what love is."

"Ya wanna know? It's yer husband refusin' to look at some cute young thing in a red dress when ya start to get gray hair and a few extra pounds from the years. It's the way he hugs ya to his heart when yer still in a paper gown on a doctor's table and he just told ya that ya cain't have kids."

She jabbed her finger at me, tears spilling down her cheeks. "It's when he looks at ya, all wrinkled an' old with yer hair in curlers, and says yer more beautiful now than the day ya met and how he'll never leave ya.

"*That's* love, Shiloh. Don't ya ever forget it. Ya might not see it in them books, but that kind a love will fill yer soul fer the rest of yer life."

The soft lines in her neck quivered slightly as she swallowed, tracing Mack's face with her finger.

I followed her with my gaze, down to his reddish hair and gigantic smile. Big shoulders and skinny neck. *"My Mack wasn't a looker,"* she'd said. *"But he loved me."*

He loved me. That word again, with that same wistful tug.

I could see it in Mack's face. The lines squinting at the corners of his eyes, his too-thick eyebrows and unphotogenic, gaping mouth. And her upturned face, looking into his with a laugh.

And yet I'd never seen a couple with so much joy in their eyes as Mack and Faye, frozen right there. *Beautiful.* He was beautiful. Beautiful in his unabashed love for Faye, his proud grin. I held my hands from reaching out.

"Why, Faye?" I wept, taking a tissue on the end table to sponge my face. "What changed your mind about Earl?"

"He's a good man. Life is short, sugar. Sometimes you've jest gotta say yes."

I glanced around the room at the soft peach-colored drapes. The patch of pale sunlight on the carpet, the emerald plants blooming in the brightly lit corner. I imagined Mack peeling off his coat in the doorway, filling the house with his booming presence.

Instead it would soon be Earl standing there, the lines in his face like a weathered barn plank: sturdy, steady, holding up the walls and ceiling with the force of his gentle smile. Surrounding Faye with his simple grace and simple ways.

Not a palace, but a barn. Not a marble slab, but a rough pine board.

The kind that surrounded Jesus when He came to earth, squealing out his first breaths in a manger for animal fodder.

The simple made holy.

Faye said something, and I forced my head in her direction. Tried to focus over my shuddering breath.

"Are you going to move to Earl's?"

"No. He's gonna move in here. There's more space here, an' his business won't hurt a lick if he comes across town."

"But I thought he didn't want to move! Stella said—" I broke off, not sure how much of my behind-her-back plans I wanted to reveal.

"He loves his house. All his kids grew up there. When I first met him, he was real straightforward about not movin', but in the end, sometimes ya gotta give somethin' up, Shiloh. That's what love's all about, ya know."

I pressed my eyes closed, trying to take it all in. The pain and memories that bloomed in a tender corner of my heart, giving way to hope. A new song. Crocuses pushing up tendrils through the snow. Something waking, blinking in a light I'd never seen.

"Greater love has no one than this: to lay down one's life for one's friends."

"Why does love have to give up something, Faye?" I took her hand, suddenly vulnerable as I ran my fingers over her ring.

She closed her hand over mine. "I reckon that's what makes a sacrifice so precious, sugar. The cost. We all give up somethin', or we stay the same, set in our ways. God left heaven fer us, doll, and died fer our sins. I guess we jest reflect the Father."

I sat there awhile without speaking, tracing my empty ring finger until Faye broke the silence.

"I reckon we'll get married right away. In the spring. March, prob'ly. No fancy weddin'. Jest some relatives an' friends, an' Earl's kids and grandkids. We might even do it here at my place, in the backyard, with Pastor Davis."

I imagined it suddenly, Faye in a pretty dress and the wind blowing those grasses in the field. All of us gathered under the blue sky. Daffodils poking up where the snow had been, reminders of glory after loss.

"Would ya mind bein' in my weddin'?"

"Me? You want *me?*" Tears choked me.

"'Course I do! Jest one little bridesmaid, an' I cain't think a nobody else I'd rather have but you."

My hands shook so much I had to scrub them on the knees of my suit, twist them together. Faye chose *me?* The cheater and copier? The one who'd written her off as backward and ignorant and mocked everybody's grits and collard greens?

She laughed and hugged me, and I sat there trying to imagine Faye as a wife. Washing Earl's overalls and kissing him over the pumpkin and tomato vines. I bet her faucets would work better than anyone else's in town.

"Why, ya ain't even told me yer news! Why are ya in a suit?" Faye put her hand on her hip. "An' me blabberin' on like this!"

She studied me a minute then slowly raised an eyebrow. "Yer good news ain't about Adam, is it?" she asked in hushed tones, lips curving into a smile.

"Adam?" I dropped the glossy portfolio of my news articles, half-dug from my bag, splatting its expensive pages across the carpet. "Kind of. Yes."

I hauled the portfolio up and plopped it in my lap, avoiding her eyes. "I've been thinking, Faye, that maybe if I stay here in Staunton a little longer I can find out if. . ."

My cell phone buzzed again, and I reluctantly reached for my purse. "Just let me get this phone call first. Somebody's called me like five times." I picked up the phone. "No, six. And it better not be the septic service, or I'll. . ."

I put the phone to my ear and listened, nodding. Then blanched, barely able to hold the phone to my ear. "What did you say?" I gasped. "You're sure he was talking about Adam Carter?"

I listened, open-mouthed, then slid right off the sofa and onto the floor, hand on my forehead.

Chapter 30

"You can't be serious, Stella. You can't be." I tried to speak, but nothing came out.

"I know. Ain't it great?" I could almost hear her grinning over the line. "I mean, when I heard they was lookin' for somebody to give a scholarship to at that new rehab center, best in the country, I jest thought a Rick right off the bat. There's a heart a gold if I ever seen one, an' I'd be tickled pink if they chose him. So then I talked to my cousin's husband, who works there, and he pulled for Rick's name. And they picked him! He's gonna get ev'rything paid for, Shiloh! All kinds'a new-fangled stuff. Things they're experimentin' with an' whatnot."

"In Atlanta," I repeated, trying to force it into my stunned brain. "With Adam."

Faye looked up then immediately slipped into the kitchen, closing the door behind her.

"Shore! Ain't that a swell setup? Adam's a real nice guy from what I seen of him, an' they'll pay for somebody to stay with Rick for two years. Room an' board. 'Cause Rick's gonna need a lotta support an' somebody to drive him to treatments and therapy and stuff. But after that, ol' Rick'll prob'ly drive himself!"

Stella giggled, sounding giddy. "An' guess what? Chris said he's even got some jobs in Atlanta for Adam—like at the Botanical Gardens and some fancy hotels. It'll be great for him, Shiloh! An' he'll still be close enough he can still check up on his work here every now and then and take some projects. It ain't more'n nine or ten hours by car."

"Nine or ten hours!" I sucked in my breath.

"Other'n his business, he ain't got nothin' tyin' him here in Staunton, does he?"

"In Staunton?" My hands shook.

"Yeah, like a girlfriend or nothin'. I mean, I thought for a while maybe y'all was sweet on each other, but I ain't seen him around in a while, and. . .I ain't wrong, am I? Lands, I'd hate ta goof this one up. I know that Harrison gal come home awhile back, from what Shane said, but I never heard any more 'bout it. Adam got a fiancée?"

"No." I put my head in my free hand. "He doesn't."

"Good thing, 'cause that'd muck up things somethin' awful. Lands, Shiloh—this is the opportunity of a lifetime for Rick! Adam's already given up a college scholarship for the fella, so ain't nothing he won't do, I reckon. God bless him."

I stammered, trying to pull words out of the air and failing.

"So you're saying that Adam can keep his job?" My heartbeat slowed slightly.

"Reckon so. He's got people workin' for him, don't he? That Gabe Castle fella? He's real good, too. Trustworthy son of a gun. Adam don't need to be there personally for everything."

"And that would free up his parents to just stay and take care of Todd. I know Adam told me he didn't do very well until Adam gave up college."

"Exactly what I was thinkin'."

Time seemed to stop. Frozen. Poised on the edge of something great and terrible, like the stillness before thunder. The sun hid for a moment, its shaft across the carpet paling and then fading to gray.

"Is it. . .really good treatment, Stella?" Tears started to quiver in my eyes. "I want Rick to have the best. Do you think. . .?"

"It's the best. No doubt about it. They had over two hun'erd people biddin' on the scholarship. And Rick won. It's like one a them miracles ya talk about. You an'. . .yer mama." Her voice choked.

I sniffled, gathering up my high heels and pulling myself back up on the sofa. Brushing off my suit. "Tell me one thing. Do they have horses?"

My question hung there in midair, echoing against the carpets and curtains and painfully smooth walls.

"Horses?"

"For equine therapy." I tried to steady my voice.

"Oh, is that what that means? My cousin's husband told me 'bout some equine center they got, top-a-the-line, but I figured that was just some fancy machine or somethin'."

I couldn't even laugh, letting the words sink in. "So they have it."

"Yeah, an' a bunch a brand-new swimmin' pools, an' they even do ski trainin'. Ain't that funny? For people who don't got no legs, or arms, some of 'em?" She chortled. "But they say it works. Reckon they could teach me while they're at it?"

I sat there in silence so long Stella "hello-ed" into the phone. I answered back, hearing the laugh track of some daytime TV show in the background.

"Do Adam and Rick know?"

"Not yet. They'll know in about two weeks, I reckon. Why, you wanna tell 'em?"

"No, no. Of course not. I'll let the rehab center tell them themselves." I wiped my face with a sticky tissue. "Thanks for letting me know, Stella. And thanks. Thanks for doing this for Rick." My sentence quivered in the middle like a too-soft Japanese noodle.

"Aw, it ain't nothin'. I had ta blab ta somebody, ya know." She tittered. "Ain't very often I git ta do somethin' for somebody else like you done for me with my cookin' for Jerry. Say, ya'll gonna come over an' help me design that stuff? I got two orders for parties this week! Can ya believe it?"

I firmed up our plans then thanked Stella again and hung up. I put my purse over my arm and pushed open the kitchen door, where Faye was brewing a pot of my favorite hazelnut coffee. Its sweetness steaming out, catching me with an unexpected ache in the middle of my stomach.

"You okay, doll?" Faye looked up from getting two coffee mugs out of the cabinet. She paused as she set them on the table.

I forced a smile. "Fine." I sat down at the table, avoiding any comment about the call. Playing with my empty mug to keep her from noticing my shaking hands. "And I've still got that news for you."

"Tell me." Faye pulled out a chair and put her hand on my arm. "Is it about Adam? I just have a feelin' you an' him. . . I don't know." She shrugged. "Maybe I'm wrong. But do ya think there's any chance you an' Adam might. . .?"

The coffee brewed. I turned my head, watching the sun flicker against Faye's frilly yellow curtains, all trimmed with delicate sunflowers.

"No," I said in as clear a voice as I could muster, clearing my throat and abruptly scooting my chair. "Not Adam. We're. . .over, Faye. And I'm done here in Staunton. I've stayed here too long already. The sooner I leave, the better."

It took all my strength to hold myself in the chair until Faye poured the coffee and we drank, and then I grabbed my purse and fled.

Snow clouds billowed low over the mountains as I turned toward town, misting over the blue curves I'd come to know so well. Flurries peppered my windshield, so thick I flicked on my wipers.

I should have guessed Adam and I would never work out. I pounded the steering wheel with my hand, head spiraling with the irony of it all: I, Shiloh P. Jacobs, had just landed a job in Staunton, Virginia, while Adam Carter would spend the next two years in Georgia.

God, how can You do this to me?

It wasn't fair. Wasn't sane. Wasn't. . .

I laughed out loud and shook my head, pausing at the intersection and waiting for the light to turn. My turn signal clicking out a mournful rhythm.

And then I spotted it: the *Yomiuri Shimbun* that Carlos had brought to Staunton. I'd told myself a hundred times to throw it away, but it still sat there, reminders of a language and world I once knew. I ached to read its pages, trace its kanji characters. But I had no time.

I started to turn my eyes back to the road then suddenly reached over and snatched it up, scouring the column again and again. I blinked. *That can't be right. Am I seeing what I think. . .?*

A car behind me honked, and I hastily threw the newspaper on the seat and punched the gas then veered into the grocery store parking lot. And grabbed up the pages of black-and-white newsprint with shaking fingers.

Chapter 31

On Thursday morning I tried to find my car. Literally. The snow hadn't let up in three days, and except Stella who showed up on my porch in her Yeti suit, kerchief and hood over her be-curlered hair, I hadn't seen a soul. Snowplows couldn't get through, leaving us all in a pale, glittering blanket and giving us an unexpected holiday.

Except I had no one to share it with but Christie.

I took a flashlight out in the yard, stomping through mounds of snow, and held the beam up to a weak blob, snow scudding like mist across its surface in the predawn darkness.

Everything slept in white, buried like lumps under a rug: the rose canes, the remains of the garden, the mailboxes. Stella's giant satellite dish stuck its head out, grinning that octagonal smile.

"I guess this is it," I said, kicking the sides of the sloping mound and digging through until I found a door handle. I brushed as much as I could off with a broom then scrubbed at the rest with an ice scraper until my hands turned raw and red from the cold.

I eased the car door open, trying not to unearth an avalanche into Mom's newly vacuumed interior, and turned the keys in the ignition. Flipped the defrost on high and hit the windshield wipers.

No luck. All I did was spin tires and waste gas. Mom's Honda had frozen into my driveway.

I heard the house phone ring and trudged back inside, Christie at my heels. "Don't bother," came Kevin Lopez's voice. "We've got a skeleton crew who can get the paper out. Just review the information packet I sent you and get started on some photo captions. Meg'll send them later today."

"If I'm stuck here much longer I'm going to *be* a skeleton!" I retorted, peeling off my hat and trying not to scatter snow all over the kitchen floor.

"Then write your own obit because we're busy," he deadpanned back.

No sooner had I hung up and stepped out of my snow-crusted ski pants than the phone rang again. "Kevin?"

"Kevin? Who's Kevin? Yer new boyfriend?" Becky snickered.

Like Sweet Potato Pie

"What about poor Adam? He'll cry his eyes out."

"Becky?" I reached out with one free hand, shivering, to fill my black Japanese teakettle with water. Heart momentarily stopping at what she'd just said. "Kevin's my new editor. I barely know the guy. And as for Adam. . ." I let my sentence expire.

"Congratulations again! We been whoopin' and hollerin' over here about yer new job!"

"Thanks." I turned on the stove, eyes darting to the folded *Yomiuri Shimbun* on the kitchen table. "Why are you calling so early?"

"Oh, I was jest gonna offer ya some septic services." She giggled.

"Not funny." I glared and opened the cabinet, searching for my favorite Japanese teacup.

"So, yer off fer today, ain't ya? I got plans fer ya!"

"Becky Donaldson, if you're dragging me to another Civil War battle reenactment, forget it! I think even the Confederates would've stayed in their tents today."

"Don't be silly! We ain't gonna see no battle. We're goin' sleddin'!"

"Sledding? Is that that thing where you slide around on a cardboard box?"

"Box? What're ya talkin' about?"

"You know, a box. You cut it open and get people to pull you across the parking lot or something." My voice trailed off. As a child I'd seen kids playing in vacant lots and behind the Chinese grocery, but I didn't like the idea of getting wet and dirty.

Becky guffawed a long time, snorting. "A box? You musta lived in New York too long!"

"Why? What do you go sledding with?" I asked crossly, turning off the stove and pouring hot water into my teacup amid a cloud of steam.

"A sled, silly! C'mon! It'll be fun. But I ain't wearin' no dress; I don't care what ya say!"

I stirred in a spoonful of bitter green *matcha* powder. "Becky. You're kidding, right? The only thing I can see of my car is a corner of the side mirror. It'll take a crane to unearth it!"

"Shucks! Tim'll come git ya. His truck's got chains!"

"Chains? Like to strap a snowplow on top? It's not going to work—hear me? Even Kevin told me to stay put!"

"So if we git there, you'll come? Adam's goin'." I could almost hear her waggle her eyebrows.

Oh no. I sighed and dropped my head into my hand. "Maybe

that's good. Maybe I can talk to him afterward and tell him."

"About the job? Shucks, he already knows! Everybody knows! Reckon ya figgered out that news travels fast, ain't ya? Adam's tickled pink."

"No, about. . ." I put down my spoon. "Okay. Yes. I'll go. I just need to talk to Adam afterward."

"Aw, we can arrange that," said Becky with a telltale laugh in her voice. "How much time ya want? Four hours? Five?"

"I think thirty minutes'll probably do it," I said so softly Becky probably didn't even hear me.

★   ★   ★

An hour later I stood on top of a hill at Mary Baldwin College, arms crossed against the wind, while Tim and Becky tried to convince me to sit on this wooden thing called a sled. Adam and Todd stomped through drifts at the bottom of the hill in coats and boots, hauling a second sled to the top. People scattered across the vast hillside, laughing and gazing up into gray clouds, which had broken into glowing chunks like bright marble. A faint hint of sun sifted through among the spitting flurries.

"Why are we here again?" I hugged myself, shivering. Tim had made it to Crawford Manor, all right. Right before the snowplows did. Scooting his pickup through snowy roads to something by Hank Williams, spinning dirty white under his snow tires.

"This is where ev'rybody comes. Look around! It's the best hill in town!"

I didn't budge. Christie pulled on her leash excitedly, and Becky let her snuffle around in the snow, tail wagging. She snorted with delight as flakes fell all around her, open-mouthed in a laugh, straining to trot down the hill. *Et tu, Brute?* I scowled.

"C'mon!" Becky rolled her eyes. "Don't be a baby, Shah-loh!"

"Todd ain't twelve yet an' he's been doin' it fer years!" Tim grinned at me, poking my shoulder. "I thought you was a tough gal!"

I glared at Tim and his shaggy mullet, which hung out from under a blaze-orange hunting cap so bright it hurt my eyes. "Do you really think this is a safe sport? If it *is* a sport? Do they have it in the Olympics?"

"Don't tell me you ain't never been sleddin' before, Yankee!" he guffawed.

"Of course I haven't."

Everybody stared at me—including Todd, who mounted the hill and dropped the sled, ears and cheeks red under his blue wool hat. "Yer serious?"

Adam grinned. Snowflakes stuck in the lock of hair that hung over his forehead, and he looked funny. Adorably so. I turned my eyes away and stared down at the hill again, trying not to think about him any more than I had to.

"I don't see any medics," I said, my voice coming out quivery. "Is this legal?"

I'd never seen Adam roll his eyes before, but he did. He thrust a sled at me and pointed. "Sit. Like this." He set his sled down on the smooth spread of white and sat down, feet in front, gloved hands gripping the sides. "It's no big deal, Shiloh. You can do this. Come on—I'll race you!"

I threw my hands up in surrender and awkwardly straddled the sled in my snowy boots and pink ski pants, gripping the rope loop at the front. Todd and Tim held my sled steady while I reluctantly sat down.

"I don't know about this. What if I break something? Is Mary Baldwin going to reimburse me?"

I flexed my gloved fingers, their soft, woolly pattern smiling back at me in pink, blue, and gray snowflakes. A pity I'd probably never see them again—crumpled with my lifeless form in the snow at the bottom of the hill.

"Haven't you read *Ethan Frome*? You know what happened to him, right?" I turned to Becky to describe in mangled detail, but I didn't finish my sentence because Tim shoved me down the hill. The wind sucked the rest of my words out of my mouth, and I felt myself sliding, shifting, and then breaking into a fast rush of wind and smooth snow.

Adam's dark coat zigzagged across my bumpy vision, getting smaller and smaller. My stomach leaped into my throat, then my mouth, and back again. I felt lighter than air. . .wind whistling around my face. . .hat fell off. . .and then suddenly it slowed.

I lurched to a stop and crumpled sideways into a soft pile of snow.

Christie barked at me, far-off, from the top of the hill.

I'm alive. I'm. . . I flexed my surprisingly unscathed arms and legs, looking up at dark forms of trees, spindly with winter, stretching into the gray sky. Falling snowflakes kissing my cheeks with tiny, frozen lips.

I'd just started to get to my feet, reaching for the half-buried sled in a drift of rough, powdery snow, when a pair of boots appeared by my head and a gloved hand reached down for mine.

"You okay?"

"I survived." I reached out as he helped me to my feet.

"You survived? Come on, Shiloh. You liked it! Your eyes are shining!" Adam grinned at me. He wiped some snow off my forehead then dusted off my hat and put it back on my head. A snowflake caught in his eyelash, and he blinked it away as he adjusted my hat. The color of his eyes matched the ridge of trees in the distance, a sort of smoky gray-blue.

"Okay. I liked it a little. Maybe."

"Whatever." His gloved fingers brushed my cheek as he pushed my hair back, and I didn't pull away. "So are you going to sue the college now?"

"Depends on how the next round goes. You never know what could happen."

You never know what could happen. Neither of us moved. Our breath misted, and I felt my heart speed suddenly, flooding my cheeks with heat.

Our faces came so close I could smell his aftershave-sweater-truck scent, and for an instant I thought he might kiss me. I caught my breath, my footing in the deep snow feeling unsteady, and he reached out to catch me.

Chapter 32

Our fingers laced together briefly as he helped me into a tramped-down area where my boots found a bit of traction.

But then Adam let my hand go. He took a step back and scooped up a snowball. And *threw* it at me! *Of all the. . .!* It splatted on my shoulder, a handful of moist white.

"What do you think you're doing?" I scooped up my own and hurled it at him. He ducked, and it sailed over his head. Adam laughed and started carrying his sled back up the hill, glancing back over his shoulder with a wave.

I put my hands on my hips then finally grabbed my sled and marched after him through the smooth drifts, scooping up another snowball with my free hand.

We neared the top laughing, red-faced. My hair hung in damp strings. I'd lost one glove, and when Adam finally found it, I could barely move my stiff fingers to stuff it on. My feet had frozen inside my boots.

On top of that, Adam baffled me. I'd never seen him so relaxed, so. . .cheerful. Wasn't he all business and no fun? Stuffy, nondating prude who rarely cracked a smile?

And why, why did he have to smile at me like this now, right before I broke the news?

"Listen. I. . .uh. . .need to talk to you about something. After this." I sniffled in the cold wind.

"Becky told me. I'm so happy for you." He reached over to brush a snowy strand of my hair back under my hat as we crowned the hill.

I stumbled in a drift, Adam's smile suddenly locking into place. My job. Staunton. Staying. *He thinks I'm staying so we can. . .*

Oh no. Oh noooo. . . . I covered my face with my hands, everything around me spinning in a white and gray blur.

"What? Isn't that what you wanted to tell me?"

Tim hollered something, waving for the sled, and Adam grabbed my sled and trotted the rest of the way up the slope, leaving me mucking through the snow a few paces behind.

"You goin' again?" Tim punched my arm, shattering the poignant moment like a broken halo. "Scaredy-cat?"

"I guess." I took wiggly Christie from Todd. "Since there's nothing else to do around here except freeze."

I did go again. And again. So many times I lost count. I raced Becky, NASCAR-style, while Tim played commentator: "Here they go fer the final lap! Jacobs in the lead headin' toward the pit, and oops, there she goes, folks, off the track!" The others cheered us on from the top, waving and shouting.

Zooming faster and faster, learning the pull of the sled and how to lean right or forward to change directions. The exhilaration of going over bumps and being, for a few short, dazzling seconds, airborne.

Becky snuggled in Tim's arms, lips purple. "Coffee, everybody?"

"Coffee." I breathed it out like a sigh, imagining the steaming cup. Cradling snowy Christie to my cheek to feel her warm breath.

"Hot chocolate?" Todd raised a hand. "Please? I hate coffee."

"No Starbucks." I rubbed my hands together, hardly believing my own words. "I've seen enough of it for a while."

"I'll see what we can do." Becky shook the snow off her knitted hat and whacked Todd with it playfully. "Hey, squirt, why don'tcha ride with us over ta the coffee shop?"

"Can I take Christie?" He cradled her carefully in the crook of his elbow, his face bouncing from Becky to Adam to me. I gave a thumbs-up.

"Deal." Becky winked at me and waggled her eyebrows, elbowing Adam. "I reckon we'll take the looooong way over. With plenty of time, if ya know what I mean. Ya won't get lost, will ya, bro?"

Adam laughed and shook his head as he opened the truck door for me. I scooted my snowy self into the truck, which smelled different than Mom's car—a combination of aftershave and musty interior and potting soil, from bags tucked behind the seat. Business flyers and a ledger sat on the dash.

I moved a jacket and clipboard and buckled up, knees shivering, until Adam jumped in next to me and turned on the truck. I plastered my hands to the vents as Adam reached over and turned up the heat.

"You know where we're going?" I felt nervous suddenly inside closed doors, not sure what to say. My voice sounded squeaky in my ears.

"Yeah. There's this one little place they love. The coffee's pretty terrible if you ask me, but don't tell Becky that."

As he glanced over his shoulder, hand on my seat back to check before backing out, I flipped down his visor and scrubbed the mirror clean. Pulled off my hat and tried to tame my hair, which stuck in all angles like I'd gone through a car wash without a car. The little makeup I'd slapped on this morning had fled with the geese for warmer climes.

Adam turned the wheel and started to move then abruptly shifted back into PARK, truck idling.

"What?" I looked up from the mirror and flipped the visor closed. I couldn't do anything short of a week-long shower and emergency call to Trixie.

"Shiloh, you're. . .you're beautiful."

Something electric tingled in my stomach, like when I went over a bump on the sled. Weightless. Floating. For a split second. I felt my mouth open, wobbly, and closed it.

"Oh no. Not now." I let my face sink into my hands.

"Yes, now." He colored a little and fumbled with his keys, which dangled from the ignition. "I think you're most beautiful when you're like this."

"No, I meant. . . Wait a second. You think I'm beautiful when I'm a mess?" I lifted a clump of hair in horror. Not sure how to undo the word tangle we'd both stepped into.

"Yes." Adam pulled a glove off and smoothed my hair with his hand. I felt the tip of his warm palm rest on my cheek.

"Is that supposed to be a compliment?"

"Yes, actually. It's just that I love seeing you this way—happy, free, not caring how you look. You're a pretty girl, Shiloh, but your heart is what shines the best."

"Thanks." I fumbled shyly with my gloves, remembering how not so long ago I'd bought thousand-dollar scarves and jackets and highlights to create some image I hoped would make me worth something. Make me forget my past.

"I mean it. You're not plastic. You're real and alive." Adam touched a strand of my hair and let his hand rest on my shoulder. "Not trying to impress or be someone you're not."

Oh the irony of his comment in light of my years of lies and debt! My hands trembled so much I knotted them together.

For crying out loud. Adam Carter certainly wasn't making my dilemma any easier.

"Adam." I forced my mouth to move. "I told you I needed to talk to you." I sucked in my quivering chest.

"About what?"

"About us."

"What about us?" I thought I heard the soft catch of his breath over the drone of the air vent.

I opened my mouth to speak, fingers cold, and then—my evil nemesis—the cell phone. Adam's. Beeping from his pocket in irritation.

I mentally banged my fist on the dashboard while he answered, eyes drifting away from me and coming to instant attention. Widening in shock.

"What? In Charlottesville? Today?"

He glanced at me with open jaw then hollered into the phone. "Go! Go! I'll take care of Todd. Just come back to Mary Baldwin! We're still here."

"What's wrong? Is Becky okay?" My hands flew to my mouth.

Adam pressed the phone off and turned to me with a dazed expression. "Tim just called," he said, running a hand through his hair. It stood up in a messy wad, damp with melted snow.

"Why? What's wrong?"

"You won't believe it!" He reached for the gearshift, jerking it into REVERSE. "Shiloh, you just won't believe it!"

And he backed out into the snowy street.

Chapter 33

What?" I shouted, throwing my hands forward into the dash and knocking Adam's stuff off. I scrambled to pick it up, mouth gaping. "Are you serious?"

"Yeah! I can't believe it myself!" Adam rubbed his hand across his jaw, eyes wide, and then laughed out loud. "That's fantastic, Shiloh! Oh, we have to pray!"

His hand found mine as he reached for the gearshift, and we awkwardly squeezed them together. "Pray hard! They've been waiting for this for years, and it's never panned out."

My eyes fluttered shut as I remembered Becky and her baby-name book. Her hand curving over her pregnant belly as if trying vainly to protect it.

"They're going to Charlottesville today? In this snow?" I craned to see out the window. A snowplow squeaked by in a patch of sun, lights flashing. Dumping piles of snow into fat, vertical drifts on either side of the road.

Adam glanced at his rearview mirror and edged out into the street, tires dropping down into glossy, hard-pressed tracks. "Right now. The interstate's supposed to be clear."

I waited, heart pounding, for Tim's truck to pull up—and when it did, I leaned forward to memorize the look of dead shock on their faces. Becky's mouth hung open, fingers clasped loosely across it.

"It probably ain't nothin'!" she finally managed, waving away some snowflakes that blew in the open window. "Don't wanna get our hopes up! We're jest gonna check it out."

"G'won!" I shouted to her, Jerry-style, waving my arm. "Git! Call us when you get back!"

I pulled open the door for Todd to climb in with wiggly Christie, letting in a blast of cold air, and scooted the seat forward so he could squeeze behind.

"So much for coffee," I joked, slamming the door and adjusting the seat back. "Not that I'm complaining."

My fingers, which wrapped around the edge of the seat, brushed Adam's as he shifted gears, and I pulled my hand away, suddenly self-conscious in front of Todd.

"Says who?" Adam glanced over at me. "Come over. We'll fix some at home while we wait."

And he grabbed his cell phone, punching in numbers at the stoplight and putting it excitedly up to his ear.

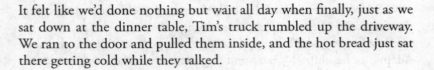

The afternoon stretched endless. Not from boredom, but from waiting. And guessing. And speculating.

And so we mixed butter and sugar for cookies and preheated the oven, recounting everything to Vanna, who sat down in shock, the unopened bag of chocolate chips still in her hand.

When she finally got the scissors, her face had a hopeful look.

"I really hope it works this time," she said carefully, wedding ring glinting in the overhead light. It matched her blond hair, shoulder length, a shade or two lighter than Adam's.

"This time? Was there. . .another time?" My head swiveled between the two of them.

"About a year and a half ago. The birth mother changed her mind and decided to keep her. I think it was a her." Adam washed a measuring cup, flour on his shirtsleeve. "They'd gone to the hospital and bought baby stuff and everything."

"Oh no." My heart sank.

"Of course it's always good when a mother can keep and love her child," said Vanna gracefully, passing the bag to Todd to measure out. "But I know Tim and Becky had a rough time with the whole process."

I could see Tim's cowboy boots walking sadly away from the waiting room at the hospital, empty-handed. The sympathy flowers. Becky's teary eyes. It still felt so raw, even for me. *Oh, Lord. . .make this their first miracle of the year!*

And I fixed my eyes on the silent phone, praying for it to ring.

It felt like we'd done nothing but wait all day when finally, just as we sat down at the dinner table, Tim's truck rumbled up the driveway. We ran to the door and pulled them inside, and the hot bread just sat there getting cold while they talked.

"Ain't so much ta tell jest yet," said Tim, obviously shaken. He sat down at the table, forgetting even to take his coat off. "They just told us the heartbreakin' story of this li'l newborn baby girl, how her mom's goin' through some hard times and can't provide fer another baby."

"Does she have a name?" I interrupted.

"Courtney." Becky twisted a napkin in her shaking fingers. "The nurses named her. That's all we know. But she was born four weeks early—jest a tiny little thing. They all thought she wouldn't make it, but she's a champ, and she did. Ain't got no problems that they know of, 'cept she needs somebody ta love her."

Her eyes watered, and Vanna reached over and squeezed her hand.

Nobody touched the lasagna. I stared into my quivering water glass, willing myself not to cry.

"So you're going back Monday? To see her for the first time?"

"That's right. They didn't have a pitcher of her 'cause of all the snow. Lady who has the pitchers on her digital camera couldn't come in."

Becky dropped the fork she was playing with, fingers quivering. I got up and poured her a cup of hot coffee, and she sipped it. "'Course if ya'll can come with us on Mondee, I'd be honored."

"You mean to the hospital?" I gasped, the coffeepot tipping in my hand. I jerked it upright. "In Charlottesville?"

"Yep."

"You wouldn't. . .mind if we came?" Adam leaned forward.

"Mind?" She punched him playfully in the arm. "Lands, it's gonna take ev'ry ounce a strength I got jest ta walk into that place, thinkin' I might be seein' my own little daughter fer the very first time!" She paused to regain her composure. "'Course it might not work out. But we gotta try, right Tim?"

"That's right, sugar." He put his arm around her. Then he seemed to remember he still had his coat on, and he shrugged it off. He ran his hand through his wild hair, eyes faraway and glazed.

"It would be so much easier if y'all'd come along. Yer family, ya know. All a ya." Becky's coffee cup clattered against the teacup, and I mopped up the spill with a napkin.

"Won't you want some privacy?" asked Vanna. "It's an important moment, Becky. Think about it."

"Privacy? What do I need privacy fer? It ain't like I'm gonna be givin' birth or nothin'," said Becky, making us all titter. "Best thing y'all ken do is make sure I don't do nothin' stupid to make 'em think I'm unfit!"

I chuckled to myself and thought fast. "Monday, Monday. . ." I doubted Kevin would give me another day off after my snow day, but maybe I could. . . "Hey, how close is University of Virginia to the hospital?"

"Shucks, I don't know. Ought not to be too far."

"Kevin wanted me to do an interview there. Maybe I could schedule it for Monday afternoon and then—"

Becky's eyes brightened, and she wiped them with the back of her hand. "Really? Ya think ya could?" She wiped her nose and pulled out her cell phone to call Faye. "How 'bout you, brother a mine?"

Becky turned to Adam, and Vanna smiled, a warm smile that glimmered over the top of her coffee cup. Becky set her cup down and squeezed Adam's shoulder, and he patted her hand.

I pretended not to notice. Instead I shook the melting ice in my glass, refracting against the clear sides like little rainbows. Vanna obviously loved Becky as much as Becky loved the Carters. Their friendship went way back—much further than mine.

I wondered, in a split-second thought, if Vanna and Cliff could ever love me the same way. Could ever think of me as a daughter, or at least a close friend—or give me that same fond smile they gave Becky.

But no. Like everybody else, Vanna would probably hate me, too, when I packed up my suitcases and left Virginia.

★　★　★

"So what did you want to talk to me about?" Adam's breath misted as he stood with me off to the side of Tim's truck. Engine running, sending up puffs of exhaust into the barren overhead limbs. A lantern bleeding pallid light across a sparkling snowdrift.

I put my hands in my pockets and turned to face him, hating to burst Tim and Becky's hopeful bubble with sour news. "I'm leaving."

"You mean like for a vacation?" Adam's brow quirked.

"No. For good." I pressed my lips together in the cold, looking away. "I've applied for a job at *Yomiuri Shimbun* in Osaka."

The look that spread across Adam's face made me stare down at my feet.

"What? You mean you're. . .?" He shifted there in the lantern light, the glow illuminating the hard lines of his eyes. "But you don't even know if you've got the job or not! I mean, I know it's what you've always wanted, but I thought. . ." His mouth hung open.

"I know the editor." I brushed my hair out of my face, shivering. "He just became editor last year, and he's always loved my work. He said"— my voice cracked, and I cleared my throat to steady it—"He said that job announcement expired ages ago, and they still haven't hired anyone. But the job is in the bag if I want it."

"You called him?" Adam sounded angry. Or grief-torn. I couldn't tell which. But his arms crossed tightly across his dark coat.

"Yes, I did. Now I just have to wait for some interviews and things. And then they'll. . .well, they'll send tickets." I swallowed hard. "I'm sorry, Adam. I didn't plan on things being. . .you know. This way." I scuffed my shoe in the snow. "I'll have to find a home for Christie, and. . ." My voice trailed off. "I'm sorry."

Adam stood silent a long time, looking down at me with an expressionless mask. Swallowing.

"So you're going to go if they offer you the job?"

"Yes. I've decided. Staunton just isn't for me, Adam. I can't stay here."

Tears had formed in the corners of his eyes, and he threw out his arms. "What about your house? You're just going to leave it?"

"No. I'm going to lose it in March anyway."

"Lose it? Why?"

"I just. . .am."

Adam gave a sort of angry snort and turned away, stamping the snow off his boots. "Is Japan what you really want, Shiloh? I mean, I tried to. . ."

I froze, unable to move a muscle. Thinking of how thousands of times I'd played that question over in my mind, always ending with *yes*. And suddenly I couldn't answer.

"I hope we can still be friends," I replied instead, tears spilling cold onto my cheek.

And with that, Adam put his hands in his pockets and stormed into the house, leaving me standing there in the snow.

Chapter 34

"There they are! I see them!" Todd called from the darkening window, face pressed toward the outside. A ring of condensation where his breath touched the cold glass.

"They're here?" I leaned forward, looping my purse over my shoulder. My scarf draped over my arm, limp as my legs from a long and sleepy wait.

Our little welcoming party in the University of Virginia Medical Center had grown: Adam and Vanna and Todd, plus Faye, plus Tim Sr. and Jeanette, plus Becky's parents, Tina and Pal. We probably looked ridiculous—all jabbering over a baby that might not be the answer to our prayers, and nobody knowing quite what to say. And yet every last one of us giddy with nerves, hiding smiles, tense with roiling delight just under the surface.

The sliding glass doors opened, and in strode Tim and Becky, looking nervous and out of place in their simple winter coats, heads gawking at the enormous, high-tech lobby. Tim's polished cowboy boots under dress pants. Becky's smiling mouth, coral-colored with fresh lipstick.

We all rose as if watching a bride escorted into the church.

Walking beside them, nodding and laughing, came a small, curly-haired woman who we assumed represented the adoption agency. Her friendly face and gentle manner instantly put us all at ease.

"I'm Hannah," she said, her brown eyes sparkling as she shook our hands one by one. "It's so nice of you all to come. Are you family or friends?"

"Family," said Becky firmly before we could respond. Cheeks white and pink with cold, bright pink scarf tied firmly around her neck. "All of 'em."

I felt my breath catch in my throat, shallow-breathed. The way I'd felt when Faye asked me to be her bridesmaid.

My eyes found Adam's from across the room, and he gave me a brief smile before looking away. I smiled back then glanced away, too, catching my fingers together to hide the emptiness I felt. Remembering his voice over the phone on Sunday afternoon, as I stood at the kitchen window looking out over lifeless trees.

"I'm sorry about the way I acted, Shiloh," he'd said. After I'd skipped church and spent the day praying, putting my final résumé together and even packing up a few boxes. "I just wasn't expecting you to move back to Japan so suddenly. Not in a million years."

I didn't know what to say. "I'm sorry, too," I replied. "I guess things sometimes work out differently than we expect." I wanted to say "hope" instead of "expect," but I refrained.

"I wish you the best. Of course we'll be friends. It might be a little awkward for a while, but we can do this."

"Thanks, Adam." I stood there holding the phone, thinking of a thousand words I wanted to say but couldn't. And hung up the phone as a dull chill settled over the house. I felt ready to move suddenly—ready to pack up and leave this portion of my life behind me for good.

I'd accomplished what I'd come for in Virginia—to settle my past and deal with Mom's house. To restart my life. And now it was time to go.

"What a wonderful and supportive family you have," Hannah was saying to Becky, and I looked up, surprised to find Adam's eyes still on me. They bounced away quickly, as did mine. "You're a lucky couple, that's for sure. I've never seen so many family members at a meeting like this!"

Tim looked around at all of us, and down at Becky, then slid his arm around her. "I know," he said mistily. "We call it blessed."

Tim Sr. swallowed hard and blinked, and Jeanette reached into her purse for tissues.

As if on cue, Hannah opened her arms in a happy gesture. "Ready?"

Tim grinned. "Let's git this show on the road."

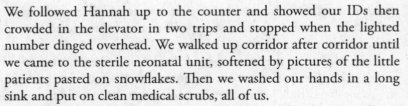

We followed Hannah up to the counter and showed our IDs then crowded in the elevator in two trips and stopped when the lighted number dinged overhead. We walked up corridor after corridor until we came to the sterile neonatal unit, softened by pictures of the little patients pasted on snowflakes. Then we washed our hands in a long sink and put on clean medical scrubs, all of us.

"We can't go in all at once, so maybe Tim and Becky can call you in separately," directed Hannah in her scrubs, looking nonplussed as if she did this all the time. "We'll let them go first and start from there."

We plastered ourselves to the neonatal window, peering in over the rows of tiny babies, doll-like, sleeping in miniature cribs and incubators. Tubes and poles and monitors lighting up with numbers lined the room. Walls decorated with little lambs and angels in soft pastels, a sharp contrast to the room's startling, hard lines of white and silver.

I put my arm on Todd's shoulder and watched a tiny girl with pale brown hair squirm in an incubator, red-faced, almost too small to be real. Courtney, perhaps? My heart fluttered. She flailed fists, hooked up to so many tubes my hands clenched in sympathy.

But of course not. The hospital wouldn't release a child in such precarious condition.

We fell silent, watching as Tim and Becky entered in their scrubs, looking around with nervous eyes. They followed Hannah through the maze of cribs, and she paused to speak to several nurses on duty. Nodding and gesturing.

Then Hannah smiled and stepped forward, motioning with her arm.

We rushed to the next window, still trying to see, and one of the nurses gathered up a little bundle from the far corner of the room. Something wrapped in a pink blanket.

She lay the bundle in Tim's arms, and a hush fell over all of us.

There lay Courtney. Skin the color of chocolate, soft black curls covering her tiny head. Her eyes, so full of black lashes, closed in drowsy half sleep. They flickered open, and she blinked, showing the darkest baby eyes I'd ever seen. Tiny pink rosebud lips. She turned slowly from one face to the other and then up into Tim's upturned face as if trying to understand.

I tried to read Tim's face, his parted lips and down-turned brow, but I couldn't tear my eyes from Courtney. Looking up, up—a long inquisitive gaze. She blinked her eyes and squirmed. The she reached out and, as if in slow motion, wrapped one tiny brown hand around his bony white finger.

Tim looked at the baby, then at Becky, and then turned to all of us with a kind of weepy astonishment on his face. He passed a trembling hand over her forehead and through those soft little curls, as if afraid she might break.

I waited for someone to say, "She's black," but no one did.

266

Only Jeanette whispered, "Lands, that's a pretty child if I ever seen one." And Pal murmured back his agreement. "So little."

I couldn't see through my tears anymore. All my makeup had run into a puddle on the floor probably, or onto my crisp white dress shirt. Adam moved a step closer, and we stood there together, side by side with Faye, unable to tear our eyes away from the glass.

"Would you like to feed her?" One of the nurses held up a bottle, her voice wafting through the open door.

Tim and Becky exchanged glances, and Tim reluctantly (and awkwardly, new father-like) passed the blanket to Becky. Courtney still clutched Tim's finger, until finally, one by one, the little fingers released.

Becky stared into her face for a moment in awe, tears dripping, and sat down in the rocking chair the nurse indicated. She expertly turned the bottle the correct way, flat part of the nipple down, and gently offered it as Courtney reached out.

We watched as Becky rocked, smoothing the baby's cheeks with her free hand. Passing her fingertips across the fuzzy curls in a kind of awe, nuzzling the baby toes that poked out from the end of the blanket.

Becky nestled her carefully so as not to jostle her still-floppy neck, face bent close. Voice low and soft. Singing. Becky was singing.

Becky's going to be a mom. I knew it. I could feel it. It burst in my heart so strongly I wanted to shout it down the corridor, waking everyone just to tell them the news.

Macy Alyssa, I wanted to whisper. *Your daughter. The name you chose, flipping through Barnes & Noble baby-name books. It was for her.*

We huddled in the hall as Tim and Becky bid the nurses good-bye. The door closed, shutting the sound of monitors and baby cries behind glass. The squeak of the rocker and whir of machines. Leaving us all in the sterile fluorescent glow of the hallway, spotless white, smelling of soap and antiseptic.

We peeled off our scrubs, nobody really knowing what to say.

Out of the corner of my eye I saw Becky cast a last glance over her shoulder to see Courtney, wiping her eyes, but the closed door and basinets obscured the crib.

Tim still leaned with both hands at the window, deep in thought.

"You okay?" I put a tentative hand on his arm.

"Huh?" He looked up briefly, trying hard to get back the goofy, carefree smile that usually lined his face. "Oh, yeah. I'm good. I jest. . ." He looked back through the glass and sighed, fingers tensing. "I ain't sure if I can do it." His voice sounded strained.

I caught my breath, feeling the hallway freeze into a hard cube of white. Motionless. "Why not?" Memories of skinheads and Southern sin poured back against my will.

Tim turned to me, and for the first time I saw his watery eyes, all rimmed with red. He played with his jacket lapel, Adam's apple bobbing as he swallowed a couple of times before speaking.

"I dunno if I can give her away as a bride."

Chapter 35

"You can thank me now."

"Thank you? For what, Kyoko?" I'd just plopped down at the computer, Skype ringing for me to answer it. Scarf still wrapped around my neck, and eyes sticky with tears.

"Go ahead. Just thank me."

I gathered Christie on my lap and scratched behind her ears, grateful for something warm and soft to squeeze in the otherwise hollow silence of the room. Even if she did gnaw on the mic first and then the chair back.

"Um. . .okay. Sure. Thanks."

"You're welcome."

"Well. . .what did I just thank you for?"

"Solving your mystery. Your riddle."

"What mystery?"

"The seeds. Something that they all had in common with you."

I leaned back in my chair, thinking hard. *Seeds. Something in common. Adam.* "My Christmas present?"

"Seems like you've put so much thought into it," Kyoko snapped. "What is it now, February?"

"Yeah. Sorry. You have no idea what's going on here. We just—"

"Save it! You're hopeless."

"But I've been taking good care of the bonsai he gave me." I let out a shuddery breath, reaching up to stir the tender baby leaves with my finger. It smiled down at me, one swollen pink bud fat with life.

"Adam gave you a bonsai?"

"A crab apple. It's beautiful. It's just getting leaves, and—"

"You didn't tell me he gave you a bonsai! Do you know what that means?"

"What?" I pushed the bonsai back and turned my head away to keep from looking at it. From remembering.

"Giving a bonsai tree as a gift is a gesture of respect and a harbinger of good fortune," said Kyoko as if quoting.

"A harbinger of. . .what? Come on. That sounds like something you'd see on a chopstick wrapper in a Chinese restaurant. And besides,

I don't believe in luck or fortune anymore. Good or bad." I cocked my head. "How do you know all that about bonsai anyway?"

"Well, I got one."

"From who?" I leaned forward. "Kaine?"

"Nope. Guess again."

Kyoko made me feel like pulling my hair out sometimes. "Dave?"

"Don't be ridiculous! Guess, Ro! Really. You'll never figure it out."

"Then why are you asking me to guess?" I snapped, shoulders sagging from the day's emotion. "Just tell me!"

She sighed. "Okay, spoilsport. Theo."

"Theo? Who's Theo?"

"Hello! Book-publisher Theo? The one who wanted to see samples of your 'Southern Speak' journal, Ro! Do you even listen to a word I say?"

"Of course I do! I just. . ." I drummed my fingers on my cheek, trying to recall. "Didn't you tell me he has a cleft. . .something? Cleft lip?"

"Cleft *chin*, Ro! A cleft chin!" Kyoko snarled. "Big difference! And yes, that's the right Theo."

"He gave you a bonsai?"

"Okay, so it was a virtual bonsai, but it could have more than virtual significance."

I put my head in my hands. "How did we get into this conversation?"

"Beats me." Kyoko fell silent. "Oh, right. The seeds."

"The seeds!" I sat up straight. "What do they all have in common?"

She paused for emphasis. "Ready for this?"

"No, but I'm sure you're going to tell me anyway."

"They're rare."

I just sat there. Christie squirmed in my lap, licking my cheek, and then tried to bite the microphone again.

"Uh. . .you're sure?"

"*Tropaeolum majus* doesn't come in that shade of blue most of the time. And your moth vine is really weird. They're rare. Get it?"

"They're rare," I repeated, wrinkling my brow. "As in. . .they're expensive?"

"No, bonehead!" Kyoko shouted. "As in YOU are!"

"I'm what?" Then suddenly it hit me. "You mean he's trying to say that he thinks. . .that I'm. . .?"

Like Sweet Potato Pie

"Yes, O thou of slow wit! Does it always take you this long to catch on to things, Ro? Seriously! Romance is wasted on you, you know that?"

My eyes hovered over the computer screen and out into space as I let it all sink in, feeling the air seep out of my lungs.

"He thinks you're one in a million. Rare. Unique. That's what he's trying to say in his plant way of speaking. You're really lucky, Ro. That farmer might not stop traffic with his looks, but he's all right."

I pounded the desk with my fist and let my head drop. "He's not a farmer! And we're not. . .anything. I don't know how to break it you, but we're done! I'm leaving. Did you check your e-mail?"

Kyoko hadn't heard me, blabbing something about love and youth. If I didn't stop her now, she'd slip right over into the *Pretty In Pink* trap, and we'd be talking about the '80s again. *Please, no! Anything but that!*

"Becky's almost a mom," I blurted, squeezing my trembling fingers together and trying not to look up at the bonsai with its pink unfurling bud. "I think she's going to have a baby really soon. Maybe even this month."

That did the trick. "What did you just say?"

"Becky and Tim. I think they're going to adopt."

"What? Ro, that's really great!" Her voice turned sweet. "Let's just hope she's as redneck as they are."

"I don't know yet. But I imagine she'll pick it up really fast."

"Before long she'll be the expert, living around Mr. and Mrs. White Bread." Kyoko snickered. "No offense, believe me! They're great. They're just. . .really funny."

"Well, it'll be tough for little Macy to turn into White Bread Junior," I said carefully. "She's African-American."

Dead silence on the other end of the line. "Um. . .Kyoko? Still there?"

I heard something thump. Then something crash, like a chair toppling over into a pile of books.

"Kyoko?" I leaned forward, nearly dropping Christie off my lap. "Hello? What's going on?"

No answer, just more banging, and something that sounded like . . .laughter? I jiggled the microphone and clicked the volume up as far as it would go. "Answer me! Are you there?"

"I'm—I'm here! I'm just. . ." Kyoko gasped for breath. Then broke off into another hysterical belly laugh, guffawing so much I turned the volume down.

"What's so funny?" I glared.

"Nothing," she wheezed, chair squeaking as she wept with laughter. "It's fantastic! Brilliant! I just have to say that that God of yours has one crazy sense of humor, Ro!" She broke off again in another round of laughter.

"Why? Because of an interracial adoption?" I scowled, not seeing the connection Kyoko obviously found so funny.

"No, because nobody on earth could have planned something that wild. Tim and Becky with. . . Don't you get it? It's awesome! It's. . .wow." I heard Kyoko pull tissues out of a cardboard box. "If that's the kind of stuff He does, count me in!"

"What are you saying?" I started to think Kyoko was the one who'd lost her mind. "You don't mean you. . .believe in God?"

"Me?" Kyoko laughed again. "God? You're funny, Ro-chan." She pulled out another tissue.

"No, I'm serious."

She paused. "Hey, I think I liked you better when you were rude and arrogant."

"Sorry." I leaned back slightly, letting the mic go limp. "I had to ask."

"Hmmph. Just don't try to foist anything on me, okay?"

"I'm not foisting anything, Kyoko. Any more than you try to foist your weird music on unsuspecting souls like me."

"You just don't have a high enough appreciation of art to grasp the raw, unbridled glory."

"Ditto."

Silence shook the line for a few loud seconds. Then Kyoko's voice: "I can't. . . Oh, Ro, you did not!" She laughed out loud. "That *was* pretty clever, actually. I have to admit."

"Just think about it, okay? Read the Bible or something." I felt grumpy. "And then you can come complain to me."

"Why, so I can become a religious nut job like you?" Kyoko's voice sounded surprisingly tender.

"You could do worse."

"It would be hard." She breezed me away with a chuckle. "But first I need Tim and Becky's address."

"What for?" I sat up straighter. With Kyoko, I could never be too careful.

"To send a baby gift, of course. C'mon, what do you think I am, a heel? They're nice! I'll help them celebrate."

"Nothing too dark or scary. No blood, no monsters, no aliens. No creepy anime comics stuff," I warned. "Nothing with skulls or weird bands or smelling like incense. Promise me."

Silence.

"What's wrong?" I drummed my fingers on the desk.

"Doggone it, Ro-chan," said Kyoko in a pitiful voice. "What is there left to send?"

★ ★ ★

I'd just stood up and was clicking the screen off when Skype beeped again urgently.

"Kyoko?" I reached for the mic again in surprise. "What's up?"

"Is this for real, Ro?" Kyoko shouted. "Tell me the truth! Now!"

"The truth about what?"

"There's this little blurb on the *Yomiuri* insider feed that says you might be coming back to Japan? To Osaka? Am I reading this right?" Kyoko's voice had turned into a cosmic roar. I could imagine the books flying off the shelves, curtains whipping. "And you didn't tell me?"

"Sit down, Kyoko." I sighed, sinking back into the chair. "This is going to take awhile."

Chapter 36

Macy Alyssa Donaldson arrived at Tim and Becky's house on Friday afternoon, a mere four days after their first introduction. We snatched up our cameras and rushed for the front window, where the sharp crunch of gravel under Becky's car heralded their arrival.

"They're here!" cried Becky's dad, taking the front steps two at a time, video camera pressed to his eye, just as Tim cut the engine and we poured out onto the front steps in coats and hats, sharp gusts stinging our cheeks. An iced tree dripped overhead, its thin glass branches clattering together like muted tambourines.

Tim jumped out of the driver's seat, beaming, and waved to all of us as he rushed around to the backseat. "Here she is, y'all!" he hollered, not even cracking his usual goofy jokes.

He swung open the door for Becky, and both of them bent over a car seat then carefully lifted out a lacy, bunny-patterned bundle wrapped in a blanket. Adjusting the blankets around her head to keep out the harsh winter wind.

And Becky walked up the front steps like a Virginia Gourd Festival queen, minus the tiara and green sash. Chin proudly held high. Tucking Macy carefully in her arms and beaming down at the little brown face.

Everybody started to talk at once:

"Atta girl!" said Pastor Davis, patting her on the back.

"Oh my lands!" Jeanette bawled into a tissue. "My li'l granddaughter!"

Gordon brayed and howled, license tags clinking, and I wrapped my arms around him to keep him still as we all made way for the newest Donaldson. Tim barged up the steps, slapping backs and stuffing everybody's pockets with Slim Jim sausage sticks in lieu of cigars.

Macy sucked a finger, curious, taking it all in.

They pushed their way into the living room, all loaded with presents and banners and flickering candles, and the crowd of faces parted, hushed, for the big moment.

"Well, welcome home, gal!" said Becky, teary-eyed, giving Macy a big smile.

274

To everyone's astonishment, Macy gave a cute little toothless grin right back, and everyone clapped and laughed.

"It's meant to be!" Tim put his arm around Becky, looking weepy.

Pastor Davis came forward with Tim and Becky's parents, all surrounding them with loving hands, and he led us in a prayer of blessing for little Macy and the entire Donaldson family as they raised her in the Lord. We mopped our faces, necessitating the quick redneck no-tissue substitute: rolls of Charmin toilet paper. Adam sniffled, standing next to me, and Tim Sr. wept unabashed.

★　★　★

As Macy settled in at the Donaldson house, I stopped by almost every day—bringing discount baby formula or a pacifier, hauling in another box of diapers bought with drug-store points, or just hanging around to hold her and brag about how cute she was. She slept deeply in my arms, silent, lashes closed, little curls tousled and pretty.

"Sleep well, love," I whispered, gently rocking her in the distinct way she liked. "I'm the aunt who's going to buy you all those loud, messy toys your parents will hate—complete with extra batteries. You'll love me. But your parents won't."

Macy didn't know it, but she'd changed me already. I'd spent hours—days, probably—scouring discount clearance racks and thrift stores for cute socks and onesies, baby rattles and teething rings that even I, Coupon Clipper of the Century, could afford. Scouring JCPenney for that perfect baby gift, fingering the gift card in my pocket.

Becky and Tim changed a little, too, turning overnight from carefree twenty-somethings to gentle and cautious caretakers, always on the listen for a whimper or a cry. Going back and forth about where to find the pacifier and passing each other bottles and burp cloths, tag-team style as always.

Becky's eyes wore dark circles from night feedings, and Tim looked pretty terrible. But I'd never seen them more full of joy and energy.

"Yer bringin' an awful lot of stuff, Yankee!" said Tim as I dumped another package of diapers on the living room floor. "Not that I mind! But ya ain't gonna hafta hock that house fer all this, is ya?"

Macy had just finished a bottle and was dozing in her crib, a sheep-shaped chew toy in her limp hand. Tim raked his hand through his hair, making it stand on end. His chin bristled with unshaven grizzle, making him look like his Civil War reenactment persona on a bad day.

"Nope. The house is still mine, especially after I turned down that last offer," I whispered as Becky carefully closed the nursery door.

"Ya got another offer?" Both heads looked up at me.

"Two, but one retracted the offer and bought somewhere else," I said, sitting on the sofa and hauling Gordon up in my lap. "I almost took the second one, but Lowell found out they have a lot of debt and not very good credit, so we said no."

"That's the right thing, gal." Tim nodded his affirmation. "No sense rushin' things. Hang in there!"

"Yeah, well, I've got about one more month to hang, and then it's a moot point." I patted Gordon, avoiding their eyes. "I've accepted it now. I just. . .didn't think things would end this way."

"It ain't gonna!" Becky protested. "We're prayin', Shah-loh! I know God's gonna come through fer ya!"

Tim waved his finger at me. "God does stuff when ya least expect it," he said, eyes boring into mine. "An' *how* ya least expect it. Don't ya ferget it, Shah-loh Jacobs! He don't always work on our time, but He's gotcha covered. Mark my words!"

"Ya got that right." Becky's voice sounded choked, and she glanced around at the baby decorations and toys still scattered around the living room. "Jest cain't believe it's fer real, ya know?"

The old me would have envied their good fortune, but not now. They'd waited years for this moment, and I wanted us all to savor it, like a faint whiff of Macy's baby powder fragrance. I felt almost like Macy belonged to me, too, the way I swelled up with pride when they held her.

"Well, thank ya fer the presents." Tim, as usual, abruptly jumped from sentimental and spiritual as easily as changing socks. He rubbed his tired face and looked at his watch. "Say, what'n the sam hill ya doin' here at nine in the mornin' on a weekday anyway? Ain't ya got work?"

"Off on some excitin' story!" Becky picked baby bottles and gift wrapping off the carpet. "Off ta interview the governer'r somethin'. Ain't that right, Shah-loh?"

"Nope. I'm going to Winchester."

"Winchester?" they both cried.

I stared at them. "The trial? Remember? Assault and battery? Getting beat up by a skinhead?"

Tim smacked his cheek. "Aw, man! Is that today?"

"Relax." I patted him on the shoulder. "I hold no grudges. You guys have a baby now."

Tim shook his head, running his fingers through his messy hair. "You been workin' out a deal or somethin' with yer lawyer?"

"The prosecutor? Yes."

"You gotta pay fer all that?" Becky looked up, horrified.

"No, thank goodness. The police filed the charges out of interest in public safety, so someone represents me. We're asking for jail time plus damages."

"I don't blame ya. I'd a hung the suckers." Tim scowled. "Bunch a boneheads if I ever seen 'em. Shucks! I really feel fer ya. So sorry ya hafta go through this, and us not bein' able to do a thing about it." He glanced toward the nursery. "I reckon we could take Macy an' ride up there with ya, if she don't—"

"No way!" I snapped, jerking the lid off a glass candy jar and snitching a miniature Reese's Cup. "Don't even think about it! I'll be fine."

"Ya ain't goin' alone, are ya?" Becky dropped the baby blanket in midfold. "I mean, it's our fault fer takin' ya to the reenactment, an'. . ." Her face started to turn all blotchy, eyes spilling over.

"Now, don't you start!" I put the lid back on the jar. "I'll have you know I have a pretty impressive escort to Winchester all lined up."

"Who, Adam?"

I accidentally banged the lid, clinking glass. "Well, yes. He witnessed the crime, so he has to testify."

"The most important witness, of course," Becky added, picking the baby blanket off the carpet and shaking it out. Eyes falling from mine. "Although it seems like mebbe somethin's not going so well in that department these days."

I avoided her gaze. "Well, not like we thought. But. . .we'll be okay."

Becky sighed. "So y'all are really done then? Over?"

"Well, we weren't dating anyway. He just said he wanted to get to know me better, and all this stuff about marriage and not kissing and. . . What?" I looked up as Becky and Tim exchanged round-eyed glances.

"Yer kiddin'." Becky's face had gone white. "The talk about gittin' ta know each other, proper-like, without all the hoopla? You serious?"

My fingers halted on the chocolate-scented foil. "Why? What's that supposed to mean?"

"Nothin'. It's jest. . .wow. He must've been awful serious about doin' things right with ya. Adam's pretty particular. Always has been with the gals—since he was a kid."

I couldn't answer. Just ate my Reese's Cup in silence, wishing Becky hadn't brought him up.

"Yeah." I chuckled, trying to blow the whole thing off. "He's kind of weird. Not necessarily in a bad way, but. . ." My smile melted a bit. "Listen, guys. I don't know how to tell you this, but I'm leaving Staunton. For good."

Tim's head jerked up, and Becky staggered, banging into the TV. She dripped down into the empty rocking chair as if her knees had given out. "No," she whispered. "On account a Adam?"

"On account of me not having any place to live in about a month." I balled up the foil, not looking at her. "I've applied for a reporting position in Japan, and the office called me last night to confirm my acceptance. As soon as they get the housing situation settled, we'll discuss ticket dates."

Nobody moved.

"I'll miss you both so much. You have no idea. I'll miss Faye. I'll miss. . .well, everybody." I swallowed, looking for something to divert my attention before I started crying.

"Well, I'll be." Tim sank his chin into his hands. "But that's what ya wanted, ain't it?"

Why did everybody have to ask me that? "Sure," I said, trying to keep my voice bright. "Then I'll finally be back in the place I loved."

The words sounded so hollow suddenly, after so many months of waiting and longing. I reached for my purse and fumbled with my keys. "How's Rick doing?" I asked, quickly changing the subject. "Any news on him lately?"

"Oh, he ate Vanna's slippers again." Becky shrugged, sniffling. "He makes such a ruckus runnin' around the house, tearin' things up an' messin' everywhere. I'm surprised they don't give the doggone fella away."

My purse sank to the floor, along with my jaw. "Excuse me? Rick Carter?"

"Oh, him?" Becky gasped. "Shucks, I was talkin' about Todd's new gerbil! Ain't he told ya about him? His name's Richard—after Richard Petty, that racecar driver—and Todd calls him Ricky." She glanced up at me sheepishly. "I reckon Rick's doin' okay. Ain't heard nothin' else."

Wait a second. Didn't Stella say. . .? My hands slipped nervously to my cell phone, wondering if I should call and demand some explanation, when Tim suddenly sat up straighter.

"Now, wait a second, honey bun. I heard somethin' about a rehab scholarship for Rick somewhere in. . .I forgit where. Somethin' that they's gonna send a representative to talk to 'em all about it this comin' week. Didn't ya hear that?"

"Naw! For who?"

"For Rick. Somethin'. . ." He rubbed his forehead. "I fergit the details, but it sounded like he hit the jackpot."

"Who told you?" My words surged out before I could stop them. "Adam?"

"Nah. I don't think he knows yet. I heard it from my friend down at the DMV. Got a cousin or somethin' who really wanted that scholarship bad, but his buddy told him they'd chose Rick Carter." He glanced up at Becky. "Don't say nothin' ta Adam yet."

"Oh, I won't. But gracious, wouldn't that be good fer Rick?" She teared up again. "Lands, all this good an' bad news at once! I dunno how much I can take!"

"Hey, how'd ya know?" Tim suddenly swiveled his head to me.

"Me? I didn't say I knew anything. I just asked about Rick." I checked my watch. "I'd better go, huh? Your parents are picking me up, Tim."

"Oh, right. Pop was there at the reenactment when them clowns—"

"Don't say it." I stood up and dug another Reese's Cup out of the jar for the road. "I'm trying to forget until I get to Winchester."

"Don't fergit," said Tim sternly. "Tell the truth. We'll be prayin' fer ya. Here. Let's pray right now. Whaddaya say, sweetie?" He reached for Becky's hand, and she reached for mine.

We prayed for protection and fearlessness, Becky wiping her eyes with a tissue as Tim said the "amen." And I blew them a kiss on my way out the door.

★　★　★

We arrived in Winchester to a sky spitting flurries, noon traffic, and patchy white cloud cover. Lunchtime came, and while I would normally be starving, my stomach had coiled itself into a tight ball. Food, for once, was the furthest thing from my mind.

Cold ice-blue skinhead eyes bored into my memory, searing me with a boot kick to the side. I pressed my hand protectively over my ribs, wondering what might have happened if Adam and the others hadn't reached me in time.

"Yankee scum." I sipped my iced tea and felt seriously ill, looking nervously around the restaurant where we stopped for lunch and wondering who lurked among the booths. If a touch of my Brooklyn accent gave me away. If Jimmy and his posse waited in the shadows to jump us as soon as we paid our bill.

I barely heard Tim Sr. pay and Jeanette put her arm around me as we walked out to the car, but I saw the concern in Adam's eyes as he glanced up at me from across the car, pencil in hand. His lap full of clipboards and ledgers and work stuff, the pale light from the clouds and telephone-pole-lined streets flickering across his sober face as he worked.

The way he'd looked at me at the edge of the battlefield, asking if I'd found Mom's precious keychain I'd gone looking for. Which is what started the whole thing.

Like Faye, Adam had always been there for me.

Loved me. The kind of love Faye'd talked about over her amethyst ring—a love that served, cared, and quietly walked by my side. Painted my kitchen. Lent me his phone. Repaired Mom's roses. And came with me now, when I needed someone the most.

"You're going to be okay, Shiloh," he said with a smile, briefly touching my arm. "Don't worry."

And deep inside, welling up, I felt something. . .*something almost like. . .*

We were getting out of the car. Walking up the street, cold wind ruffling my unfeeling skin and interrupting my thoughts. I took a deep, shaky breath and gazed up at the imposing courthouse, trembling under my trim navy-blue peacoat that was supposed to mean business.

Inside smarted with cold, with hard lines and stark white paint. Echoing footsteps and a frightening smell of wood, varnish, and nervous whispers. A distant cough reverberated from one of the closed rooms.

Commonwealth's Attorney Clyde Argenbright strode toward me,

dressed in a dark gray pin-striped suit. He shook hands and spoke in low tones about something. I don't know what; he might as well have recited the *Farmer's Almanac* from 1872.

"Two of them are brothers—Jimmy and Beauregard Hooton. Goes by Bo," Clyde was saying, and I tried to tune him in.

"Beauregard? Like the Confederate general?"

The fact that I knew that stunned even me. Out of the corner of my eye, I saw Adam hide a smile.

"Uh. . .yes. Probably." A flicker of mirth darted across Clyde's unsmiling gray eyes. "Jimmy has a record already, and since he'd failed to show up for a larceny hearing a few months before your incident, he went to jail. They scrounged up some bail from somewhere on the condition that he show up today. The other guy's a local. Name on his records is—"

"Travis."

"How did you know?"

I rolled my eyes. "Lucky guess. He's the one missing a tooth?"

"That's him. Travis Truxell."

"What about the skinhead?" My hands twined together, fingers suddenly stiff.

"Jeb Tucker. He's got a record in another county."

I found myself seated in a chilly courtroom on a hard bench, shivering despite my best efforts. Turning to see the judge on her bench, graying hair cut in an attractive style but hard, steely eyes that did not smile back.

I remembered the taste of dusty bandana in my mouth.

And then the courtroom door squeaked open.

Chapter 37

"The skinhead didn't show?" demanded Trinity, setting down her tea mug so hard it nearly sloshed.

"Nope. Just the other cronies, who didn't have much of a defense."

"That's nuts! You mean he's still out there somewhere?" Trinity frowned, glancing around the Starbucks where I used to work. With its familiar stacks of mugs and teas and the tables and chairs I used to scrub.

Now I sipped a hazelnut mocha like any other customer, hair pinned up in a messy bun. Sleek brown boots and emerald-green belted sweater, nice jeans. Not an apron in sight.

"Yeah, the creepo." I stirred my coffee, resting my spoon on the edge of my dish. "But the judge swore out a warrant for his arrest, so when they do get him, he'll probably do longer jail time. Since he's the one who actually kicked me."

"Good! He deserves it." Trinity squeezed my arm. "How about the others?"

"Jail. Fifteen days each. The skinhead is supposed to reimburse me for my emergency-room visit, too, but since he didn't show, I guess not."

"You're a brave woman, Shiloh. Facing them down like that."

"Me? Be serious, Trinity. I only went because I had to. And if they pick up the skinhead at a traffic stop or something, that means I'll have to go back to court again. But it'd be worth it." I leaned my head on my hand, playing with a silver-drop earring. "I didn't like seeing those guys again, though."

"Were you scared?"

I shrugged. "A little." My voice trailed off, remembering their stares of hate. Their formerly messy hair unnaturally sleeked and side-combed, the attempt at professional-looking suit jackets that failed completely. I almost felt sorry for them.

Not that sorry, though, when a grandmotherly relative called me a nasty name on our way out the courtroom doors. Wearing, I might add, something that looked an awful lot like a skirted bathing suit under her coat, coupled with bulging turquoise leggings.

Like Sweet Potato Pie

Sheesh. Maybe Kyoko's right about this place! I picked up my coffee cup again, enjoying the rich, slightly bitter meld of espresso, foamed milk, and a hint of sweetness.

"So what are you going to do now? Stay here in Staunton with that nice new job of yours?" Trinity dunked her orange spice teabag a couple of times and dug it out with her spoon.

"It's not that nice. And no." I avoided her eyes, running my finger along the smooth mug handle. "I'm just waiting to hear back about housing, and then I'll move to Osaka." I sipped, feeling a painful stab at the thought of Christie's chew toys. "You don't want a puppy, do you?"

"Me? I can't have a dog, Shiloh. My cousin's allergic."

"Well. I'm looking." My voice came out mournful. "Although it's harder to give her up than I thought."

"But the Osaka job's good news, right? I guess you'll be leaving soon." She sighed. "Like everybody else. First Jamie, now you. But good luck. I mean it."

"Thanks. I'm already boxing stuff up."

"What about your job at *The Leader?* Have you quit yet? After what, a couple of weeks of work?"

"I won't quit until I get the tickets. But then, yes. I'll talk to Kevin and resign." I stared into the mug. "But. . ."

"But what?"

"But I'm glad I came to Staunton." The reflected lights in my foam-covered coffee jiggled as I picked up the mug, emotion suddenly clouding my throat. "My life changed here. I discovered love here."

I sipped, not trusting myself to speak more.

"Love. You mean like Adam?"

"Adam?" The mug jerked, sloshing against my lips. I put it down and reached for a napkin. "Sure. He's a nice guy." I wiped my mouth and then my mug, remembering how he'd sponged cream off the side of my coffee cup in Tastee Freez with his napkin. "But. . .I really meant Jesus. I never knew anyone could love me so much. Could. . ."

I broke off, teary-eyed, and sponged my cheek in irritation with my napkin. *What's the matter with you, Shiloh? Trial stress? Too-late nights working on news stories? PMS?*

Instead of finishing my sentence I dumped another sugar packet in my coffee, watching the crystals dissolve. *Definitely PMS.*

"Jesus." Trinity's mouth made a straight line. Eyes turned down. Stirring her tea, chin in hand.

I dabbed my eyes again, feeling the same boldness that had steadied my shaking knees in the Winchester courtroom. "I never knew what love was until I gave my heart to Jesus. He changed everything."

"Changed everything how? By giving you a man who loves you and a new job?"

"No. By forgiving everything I've ever done and letting me start over again with Him."

Trinity started slightly, but enough to make her chair scrape. She sipped her tea in silence a long while then shrugged and picked at some lint on her jacket. "I don't know, Shiloh. It ain't that easy for me to believe."

"Sure it is. Like Faye told me—sometimes you just have to say yes."

"It's not that simple."

"Yes and no. You read and pray and see the truth, and then you make the choice to give up your old ways. And put on His instead."

"You Christians." Trinity rolled her eyes, the pensive expression turning hard.

"Yeah. I know. We're a bunch of pains in the neck." I lifted my coffee cup to my lips with a slight smile.

Trinity's laugh surprised me, dimpling her cheeks delightfully. "I didn't mean that. It's just. . .well, you know Grandma. She's always yakking about 'Jesus' this and 'Jesus' that, and now you! You ever watch pro wrestling? It's like tag team."

I grinned, picturing Tim and Becky. "Tag team isn't always such a bad thing," I said, gently patting her arm. "Especially if the people tag-teaming really love you."

My watch had stopped. I flicked the crystal then groaned and unclasped it from my wrist. So much for all that money I'd plunked down at the Gucci counter. The cheap Wal-Mart special I'd bought for swimming eight years ago? *That* still worked.

I was digging through my purse in search of my migrating cell phone when I heard Trinity sniffling.

I froze, hand still in my purse. "What's wrong? What did I do?"

Trinity sponged her eyes, careful not to dab her makeup, then wiped her nose. "PMS," she muttered.

"Good. That makes two of us." I turned my cell phone to see the time then breathed out in relief. Still half an hour before my lunch break ended.

"And all that stuff you said about. . .you know."

"No, I don't. What?"

"About Jesus, Shiloh. I don't even. . .well, believe in Him. Exactly."

"That's all right. He knows that, too, and still loves you." I was blabbering, but for some odd reason I didn't care. Or stop. "Just tell Him the truth, Trinity. Tell Him you don't yet, but you want to."

I saw tears glitter in her eyes again, and her graceful throat flutter as she swallowed. "I've gotta go," she said abruptly, collecting her purse. "Work. You know how Jerry is."

She pushed the gift bag across the table that had my scarf in it, and I pushed it back. "Keep it."

"What?" Trinity shoved the bag in my direction. "You bought it in Japan."

"No. You keep it." I shoved it again and picked up my coffee cup.

"Why? So I'll become a Christian?" she asked a little warily, fingering the soft fluff.

I made a face. "Give me a break, Trinity. So you'll have a warm neck. Although as warm as it's been lately, you might have to save it for next year."

"Tell me about it. I've worn short sleeves all week."

Trinity took the scarf out and wrapped it around her shoulders, the soft gray color complementing her charcoal jacket and silver earrings. "Really? You're sure?"

"I'm sure. There are more important things in my life now than scarves. I promise you that."

Trinity rose and hugged me, her voice trembly. "I don't know how to say this, Shiloh, but I really needed someone in my life like you. You. . .you give me hope."

Her lips quivered, and she pulled her sunglasses down over her eyes and fled out of Barnes & Noble, not even bothering to wave good-bye. Doors closing behind her in a glint of pale winter sun.

I stared at her retreating figure. "Hope for what?" I said out loud, but Trinity had vanished.

I finished my coffee alone, fingering the soft ivory scarf Vanna Carter had given me for Christmas. Simple. Hand-knit. I pressed it to my nose; it smelled like vanilla, fireplaces, and cinnamon.

Funny how I'd just replaced an expensive Japanese boutique buy with something I could probably sell for five bucks on eBay. And yet it seemed, sitting there at the empty table with memories of snows and Christmas and Adam wrapped around my neck, that I'd come away with the better deal.

My cell phone vibrated loudly on the table, and I answered.

"This is the office of James Reuben Prufrock III, Attorney at Law, returning your call. How may we help you?"

"Well, it depends," I said, jerking myself up straight. "On whether one of your clients is still threatening me."

Pause. "Which client, ma'am?"

"Ashley Sweetwater."

I waited an eternity while the receptionist typed. Asked me to spell and respell the name. Asked where Ashley lived and how to spell her maiden name.

And then she finally came on the line again. "I'm sorry, ma'am. We have no one by that name in our client file."

"You what?" I sloshed coffee over the rim of the mug.

"I'm sorry. She's not listed with us."

I dragged my hand through my hair in disbelief. I mean, I knew Ashley had no qualms about lying, but forgery?

"You mean you've never sent a letter to me, Shiloh P. Jacobs, in the name of James Prufrock himself? Signed?"

"No, ma'am. I'm sorry. I don't have your name on file either. You must be mistaken."

I hung up the phone, shaking with anger. "Oh, I know who's mistaken, all right," I muttered, scrolling through my phone number list until I came to Ashley's number. "And she's going to hear from me."

I grabbed up my things, the once-sweet coffee tasting bitter in my mouth as I drained the last sip. And stormed out the glass doors like Trinity had gone, pausing at a potted tree just starting to push out pale green buds. Away from patrons. Away from everybody.

A square cement planter encircled the tree, so I leaned against it, phone still shaking in my hand, facing the outside of JCPenney as I gathered my words. Preparing to speak. To accuse, and rightfully so. To yell. To tell her exactly what a rotten half sister she was and how we needed to go our separate ways.

And as I looked up into the wide pane of glass, I saw it: a powder-blue baby set in the display window. Fluffy bunny slippers and pajamas. A stuffed blue duck tucked in the pocket. A fuzzy bath towel wrapped around the whole thing.

The strangest thing of all—my own image layered over it in glass. Blinking back tears. My coat buttoned against the harsh wind.

The two reflections merging curiously into one.

And that old gift card from JCPenney screaming at me from my purse.

I started, mouth sputtering. *Oh, no, no, God. I don't think so! Don't even. . .*

I stood there in the wind, not quite believing what just went through my mind. And feeling like a hypocrite for everything I'd just said to Trinity about God forgiving me—and now, not twenty minutes later, taking it back.

"But God," I whispered. "I feel nothing for Ashley. I have no love."

Adam's voice echoed back to me from across the months: *"God can raise the dead."*

All at once I pushed off the planter, throwing my purse over my shoulder.

Chapter 38

It took three days to write the letter. Poring over the words by lamplight, contacts exchanged for old Prada glasses, eyes strained from too many hours of staring at a computer screen.

But I wrote it. I told Ashley I knew. That she could stop hiding, stop bluffing.

And I told her she'd hurt me. Deeply. And it would be a long time before I could trust her again, if I ever did.

In my own handwriting, on pretty Japanese paper. I stared at the lines, remembering the letters Mom had written me back in Japan. Most of which went unanswered, or in many cases, simply unread.

I ended my letter by telling Ashley the truth. That I did not want to forgive her, but since Jesus had forgiven me, I couldn't say no.

And I sealed up the envelope and tucked it in the package, which I wrapped in pale blue paper.

★   ★   ★

"Is Clarence in?" I wiped cold rain off my sleek black-silver jacket and shook my umbrella out the door.

Lee Ann the receptionist glanced up at me, face wrinkling into a scowl of dead hate, and turned stiffly back to her work. She swiveled her back to me in emphasis.

"Well." I coughed back a laugh. "Thanks for the help."

I don't know why, but Lee Ann's coldness struck me as funny. I should have been offended, but it had become a sort of game to me. Not a spiritual one, mind you. More of an internal bet. I kept a tally list on my cubicle wall of her jabs—and sometimes complimented her shirt or her hair just to add another tick.

Sick, I suppose. But that's what served for humor in a setting where I wrote up custody battles and domestic disputes.

"Clarence?" I rapped on the mail-room door and pushed it open.

"Heya, Shannon." He shut the microwave and punched in eleven seconds. I'd heard about this "eleven seconds" quirk; apparently it was true.

"Shiloh." I held out my package. The second one I was sending to Ashley with, so far, no response. "Could you weigh it for me?"

"Oh, sure, sure." The microwave dinged, and Clarence pulled out his cracked I'M-NOT-IRISH-BUT-KISS-ME-ANYWAY mug. He grinned as he took a sip, his wrinkled cheeks bulging against wild whitish-gray hair. "Now we're talkin'. Eleven seconds does it just right."

"Root beer. You heat root beer in the microwave." It came out as a statement rather than a question.

"Yep. Nothin' better in the world. Wanna try some?"

"No thanks." I handed him my box. "I'll just. . .mail this and get back to work."

"What's in it this time? More baby stuff?" His grin widened into something bordering on a leer, and he shook the box.

"Yes." I checked my watch. "If you don't mind, I'm kind of in a hurry."

The name *Clarence* conjured up images of a charming, elderly British gentleman, but Clarence Toyer was neither charming nor British. Although he did wear a bow tie. Every day. Each day's uglier, if possible, than the previous. One so hideous that the office secretary spilled a cup of coffee when she saw him.

"You havin' a baby, Sherry?" Clarence's teeth gleamed yellow like an old piano.

"If I were, why would I be sending stuff to Chicago?" I slapped the bills down on the table as the meter rang up the postage. "And my name's Shiloh."

Big, big, big mistake.

I learned that day that Clarence was also the source of every major rumor that spread through *The Leader* staff.

"This is ridiculous!" I threw down my pencil when Meg the photographer came by to congratulate me on my supposed pregnancy. Meg, mind you, christened "Mary Margaret" by her staunch Irish parents in hopes of devoting her to the church as a nun. Fat chance for that. "Why would Matt say something like that?"

Meg tilted her head sideways, her nearly waist-length hair splaying over her rows of hemp-braided necklaces and beads. "I dunno. Said he heard it down in the mail room."

I opened my mouth to spew out a torrent of threats when I caught a whiff of something pungent and foul drifting from Meg's mug.

"What is that?" I turned my head to gasp fresh air.

"Sassafras and cayenne pepper." Meg peered into the darkish depths. "Mixed with some homemade brew my boyfriend Cooter makes in a still."

She shook the mug at me, making the tiny bells on her billowy bohemian-print skirt jingle. "Want some? It's better for you than your Japanese green stuff. In fact, tea leaves are probably carcinogenic, too. And if you are pregnant, by any chance, then—"

"I'm not pregnant, Meg!" I gripped my head in my hands. "That package was for my half sister! Next time I see Clarence I'll. . ."

"Did you deny it?"

"What? Of course not! I didn't think he meant it!"

"You have to be really careful with Clarence." She smiled down at me breezily as if this happened all the time. "Deny *everything*. You're a reporter, Jacobs! You should know that. Even if you're lying, there's always some sucker out there who'll believe you if you deny it."

I threw back my chair and grabbed the marker under my white message board. And wrote I'M NOT PREGNANT! in big block letters. "There. Is that denial enough?"

I slapped the cap on the marker then refilled my green-tea cup and tried to focus on my newest crime story—a drug and firearms arrest in Verona. I was staring at the screen, trying to come up with a lead, when the desk phone rang.

I answered with my usual "*News-Leader*-this-is-Shiloh-Jacobs" bit, still punching in stuff on my keyboard with my left hand.

"Uh. . .hey."

The office froze to an eerie silence. "Ashley?"

"Yeah." A weak laugh bleated across the line. "It's me."

I took a breath, willing myself to say something nice. Something civil, at least. "How did you get my work number?"

A baby jabbered in the background, filling in the dead weight of the line while Ashley stayed there, not speaking. "Do you want me to hang up?"

"No, no. I was just. . .curious."

"Google search."

We just sat there not speaking until I felt uncomfortable. "Did you. . .uh. . .get the. . ."

"The package? Yes. Thanks. That was really. . .you know. Nice. Of you."

For goodness' sake! We sounded like robots on an awkward first date. I scrunched my eyes closed and tried to think of something to say.

"I. . .uh. . .just sent another package for you." I fiddled with my pen. Picked up my teacup and sipped it nervously.

"Really? Well, you don't have to send it, you know. If you don't want to."

"Well, I want to. Is that all right?"

"Why, Shiloh? Why are you being so nice after everything mean you said in that horrible letter?"

"Mean? You were the one who called me a selfish monster, as I recall."

"And pregnant," tittered Meg on her way to the watercooler.

I glared at Meg and scooted farther inside my cubicle. Pressed the phone to my ear and quieted my voice, even though the Dilbert comic strip promised that attracted eavesdroppers in droves.

"Mom did write a letter about Carson and wanting to get to know him better," said Ashley, her voice hard and reluctant, like pulling out splinters. "She said she'd changed and wanted to be different, and. . . Whatever. Maybe she didn't mean to include him in her will. I must have. . .you know. Misunderstood her intentions."

"Oh. Misunderstood." I rolled my eyes.

"Anyway, I just want to know why you suddenly decided to be nice."

I let out a long sigh, setting down my teacup so hard it almost spilled. "Ashley, it's not that I suddenly decided anything. I just wanted Carson—and you—to know I still care about you." It was hard, but I got it out.

"You didn't sound like it last time."

"Why, because I'm not going to fork over my inheritance to you? You lied to me. You forged papers. You have no idea what stress that's caused me over the past few months."

"Oh, please. You're always so dramatic. I don't want your inheritance or Mom's dumb old. . .Mom's house, okay? *Your* house. Forget it. Keep it. I could care less."

"Then what do you want? What did you mean by all that lawyer garbage?"

"Nothing. Forgive me," she said with a sarcastic laugh. "I didn't know family had to hold a press conference to ask questions! But then again, you probably don't consider me family anyway. So be it."

Oh boy. I put my head in my hands and offered up a quick prayer for God to FIX THIS, fast. For Him to make something out of our mess before it got any way worse because our conversation was already skidding downhill. Sort of like sledding at Mary Baldwin, but with sharks at the bottom instead of snow.

I tapped my pen on the desk as I racked my brain to think of something, anything, that could make sense of Ashley's twisted logic. She had a scheme of some sort; and as usual, I had to figure it out.

Expenses. Expensive. I recalled the way she'd repeated that word on the phone.

"Ashley, are you guys doing okay financially?" I blurted. "It's none of my business, and you don't have to tell me if you don't want to. You just seem to be. . . Ashley?"

I heard what sounded like sniffling on the other end of the line. "Hello?"

"I'm here," she snapped, voice choked.

"Well." I scratched my head. "I don't know what's going on over there. Can you. . .um. . .help me out? Everything okay?"

If I'd ever believed in the power of God, it was right at this moment. The old me would have hung up on Ashley and thrown the phone out the window by now.

"Everything's *not* okay!" she retorted angrily. "Wade lost his job. He got laid off six months ago and still hasn't found a job. And I quit mine to take care of Carson. So for your information, no! We're not okay. Wade's going to run out of unemployment soon, and we still have nothing."

I hesitated for a second to judge if Ashley was lying again. But my gut told me that for once, she spoke the truth.

"Wade lost his job?" I ran my hand through my hair. "Ashley, why didn't you say something?" Fresh anger seethed through me.

"I tried to! But you didn't want to hear it!"

"That's not what happened, and you know it!" I shook my head. "Did it ever occur to you that if you'd just asked, maybe I'd help you?"

I heard more sniffling on the other end and then the baby gurgling morph into a cry. Plaintive at first then loud and angry. Ashley covered the phone, speaking to a muffled male voice I could barely make out. *Wade.* Indeed at home and not at work.

"No. The other one. Over there."

"Huh?"

"Sorry. I'm talking to Wade." Ashley sniffed again then made a nose-blowing sound.

"I'm really sorry, Ashley. I thought you guys had plenty of money. I mean, you have your own house."

"Our own house? We've got a fixer-upper, Shiloh! Have you ever seen the pictures? And it needs more fixing-upping than we can deal with right now. We're behind on the roofing payments. The furnace keeps going out."

"What about Dad? Hasn't he helped you at all?" I knew Dad had a fairly close relationship with Ashley—at least closer than I did. Which meant they actually spoke.

"Dad bought us this house," said Ashley bitterly.

So Dad gave Ashley a house, and Mom gave me one. Funny. Perhaps Mom left me the house on purpose, to ensure I was cared for, too.

"Dad's done a lot for us, Shiloh. I can't keep asking for more, especially now that he's putting Tanzania back through school. She's decided to be a doctor. And of course he pays for Sam and Sarah to go to private school."

"Who?"

"Tanzania's kids."

Wow. Ashley'd just told me more information about my paternal side in one minute than I'd heard in three years. I opened my desk drawer, still trying to take it all in, and pulled out a package of seaweed-flavored Japanese *osembei* rice crackers.

"What about Wade's family?" I asked in midcrunch.

"They don't have money. They gave us a sippy cup as a baby gift. Really, Shiloh. A plastic one from Wal-Mart."

The baby wailed again, and Ashley blew out her breath angrily. "Listen, you can just forget all of this, okay? I don't know why I called. I guess I just wanted to say I'm sorry and thank you. And. . .that's it. Have a nice life, okay?"

And she hung up.

I sat there staring at my computer screen, unseeing, cursor blinking away at the end of my last line of text. The sound of tittering startled me.

"Congratulations, Shiloh!" Matt the intern poked his chubby head into my cubicle. His shoulder-length hair shivered as he reached for my limp hand and pumped it.

"Congratulations for what?" I bit into another rice cracker and glared. "Having my half sister hang up on me?"

He gave my crackers a look and stepped back, the way I did with Meg's stinky tea mug.

"Well, if you think that's a congratulatory event. By all means, imbibe in the festivities."

Great. Matt the vocabulary show-off. I'm not in the mood for it. "Rice cracker?" I held out the package.

He grimaced. "No thanks. But congratulations."

Congratulations on what? Being the weirdest person on staff? No, that would go hands down to Clarence.

I rolled my eyes and turned back to my crime story, but after the third or fourth person had giggled outside my cubicle and put presents on my desk (mostly junk around the office like paperweights and coffee creamer, but still. . .), I got worried. I went on patrol around my cubicle and found nothing unusual. Until I saw my message board.

Somebody had erased NOT.

Chapter 39

When the snow finally melted in giant, gaping patches, I noticed the grass underneath: fresh and green, alive with glorious, tender life, all spangled with opening crocuses like fallen stars. Everything bloomed in an unexpected early warm spell—fragrant yellow daffodils, lacy pink redbud trees, peach and apple blossoms. The trees budded and began to unfurl delicate leaves, and I threw my head back to inhale lungfuls of fresh spring air. Joyful throbs of light after too-long winter.

Yomiuri Shimbun called to tell me they'd resolved the housing issue and would send tickets within two weeks. I scheduled a meeting to give Kevin my notice Wednesday morning and begged Becky to take Christie for me until she could find a good home.

The mountains turned to green lace. Creeks swelled with melted snow.

And my favorite of all: grape hyacinths that poked up through the winter-bare earth of my flower bed, perfuming the air with their little purple-blue spires of chubby bells.

I told Faye if I ever got married I'd use nothing but grape hyacinths and Mom's roses. Just thousands of them, stuffed in every vase, jar, and bouquet imaginable.

"Daffodils," said Faye. "That's what I want."

Good thing because they're everywhere. Rivers of yellow, spilling along the roadsides in butter-colored bliss.

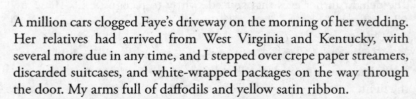

A million cars clogged Faye's driveway on the morning of her wedding. Her relatives had arrived from West Virginia and Kentucky, with several more due in any time, and I stepped over crepe paper streamers, discarded suitcases, and white-wrapped packages on the way through the door. My arms full of daffodils and yellow satin ribbon.

"Oh my lands!" Faye rushed through the house, trying to remember where she'd put the ice or the clear nail polish for Aunt Fanny's fraying stockings. She'd just had her hair done, and her chic floral dress sparkled. New, I might add. I helped her buy it.

"Shiloh, honey, thank goodness yer here! How do I look?"

"Gorgeous." I hugged her tight and tried not to think about how our afternoons would change. Our phone calls, our coffee visits. Faye would still love me, with all the tenderness of her great heart, but I'd be a distant second now. All as it should be.

"And you in that yella dress I picked out!" She put her hands on her hips and shook her head at me. "All the single fellas'll be buggin' their eyes out! Especially—" She started to say Adam, I figured, but stopped herself. "Well, anyway, you'll look real pretty."

"Not as pretty as you. Earl's probably trying to peek in the window just to catch a glimpse. Now, don't you dare let him see you in your dress, Faye!"

"Don't be silly! That's an old wives' tale about good luck an' whatnot. I don't believe in that mess."

"Neither do I, but it's your wedding! You have to make him wait." I said it so sternly that she laughed again. "Promise me!"

When she did, I pulled out a little wrapped box.

"For me?" Faye's eyes rounded behind her glasses.

"Well, I'm certainly not getting married." I held it out. "Please open it."

"Aw, sugar, ya didn't need to do that."

"I want to. And there's. . .an explanation."

"What?"

"Open it."

Faye graciously took the package then tore off the springy rose-patterned paper and lifted out a velvet box. Opened the lid to reveal a pair of delicate amethyst-drop earrings, just the shade to match her dress and ring.

"Oh, doll, these are jest beautiful! These are. . ." And then I saw it. The delight in her eyes that shifted swiftly to recognition. "These are Ellen's, honey."

"My mom's. I know."

"They were her favorites. She used ta tell me. . ." Faye's blue eyes started to tear up, and she lifted one of the earrings, turning it in the light.

"That I always loved it when she wore them. I remember." I swallowed the bulge in my throat. "Please put them on." My fingers shook as I took off the silver backing.

"Now? Are ya sure? I can't take yer mama's special jewelry, sugar."

"You're not. I'm giving them. Please. Do it for me."

Faye sniffled as she took out her pearly studs, replacing them with the amethyst drops. They looked so elegant, dangling by her hair. Just like they used to sparkle by Mom's so many years ago.

"You're my second mom now, so I thought they'd suit you just fine. I was right. You're beautiful." I squeezed her hand. "Go make Earl proud. And Mom, too."

Faye put an arm around me, and we just stood there a minute, looking out over the mess that was now her house. Suitcases and bags and wedding presents everywhere. Ribbons and shoes and potted gerbera daisies.

For a moment I could feel in my soul the goodness of God and how special Faye was to me. And somehow I to her. Resurrection again! And what better way to celebrate the resurrection of my life— and Jesus'—than just before Easter, with two people I loved pledging their lives together.

Before I could speak again, a noisy car pulled up, people laughing and shouting and banging doors, and Faye introduced me to funny relatives from Kentucky who didn't speak any form of English I'd ever heard. And the moment slipped away.

But I stored it in my heart, like the memory of Mom wearing those pretty amethyst drops to an art show, arm-in-arm with me.

★   ★   ★

I lugged my stuff to an empty bedroom then put on my dress. I smoothed my hair down under a wide, white headband, bangs swept to the side, and sprayed on a fruity shine serum. Put in little daisy earrings I'd bought from an art bazaar. Spritzed on springy perfume and stepped into white-and-linen wedge-type sandals. And then I headed out to put together the daffodils for Faye's bouquet.

My arms overflowed with yellow when Tim and Becky arrived. Becky in a smashing pale blue-and-white gingham checked dress, and Macy in something mint green and lacy. We all looked like a bunch of pastel Easter Peeps.

"Hold these," I ordered Tim, handing him the daffodils. "I need to tie on the ribbon."

He jerked his hands back as if bitten by a snake. "Flowers? I ain't holdin' no flowers!" he groused. "They's gonna make my hands smell all sweet!"

"Heaven forbid." I rolled my eyes. "Tie the ribbon then."

For a new dad, Tim had picked up on the ribbon-tying awfully quick. He made nice big loops and left long, yellow, satiny curls hanging down as I instructed him.

"You're going to be good at hair," I said, watching his steady hand as he fixed the bow. "Just wait 'til you get into braids and barrettes."

"Shoot, Yankee! I don't know nothin' about all that! I'm just gonna take 'er fishin'. Ta heck with hair!"

"You say that now."

Although Tim did sport a striped Western-style shirt and cowboy boots. Bolo tie. Vic Priestly NASCAR baseball cap. Maybe I was wrong.

"You're going to wear a baseball cap to Faye's wedding?" I took back Faye's bouquet and wrinkled up my nose.

"Shucks, why not? Ain't no black-tie affair." He grinned. "I might take it off when she comes down the aisle. Mebbe."

Adam at least put on a shirt and tie, but when he arrived I found myself so knee-deep in fixing the gift table, setting up chairs, and lining the aisle with white and yellow gerbera daisies that I could barely say a civil "hello." Instead, to my surprise, he jumped in beside me—tying silky, transparent crepe ribbon along the aisle, looping it from folding chair to folding chair, and then set out more chairs and stacked more gifts while I wrote down the names.

Then Adam disappeared to his truck and returned with mounds of flowers: super-fragrant Easter lilies in creamy white, pink-speckled stargazer lilies, and potted tulips and hyacinths. We stacked them around the simple arbor where Pastor Davis would speak then set to work tying stems of lilies into the arbor.

"The arbor still looks bare," I said, tilting my head.

"I know." Adam studied it, chin in hand. "Like it's got holes in it."

"Any ideas?"

"Just one."

"What?"

"Come with me." He held out his hand a bit hesitantly, and I awkwardly grasped it as we hurried across the grass toward the woods. Me trying not to fall in my sandals and ruin my dress.

We saw them at the same time: redbuds and dogwood trees, blooming pink and white in the riot of new greens. Adam pulled out his pocketknife and sliced off slender twigs full of blooms, handing them down to me.

"Are you sure? This one looks like poison ivy." I jerked my hands away from a flowerless green vine.

"It's Virginia creeper. Five leaves, not three." Adam's voice sounded distant, almost cold. "It's a weed, but I think it'll work to cover the bare spots on the trellis."

I didn't know what else to say, so I pretended great interest in the wedding party, bright spots in the distance through the trees. A chilly wind blew, scattering fuchsia redbud blossoms across the ground.

"So you heard the news about Rick," said Adam finally, grunting as he shimmied partway up a small tree to cut a few more stems.

"That he's going to Georgia? I heard. Congratulations. I would have called, but. . ." I shifted the branches in my arms, not sure how to explain myself.

Adam didn't look at me. I watched his knife slice off a branch, and then he dropped to the moist, mossy ground, brushing himself off. "No. He's not going."

"What?" I hollered, flinging my arms up in the air. The branches went everywhere, and Adam bent to scoop them up. "What do you mean he's not going?"

"I mean he's not going." Adam clicked his pocketknife and stuck it in his pocket, throat bobbing as he swallowed. "And that's that." He lifted his eyes to mine in a split-second ray of blue then looked abruptly down at the branches. Kneeling down to gather them up one-by-one, and shaking off the dirt.

I squatted down awkwardly in my dress, ignoring the scattered blooms. "Why, Adam? Why isn't Rick going? He won that scholarship! He was supposed to—"

I broke off at Adam's silence as he smoothed the branches then piled them together and held them out to me. I clumsily stood and put my arms out.

"Rick asked them to give the scholarship to a buddy of his who's worse than he is." He stood and sifted through some boughs, struggling with his words. "The guy burned something like seventy-five percent of his body and lost a leg and an arm. He lives in Marietta, Shiloh. That's less than an hour from the rehab center." He let the twigs go. "Rick says he can make it. And he's afraid his friend won't without help."

"Rick." Tears welled up as I arranged the branches in my arms, gently patting the blooms. "He's really a hero."

"He is." Adam turned away, ducking under a thick limb. He held it out for me and I walked under, as if stepping under a wedding arch.

"So you're going to Atlanta without him? I heard you have some work lined up there." I smoothed my hair where twigs grabbed at it.

"No." Adam turned suddenly to face me, hand trembling on a rough tree trunk. "I'd already told Rick I couldn't go with him."

"You what?" I cried.

"Don't drop those again!" Adam scolded, taking the bunch from me. "We've got to hurry. The arch isn't done yet, and. . ." He checked his watch and marched through the lush spring thicket, leaving me stammering to myself.

I came to my senses and stomped after him, trying not to fall on the roots and twigs. Wondering how in the world Adam and I always ended up in the messy woods with too-nice clothes.

"You're staying?" I grabbed my head in my hands.

"Yes. And I've been accepted at James Madison University in Harrisonburg. I start in the fall." He kept his eyes on the tree above him, pulling down a creamy white, bloom-laden bough. His voice thin and tight.

I swiveled my head, feeling like two semitrucks on Interstate 81 just hit me at the same time. "School? You're going back to school?"

"Engineering. Don't ask me how I got in. It's a miracle. My scores aren't that good anymore now that I've been out of academics for so long." He whacked off the stalk of dogwood with more force than necessary.

"Congratulations, but. . . What am I saying? How could you abandon Rick?" I practically shouted.

"What? I didn't abandon anybody." Adam whirled around. "It took me two full weeks to decide, Shiloh. And in the end I realized that I've got my own life to lead, and Rick is man enough to understand. He knows I love him more than just about anyone on earth." He waved a free arm at me. "If anyone did any abandoning, it's you."

"Me?" I stepped back angrily. "Just because I applied for a job in Japan?"

"Yes. I'm happy for you. Don't get me wrong. I know it's your dream, and I'm. . .well, proud of your work. You were always too good for this town anyway. I'm not your type. None of us are."

I clenched my fists, my breath coming fast. "No, you're not! And I'm not yours. So what?"

Adam barely seemed to have heard me, turning away slightly to shake his head. "All we have here is. . ." He lifted a lifeless arm and dropped it, gazing out through the trees at the field, which bordered a fenced-in cow pasture. "You know something? Part of why I stayed is to make something of myself. For you. To see if I could change your mind, and if not, at least start living my own life as a man on my own two feet. Go back to school. Start my life over."

"What did you say about me?" I felt the color drain out of my face.

"Becky said you didn't seem happy when you talked about moving back to Japan. So did Faye and everybody else. I could see it a mile away, Shiloh—crazy as that sounds, it's not what you want." He ran a shaky hand over his face. "Except I was wrong. It is. You don't even speak to me anymore, and you're packing up. So be it." He flung an arm in my direction. "You couldn't wait to leave Staunton anyway."

"What? I took a writing job here, too!" I put my hands on my hips.

"Until you could leave."

"No. Not exactly." Heat rushed to my cheeks, thinking of why I'd signed on with *The Leader*. Hoping to sort out things with Adam. "I had more reasons than that."

"Why, then?"

"Well, for starters, so I can have a place to live," I snapped. "Unless I can come up with an absurd amount of money in a week and a half."

"Why? Why do you keep saying that?"

I spat out a sigh, looking away. "My stupid back taxes, okay? The IRS is going to take the house, and I'll be homeless. You've got your family, Adam. I don't have anybody."

"You have more people than you think you do," his voice shot back, fraying with emotion around the edges.

I flinched, crossing my arms tightly to hide their shaking.

"And that's not the only reason I took my job at *The Leader*. I knew what I was doing. I took it because. . ." I swallowed, turning to meet his gaze. "But before all that, I want to know one thing."

"What?" Adam stood there, branches poking out of his arms and eyes dark with sorrow or anger—or both.

"You said part of the reason you decided not to go to Georgia with Rick was to make something of yourself. What was the rest? Why did you decide to stay?" Adam didn't speak for a minute, pursing his lips. Then he turned around, marched straight toward me, his face coming so close to mine I had to tip my chin up to see his eyes.

"Because I love you, Shiloh," he whispered, mouth quivering. "That's why."

And he turned on his heel and stalked through the trees, leaving me standing there in the glen full of green.

Chapter 40

Everything spun. I stormed back through the grass, stumbling twice, and pushed my way through dozens of camo- and plaid-clad relatives, gathered in clumps talking about bow hunting and how to skin a rattlesnake. I needed nothing but a bathroom with a lock on the door. And maybe a psychiatrist.

Here I stood in my yellow dress in the middle of Faye's carpeted hallway, a folded acceptance letter from *Yomiuri Shimbun* tucked in my purse to show Becky and Tim.

"Please confirm with the human resources office to schedule your flight," the letter read in crisp, formal kanji.

Finding all the bathrooms occupied with shrill-voiced women heating curling irons and issuing clouds of hairspray, I shut myself inside a spare bedroom closet and leaned against the door, trying to calm my shaking nerves. Pressing a tissue to my eyes and willing myself not to cry. Not to smear my makeup.

Of all the absurdities: I, Shiloh P. Jacobs, was offered free tickets to Japan while Adam stood there in the woods and said he'd stayed in Staunton for me.

What on earth am I supposed to do NOW, God?! I held my head in my hands, trying not to scream.

Life, as usual, had thrown me an oxymoron.

I pressed my eyes closed and tried to pray. Then I took a deep breath and stepped through piles of shoes and shopping bags, dodging two kids in coonskin caps throwing a deer antler back and forth while a hefty, red-faced aunt yelled at them to stop.

I didn't stop until I came to the wedding arch. Adam had finished the lower part of the left side already, and he barely turned when I appeared. The yard already full of people.

"Can I help you finish this, Adam?"

He gave me a brief side look then handed me a thin roll of black tape and scissors. I snipped off a length and tied it around a pink-flowered bunch of redbud, fluffing the blooms into place. Working our way up one side of the latticework, and when the trellis went over my head, Adam brought me a folding chair.

The tape ran out. I excused myself and headed into Faye's house then returned with a bag of rubber bands, wire bread-bag ties, and even a few hair elastics from my purse. I stepped off the chair and surveyed our work then scooted it forward and blended in a few ugly spots, slipping in lilies and stray gerbera daisies.

The Virginia creeper vine wrapped easily, covering the rest of the spots like a leafy green scarf.

It worked. It was magic. I stepped back to survey our work, and Adam gave me a brief smile, arms crossed.

I nodded in satisfaction. We'd accomplished something great together, Adam and I. Two people, one purpose. We made a great team. The thought reverberated through me with unexpected warmth.

Just before Becky appeared by Adam's shoulder, saying that Faye needed his help.

I watched him go, wishing I could say something—anything—to fix this mess, and instead keeping my lips pressed shut, not even daring to say his name.

★ ★ ★

Before long, guests—including a rare cigarette-less Stella in an actual dress, not a housedress—began to fill up the folding chairs. Earl stepped out of his car in a suit, looking starched and pressed and nervous, but not without his beaming smile. He shook hands with all of us, making small talk with Faye's relatives in true, understated Earl-style.

His son's family pulled in right behind him, unloading children and presents, and one of the violinists started to tune up.

I finally found Faye speechless at the kitchen window, staring out with a gaping mouth while a dozen voices talked and laughed behind her.

"Land's sakes, what've ya'll done?" Her hand trembled as she pressed it to her lips, pushing the curtains back. "Where'd all them flowers come from? I didn't order all a them!"

"Do you like them?"

"Like 'em? They look like they come out of a magazine!"

"Well, then, that's all you need to know." I grinned at her. "And don't look now, but your groom's here."

She dropped the curtains and laced and unlaced her hands then immediately tried to cover it by straightening stuff on the counter. "Is he? Well, I'll be. How does he look?"

"Like a million bucks, Faye. Just like you. Now don't you let him see you in your dress!"

The violinist began to play. Soft, straining notes of "Pachelbel's Canon," wavelike and so throbbing it almost hurt. It seemed too refined for our country gathering, with Faye's young nephews having burping contests and crunching Cheetos and the older guys wearing cowboy hats with feathers in the brim and describing field-dressing techniques.

But somehow, like the Virginia creeper on the trellis, it melded together beautifully.

"Here are your flowers." I took the daffodils out of their vase and wiped the ends. "Don't be nervous. Just stand up straight and walk like you're a queen."

I was bossing again. "Sorry, Faye. It's your day. You do things however you want."

Faye looked up from the bouquet in surprise. "Doll baby, this is one of the best days of my life, ya hear me? I could walk on my head and still be happy!"

I bit back a laugh. "Do you have all the something-borrowed and something-blue stuff?"

"I got my man borrowed from the Lord an' his are the bluest eyes I ever seen." She bent closer, smoothing my hair. "Listen, Shiloh. Before all this gets goin', I need to tell ya somethin'. Somethin' kinda important."

The singing notes of the violin shifted. *My cue.* Urging me forward.

"What did you want to tell me?" My head wavered in the direction of the music. "There's no time now. You'd better tell me afterward."

"There won't be no afterward. We're goin' to North Carolina straightaway."

Somebody rushed past the glass square in the door to find me, gesticulating frantically, and I put my hand on the doorknob. "The wedding's starting, Faye! Tell me later."

"Wait, sugar!" Faye rushed to stop me. "Ya forgot yer bouquet!"

"My bouquet? I thought I was just going to walk."

"Adam didn't think so." Faye reached for something in a vase, fluffing the ribbon. "I was tryin' ta tell ya. He wanted me ta give ya this."

She handed me a little bouquet of small daffodils and cobalt-blue grape hyacinths, all wrapped in yellow ribbon just like Faye's. All day long I'd told myself I wouldn't cry in front of Faye, but now she and the flowers morphed together in a shimmering radiance.

"Grape hyacinths are my new favorite flower," I blurted, steadying my shallow breath. "Ever since I found them in my flower bed. He planted them last year."

"I know." Faye beamed back at me. "He told me that, too."

The music outside rose in throbbing circles, spinning toward a heady pinnacle. Frenzied footsteps clacked through the house, desperate to hunt me down, and probably mount my head on a wall next to somebody's six-point buck. A fist pounded on the locked side door.

Through the window I saw faces turn. Horrified aunts half-stood in their chairs, whispering together.

Faye barely caught my arm as I rushed toward the door, the fragrance of grape hyacinths making me light-headed. "He loves ya, Shiloh," she whispered. "Don't forget that."

"Who loves me?" My heart knocked as loud as my knees, which quivered like Japanese pudding.

"Adam Carter." She stepped closer. "You know who. And I told him—" She paused suddenly, fingers twisting together.

I couldn't breathe. "Told him what?"

"Somebody spilled to you about Rick before Adam found out, didn't they?"

I dropped the bouquet. Right there in a beautiful blue-and-gold smush on the floor.

"Why do you say that?" I picked it up with shaky hands, trying to smooth the smashed petals.

"That day you sat in my livin' room. The phone call. I remember." Faye's eyes bored into mine. "An' if I'm wrong, you'd better say so right this second because I done told Adam. While you was finishin' up the arch."

My mouth opened and closed. For a split second I forgot the music. The flowers. Everything.

"I think y'all could be real happy together, you an' Adam. A man who loves God and loves you is a real find. Maybe even worth leavin' everything for."

"How am I supposed to do that, Faye? I've got no house. I've got. . .nothing. Nothing but a job in Japan."

"God can find a way. He always does."

Whispers droned from the folding chairs like worried honeybees, louder and angrier. The side door flung open with the rattle of a key, and a clump of women rushed inside, nearly bowling us both over. Somebody grabbed my arm, sputtering, "Where the tarnation you been? I oughtta tan yer hide! Ain't ya comin'?"

Faye pushed me through the open door, and I stumbled into the bright sunlight, barely seeing the blur of faces turned in my direction. The indignant voices died into soft sighs of relief, and people sank back in their chairs.

The violinist spun quivering notes across the breeze-trembling grass, note by smooth and painful note, as I walked through the folding chairs. Step and slow step. Past the silk Adam and I had hung along the aisle. Past the yellow and white of gerbera daisies.

Each step perfumed by the little bouquet of indigo and yellow, clutched tightly in my nervous fingers.

The arbor dripped blooms in pink and white, thick with leaves. At the base crowded pots and pots of fragrant lilies and colors, making the whole scene flower like a garden come alive.

And there off to the side burned those blue eyes of Adam's, looking right into my heart with unexpected tenderness. He sat next to Tim and Becky, holding Macy on his lap and entertaining her with his truck keys. Not dazzling. Not polished. Too young and too plain.

But never before had he looked so dear to me, a familiar face radiating joy.

"This is now bone of my bones and flesh of my flesh. . ."

I hadn't even thought Adam handsome when I met him nearly a year ago, holding a gas can and covered with mulch. The day of Mom's funeral, which had now become a tender memory.

"That is why a man leaves his father and mother. . ."

Pastor Davis smiled at me, and I walked under the fragrant arch, breathing in the sweetness of its flowers on the cool breeze. Leaves and petals quivering, light dancing over their curves.

Over to my right stood Earl, arms stiff in his pressed suit, but his smile fresh and alive. He winked at me, and then I saw his eyes quickly drift over my head and back to the house.

The violinist drew out his last silken note.

I took my place next to Pastor Davis and turned as the violins raised their bows for the wedding march.

". . .and is united to his wife. . ."

Everyone stood. Faye emerged from the house in her heels and dress, the yellow ribbon on her daffodils fluttering. Just as I'd imagined. Walking toward Earl with a glow on her face.

Walking toward a man who, though not her kin or blood, would become her family.

She stopped at his side, and he reached out and took her hand. I watched his fingers wrap around hers, covering the lines and scars of the years with his caressing palm. Her eyes as they met his in a happy, nervous smile.

When I peeked into the crowd again, Adam wasn't watching Faye and Earl. He was watching *me*.

". . .and they become one flesh."

Chapter 41

"Fishing," he whispered in my ear as soon as the ceremony had dissolved into a kiss, cheers, shouts, and laughter. Gobs of people milling about, starting the fire for the barbecue and setting out an enormous homemade spice cake. The crooning violins were replaced with fiddles and banjos, whole rows of people stamping their feet and clapping in time to the rollicking tunes.

"Fishing?" I jerked my head up from the punch bowl where I stood serving something pink, fizzy, and lemony, clogged with ice.

"Tuesday afternoon." Adam took his keys out of his pocket. "Can you get off work?"

"Work? I—I don't know. I can try. I'd planned to talk to Kevin on Wednesday about. . .well. . .stuff, but. . ." My heart pounded, picturing the letter from *Yomiuri Shimbun*. "He does owe me some time off, though, after I worked all last weekend."

"I'll pick you up Tuesday afternoon then. Around three-ish."

"Wait, what?" I gasped, dropping the ladle and grabbing a towel to dry my hands, rushing after him.

"That's it. I have to go. Can you call me if you're able to get off work?" Adam waited for me to catch up, but he didn't stop walking.

"Sure, but. . .what's this all about?"

Adam paused only briefly before unlocking his truck door and swinging it open. "Do you trust me, Shiloh?"

I stood there with the towel in my hands, looking up into his blue eyes. A tenderness there, mingled with something almost like tears.

"Yes."

"Well, then, I'll see you Tuesday." And he waved good-bye, pulling out of the driveway in a thin cloud of gravel dust.

I didn't see Adam all weekend. Not even Sunday, when I gathered after church with Becky and Tim to gush over Macy and gossip about Faye's wedding. I barely slept Monday night, staring up at the dark ceiling and thinking of Adam. Of Osaka. And what in the world I was supposed to do now, with all this mess roiling around in my head.

Kevin gave me the whole day off Tuesday, but I couldn't bring myself to pack any more boxes. Just sat at the table and flipped through my Bible, letting the Psalms soak into my heart, and then prayed until I slept, head right on top of the crisply folded letter from *Yomiuri Shimbun*.

★　★　★

"You're taking me to the same place we went the first time," I said, peeking out the open truck window. "A year ago." All the trees leafed out thinner than the thick summer foliage I remembered, like green lace, spring-delicate and spindly.

"Almost a year. Right." Adam parked the truck on a wash of apple-green grass and got out then came around to let Christie down and grab her leash.

The wind still rippled with cold, so I shrugged on my jacket and scooted out, coming around to the back where Adam stored all his fishing rods and gear.

"Why did you want to come here today?" I asked, shielding my face as a cold breeze blew my hair all wild.

"Because I could talk to you here. And we need to talk." He set a tackle box on the ground, and I started to pick it up.

Adam glanced up briefly. "That's okay. I'll get it."

Southern male bravado. I rolled my eyes. Adam apparently saw it because he paused in midswing of his truck-bed door. "Because I've got something else for you to carry." And he abruptly pulled an envelope from under his jacket and stuck it in my hands.

"For me? What's this?" I turned it over. It stared back at me blank, unaddressed.

"Wait 'til we sit down and you can open it."

We hauled our stuff to one of the picnic tables where I'd first cried over pecan pie, down by the trees and near the lake. The water stretched smooth and silver against the green landscape, mirroring streaky clouds in its shining surface.

Adam put all his fishing gear on the table and sat down on the bench then started threading a lure on his line. Not looking up from his tackle box.

I hesitated a minute then sat down next to him on the wooden bench and slipped off my sandals, scrubbing my bare toes through the still-cold spring grass. Christie sprawled out beside us, soaking up the sun.

"So what is this? Can I open it?" I held up the envelope.

Adam's hand—the one with the scar across his knuckles—wavered on the fishing pole, and he finally put it down and turned to face me. "Go ahead."

I paused a minute at Adam's expression, his eyes dancing like blue fire, bright and proud. And also. . .sad.

"What?" I started to put the envelope down. "Why are you looking like that?"

"Just read it."

I slipped my finger under the envelope flap as he reached down to pet Christie then glanced up suddenly. "Oh. I forgot to tell you. Your EDEN LANDSCAPING sticker came off your truck again."

"Yeah." Adam scratched his hair with his free hand and looked away. "I know."

"You've really got to get that thing fixed, you know?" I pulled a folded paper from the envelope and opened it, swinging my legs around the end of the bench. "It's your logo. Your—"

The words *Internal Revenue Service* stopped everything else that intended to flow from my tongue. I shut my mouth, eyes skimming the rows of black type.

"This is a fax." I raised my head briefly at Adam. I leaned forward to read it again, perched on the edge of the bench.

"It is. Keep reading."

And then I saw my name. Everything around me started to wobble. Adam reached for me, but he wasn't fast enough. I found myself facedown on the grass, Christie frantically licking my cheek.

Chapter 42

What is this?" I croaked, pushing myself up with my arm and wiping dog slobber off my cheeks. Clawing for the paper, which had fallen out of my hand and scudded in the wind.

Adam grabbed for the fax and stuffed it back in my fingers. "It means what it says." He swallowed hard. "Did you read. . .everything?"

"That my back taxes are paid off?" My voice wobbled. "I don't understand, Adam. Did you borrow some money or something?"

He knelt down next to me, fending off Christie's tongue with one arm and finally convincing her to lie down in the grass so he could rub her belly. "No. I didn't borrow anything."

"Well, what did you do? You don't have stocks, do you? Bonds? Or some secret stash I don't know about? Did you win the lottery?"

Adam, gambling? Of course not. But none of it made sense. I stared back down at the paper, straightening it in the breeze.

"I sold my business."

"You WHAT?" I shrieked. So loud that Christie rolled over, ears pricked. "Adam, you didn't!"

"Gabe's wanted to buy it for a while, and with that top-dollar project I'm supposed to do in July, I put the price up." He brushed a hand through my hair, not meeting my eyes. "I called the project manager and told him I'd still do the plans like I agreed, but that Gabe would take over Eden Landscaping and be doing the actual work."

I sobbed. The long, loud kind where I could hardly breathe. Adam tucked me against his chest, and I stayed there, not hearing anything but the sound of my racking sobs.

"It's not that bad, Shiloh," said Adam, his cheerfulness sounding forced. "The name still fits. Gabriel. The Garden of Eden had an angel, too, remember?" I felt his shoulders shrug. "True, maybe he was driving Adam and Eve out with a fiery sword, but it still fits. It's not like his name is Nash. . .or. . .or Tyler. Then he'd have to change it completely."

I couldn't even reply. Just thinking of those beautiful truck decals on somebody else's dusty SUV made me feel like heaving.

He played with a blade of grass, rolling it between his fingers.

"That's why I needed until this afternoon—a business day—to arrange everything. Oh, and there's one more thing. I got a job."

"A job?" I bawled, face running. "What job?"

"At UPS. You know. With the ugly brown shorts." He laughed, and it sounded a little forced. "Some day work, but mostly evening duty, delivering packages and stuff. Who knows? Maybe I'll show up here to deliver something from Japan."

I froze, hand sponging my wet face. "What did you just say?"

"About Japan? I just mean that if—"

"No. About evening duty. You're going to school, Adam! You got accepted! You told me. . ." I backed away from him in horror, fresh tears forming in my eyes. "Please don't tell me you. . ."

Adam didn't answer. He didn't need to. I saw it pass swiftly through his eyes like a kid with his leg gashed open, laughing over the pain that it doesn't hurt a bit.

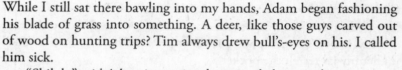

While I still sat there bawling into my hands, Adam began fashioning his blade of grass into something. A deer, like those guys carved out of wood on hunting trips? Tim always drew bull's-eyes on his. I called him sick.

"Shiloh," said Adam in a voice that sounded strained.

I looked up, eyes streaming.

The grass formed an *O* shape, a neat circle.

"I know this isn't what you deserve, but. . ."

I didn't hear the rest of what he said. It wasn't a circle. It was a *ring*. There in his palm, green, smelling of fresh afternoons and sunlight and all the moments two people could share in a lifetime.

My old days in Japan swirled like a kaleidoscope, flashing colors and memories like ripples on the lake. Circles spreading out and out, like a word that, once said, can never be taken back.

Instead of steak and wine like my first proposal, I stared down at a feathered orange lure sticking out of the tackle box. And a rumpled, tear-stained fax.

"Shiloh?" Adam held out the ring. "Would you maybe consider . . .well, me?"

"You mean it?"

"Marry me. Please."

Down in the ripples I saw our reflection: two faces together, shimmering against the sky as if we formed one single person.

"I don't know, Adam." I gulped, tears stinging my eyes. "I've made a lot of mistakes."

"Haven't we all?"

"No, I mean. . . I've been engaged before, and had too many boyfriends, and. . ." I broke off, wiping my eyes. "I'm not like you, all clean and pure, waiting for the right person since I was a child. I'm afraid you'll. . . I don't know. Regret it."

Adam didn't look away. "None of us are all clean and pure, Shiloh. And I didn't ask you to be me. I'm asking you to be you and marry me. Regret it? No way." He brushed his fingers through my wind-blown bangs. "Besides, what if you're embarrassed to be with me? I'm young and poor. I don't even have a college degree, and you're half-way through your master's. Didn't you interview the prime minister of Japan? Your Cornell friends would eat me alive."

"Who cares about them?" I leaned into the curve of his neck and shoulder as he turned my head gently to brush his lips against my hair.

"Then marry me."

As I murmured my yes and Adam leaned forward to slip the ring on my finger, the acceptance letter from *Yomiuri Shimbun* crackled under my jacket, in the pocket.

"What's that?" He wiped my moist cheek with his thumb.

"Nothing," I said, stuffing it back in my pocket. "Nothing that matters anymore."

I watched a leaf that had shimmered on the surface of the lake slip beneath the water, twinkling like my old dreams of Japan and fame, down. . .down. . .down. . .until I lost it beneath a shaft of sunlight.

"Go forward," Beulah had told me. *"Don't look back to Egypt."*

And for the first time in my life, looking into the face of Adam J. Carter, I realized that I had finally found home.

Chapter 43

Tim and Becky threw such a commotion that I'm surprised someone didn't call the police. Screeching into my driveway at breakneck speed, honking and hollering all the way. Lights flew on up and down the street, and a couple of people yelled back congratulations. Stella put on her Elvis records as loud as they would go, dancing on her front porch in her flowered nightgown until two a.m.

When the commotion died down, I called Faye on her honeymoon, against protocol. Called Kyoko, who yelled at me for forty-five solid minutes.

"Fishing?" she roared. "He asked you while you went fishing?"

Fishing. Fish. Jesus and the miraculous catch. I slapped my forehead, staring at the Greek fish tile Adam had given me.

"I love him, Kyoko," I said. "I just. . .do."

And Kyoko promptly burst into tears.

I even e-mailed Ashley, of all people, and she called me immediately—up with a late-night feeding. Giving me bleary, if not tepid, congratulations.

"Have you called Dad?" she asked in her bossy tone of voice. "He misses you, you know. You ought to call him. It's earlier in Cabo San Lucas. He's on vacation. You could still catch him awake."

"Maybe," I said. But I just sat there, staring at the phone.

It took me days to come to terms with what Adam had done, especially after he cashed in his final payment from selling Eden Landscaping to buy me a simple silver band, stoneless, to replace the ring of grass.

So I racked my brain for any possible way to find enough money for Adam to go to college in August. I prayed and clipped coupons. Ate cheap ramen noodles and carpooled with Meg for a while, leaving my car parked in an empty lot. Until somebody tried to jimmy the lock, scratching up my door, and I decided to drive myself.

But no money came. Instead I found myself at the kitchen table, bent over a stack of forms, calculator, and checkbook, when I realized I'd forgotten to pick up the mail. The days popped with craziness—calling Tim Sr. and Jeanette and Beulah. Telling everyone at work and arranging days off. Trying to decide on a honeymoon spot that wouldn't cost a fortune and haggling over dates. And breaking the news to *Yomiuri Shimbun,* bowing repeatedly as I apologized over the phone, tears in my eyes.

I just hoped I could still keep my electricity on, so behind was I on bills and late fees from some of the newest collection agencies that had caught up with me.

Besides bills, the rest of the table was crowded with steno pads, papers, and tapes of the local school board superintendent scandal, which had turned out to be a huge story.

All of this in the middle of driving out to Craigsville and Augusta Springs to do crime stories about stolen tractors (really), marijuana plantings, and illegally poached deer, among other things.

"Come on, Christie," I said, putting down my pen and opening the front door into a glowing peach sunset. "Let's see if God's going to send us a million bucks."

I trudged through the grass and pulled open the mailbox door then drew out a thick padded envelope with something hard inside. I checked the return address, which I didn't recognize, then sat down at the kitchen table and slit the envelope. Reached inside.

And pulled out a book. WITH MY NAME ON IT.

"What on earth is this?" I threw it on the table.

I blinked and shook my head, but didn't wake up; my name in curly script on glossy card stock and underneath, Mom's. *To Live and Die in Dixie* read the spiral-bound cover. Decorated with a whimsical, artsy painting of a Rebel flag all made up of flowers and boots and things. My jaw dropped as I turned the pages, not prepared for what I saw.

Inside, in a page-a-day format, unfurled "365 Days of Dixie"— starting on January 1 and ending on December 31. And under each day's heading flowed something that looked astonishingly like my writing. Stuff about mullets and cowboy boots and the number of people named Travis. Complaints about belt buckles and fatback.

Half of the entries weren't mine, but they rang strikingly familiar, whispering deep down in my soul: *"Even though the canes are bare, life stirs beneath the surface. How do I know? Because that's what faith is. Belief in an unseen God. Belief in grace and second chances even when all else shouts otherwise. . . ."*

The other entries boasted humorous and interesting facts, such as the origin of root beer, the history of grits, some recipes, and curious items from *Farmer's Almanacs*. All with whimsical, folkish drawings.

I stood there like an idiot, staring, and then grabbed the envelope and scrutinized the return address again. *Theodore Baxter. Theo. Kyoko.*

I flew into the library and dialed, not even bothering to sit down. "Kyoko, what have you done?" I shouted, still holding the book.

"What are you talking about? The thing I sent couldn't have gotten there yet, and besides, you didn't tell me not to send anything weird or scary *to you* as a present. You just said not to send it to Tim and Becky."

My jaw wobbled, and I lost my train of thought. "You. . .sent something weird?"

"Well, that's what you're talking about, isn't it?"

"A book?"

"No, not the book, the. . . What?" I heard her gasp audibly. "You got a book? Theo sent the galley already? Oh my goodness, Ro-chan—tell me!"

"The what? Wait a second—you know about this?"

"Well. . .um. . .a little something. Maybe," she replied smugly.

"Maybe?" I howled. "Kyoko, there's a book sitting here with my name on it! Are you going to tell me what's going on or not?"

"Okay! I confess. I snooped. At. . .um. . .your house. I'm sorry, Ro. But it was unavoidable. Sort of."

"So you read my stuff when you came? And Mom's journal?" I shook my head in disbelief. "I don't understand."

"Okay, okay, Ro-chan." Kyoko's voice lost its sarcastic edge. "It's like this. You told me about your 'Southern Speak' notebook, and I couldn't pass it up. You're hilarious, Ro! Really."

"Are you joking?"

"Nope. I copied it at Kinko's. Sorry." She snickered sheepishly. "Then I found your mom's journal lying out on the table. I swear, I thought it was yours at first, and you left it open, so I assumed you didn't mind. I'm so sorry, Ro, if you think I'm invasive or anything. I can talk to Theo and it'll be ancient history. Just like that." She snapped her fingers. "After all, it's just the preprint version, so we can scrap it if you want. But I had to try."

"No, no. It's okay. I'm just. . ." I looked back down at the book in my shaking hands. "Wow. A book?"

"Hey, if Boy George can sell memoirs, you can write a book. I rest my case."

I paged through the book, half listening. "Boy George? What does he have to do with anything?"

"Forget it, Ro." Kyoko chuckled. "So, do you like it? If you do, it's a go. You can look over this version and approve it, and we'll finish the cover design, send it to printing. Publicity and all that. Theo says he'll talk royalties with you. And payment of course. An advance. You are, after all, the author."

My knees felt weak, and I staggered into the chair.

"Ro? Hello? Earth to Ro-chan?"

"I'm here, Kyoko. I. . . Did you say payment?"

"What, you think authors do their stuff for free?"

"No, I just meant. . ." My heart suddenly sped up. "Kyoko, tell me something. Do you think I might get like. . .a couple thousand dollars?"

"A couple thousand? Sure. I mean, you're a new author and all, so Theo says if you sign the contract, they'll probably start you off at—"

"No. You don't understand. I need it now. Right away."

Kyoko paused. "Well, that's what an advance is," she replied, as if I were exceptionally slow-witted.

I bowed my head onto the keyboard, typing rows of letters. "So I might be able to get it before August? Before Adam's school starts?"

"August?" Kyoko chuckled. "I can probably get it to you next week, if you want. Theo's pretty into me, you know."

"What about Kaine?"

"Kaine? Forget him. He has no taste in music. He called Siouxsie and the Banshees a 'lame girl band.' I'm quoting, Ro. Can you believe it?"

I wanted, as usual, to ask Kyoko whom she was blabbing about, but she saved me. "Know what Theo sent me this week? A virtual Grubschmitter. It was amazing. He designed it himself."

Okay. Maybe she didn't exactly save me. "A. . .a what?"

"A Grubschmitter. Haven't you ever played Doom before?"

I raised a shaky hand to my head.

"It's this really creepy computer game, and they just released this new evil monster character that slays other creatures with a—"

"Stop!" I shrieked, pressing my hands over my ears as Kyoko protested how there wasn't anything wrong with it, and if I hadn't ever played it I couldn't pass judgment, and how it reminded her of this '80s band where the lead singer's hair looked like an overgrown bush, and. . .

Like Sweet Potato Pie

"So you like the book?" Kyoko asked, from somewhere in the depths of her diatribe. "We started to call it *Song of the South,* but then I thought of the current title. Sort of a life-and-death theme, if you don't mind me saying so. Since it'll be a posthumous publication for your mom. She's a really good writer, too, Ro. I never knew that. You must take after her."

"Life and death," I murmured, remembering the grave on a green hill. Her final glorious moments. "It's perfect."

I tried to thank Kyoko profusely, but she made gagging sounds and threatened to hang up. Started reading the Japanese phone book.

"Kyoko, what's the other thing you sent me?" I asked suddenly, remembering. "That thing you mentioned when I first called?"

"Oh, listen!" she replied. "I think my cell phone's ringing. Gotta go!" And she promptly hung up.

★ ★ ★

I stood out on the porch a long time after calling Adam, praying up into the starry night sky. Not with words but with my whole soul, clutching the book to my heart. Crickets began to whisper.

God, You are too good to me! I thought, watching a shooting star explode over the mountains. A brilliant streak that glowed for a moment and then burned out into blackness. When I closed my eyes, I could still see the faint streak, luminous, like a memory.

One last flourish, Mom had written. Life is so short, so fragile. And yet we hold it in our hands like a gift, making each moment our brightest and best. Giving our all to God until our last petal falls, and still we sing. One last flourish on this earth, to love, to live, and to open doors.

I still had one more phone call to make.

I picked up Adam's cell phone, still warm in my hand, and dialed my dad's number.

317

Discussion Questions

1. During Shiloh's first visit to church she senses she's losing her grip on "who she is"—leaving her trapped between the person she was in the past and the person she's becoming. Has this ever happened to you? How did you come to terms with your "new" self?

2. When Shiloh's world begins to shake, she says, "Wasn't God supposed to... start me off easy?" Have you ever felt like this? What does the Bible say about the troubles Christians face in life (see John 16:33, James 1:2, 2 Corinthians 12:7-10)? Do you think it is unfair of God to test believers in this way? What might happen if God prevented Christians from deep suffering? Can you list any good that comes from suffering and difficulty in our lives?

3. At the beginning of the book, Shiloh is afraid to tell Kyoko that God has changed her life. What is she afraid of? Have you ever felt this way before—and if so, why? If you've ever experienced this, what did you do to face your fears, and what was the result?

4. Jamie Rivera tells Shiloh not to worry about being Kyoko's friend as a new believer, but to "be yourself—yourself with Jesus." What does she mean by this? What kind of impact do you think this kind of lifestyle and friendship could make on a person like Kyoko? Conversely, what actions or attitudes might have a negative impact?

5. Beulah says that God plans every detail of our lives, including where we work and who we meet. Do you believe this? Have you ever seen evidence of God's obvious planning in your life, even when all your choices seemed "random"? What does this tell us about God and His care over the details of our lives?

6. At one point Kyoko suggests that Shiloh date Shane Pendergrass just to take advantage of his money. Do you agree with her suggestion? How does Shiloh reply to her? Have you ever been tempted to do something you know isn't the best choice in hopes that the ends will justify the means? List some consequences that could come from Shiloh deciding to follow Kyoko's advice.

7. Throughout the book, Shiloh often comments that Adam isn't handsome and isn't "her type." How important do you think these

qualities are when choosing a good spouse? List some qualities that are essential when choosing a good spouse, and explain why each one is so important. Do you see these values reflected in most searches for love and romance around you? Why or why not?

8. Carlos calls Shiloh "stiff" when she refuses to let him stay at her house or go up to his hotel room with him. Do you think this is a fair assessment? Why do you think she makes these refusals, and were they good or bad choices? If Shiloh had given in, how might the book have ended differently?

9. When Shiloh is standing outside the hotel with Carlos, she mentions how "easy" it would have been to go back with him and to believe the things he says even knowing they're lies. Have you ever been tempted to do this? Why do we sometimes willingly choose to believe a lie? If we give in to this temptation, what have we sacrificed, and what impact can it make on the course of our lives? What should we do in a similar situation? Does ignoring the truth make it become somehow not a reality?

10. When Shiloh meets Carlos, she's on guard against the influence his dazzling good looks and charm hold over her. Have you ever noticed the "power" good looks carry in relationships, literature, movies, business, and even in society? Why do you think this is? And why do you think we crave a spouse with good looks? Do you think good looks always reflect good hearts? What importance does the Bible give good looks (see 1 Samuel 16:7, Proverbs 31:30, 1 Peter 3:3-5) and what does it tell us to focus on instead?

11. Beulah tells Shiloh that Satan would like to destroy her life and witness simply because she believes in Jesus, and not because she's an important pastor and missionary. Do you believe this? In what ways could Satan be successful in ruining the life of a normal, everyday Christian, and what effect would it have on those around her? What steps does Beulah give to guard against this? What else could a person do to remain strong in the Lord even against Satan's schemes?

12. Toward the end of the book, Adam and Shiloh each sacrifice something for the other. What do they give up, and what is the personal cost? Do you think they gained more by giving up than they would have otherwise? Why do you think love so often involves sacrifice?

13. In terms of a possible marriage partner, do you think Shiloh made the right choice when choosing Adam? What good qualities did he show, and why are they so important? In what areas did he seem to offer less than Carlos, and in what other areas did he offer more?

About the Author

Jennifer Rogers Spinola, Virginia/South Carolina native and graduate of Gardner-Webb University in North Carolina, now lives in the capital city of Brasilia, Brazil, with her husband, Athos, and their son, Ethan. Jennifer and Athos met while she was serving as a missionary in Sapporo, Japan. When she's not writing, Jennifer teaches English to ESL students in Brasilia. Find out more about Jenny at www.jenniferrogersspinola.com.